kiss them goodbye

Also by Stella Cameron
in Large Print:

About Adam
Mad About the Man
Cold Day in July
7B
Finding Ian
More and More
Guilty Pleasures
Pure Delights

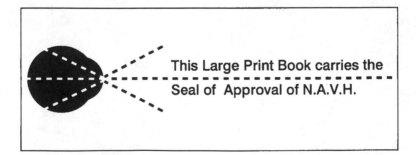

STELLA CAMERON

kiss them goodbye

Thorndike Press • Waterville, Maine

Published in 2004 by arrangement with Harlequin Books S.A.

Thorndike Press® Large Print Core.

The tree indicium is a trademark of Thorndike Press.

The text of this Large Print edition is unabridged.
Other aspects of the book may vary from the original edition.

Set in 16 pt. Plantin by Liana M. Walker.

Printed in the United States on permanent paper.

Library of Congress Cataloging-in-Publication Data

Cameron, Stella.
    Kiss them goodbye / Stella Cameron.
      p. cm.
    ISBN 0-7862-6286-9 (lg. print : hc : alk. paper)
    1. Murder victims' families — Fiction. 2. Plantation
life — Fiction. 3. Louisiana — Fiction. 4. Resorts —
Fiction. 5. Large type books. I. Title.
PS3553.A4345K57 2003
    813'.54—dc22   2003070318

For the Seventy-Niners plus two,
adventurers all.

As the Founder/CEO of NAVH, the only national health agency solely devoted to those who, although not totally blind, have an eye disease which could lead to serious visual impairment, I am pleased to recognize Thorndike Press★ as one of the leading publishers in the large print field.

Founded in 1954 in San Francisco to prepare large print textbooks for partially seeing children, NAVH became the pioneer and standard setting agency in the preparation of large type.

Today, those publishers who meet our standards carry the prestigious "Seal of Approval" indicating high quality large print. We are delighted that Thorndike Press is one of the publishers whose titles meet these standards. We are also pleased to recognize the significant contribution Thorndike Press is making in this important and growing field.

Lorraine H. Marchi, L.H.D.
Founder/CEO
NAVH

★ Thorndike Press encompasses the following imprints: Thorndike, Wheeler, Walker and Large Pr int Press.

We were three.

We took our names for their meanings.

Guido, the leader.

Ulisse, the hater.

Brizio, the craftsman.

We were young and wild. We killed cheap. A trio of urban mercenaries.

A game? Yes. A game of hide, seek and destroy. It eased the boredom while we waited for a purpose and no one ever knew; no one ever found out.

Until Ulisse betrayed Brizio and Guido broke the pact. Guido found a conscience and confessed to another.

Guido died a perfect death: slow agony, a traitor's reward.

Ulisse, ah Ulisse. He still plays the game of hide-and-seek, but waits patiently to destroy again, to avenge.

I am Brizio the craftsman. My skill is sublime, the results perfect. I open like a surgeon, swift and sure, but I never close the wound.

See them bleed.

I might stop, but I am forced by Guido's confessor to continue. This so-called man of honor blackmails me to kill for him.

For now I enjoy playing his game.

Excitement swells, beats beneath my skin. My beautiful knife is ready to cut again. Already I see the fear, the blood, hear the pleading, smell the fecund odors of terror.

Kiss them goodbye.

1

The first day

Hay-ell. Saved by the bell, or the egg he guessed he should say, the golden egg. That big and unexpected dude had gotten itself laid in the nick of time, and right at the feet of Louis Martin, Attorney At Law, of New Orleans, Louisiana.

Driving to Iberia, just about through Iberia until the parish all but ran out and melted into St. Martin Parish, wasn't Louis's idea of a good time, but he wanted to make this trip. He had good reasons, the best of reasons.

There'd been a fire in the Patins' famous New Orleans restaurant and David Patin — owner and the glue that held the business together — had died. Nobody guessed David had hidden huge losses and brought the business so low it would have to be sold. Except for Louis, who had known all about it.

9

Louis rolled the driver's window of his powder-blue Jag down a crack to let in a sideswipe of warm September afternoon air scented by the eucalyptus trees that arched over the roadway. To his left, Bayou Teche made its sluggish, slime-slicked way past banks where bleached cedars dripped Spanish moss.

An okay place to visit, he guessed, but he belonged in the city and the minute he'd given David Patin's widow, Charlotte, and their daughter Vivian the good news, he'd be heading east once more. East and New Orleans before nightfall. He would lock himself away with his memories and dreams. There would be even more to think about.

His destination was Rosebank, the house David had inherited from his older brother, Guy, not more than a couple of weeks before his own death. Guy had planned to leave the property to a preservation society but changed his mind on his deathbed, possibly because he knew about his brother's financial mess and wanted to help.

Louis slowed to a crawl to drive through a village bleached and dried by sun and etched with moss. Aptly named, Stayed Behind had died but no one had thought to bury it yet.

A general store with wide slat siding weathered to the color of bones, a scatter of single-storied houses, brown, gray, green, on blocks, their porches decorated with refrigerators, swings and dogs, and not a soul in sight. Louis itched to slap his foot down on the gas but figured that somewhere there were eyes watching and hoping he'd do just that. He surely didn't see any way for the folks around here to bring in a little revenue other than from speeding tickets.

Honeysuckle or jasmine — he'd never been too good at recognizing flowers — or some such cloying scent made him think of hot honey dropped from a spoon. Sweet, golden, and sticky.

He took a bite from the hamburger balanced on the passenger seat beside his briefcase and chased it with a clump of french fries.

In what felt like seconds, Stayed Behind receded in his rearview mirror. There wouldn't be another settlement before he got where he was going. Occasionally he caught glimpses of fine old plantation houses set back from the road and surrounded by mature gardens. Trees shaded most of them and if you looked quick enough, each facade might have been a black-and-white photo missing only the stair-step lineup of parents and children dressed in white and posing out front.

The next perfumed attack was easy to recognize, roses, banks of white roses intended to be clipped into an undulating hedge but shaggy today. Louis slowed a little and leaned to peer over the wheel. The gold signet ring on his left pinky finger felt tight and he twisted it through a groove made by swelling. The heat made his head ache.

Rosebank. Guy Patin's shabby pride and joy sat on a deep five acres surrounded by hedges like this one. Charlotte and Vivian had told him they intended to make the place pay. Something about a hotel. He didn't remember the details exactly because he had other things on his mind, like how he'd make sure Charlotte remained his client. After all, he couldn't see how two women alone would turn a rambling old house into anything, particularly when they had no money to speak of. Although Charlotte had agreed to the first loan he'd arranged, she wouldn't hear of taking another and the money was running out.

But Guy's treasure hunt had come to light exactly as the man had planned and the little ladies should have no financial difficulties once they secured their windfall. They'd have to find it — darn Guy's perverse fascination with intrigue — but he had promised that the sealed instructions now in Louis's briefcase would require only clear minds and perseverance to follow. The envelope, with a cover letter to Louis, had arrived from Guy's lawyer two days previous. Apparently these would never have been revealed unless there was danger of Rosebank passing out of Patin hands. The lawyer had been left instructions to decide if this was ever the case and apparently took his duties seriously.

White stone pillars topped with pineapple-shaped finials flanked the broad entrance. Louis swung past an ancient maroon station wagon, a Chevy, and onto the paved drive. He braced his arms against the steering wheel to ease his cramped back. The quack said Louis needed to lose God knew how much weight. Garbage. He might be softer than he used to be because he was too busy to work out, but it wouldn't take so much to tighten up those muscles.

Beneath the avenue of live oaks that framed the driveway, a tall figure walked toward him on the verge. He wore all black except for the white clerical collar visible at the throat of his short-sleeved shirt. Louis felt a pang of irritation at the man's cool appearance. Then he remembered. The handsome face, dark curly hair and broad shoulders belonged to Father Cyrus Payne of St. Cécil's Parish in Toussaint, a town just over the line between Iberia and St. Martin parishes. He'd been visiting Charlotte and Vivian the last time Louis came down.

Money-grubbing man of God. Probably fishing around for fat contributions. Well, Louis would find an opportunity to make sure the ladies didn't waste money, or anything else, in that direction. It was his responsibility to guide them now.

Father Cyrus waved and smiled and Louis grudgingly stopped the Jag. He rolled down his window again. "Afternoon, Father." Curtness would be wasted on this heartthrob ray of sunshine. Louis bet that those clear and holy blue-green eyes only had to look sincerely at all the sex-starved wealthy widows, or bored wives — and their daughters — around these parts to make sure he got plenty. Louis didn't believe abstinence was possible.

"Good afternoon," the priest said, ducking to look at Louis. "Mr. Martin, isn't it? Louis Martin?"

Louis made an affable, affirmative sound.

"Well, welcome," Payne said. "Charlotte and Vivian will be pleased to see you. They

14

mentioned you were coming."

The guy was too buddy-buddy with the Patin women who were both good-looking. He checked his watch. "That's right. I'd better get along or they'll be wonderin' where I am. Afternoon to you, Father."

"And to you." The priest nodded and straightened his long, muscular body before setting off for the road.

Louis eased the car onward, but watched the man in the wing mirror, disliking every easy swing of those big, wide shoulders. Oh, yes, he'd surely have a word with Charlotte and Vivian. He drove around a bend and lost sight of Cyrus Payne.

DETOUR.

What the fuck? Sweat stuck his shirt to the soft leather seat. He closed the window and turned up the air-conditioning.

A homemade detour sign, nailed to a stake and stuck into the soil beneath a large potted laurel bush pointed in the direction of a side road through thick vegetation. The holy man could have warned him.

Crawling the car between brambles he was convinced would scratch his shiny new blue paint, Louis squinted through the windshield and sucked air through his teeth at the sound of scraping branches.

He stuck to the narrow, overgrown track,

15

jogging right, then left, and right again.

DEAD END.

"Freakin' crazy." He stomped on the brakes. This wasn't helping him get back to New Orleans before dark and he didn't see so well at night.

Knuckles rapping glass, close to his head, startled Louis. He swallowed the bile that rushed to his throat, turned, and stared at the masked face of a man who hooked a thumb over his shoulder and indicated he wanted to speak to Louis.

Sucking in air through his mouth, Louis threw the car into reverse only to back into something. He looked in the rearview mirror and saw a tall shrub falling, a tall potted shrub that hadn't been there seconds ago.

The man hammered on the window and gestured for Louis to stop.

Louis put the car in Park and rolled the window down an inch.

"Allergies," the man shouted, pointing to his covered head. "This thing works best for keeping stuff out. Damned hot though."

Reluctantly, Louis lowered the window all the way. He felt sick.

The man pushed his head abruptly inside the car. Alarmed, Louis drew as far away as possible.

"You lost?" the man said, repeatedly scratching his face through the dark mask. "You —"

"Dead end." Louis pointed to the freshly painted board and added, "Wouldn't you say that's a redundancy? I'm not lost, just pissed. I'm a busy man. I don't have time for paper chases. I'll just get that thing back there out of the way and turn around."

"No need for that," the man said and opened Louis's door. He placed himself with the door at his back so Louis couldn't attempt to close it. "Just follow my directions and you'll get where you're supposed to go."

The voice was expressionless, serene even, and with the power to raise hair on the back of the neck. "I'll do just fine," Louis said. He screwed up the courage to say, "Can I give you a lift?" even as he prayed the fellow would refuse.

He did.

"I'm goin' to be your guide, Mr. Martin."

Louis shivered. "How do you know who I am?" Instinct suggested he should hit the gas and shoot backward out of there, no matter what he had to drive over, only he could likely kill this menacing nuisance. It might be hard to convince a judge that a person with no visible means of making

17

trouble, had scared the shit out of Louis who then acted in self-defense.

"Pass me the briefcase."

Louis's throat dried out and he coughed. He moved his right hand to put the car in reverse.

"You don't want to do that again. Turn the car off. Give me the briefcase and I'll let you go."

Louis didn't believe him and his hand continued to hover over the gearshift. The inside of his head hammered.

The man reeked of rancid sweat and when he pressed even closer, Louis turned his head away.

What had to be a gun jabbed into his ribs and the sharp point of a knife, pressed gently against the side of his neck, ensured that Louis didn't make any more moves. "Turn off the ignition."

Louis did so.

"Good. Now the briefcase. Slowly. Keep your left hand on the wheel and pass over the case."

That was when Louis saw that the man wore tight-fitting gloves.

"No. I've changed my mind. Put it on your lap and open it."

Louis did as he was told. He shifted slightly and felt the blade open a nick in his

18

skin. A trickle of warm, silky blood drizzled from the wound.

"Open it," the man repeated in his soft voice. "Thank you. I want the envelope. You know the one."

Oh, my God, I'm going to die. Louis's hands shook as he opened the case wider. The Patin file, and the envelope in question were all it contained.

"Good. Really good. Remove the envelope, then close the briefcase and put it back on the seat. Good. Now throw the envelope out of the car, backward, away from the door."

Louis made himself chuckle. "I was bringing these to you all the time. Yes, indeedy, these would have had your name on them if I'd known it. You're going to do what I should have thought of — find a fortune for yourself. The Patin women don't know a thing about it, y'know. I was supposed to tell them today. I can be a friend to you. I can make it easier to get what you want."

"Throw it out, please."

"We need to study the map in there. Honestly, I've wanted to do this, to take what they don't know they've got coming. You may not find it on your own, but with me it's a cinch. I'll —"

"You're making this more difficult. I'd be

so grateful if you'd do as I ask. Then we'll discuss your kind offer."

Hopelessness weighted Louis's limbs. The freak's painful deference only increased the menace. Louis tossed the envelope on the ground and the man kicked it away. "Now," he said, returning his whole attention to Louis. "Why don't you tell me all about how you can make my job easier?"

"There's treasure. It's hidden at Rosebank."

Slipping the knife from his right to his left hand, the man settled it against the other side of Louis's neck, the right side. "I'm sorry, but it's news I want and you don't have any, do you?"

There hadn't been a gun. The guy had faked it just to make doubly sure Louis didn't try too hard to escape.

"It's not easy to think straight like this," Louis babbled. "But I do know things you couldn't know. Give me a chance to look at the map with you. Get in the car and we'll go over things. Charlotte and Vivian know me. They trust me."

"Stupid of them but never mind. They'll have me and they already trust me."

"But —"

There wasn't a lot of pain. The knife blade sliced deep into his neck, just the right

20

side of his neck, and he flopped slowly sideways. Thunderous pulsing roared in his ears and he saw red, red everywhere. His blood pumped from the carotid artery in gushes. It hit the windshield and splattered over the lovely ivory leather interior of the car.

Red and black. Bleeding to death. Life draining out.

Louis opened his mouth but couldn't speak.

He slid until his head rested on the briefcase.

"I'm only doing my job," a distant voice said. "Brizio always does his job."

Louis convulsed. His mouth filled with blood. No pain at all now, just soft, gray numbness gathering him in.

"Sleep tight. This is your dead end, sucker."

2

"Vivian Patin, I'm your mother. You have absolutely no right to speak to me in that manner."

Charlotte paused to peer down the passageway leading from the big, antiquated kitchens to the hall and the receiving room where their next-door neighbor, Mrs. Susan Hurst, waited for tea. After taking no notice of Charlotte and Vivian since they moved in months earlier, she had appeared on the doorstep today, just appeared without warning and invited herself for tea. Imagine that. With a plate of cookies in hand, she'd showed up to be "neighborly."

"Mama," Vivian said in a low voice but without whispering. "I'm a little old to be treated like a child. Now tell me what you've been up to. No, no, don't tell me you haven't been up to anythin' because I can tell. Guilt is painted all over your face."

Her mother's pretty, fair-skinned face and innocent, liquid brown eyes couldn't hide a thing from Vivian. Charlotte Patin feared nothing and would dare anything. Her close-cropped gray hair and petite frame added to the impression that she was a dynamo. In fact, she rarely stood still and she hatched a plan a minute. And Vivian adored her. She also knew that her mother was putting a great face on her grief. She and Vivian's father had lived a love affair. Mama was brave, but David Patin had only been dead a year and Charlotte's odd, empty expressions, which came and went without warning, made lumps in Vivian's throat.

"Mama, please," Vivian said gently. "I know whatever you've done is with the best intentions. But — and I'm beggin' now — put me out of my misery."

Charlotte hushed her and leaned out of the kitchen door once more.

"Just tell me what you're up to," Vivian said. "I'm worried out of my mind about Louis Martin. Where can that man be? That should be all you care about, too, but you're up to something else. You got off the phone real quick earlier." Her mother in a stubborn mode was a hard woman to break down.

"I'd better call Louis's offices in New Orleans and see if he ever left," Charlotte said, knowing she was going to be on thin ice with Vivian. "I don't hear any hammerin' or bangin' in this house, do you? No? That's because workers have to be paid and we're about out of money." A mother had to do what a mother had to do and right now this mother had to safeguard the little surprise she had planned for the evening.

Vivian shoved her hands into the pockets of her jeans. She decided they were better there than taking out her ire on some innocent dish — particularly since most of the dishes around here were actually worth something. "Don't try to distract me with what I already know," she said, raising her voice a little. "Tell me the straight truth."

"She'll hear you," Charlotte whispered. "She's only here because she's a nosy gossip who finally decided to come and poke around. That woman will run straight from our house to chatter about us to her cronies. She behaves like the lady of the manor visiting the poor on her estates. I can only imagine what she'll say about us."

"If I shout at you, she'll have a lot to say."

"Oh, all right, I give up. You have no respect. I called that nice Spike Devol and invited him to dinner this evenin'. A

24

handsome man like that all on his own. Such a waste."

Vivian took a calming breath. "He has his daughter and his father," she said while she turned to water just under her skin, all of her skin, at the mention of that man. "Anyway, I'm sure he didn't accept. Why would he?"

For a smart woman who, until months ago, had managed an exclusive hotel in New Orleans, Vivian, Charlotte thought, could be plain stupid. "Well, he did accept and he'll be here around seven. He may be a deputy sheriff and we know the pay's not so good, but I hear he does well with that gas station and convenience store his daddy runs for him, and now he's got his crawfish boilin' operation."

She watched for Vivian to react and when she didn't, said, "He's obviously not afraid to work and he's had his hard times with his wife leaving him like that. For a *bodybuilder.* There isn't a thing wrong with Spike's body as far as I can see. Of course, I haven't seen —" Vivian's raised eyebrows brought Charlotte a little caution. "Well, anyway, he's just about the best-looking single man in these parts, and quiet in that mysterious way some strong men are. I'm tellin' you, Vivian —"

"Nothing." Vivian hardly dared to speak

25

at all. "You are telling me nothing and from now on you won't make one more match-making attempt. Y'hear? I can't imagine where you got all your personal information about him."

"You like him, too. You have since you first met him. That had to be a couple of years back. I've seen how the two of you talk —"

"Not a thing, Mama. You will not do or say another thing on the subject. Give me that tea." With that, she snatched up the pot. "Bring the cups and saucers and help me get rid of this woman quickly."

"He had a disappointing thing with Jilly at the bakery in Toussaint — All Tarted Up," Charlotte said from behind Vivian. "I guess everyone thought they were goin' some-where but it didn't work out. They're still good friends and I always think that says a lot about people."

"I know that," Vivian said.

"Father Cyrus and Spike are good friends so Spike must be a good man."

Vivian faced Charlotte, pressed a finger to her own lips and said a fierce, "Shh," before hurrying on, crossing the hall with its tow-ering gold relief plasterwork ceiling and walls hung with faded chartreuse Chinese silk. She entered the shabbily opulent receiving room. With a big grin, she said, "Here we are, Mrs. Hurst. If I say so myself, my mother and I make the best tea I ever tasted." She grinned even more broadly. "But then, I only drink tea when we're at home together."

Apparently Mrs. Hurst didn't see any humor in what Vivian said. She looked back at her from a couch covered with threadbare gold tapestry and supported on elephant foot legs. Mrs. Hurst's glistening pink lips hung slightly open and vague confusion hovered in her blue eyes. The woman could have been as young as forty or approaching sixty. It was hard to tell but everything about her was pretty tight, with not a wrinkle or sag in sight. She did have a nineteen-year-old daughter, Olympia, but that didn't really give much of a clue to the woman's age.

Vivian remembered to pour tea into three cups.

"*Hot* tea?" Mrs. Hurst said with horror in her voice. "Well."

"We drink hot tea in the afternoon," Charlotte told her. "My English grandmother taught us the right way to do things. Hot tea on a warm afternoon. The tea makes your body temperature higher. Brings it closer to the temperature of the air and you feel cooler. Anyway, Grandmama would turn in her grave if I served you *iced* tea at this time of day."

Without further comment Mrs. Hurst accepted her tea. Vivian caught her mother's eye and winked. Mama's grandmothers had been French and Mama liked hot tea — that was all there was to it.

"We are so happy at Serenity House," Mrs. Hurst said. With her younger, handsome husband she lived at the estate that bordered Rosebank to the north. They'd bought the place some months earlier and the building had swarmed with architects, contractors and workmen ever since. Susan Hurst reached for one of her own cookies but thought better of it. "We're still renovating, of course, but the house is already beautiful. Do please call me Susan, by the way. Dr. Link would like me to take his name but when we were married I chose to keep Hurst because it's Olympia's name. Anyway, I believe a woman should have some independence, don't you? Without appearing strident, that is."

On the surface Susan's accent was almost Southern, but that was forced and phony and spread on over something Vivian didn't recognize. "A woman should never be strident," she said, and found herself looking at her mother again.

"Never," Charlotte said. She stood behind Susan. Making outrageous faces at Vivian, she took one exaggerated step backward, then another forward to her starting position. "Never strident." Vivian's mother had an irrepressible sense of fun. "I thought your house was called Green Veil."

Susan managed a haughty toss of the head. "It's called Serenity House now. Much more refined and appropriate. I'm sorry to see the work on this place slow down so. It's huge. Such a maze of wings and outbuildings. I'm sure you'll be relieved to get rid of this Asian jungle theme. Monkeys and pineapples *everywhere*." She shuddered discreetly.

"Guy Patin was still in residence when we bought Serenity or we might have looked at this — even if it is in a terrible mess. And the grounds are horrible, you poor things. Give me the word and I'll send my head gardener over to talk to you. I know he and his crew could give you a few hours a week, or suggest another crew who can. Make sure you don't get those people who work on Clouds End. Marc and Reb Girard's place. All that overgrown tropical look wouldn't appeal to me.

Vivian had seen Clouds End and her ambition was to have Rosebank look just as lush. The Girards were nice people and had welcomed Charlotte and Vivian to the area. Marc was an architect and Reb the town doctor in Toussaint.

"Rosebank was never on the market," Charlotte said. "You probably noticed right away that we're also Patins. Guy was my husband's brother and the house was left to us."

"Of course I knew that," Susan said. "Silly me to forget. We've been so busy for such a long time these things slip my mind sometimes."

"We like what you call the jungle theme, y'know," Vivian said. She might as well show the woman they weren't easily intimidated, especially by money. "We're going to keep it. It'll be made wonderful again, of course."

"Poor thing." Susan patted Vivian's hand as if she didn't take a word seriously. "I can see you're overwhelmed. Let me help you. Did I tell you our pool house is just about finished? It's all marble. Very Roman and wickedly decadent, but almost edible." She hunched her shoulders. "Morgan and I want you to use it whenever you have a mind. We know the pool here isn't usable."

"Thank you," Vivian said, making a note never to have a mind for a swim in Susan's

30

decadent pool. "We do have a gardener and we're very pleased with him." Gil Mayes might be seventy-two and a bit crippled by gout but he showed enthusiasm for the work. Unfortunately he moved slowly and the gardens were big, but more men couldn't be afforded yet, not until some serious money came in.

Susan said, "Hmm," and flipped back her artfully shaggy red-streaked brown hair. Good-looking, sexy even, her mannerisms were naturally provocative. "I hope you won't think me too curious, but after all we are neighbors. There are rumors about your having some *intentions* about this place — not that I believe a word."

"Of course you don't," Charlotte said. "And a very good thing, too."

If Susan didn't know their intentions perfectly well Vivian would be amazed. And Mama might enjoy her banter but afternoon crept toward evening and she glanced repeatedly toward the front windows. Vivian knew her own uneasiness was for the same reason that her mother was edgy. Where was Louis?

"It may be crude to say so, but I come from money," Susan announced. "Might as well have honesty among friends. I'm accustomed to a quieter, more gracious mode of life. It's true that I've had my share of the so-cial whirl in Paris, London, Milan and New York, of course, but I need the life only a true Louisiana lady knows how to live. Quiet. Refined. I'm sure you know what I mean. Soon Serenity will be perfect and I expect a good many visitors — friends — who expect a certain atmosphere at a house party."

Vivian said, "I thought you wanted peace and quiet, not a load of uppity visitors."

Vivian spied Boa, short for Queen Boadicea, her hairless Chihuahua. The tiny dog had roused herself from some hiding place and stood in the middle of the green silk rug with one minuscule paw raised. Her black eyes shone while she watched Susan. Like her namesake, Boa just didn't accept her limitations.

"I didn't know you had an animal," Susan remarked. "I prefer big dogs myself, not that I have any." Her nose wrinkled. "They just aren't clean."

"That always depends on the dogs you hang around with." Vivian made sure she sounded sweet. "Come to me, sweetie pie. Come to mama."

Her daughter, Charlotte thought, could be charmingly snippy. "I'm sure you're very happy at Green Veil, Susan."

32

"*Serenity* House." The woman corrected Charlotte firmly. "Just to put my mind at rest, tell me you don't intend to turn Rosebank into a hotel with some sort of, well, trendy restaurant."

With Boa under her arm, Vivian had strolled to the windows and peered out into the rapidly darkening grounds. She heard Susan's question and winced a little, but she couldn't concentrate on anything but Louis's failure to show up. Anger had begun to replace concern. He obviously wasn't coming now and the way he'd treated them was just plain rude. Louis had always been polite, kind even, but she guessed they might not be important to him if a more valued client needed attention.

She realized there was silence in the room and turned around. Mama was eating a cookie, toothful by toothful, with the kind of close attention that spelled avoidance. Vivian recalled the question Susan had asked. "This will become a hotel, a good hotel, and we will be opening a restaurant in the conservatory. We intend to pull in clients who aren't necessarily staying with us. My mother and I have a lot of experience in the business. I managed Hotel Floris in New Orleans. My parents owned Chez Charlotte. They ran it together and it was a huge success. I thought everyone in the area knew our plans."

"A *hotel?*" Susan set down her cup and saucer and pressed her fingers to her cheeks. "I thought it must be a joke. Say you aren't serious. Why, at your time of life, Charlotte, you should be taking things easy and enjoying yourself."

"I will enjoy myself — doing what I like best. Vivian, it's five-thirty."

The heavy significance in Mama's voice meant she was reminding Vivian that they would have a guest for dinner and that Susan Hurst needed to leave.

Susan wasn't hearing anything that didn't relate to the reason she was here — to try to influence Charlotte and Vivian onto her side. They would, if she had her way, come to realize that Susan was a superior person who should not be thwarted in any way.

"We have traditions to uphold, we Louisiana ladies. The reason I moved here — what I want from life — is to recreate a way of living that's in danger of disappearing. I know both of you understand what I mean. Louisiana ladies, and houses like this, are about grace and holding out against progress." Susan turned up her nose and turned down her mouth. "It's up to us to keep certain standards alive. With something like a hotel, you could get *any* sort of person wandering about and most of them just wouldn't fit in."

Charlotte sat beside Susan and rested her hand on the back of the woman's right forearm. "Now you calm yourself and trust our good judgment. We intend to make sure our business doesn't endanger anyone who lives around here." The devil had gone to work on her. "Why, we've already started looking for a reliable firm of uniformed guards to patrol the grounds — especially when we hold outdoor concerts that will draw lots of young folk."

"Concerts on the grounds?" Susan said weakly.

"Oh, yes," Vivian said, her expression angelic. "We've already reserved dates with some of the best known zydeco bands around — and some swamp pop, of course. And we're in negotiation with one or two popular groups — hip-hop will really bring in the crowds."

Susan was no fool. She narrowed her eyes and cast suspicious glances at each of them. "I think you have very strange senses of humor."

Vivian didn't argue. She did look at her watch, then at her mother. They were running short of time if they were going to prepare dinner. Boa nuzzled her neck but repeatedly arched her little back to cast a suspicious glare at Susan.

The phone rang and Vivian went into the hall to answer.

"Vivian," the voice at the other end said. "It's Madge at the rectory. Father Cyrus asked me to give you a call." Madge was Cyrus's assistant.

"Is something wrong?"

"No! Why would there be? He said you were having a meeting with a New Orleans lawyer earlier this afternoon and you said you'd call and let him know if the news was good. He wanted me to check in with you."

Vivian yanked on the bottom of her too-short T-shirt. "Now I feel guilty. I should have gotten back with him. We waited all afternoon but Louis didn't show. Guess we'll call his office in the morning. Maybe there was a muddle up over the date. Tell Cyrus we'll talk to him tomorrow, would you?"

Madge agreed and hung up.

And the doorbell gave a rusty buzz.

Charlotte got to her feet at once. "Louis. He must have gotten lost, poor man." She looked at her watch. "Oh, my, it's almost six."

"I'm going to the door," Vivian said,

frowning. "This is turning into a messy evening."

Charlotte waited for Vivian to add that it was her mother's fault but she didn't, although the look in her green, almond-shaped eyes said it all.

"I suppose I should leave," Susan said, her attention on the hall and curiosity oozing from her pores. "I'll slip along now. Don't forget how convenient that path between the two estates is. Come over anytime, anytime at all. You'll fall in love with Morgan — and Olympia's a charmer —" She didn't as much as blink when Charlotte put a hand beneath her elbow and eased her to her feet. "Olympia is a beauty. She's considering the Miss Southern Belle Pageant. I've tried to dissuade her but you can't stand in children's way, can you?" Her long sigh wasn't convincing.

Vivian opened the front door.

Rather than Louis Martin, Deputy Sheriff Spike Devol stood there, a broad-brimmed black Stetson covering his hair, his eyes very blue in a tanned face, and with a bunch of flowers in each hand. Rather than say, "Hi," or "Good evening," or even, "Here's looking at you," he studied the flowers as if he'd never seen them before and raised and lowered them as if figuring out how to get rid of them.

Behind Spike, bands of purple streaked the setting sun, shading his face but backlighting him with gold. The deputy was in his thirties, with the mature, muscular body of a man who knew all about being physical. His shoulders and arms and his chest filled a crisp, dark gray shirt to capacity, but his hips were slim. His legs weren't so slim. Once again long, well-developed muscles strained at his clothes, in the best possible way. Vivian felt a definitely sexual thrill.

"Hi there, Spike," she said, making sure she sounded pleasant but detached. "Mama said you were coming for dinner." She felt Susan Hurst arrive at her side and knew she'd heard what Vivian had said.

"I'm Susan Hurst. I live next door at Serenity House," Susan said with a new, husky sound in her voice. "I'm just going to pop along the path and go home. So convenient."

"That's nice." Spike had a deep voice, deep and soft and impossible to read. There was something a little different about him than Vivian had noticed on the previous occasions she'd run into him, but she wasn't sure what — other than his being out of uniform.

Finally he grasped both bunches of flowers in one hand and took off the Stetson. "Evenin' Vivian," he said.

Susan Hurst still hovered.

"Take care," Vivian told her. "Best make it home while there's still enough light. It looks like it could rain, too."

Susan didn't look happy, but she gave a stiff smile and trotted off, her very nice behind swaying in tailored white slacks.

"C'mon in," Charlotte said from behind Vivian. "You're never going to believe this but Susan Hurst's visit was a surprise. We haven't gotten far with dinner yet, but it won't take too long."

"I'm early," Spike said in that still voice of his. "I'm useful in the kitchen. I'll give a hand."

Vivian stood aside for him to enter and her heart — or the vicinity of her heart — squeezed. As he passed her he looked sideways and down into her face. The faintest of smiles pushed dimples into the creases beside his mouth. His sunstreaked hair, she noticed, had a way of standing up on end in front.

Down girl, down.

"We wouldn't hear of it," she said when she found her voice. "What do you like to drink? Make yourself comfortable and we'll show you how quickly we can get things done."

"Thank you, ma'am," he said, inclining his head and broadening his smile enough to deepen those dimples and show very good teeth. He actually made Vivian feel small and feminine and she'd never thought of herself as either.

The phone rang again and Charlotte hurried away, apparently to answer it in the kitchens although she could have done so in the hall. Mama was still in matchmaker mode, but then, she'd been trying to marry Vivian off for years.

"If it won't upset you," Spike said, "I'd like to help. I'm not good at sitting still and doing nothing."

"Neither am I," she told him emphatically. "I guess it's because my parents were always busy."

He only nodded and suddenly thrust both bunches of flowers into her arms. Boa had disappeared at the sound of the doorbell — guarding wasn't one of her duties — but she chose this moment to skitter into the hall and make a dash for Vivian, screeching to a halt with all four feet braced in the forward position.

"Nice dog," Spike said, with a look that suggested he wasn't sure Boa was a dog at all.

"Thank you," Vivian said, and smiled at him. "Nice flowers. I don't remember the last time someone gave me any."

His smile dropped away. "You should be given flowers every day." Immediately he colored under the tan and the result was disarming. "I thought you could share them with your mother. How is she doin'?"

For an instant she didn't understand. Then any last reserve against this man melted. He wasn't just a tall, good-looking piece of manhood, he was thoughtful. And that was a killer combination. Almost no one here mentioned their loss. "Mama's strong, but she and my dad just about grew up together. It's hard and it's going to be hard for a long time. Especially because of the way he died."

Spike slid the brim of his Stetson through his fingers. "There's nothing anyone can say to whitewash that. I'm real sorry. Not that it helps."

David Patin had burned to death in the fire that destroyed Chez Charlotte. "Kindness always helps," Vivian said feeling the too familiar desire to be alone again.

"Vivian!" Charlotte came from the kitchens and her face was too pale. "I don't know what to make of it. That was Cyrus. He says when he was walking toward the

41

road, to his car, he saw Louis Martin — driving a brand-new powder-blue Jag."

Vivian's mind became blank.

"Y'hear me?" Charlotte said, her voice rising. "That wretch Louis drove all the way here — Cyrus spoke with him — and then he must have decided he couldn't be bothered and left again."

3

Charlotte marched back to the kitchens while Vivian and Spike shared an uncomfortable silence.

"Louis Martin is our lawyer," Vivian said. "He was due here this afternoon but he never showed up. We decided he'd forgotten the appointment. Now I don't know what to think."

"I think your mother's right. He drove here then changed his mind. Maybe he got a message and had to turn around."

"Without taking the trouble to tell us?"

Spike looked at Vivian again and was uncomfortably aware that each time he did so was more disturbing than the last. He liked looking at her but she made him heat up. Ah, what the hell, he'd accepted her mother's invitation because he wanted an opportunity to be with Vivian long enough to see if there was really a spark between them.

There was a spark.

"Should we check on your mother?" he said.

Vivian nodded and walked ahead of him. Her straight black hair slid around her shoulders. She was one of those women with a tiny waist but plenty of curves north and south. But it was her face he'd kept right on seeing from the first time they'd been introduced, at Bigeaux's hardware store in Toussaint. Her eyes were unforgettable and he'd spent serious time considering her full mouth. Exotic might be a fair classification, not that he thought she'd fit too easily inside any boundaries.

His father's sour reaction to this visit wouldn't leave him. Homer Devol didn't have much use for women and he didn't think Spike had any reason to think of them kindly either. Homer's parting words this evening had been "Don't listen to me, then. Go on and make a damn fool of yourself, you. They're old money and anythin' between you will look like you're tryin' to get above yourself."

Spike had come anyway, even with Homer's "Don't you go bringin' another woman around if she ain't gonna stay.

Wendy don't need that."

He wouldn't do anything to hurt five-year-old Wendy, no way. But he was a man with a man's needs and he'd been alone too long.

Charlotte Patin had heaped fresh vegetables onto an enormous and worn cutting block in the center of the kitchen. The room was big and at the apex of the high ceiling was an old-fashioned window that could be opened with a chain on metal cogs and pulleys when the heat got too much. What looked like the original spits were still in a fireplace that had to be more than six feet wide.

"Okay," Charlotte said. "If you want to help, Spike, chop those."

He started rolling up his sleeves. "No problem. I'm an expert."

"Spike brought us flowers, Mama," Vivian said, not liking the harassed expression on her mother's face.

Charlotte gave him a sweet smile. "Thank you. They're lovely. We need something bright and cheerful around here." She returned to pulling food out of the refrigerator.

Foreboding slipped over Vivian like a cold shroud. What would make Louis turn away when he'd already gotten here? "Will you excuse me for a few minutes, please," she said, avoiding Spike's serious glance. "I'll be right back."

She hurried from the kitchens with Boa at her heels. Where she thought she was going, she didn't know, but she had to get somewhere and breathe outdoor air while she thought.

On the other side of the main hall from the receiving room was a small, even more shabby sitting room with disappearing corners that made it seem rounded. Uncle Guy hadn't been well for some years and he'd let Rosebank go, but she and Charlotte would make it beautiful again. Vivian raised her chin. She couldn't give up now. They'd find the money to carry on the renovations. This place was their only chance to make up for what they'd lost.

In the sitting room she picked up the phone beside a gilt chair with an unraveling cane seat. She called directory enquiries for New Orleans and gave the name of Louis's firm — never expecting to get a response at this time of day.

"Legrain here."

She almost hung up. "This is Vivian Patin. My mother and I are clients of Louis Martin."

"Well yes, Ms. Patin. I know your name.

I'm Louis's associate, Gary Legrain. I believe we've met."

She didn't remember. "Did Louis set out to visit us today?"

A short silence. "Why, yes. He left this mornin'."

"He didn't get here."

More silence. "That's not possible. If something had happened, a car accident or whatever, we'd have heard."

"I was hoping he'd gone back to his offices," Vivian said, the cold feeling intensifying. She hadn't considered Louis getting in a car wreck after he turned back.

Gary was quiet for too long before he said, "He didn't come back," and sounded funny.

"Could he have gone home? Felt ill perhaps and decided to call it a day? Maybe Mrs. Martin —"

"There isn't a Mrs. Martin anymore. He has grown children but he lives alone — except for staff. Let me call them and get back to you."

"Don't call," Vivian said. "My mother's a bit anxious. I'll call you in five minutes."

They hung up and she waited, praying Mama wouldn't come looking for her. Fortunately, when Mama cooked, she tended to forget everything else.

Vivian called Gary Legrain again.

"He isn't there," the man said and although he was obviously trying to sound unconcerned, she'd unsettled him. "Look, this isn't too comfortable to talk about and the last person I should say anything to is a client but I don't know what else to do."

Vivian waited.

"Ms. Patin, recently I've been happy to know that Louis has a new companion in his life. Well, this is . . . hmm, apparently they don't like to be parted. If I had to guess —"

"You'd say Louis got to our front door and was overcome by a mad need to bang his girlfriend? Yes, I understand. When you see him, Mr. Legrain, please let him know I'd like to hear from him."

"Ms. Patin, I'm sure it wasn't quite like that."

"Are you? Thank you for your help." She hung up, disconcerted by her own bluntness and embarrassed at her sharp treatment of Gary Legrain who had been doing his best to smooth things over.

She and Charlotte didn't want to take on more loans, not without being certain Guy hadn't planned this whole thing. He'd been principled, but a joker. It would be like him to let them have a taste of really wanting the place and not being able to afford it before help showed up in some form. When Louis had set up today's meeting, he'd alluded to a considerable infusion of funds from Guy's estate, "In a strange way."

Each time Vivian confronted the mess that was her life she thought about her father. He must have been frantic to put his business to rights. Family, his wife and daughter, came first for David Patin.

She heard laughter, actual laughter from the kitchens and felt a rush of unfounded jealousy. Hearing her mother laugh should make her happy. Hearing Spike laugh did give her a lot of feelings, feelings she had no time for.

Snatching the flashlight they kept at the bottom of the staircase in the hall, Vivian slipped quickly and quietly through a maze of corridors lined with closed doors until she found the one that led into an overgrown formal garden at the back of the house, behind the south wing.

Warmth still clung to the evening and the sweet, sultry scents of honeysuckle and clematis blossoms sweetened the air. Crickets and frogs had taken over the soggy grass and sang out their raucous chant.

She walked around the perimeter of the south wing, continued to the end of the west wing and finally reached the front of the house. Rosebank was shaped like an "H" set out at an angle, and with what would be the cross stroke of the letter joining the north and west wings to the east and south wings. Outbuildings nestled into the central courtyards on either side. The original stables, their wide gates flanked with columns to match those at the front of the house, were used as the garage.

Susan Hurst had been right when she said the place was huge. But that would be useful if the renovations could start again and move ahead steadily. Just ten guest rooms were all she felt they had to deal with to get started. Ten rooms and the restaurant they planned for a detached, wonderfully preserved, conservatory.

Damn, damn. If only they'd get some breaks. Even little ones would lift their spirits. Vivian left the shadow of the house and headed down the tree-lined driveway on the left-hand verge. She could have made her way nicely without the flashlight but liked using it. One of the things she loved about being here, had loved since she used to visit Uncle Guy when she was a kid, was how safe it felt. Year to year nothing changed.

There was a softness out here that took some of the pressure off her chest.

What did she expect to find at the end of

the drive? Louis Martin with some excuse about a flat tire?

She ought to go back.

Rustling overhead made her pick up Boa who continued to try to keep up with her mistress. Crows, Vivian's least favorite birds, flew, black blotches against a leaden purple sky where the already set sun still threw up a faint patina from behind a hill.

Just to the gates and back. She needed a walk. Louis was with his lady friend, darn him. She tried to imagine him in the throes, so to speak, and shuddered, then felt nasty.

Only the crickets, the frogs, and a host of gentle evening sounds reached her through the first spatter of raindrops on leaves, but she didn't linger. Once she'd looked up and down the road, and felt foolish for doing so, she walked back, swinging her flashlight from side to side.

The crows puzzled her. They tended to settle by now rather than go on the wing with such determination. Boa grew stiff in her arms. The dog moaned, then set up a thin whine.

Vivian's spine prickled. Yelping, taking her by surprise, Boa shot from her grasp and took off between two trees and into the undergrowth.

"Boa? Sweetie? C'mon back." Shoot, Boa

never got it that any animal she decided to chase off was likely to be bigger than she was, and mean. She followed the dog and shone the flashlight where Boa seemed to have disappeared. The tangle of overgrown shrubs formed an impenetrable barrier, unless you happened to be a five-pound dog.

A side road toward the north turned off a few yards ahead. It was designed for a grounds crew to access some of the more remote areas. Vivian ran toward it. She might be able to head Boa off from there.

Where was it? Oh, c'mon, where was it? She began to sweat, and feel sick. It was small, not much more than a track that allowed for a single vehicle, but where was it? Ranging back and forth, she searched but couldn't find where the track veered off.

Boa's eerie wailing continued to reach her and she took some comfort in that. Then Vivian stood still and gauged where the track should be, and was, of course. She was too upset to be sensible.

"Boa," she called, but without any energy.

She found it, the place where she could see the track pass through the verge. And it was exactly where she'd thought it was, only there was no break between shrubs anymore. Her stomach clenched and she looked toward the house, considered going for company if not for help. And she'd look stupid and everyone would think she was overreacting. She shone the flashlight carefully along the area. Three big laurel bushes in tubs stood, closely side-by-side, and hid the little road completely.

Gil must be experimenting with some different looks.

Vivian squeezed between two tubs. Layers of pewter-colored clouds darkened the purple sky and no hint of the dead sun remained. She swung her flashlight. Critters skittered away from the light. She saw the sleek, white body of a nutria, its long rat tail fat as it slithered out of sight. She hated this. In many ways she was a city girl, not a country girl. If an alligator showed up she really would lose it.

Boa's complaints had grown quieter but they were still steady, and not too far away, Vivian decided. She would not leave her dog alone out here. "Boa? Come here girl." The dog didn't rush to her and there was no choice but to go on. What could be so scary about walking through grounds she was growing to know well?

A glint. A flicker of light passed over a smooth surface, and Vivian aimed her light in that direction.

She stopped walking and peered ahead.

The top of a car, pale and glossy and only yards away.

Boa, bursting from the bushes, barking wildly and rushing at her, raised Vivian's spirits. She'd grab the dog and run for it.

Before she could reach Boa, the dog dashed away again, her barks changing to a wail.

"Is there anyone there?" Vivian called tentatively. "Hello, who's there?"

Large raindrops beat hard on the top of her head and her face. Clouds extinguished a struggling moon and a breeze picked up.

She didn't take foolish risks, but how could she be in danger here? For all she knew, there'd been an abandoned car here all along. She certainly hadn't been all through the tangled grounds.

Sometimes snakes infested old cars.

That stopped her. She couldn't stand snakes.

Snakes could kill Boa so easily.

Vivian discovered all that stood between her and the vehicle were two more tubs of laurel, one of which had fallen against the other. Boa ran out and away again as if she were trying to lead Vivian. She hesitated. The laurels were intended to hide something — the car.

"Okay, I'm coming, Boa." Rain became

steady and harder. She'd likely be soaked in a few minutes. "Boa!"

No one lay in wait. If they did, she'd feel their presence and she didn't.

The car, a new Jaguar in a pale shade, stood with its nose into the scrub on one side of the track. Not a sound came from it. Why would it? But why would someone abandon a new Jaguar in . . . Hadn't Cyrus said Louis was driving a new blue Jaguar?

Vivian backed away. She patted the waistband of her jeans, only to discover she didn't have her cell phone.

Rustling made her skin crawl and she looked up to see crows, undaunted by the rain, lining the branches above. More birds perched on the rim of the driver's door which stood open. These sentinels took it in turns, crying out and complaining, to hop down into the car. Each one then flew to the branches with something pale in its beak.

Vivian held her breath. The birds creeped her out. She could go to pieces, or she could keep calm and see what this was all about.

The flashlight picked up dark splotches on the car windows. Vivian had no idea what they were and walked gingerly around to the driver's side.

She saw a trousered leg — already soaked — and foot, minus its shoe, trailing from the vehicle. Drawn on by determination and horrible fascination, she inched closer. Dripping, Boa sat by the foot and her wail became an unearthly screech.

Death, that's what made dogs howl like that.

Vivian ducked to look inside the car, and immediately retched. She turned aside and threw up until she felt empty and weak. Despite the downpour, sweat slid over her skin, cold, clammy. Her legs trembled. Once more she made herself look in at what was left of Louis Martin.

The remains of a discarded bag of hamburgers and french fries added the smell of rancid fried food to other disgusting odors. This food was the crows' spoils.

Louis's neck had been slashed so deep his head rested at an impossible angle on top of his briefcase and the dark splotches she'd seen were his blood. Blood everywhere, blood that turned his shirt and jacket black.

Across his chest rested a single white rose.

4

Rain came through the windows in the kitchen ceiling. Spike waited for Charlotte to notice but she was busy making pastry, a hazelnut crust for a leek and Brie pie. He was used to simple meals, quickly prepared, and only Wendy kept him just about on the straight and narrow with the main food groups.

He closed the windows.

Vivian had been gone half an hour or more. It wasn't his place to mention this to Charlotte.

The vegetables he'd finished cutting up were in a pressure cooker and he'd cleaned the chopping block. Everywhere he looked he imagined Vivian there, doing whatever she did, and the feelings he got disturbed him. He wasn't a man who moved fast when it came to women, not anymore. Once he'd

made that mistake . . . no, not a mistake —
his haste had given him Wendy.

"Vivian goes off on her own like this,"
Charlotte said without looking up. "Always
has. She thinks a lot and likes a little time
alone sometimes. She's unusual in the kind
of way that catches a person's interest."

"I can tell she's unusual," Spike said with
honesty.

"She doesn't have a temper, mind. Just
never gets cross. Very easygoing, very reliable. A good mind, too, and creative."

Spike said, "I'm sure."

"Never a bad word about a soul," Charlotte continued. "Heart of gold and the patience of a saint."

He crossed his arms and rested his chin
on his chest. If he didn't know better he'd
think Vivian's mother was giving a commercial message about her girl.

From the corner of her eye, Charlotte saw
Spike lean against a counter and seem deep
in thought. She had good instincts where
men were concerned. She'd always been
able to pick out the good ones and she was
sure Spike Devol was one of the best. David
had been the best of all and she'd picked
him for herself. Fortunately he'd picked her,
too, and they'd made love at first sight a reality.

58

She blinked back tears she rarely indulged and finished rolling out her crust.

The silence grew too long for Spike. "Is Vivian your only child?"

"One and only. We would have liked more but it just didn't happen."

"Maybe there's just one child meant specially for some of us?" he suggested, feeling awkward.

"I'd like to meet your Wendy," Charlotte said. "I hear she's a sweet one. But you're young, you've got plenty of time to have more beautiful children. Would you like more?"

Charlotte Patin asked her questions easily so even the real personal ones didn't sound out of line, not too much out of line. "I can't think about that now. Between bein' Deputy Sheriff and runnin' a business — and keeping up with a busy little girl and an ornery, well, with my dad — there isn't much time left over."

"But you wouldn't mind having more?" The crust moved magically from a board to cover a full pie dish. "Sometimes more are easier, or so I've been told."

"I guess I wouldn't mind," Spike said with the sensation that he'd finally said what Charlotte wanted to hear, although if she was matchmaking he couldn't understand why. Vivian could have any man she wanted and even if she were attracted to him, which he just thought she might be, she wouldn't be interested in getting too close to his baggage.

"Better get on with it, then," Charlotte said. "It's best to have your children when you're young so you're still young when they leave you. Then it's time for the second honeymoon, the one that keeps on going."

Spike's smile charmed Charlotte. She decided he made her feel a whole lot younger herself. Dimples like that, and those teeth. His children couldn't help being handsome — any more than Vivian's could.

"I do believe you're laughing at me, Spike Devol," she said, tipping her head on one side.

"Just smiling at the thought of beautiful babies," he told her. "Now that's a picture worth smiling about. When you hold your own baby for the first time —" he shook his head "— you feel the happiest you ever felt, then sad at the same time because that moment is too short. I like having the memory."

Well, Charlotte thought, if he wasn't the nicest man she'd met in a long time. Not opposed to more children either and a hard worker. It was time Vivian married and had

some grandchildren — children that was, grandchildren for Charlotte who was wasted without any. She decided not to mention Spike's father. She'd already heard Homer's reputation around Toussaint. Word had it that he was a bitter man with no time for women.

"Everyone says your dad idolizes little Wendy," she said. Couldn't be any harm in saying that.

"She's the only one he gives a damn about."

Charlotte looked at him and smiled a little. He blushed easily and she liked that. "That must be what he wants you to think. I never did meet a parent who didn't love their own child."

Spike wasn't so sure about that but he kept his own counsel. "I can watch things here if you want to go check on Vivian." That sounded nonchalant enough. He was beginning to worry she'd hidden herself away because she didn't want to be around him.

"No need," Charlotte said lightly. "She probably decided to shower and change. The day kinda got away from us."

Spike spent a few satisfying moments considering Vivian in the shower, then rubbing her skin dry until it turned pink.

The front doorbell rang and the heavy door opened, then shut with a reverberating thud. Eventually a voice he recognized as belonging to Cyrus called from the passageway into the behind-stairs area, "Charlotte, where are you?"

"In the kitchen," she called back. "Come on in."

Cyrus entered, his black hair plastered to his head and his shirt stuck to his shoulders and chest.

"You're soaked," Spike said. "It must be tipping down to do that on the way from your car."

"Come stand by the oven," Charlotte told Cyrus. "Let me guess, you won't listen to reason because you know everything, so that beat-up Chevy of yours is parked out by the road yet again."

Cyrus looked sheepish. "Be nice to my Chevy," he said of the maroon station wagon he'd driven for years and which several parishioners managed to keep running most of the time. "I park it there because it's easier if I need a tow truck." His shirt started to steam a little in the warmth from the oven. "Remind me to fill you in on Ozaire Dupre, Spike. He's hopping mad about you taking food out of his family's mouths . . . his words. Exaggeration, of course."

Spike ground his back teeth. "There's enough boiling business for both of us in this town. He just thinks he should get it all. Okay, we'll get to him later." Ozaire was the custodian at St. Cécil's and his wife, Lil, kept house for Cyrus. Spike didn't know how anyone could put up with them.

"Put your troubles aside, Father, you're in plenty of time for a good, hot meal," Charlotte said and grimaced. "We had company that didn't want to go home and she made me late with dinner."

"I've eaten," Cyrus said. "Thanks anyway. Madge made us muffulettas that must have weighed a pound apiece. That girl can make magic with a mess of oysters and mudbugs."

"She surely can," Spike agreed. Cyrus and Madge sometimes troubled him. The priest was married to his calling and his church and Madge served the man and his passions with cheerful efficiency, but Spike had known both of them too long not to have felt the bond between them, the un-requited love — at least on Madge's part, and Cyrus's affection and protectiveness toward her.

"You hung up on me, Charlotte," Cyrus said.

Spike watched the woman's facial expression with interest. He'd swear she had no recollection of hanging up on Cyrus.

"I did not," she said. "Well, maybe I didn't exactly say goodbye but you shocked me when you said Louis had come to Rosebank and left without seeing us."

"But you're okay, just disappointed?"

"Mad would be closer," Charlotte said. "Just wait till I talk to that man."

This time it was the phone that jangled and Charlotte plucked a cordless off the wall. "Rosebank." The look on her face put Spike on alert. Cyrus also watched her closely. "What's wrong?" Her voice rose. "You sound as if you're outside. Where are you calling from? Your cell phone's here by the sink. No, I won't put Spike on the line. Tell me what's goin' on right now."

She listened for not more than two seconds before thrusting the receiver at Spike. "She'll only speak to you. I don't know what's happened."

"Hey Vivian," he said. There was no reason to be elated she'd asked for him but he was anyway.

He could hear her teeth chattering but she didn't answer him. Boa yapped in the background.

"Vivian?"

"Yes, sorry. Something awful has happened. I need help."

"Stay calm," he said out of habit. "Where are you?"

"In the grounds out front of the house."

He stopped himself from asking what she was doing there. "Are you hurt?" He headed for the front door, catching up his Stetson as he went.

"I'm fine. No, I'm not fine, I'm scared. It's Louis Martin. He's been hurt."

"I'm on my way. Guide me to you. Hang on." He turned back and said, "Cyrus, stay with Charlotte and be ready in case we need to get more help."

"Please hurry," Vivian said. "It's terrible, I can't leave. You can't leave someone like this."

"That's right," he said. "I'm coming to you. I'm outside the house now. Standing on the steps."

She gave him directions and he followed them, quickly getting drenched himself. Each time he looked at the ground, water ran from the brim of his hat. Edging between potted laurels, he saw the flashlight she'd told him she had. He still had to walk a winding track to where a couple more laurels blocked the way. Then he pushed through and saw a car. He turned his own flashlight on Vivian who leaned against the trunk of the vehicle, her head dropped forward and a phone pressed to her ear. She held a destroyed white rose in the same hand. He turned his phone off.

"Hey, hey," he said, running to her. A man's leg extended from the open driver's door. "Everything's okay, sweetheart. Here, hold on to me. Let me use your phone to call for the local law then I'll get you into the house." He considered putting his Stetson on her but she'd only be more uncomfortable with her wet hair pressed to her head.

Vivian fell into his arms. "You are the law."

"This isn't my jurisdiction. One way to make sure you don't get along with the guys in a neighboring parish is to interfere with their turf. And, unfortunately, I have some history in Iberia. I worked here once and managed to step on the wrong toes."

"You're the law," she repeated as if he hadn't spoken. "Louis is dead. I checked. He doesn't have a pulse. They slit his throat. There's blood everywhere."

Spike held her face against his shoulder and bent to see inside the car. "You looked for a pulse?"

"There isn't one."

"You've got guts." The corpse wasn't a pretty sight. Spike wished he could have spared Vivian this. He eased back and

66

looked into her face, what he could see of it. Her hair obscured all but the spaces she'd made to see and speak. "Your mama said your phone was in the kitchen."

"This is Louis's."

He swallowed. "Where'd you find it?"

"In his briefcase. I had to pull it from under his head. It was awful. I thought it was going to . . . fall off," she finished in a whisper.

"Hush." All he could think of was how badly she'd interfered with evidence. "The thorns on that rose are going to mess up your fingers."

"They . . . I mean whoever did this left the flower on his chest." She swallowed and swallowed as if she would vomit. "They — someone kissed him on the cheek. I don't think they did it with lipstick. I think they put their mouth in his blood."

Shee-it. Sick bastard had set the scene all right. Too bad Vivian had been the one to stumble on it. He'd dealt with these situations before and he knew to expect her to have problems dealing with what she'd experienced. His next thought was about Errol Bonine, the lazy detective who would definitely be assigned to the case. Wait till he saw what had been done to his crime scene. And finding Spike in the vicinity

67

would only make the slob's night.

Running with mixed water and blood, and obviously covered with Vivian's prints, the victim's phone was so contaminated Spike figured he might as well use it. If the instrument had been in the briefcase, with Martin's head on top of it, chances were the killer never touched or even saw it. He held it between finger and thumb to call the police, was patched through to Bonine at home, and had to listen to the ass's warnings not to put his nose into Errol's business if Spike knew what was good for him. Officers would be arriving to make sure nothing was touched and nobody left the scene, Bonine told him, but Spike should fill in until they got there.

He clicked off and turned back for the house, supporting Vivian and with her little dog running circles around them. "Cry if you need to," he said. "Sometimes it helps. You're in shock. Bound to be."

She didn't answer him.

"Whoever did that was trying too hard."

"What do you mean?" Her voice sounded faint and choked.

"He — if it was a he and the chances are it was — he went overboard with the setup. Made it almost comic."

"Not funny," she mumbled.

"Not funny," he agreed and tried to brush more of her hair out of her face.

She clung to him fiercely enough to dig her nails into his flesh. "Like a serial killer. They do things like that, don't they? Leave the signs each time they kill because they want people to know it's them."

"Some do," he said. "Although they don't do much singing until they're caught and want bragging rights behind bars. But let's not think about this being a first killing with more to follow. Could be isolated and the perp tossed in the window dressing to throw us off."

"Spike." She looked up at him. "I want you to do this, not a stranger."

If he had time for the luxury, he'd be flattered. "I'll give you any personal help you'll let me, but I have to defer to the local guys."

"Will you be with me when they come?"

He groaned inwardly, anticipating Errol's sneering displeasure. "If you want me, I'll be there."

"I want you."

Timing had never been his friend. If he was going to be as much help as he could around here, he'd have to make sure he kept his head clear and his hormones under control. Hell, that shouldn't be hard. He was a professional.

He'd barely steered Vivian into the hall, and confronted Charlotte and Cyrus, when the sound of a siren reached them.

Cyrus said, "Bad?"

Spike nodded and said, "That'll be a patrol car. The officers will start sealing off the — they'll do their thing."

"Oh, Vivian." Charlotte reached for her daughter, but if Vivian noticed she chose to ignore the gesture.

What Spike felt was entirely too conflicted to be appropriate. That would change and quickly. "Let your mother help you get dry," he said. "I need to speak with the police. Charlotte, I also need a plastic bag right now."

Vivian dropped her hands at once, but she shook her head, turning down any assistance from Charlotte, who didn't waste time arguing. She sped away and returned with a self-sealing plastic bag and opened it for Spike to drop Louis Martin's phone inside. He set it on a marble-topped demilune table and rested the mangled rose on top.

"We could go into the kitchens maybe," Cyrus said — ever the diplomat. "Get out of the hall so we don't look like we're hovering."

A young officer arrived at the door. Spike expected him to ask exact directions to the

70

scene and to tell them they should all remain in the house. The man looked at Spike as if he knew him and said, "Detective Bonine said you'd make sure nobody leaves before he gets here."

He left and they turned to get out of the hall.

They never made it to the kitchens before Errol Bonine clomped in without so much as a knock. "Detective Bonine," he said, flashing his badge around. "Who found the stiff?"

Errol watched too many big city cop shows and subtlety had never been his middle name. His partner, as slim and fit-looking as Errol was paunchy — and sloppy — looked vaguely apologetic. Spike figured Bonine had cowed the younger man into being no more than his errand boy.

A few years earlier Errol had tried that on Spike and found out he had a maverick on his hands, a maverick with brains. From that day on, stomping on anyone who might make it easy for Errol to keep up his cozy arrangements with the local muscle had become Spike's reason to live.

Eventually Spike had taken a walk down an alley. He didn't remember that alley so well when he woke up in hospital, beaten to a pulp. He'd been told he was fired for jeopardizing the reputation of the force, and pressured out of New Iberia.

"Best get over the shock," Errol said to the company, yanking his tightly cinched pants higher under his belly. He wore a heavy khaki duster which probably accounted for his redder than usual face and the sweat running from beneath his greased-back gray hair and down his shiny jowls. Errol had always loved his duster and apparently thought it turned him into a romantic figure, a cowboy cop, although he never let anyone forget he was a detective. "Givin' in to weakness slows things down. Who found the body?"

"I did," Vivian said in barely a whisper.

"You didn't say who you were," Spike said to Errol's partner.

The man fumbled to produce his badge. "Wiley. Frank Wiley."

"Good to meet you," Spike said and deliberately raised his voice a notch when he added, "Spike Devol. I'm Deputy Sheriff over in Toussaint and thereabouts."

Errol had actually been too pumped up with showing how important he was to notice Spike in civilian clothes. He noticed him now. "I forgot to ask you on the phone. What the fuck you doin' here, Devol? You know what I said I'd do to you if I caught you messin' in my territory."

"Aw, that's nice of you Errol, but I wouldn't hear of you putting yourself out," Spike said, making sure his face didn't show what he was thinking. "Good evening to you. I'm a guest here. Just happened to show up on a bad night." He didn't want trouble in front of Vivian and Charlotte — or Cyrus for that matter.

Errol's mustache, which stuck straight out to begin with, bristled and brought unpleasant memories back to Spike. Errol said, "You seen the body?" Suspicion narrowed his eyes.

"Yes. As she already told you, Miss Vivian Patin here found it when she was looking for her dog. Then she called in here for help." Might as well get the first round of rage over. He angled his head at Louis's phone in the plastic bag and said, "I went out. That's the victim's cell phone. The rose is also from the scene."

Errol's chubby hand settled on his notebook and he looked from the phone to Spike. If possible, his face turned an even deeper shade of puce and puffed up. "I hope you're tellin' me the victim was in this house and left that behind," he said.

"No," Vivian said in a firmer voice. "He was on his way here but never arrived."

73

Cyrus stepped forward and extended a hand. "I'm Father Cyrus Payne, Detective. St. Cécil's in Toussaint. The unfortunate dead man is Mr. Louis Martin from New Orleans. He's a lawyer and deals with Charlotte and Vivian Patin's affairs."

Errol sneered and managed to convey a "who asked you and who cares about the small stuff?" expression. "I was," he said, "asking how that phone got into this house."

"It was in Louis's briefcase," Vivian said in a rush, ignoring Spike's attempted signals to keep quiet. "I'd left my phone in here and I figured he had to have one somewhere. I couldn't leave his body, could I? I found the phone in his briefcase which wasn't an easy thing to do because his head was resting on the case and his throat has been cut so there's a lot of slippery blood around. And Louis's head is heavy."

She caught her breath and swallowed loudly enough for Spike to hear.

"I did put the briefcase back in pretty much the position I found it." Her speech slowed and she blinked rapidly. "Um, I don't suppose I should have touched anything but I could only think of getting help. There's a kiss on his face — made with blood, I think."

Charlotte backed up and sat on the

bottom step of the stairs. She held her throat.

Vivian rushed on as if she was bent on making things as bad as possible for herself. "Now I think of it, I do think the killer may have taken something out of the briefcase because the only thing in there was a folder with our name on it and a single piece of paper in it, an agreement for us to sign, inside. And the phone, of course. There was supposed to be something else, or we expected something else, but it wasn't there." She paused for breath again and frowned. "The phone could have been touched by the murderer then, couldn't it? Oh, dear."

"Wiley," Errol said softly. "Call for some backup — including a female officer. Stay here until the others show up. We need a search warrant."

"Why?" Spike said. "What the hell are you talkin' about?"

"I run a tight ship. Unlike you, I cover all my bases — officially. But since you're here, I'm goin' to ask you to do some scut work, Devol. Might make things go easier on you. Call and arrange a search warrant. Tell 'em we got a body outside and the deceased's cell phone — covered with his blood — in the house. We gotta make sure there ain't no more of his effects mysteriously hanging around here."

Spike opened his mouth to tell Errol . . . to remind him that Spike wasn't paid by anyone in Iberia anymore. Instead he said, very carefully, "They aren't going to take that request from me — even if I was prepared to make it. Don't you think you might want to start at the crime scene? You know, the one where there's a body, and get things taken care of there?"

"Wiley, don't let these people out of your sight," Errol snapped. "Devol, I'll speak to you outside."

"By all means," Spike said. If Errol wanted a fight it could take place outside, away from Vivian and Charlotte. Cyrus was a different matter; he was no stranger to violence, but he was needed with the women.

Before Spike and Errol could get to the door, the wheels of another vehicle crunched to a halt in front of the house, a door rattled open and shut, and fleet footsteps rushed to the steps.

L'Oiseau de Nuit, locally known as Wazoo, whirled her small, black-clad body into the hallway. Spike groaned but Cyrus thumped him on the back and said, " 'Evenin' Wazoo. What brings you this way?"

Wazoo, arms extended to make the best of

trailing filmy sleeves, allowed her eyelids to droop and made unintelligible sounds. A flamboyant medium from New Orleans who had descended on Toussaint a little more than a year ago, she had set up permanent shop in the twelve-room Majestic Hotel where, according to local gossip, business boomed.

"The sight," she said, opening her dark eyes and looking intently at Errol Bonine. "A blessin' and a curse I'm tellin' you. Death am here. I felt it — and maybe saw a thing or two — and I come right here to do what I the only one can do. I need to talk with him on the other side now."

"Go home, lady," Errol said. "Do it before I change my mind about letting you leave at all. Just climb on your broom and fly away." He made flapping motions with one hand.

Promptly, Wazoo descended to sit cross-legged on the floor with her many-layered dress floating about her. "I feel evil in the house," she said. "I must stay to protect the innocent."

"Shee-it," Errol said with great feeling. "Devol, make yourself useful and call the station for more backup. Wiley's got his hands full."

"Dial on the way to the scene," Spike said, walking out of the door. "You'll have seen lights being set up when you arrived so you know where it is."

"I told you to make a call."

Spike smiled engagingly. "You know the number, I've forgotten it."

He glanced back at Vivian who gave him a pretty encouraging smile for a woman who had a right to feel she'd joined the circus, and he warmed up around the knots of anger that were eating him up.

5

Cyrus had pinned Errol Bonine's partner as a man who would do whatever he was told, but he'd been wrong. As soon as Spike left with Bonine the younger detective withdrew a distance from everyone else. And Wiley, a lithe brown-haired man with a thoughtful face, showed no intention of continuing Bonine's badgering ways.

Evidently Charlotte had come to a similar conclusion. She said, "There's hot coffee in the kitchen. Would anyone like some? You, Detective Wiley?"

A smile turned him into a pleasant and engaging man. "I would be forever in your debt, ma'am." When Charlotte turned away, Wiley said, "Why don't we all go into the kitchen?"

Everyone, including Wazoo, did as he suggested and Cyrus doubted any one of them resented Wiley tipping his hat to his partner's instructions to watch over all of them.

Cyrus walked behind Wazoo and when he saw the opportunity, caught her by the arm and turned her gently toward him.

She looked at his hand on her arm. "You don't wanna do that, God man. Your magic not strong enough to fight with mine. Could be, I hurt you without meaning to." She looked directly into his face and he realized again that she couldn't be more than thirty-five or so and without the bizarre getup, she'd be a pretty woman. For an instant her eyes were unfocused, then she said, "Kisses of blood," and dropped her head back to send up thin moans, "the devil's work."

With his free hand, Cyrus moved her tangled hair, revealing a wire running from an earpiece, undoubtedly to a radio hidden somewhere on her person. "Get pretty good reception on that thing, do you? It's probably a big help to your magic and invaluable when you need to *see* the exact location of bad news."

"You don' know what you sayin'. L'Oiseau de Nuit jest helpin' out, me. People are grateful for that."

Cyrus waved her ahead of him to the kitchen thinking, *and there goes voodoo's answer to an ambulance chaser.*

6

Spitting tacks without moving your face took talent. On the other hand, Spike thought his face might crack if he twitched a muscle, that and he'd start spilling what he thought of Errol Bonine.

"Never saw such a screw-up," Errol told the gathering in the kitchen.

Spike caught Frank Wiley's eye and did his best to ease up on the rage when the man winked at him.

"Crime scene folks are out there now. Reckon it'll take 'em forever and it don't help that just about everythin's been handled." He eyeballed not Charlotte, but Vivian, and said, "I'm gonna be talkin' to you and everyone else here for a few hours, then I'll give you a break tonight but things are gonna get hot and heavy in the mornin' — late mornin' on account of I got other duties first."

Drinking and sleeping, Spike thought.

Vivian nodded but didn't speak to Bonine.

"I don't want any of you gettin' the idea I'm thinkin' you're a suspect. Reckon all we got here is a random situation and we'll never find out who did it."

Spike chewed his tongue. He'd heard Errol spout the same advance excuses for his own incompetence before. A man who just wanted to pose and draw a paycheck didn't cotton to the kind of hard work that went into successful investigations.

"Could be somethin' else, but I doubt it. But you —" Errol pointed at Vivian "— you made a lot of work out there with your messin'. Don't keep me hangin' around when I get back tomorrow, y hear? Be here when I need you and say your prayers I don't have to take you in —"

"Can it, Bonine," Spike said. Enough was enough. "She's an innocent bystander who happened on a corpse. Leave her alone."

"You're forgettin' your place, sonny," Bonine said, smiling in a way that let Spike know the man enjoyed baiting an old enemy he'd decided was powerless. "Keep it zipped or I'll have to speak to someone in Toussaint. And pour me some of that coffee."

"Wipe your own ass," Spike said through his teeth and instantly rubbed a hand over his face. Of all the things to say in front of Vivian and her mother — and Cyrus.

He needn't have worried about Cyrus, who laughed like he'd bust a gut and said, "Never heard such language before. Your penance is to call for senior bingo next month."

7

The second day

Vivian had debated whether she should tell her mother she'd decided to go to Spike's place, even if it was two in the morning, and take him the dinner he never got to eat. She needn't have worried about Charlotte's reaction because she behaved as if the mission were all her own idea.

A deputy stood guard at the entrance to Rosebank, the driveway was lined with official vehicles and there were floodlights in the area where she'd found Louis. Only the police and the experts were allowed in or out of the main driveway. Since no one paid any attention to the second gate that led from the back of the property to a side road and Vivian's green van was parked in the yard of the old stable where it couldn't be seen from the front of the house, leaving hadn't been a problem.

After five hours during which his partner and a female officer made sure Vivian and Charlotte, Spike and Cyrus didn't have a chance to talk to one another in private, the hateful Detective Bonine had abruptly stopped his round of interviewing them, one by one. Spike and Cyrus had been dismissed with warnings to "be available." Vivian and Charlotte were told, "It's in your best interests not to plan any trips." Bonine had pulled Vivian aside and said, "I'll be back," before scuffing from the house.

Spike had left about an hour earlier so he could only have been home half an hour at most. He was probably looking for something to eat right now.

The rain had stopped and the moon shone clear, even if it was banded with cloud. Driving north into St. Martin's Parish Vivian tried to concentrate on how much she'd grown to like this quiet place. Visions of Louis, dead in his car, pushed their way in but she moved them aside quickly and found that thinking about Spike's face took her in a whole new direction.

If she hadn't been distracted she'd have made sure he took the food with him.

Yeah, and who was she fooling? Seeing the leek pie in the refrigerator and the color-frosted sugar cookies shaped like Raggedy Ann and Andy baked by her mother for Wendy had lifted Vivian's spirits and made her hands shake with anticipation. That was one convenient excuse to do what she wanted to do: see Spike again. She couldn't wait to see him.

Up ahead she could already see the black and white sign in front of *Devol's, St. Martin's First Gas Stop. Store Out Back. The Bayou Provisioners. You Want It, We Got It. We deliver anywhere. And Eats.* On the other side of the board, *Last* replaced *First.*

Vivian's courage fled. Driving from Rosebank to Spike's place took about half an hour, which meant that instead of being, "only two in the morning," it was now, "only two-thirty in the morning."

Idiot woman. How did she think she was going to get to Spike without waking up Homer and Wendy? And what made her imagine for one moment that the object of her fantasies would be delighted if she dropped in on him when he probably had to be on duty early?

Apart from a single bulb at the corner of the building, the gas station lights were off. The store, set far back from the road, was also in darkness and she couldn't see the house which she thought was closer to the bayou.

Spike's Ford sedan, complete with insignia on the trunk and front doors, stood beneath the gas station light. Pretty good deterrent to troublemakers.

Vivian pulled her van in, considered for a moment whether she had the courage to walk boldly to the house and leave the food on the gallery — with a note on top — and decided she certainly did.

If the striped moon weren't still casting some light, it would be difficult to see without a flashlight and she'd run the risk of disturbing someone.

The only sounds were of rustling leaves and buggy nightlife with voices way too big for their size.

Once past the gas station and beside the store, Vivian saw the dark outline of Spike's house. Bigger than she'd expected, it stood on substantial stilts. The gallery had to be on the other side, facing the bayou. The part of the building she approached probably contained the bedrooms.

A little jumpy, she hurried around the house, skirting a light-colored van as she went and, sure enough, two wooden chairs glowed white on a screened gallery — between them stood a miniature version. Wendy's. Vivian swallowed. Intruding here without an invitation was a dumb idea.

The dishes she'd brought were stacked in a plastic crate with wire handles. A picnic table sat out front of the gallery. She placed the crate there and backed away, wiping her hands on the legs of her jeans.

Oh sure, that would be there in the morning.

Animals around here were too well-mannered to eat every scrap and spread dishes and debris in all direction. Then there were birds. Like the crows that had hung out around Louis's body, diving in for pieces of his hamburger and fries. She couldn't expect to forget too easily.

She stared at the back of the house again. The complete lack of lights surprised her, but it could also prove convenient.

Hiking the crate from the table, she hunched over and approached the steps to the gallery and door. On the balls of her sneaker-shod feet, she climbed the wooden stairs, unnerved by a sensation that she ought to check behind her. She wasn't easily frightened, or not usually.

On the gallery, against the split log wall and right by the door, Vivian eased her burden down once more. She'd forgotten to write a note but he'd know where the food was from.

"Don't move."

The whispered order might as well have been shouted. Vivian stumbled and landed on her knees. A light snapped on, a light with a blinding beam that settled over her like a stage spot.

"You drove here alone? You walked around out here in the dark alone?"

"I'm not twelve."

He looked skyward. "There's a murderer on the loose around here. And in case you've forgotten he killed at Rosebank — right at your home — and you don't know what he came for. Only to kill Louis Martin? I doubt it. Could be he wanted something in the briefcase and that was it. We don't know, though. Could be he wanted to get at you." He held a gun against his thigh. "Didn't anyone stop you when you were leaving? No, obviously they didn't. Damn Bonine's sloppy hide."

She shivered and crossed her arms under her breasts.

"Goddammit!" Spike turned down the beam and hurried to her on silent feet. He stuffed the gun into the waist of the jeans that were all he wore and hauled her up with one hand. He dropped his voice. "What do you think you're doing? Why? Why would you do something as stupid as creeping up on my house in the early hours of the morning? Damn it, Vivian, I'm . . . You could have been killed."

When she could moisten her mouth enough to speak, she said, "You didn't have dinner. I decided to drop the food by for you to share with your family."

"Keep your voice down, I won't have Wendy scared for nothing." With that he bundled her down the steps to the warm, damp grass and away from the house.

For nothing. He was right, but she still felt bad to hear him refer to her that way. "I'm really sorry," she said in a soft voice. "I stayed up because I knew I wasn't going to sleep. To be honest, I didn't think it through before I got in the van. Forgive me, please. I'll go now so don't give this another thought. I am sorry I woke you up."

"Ah hell," he said and released her arm. "Nothing's simple, know that?"

"Yes."

Spike recognized this as proof that there was no way he could let her know how he really felt, not now and maybe never. His life wouldn't mix with any woman's. He touched her face and she recoiled. "Oh great," he said. "I frightened you. I frightened *you.* That makes me feel like hell."

"No, no, don't. You were only guarding your family and property. I put you on alert and a man like you goes on autopilot then, you have to. You thought I was . . . I'm an intruder." She gave a short laugh. "I'm not doing too well with the law, am I?"

If he argued with her, he'd get himself in deeper water. "It's too warm," he told her. "Feel like something cold to drink?"

"We'd wake someone up. Thanks anyway."

"No, in the store. No one will hear us there."

A woman could put some spin on a comment like that. Unfortunately he was simply trying to recover balance for both of them by being polite and pretending he was already over her mistake.

"C'mon, Vivian, don't make me suffer because I was an ass. Let me try to make it right so I can quit kicking myself."

She looked at the shadows that were his face, and the unreadable gleam in his eyes, and smiled. "I can't believe what I did." She clapped her hands to her cheeks and shuddered.

"Come with me," Spike said, "Gimme a break, okay? I want a cold drink and I want you with me while I have it. And we need to get some things straight between us — or I think so."

She thought so, too, but didn't pretend to herself that she'd like the result. "If you're sure you want to do that, I am, too."

Spike was more than sure he wanted to snatch at least this opportunity to be alone with Vivian. He was long past the age of buying a girl a soda and expecting nothing more than conversation and his own sexual frustration.

It would have to do.

Homer kept a spare key in one of the pots of flowers that hung from the eaves all around the store. This was one time when the idea didn't irritate Spike.

He opened up and put a hand at Vivian's waist to usher her inside.

"Oh," she said in a small voice while she backed up against his hand. "It feels strange in here. You aren't supposed to be inside stores when they're closed."

It didn't feel out of place to slide his hand around her and splay his fingers to span her ribs. She stood so close he felt the warmth of her body.

"I didn't know your shop was so big," she said and her voice sounded real small. "Why do all the freestanding displays look weird just because there isn't much light? They aren't scary in daylight."

He didn't think what he was doing until his mouth touched her hair. He whispered in her ear, "Things we aren't used to. The ordinary becomes mysterious when the context is out of whack." They stood still like that, he with his hand at her side and his mouth close to her ear — and the sensation of her bare arm against his chest, Vivian soft and angling her head to bring her face closer to his.

Spike needed his legendary willpower to stop him from kissing her ear, her cheek, and turning her in his arms, and letting things go wherever they might.

Her white tank top didn't reach her waist and the skin he touched there felt forbidden — and wonderful.

A deep breath expanded her chest and she walked away from him into the store. For an instant he felt cold at the loss of her, but he gathered his wits quickly enough and followed inside, closing and locking the door behind him. Wendy slept deeply and Homer had a history of being hard to rouse. The chances that he and Vivian would be interrupted were more than remote.

Spike hadn't inherited Homer's tendency to slip easily into oblivion. He slept only a fraction beneath consciousness and awoke with eyes wide open as if he'd been alert all the time. That was usually a good thing but forgetting he'd pointed a gun at Vivian tonight wouldn't happen anytime soon.

"A person could do all their grocery shopping in here," she said, her eyes evidently adjusted to the gloom. "That's great. I bet you do a great business."

"Fair. The big grocery stores are our competition but there isn't one of those too close. The business with the folks who live along the bayou is a plus. So are the houseboats. The sandwich and ice cream bar is a little gold mine. Hey, c'mon and sit down."

Each time Spike got close to her, Vivian struggled against touching him. His torso shone slightly in the semidarkness and she saw that the hair on his chest was surprisingly dark. Muscular and hard, what she could see of his body made her feel cheated out of what she couldn't see. He walked away on bare feet.

Did he sleep naked?

Did he leap up and into a pair of jeans — and nothing else — if he had to? His hand at her side, where he had gripped her naked skin, had excited her almost as if he'd pressed between her legs. The flare of sensation she'd felt had given her an instant's fear that she would disgrace herself by climaxing right then, standing beside him. She had responded to men before, but not like this.

He stood beside a shiny wooden table with two chairs, one of about five tables of various shapes and sizes. She sat in the chair he pulled out for her and looked up at him where he stood over her.

So serious. So many questions in eyes gone to navy-blue in the surreal cast of light. "What do you like?" he asked, leaving her and going to a refrigerated case. "We carry about everything."

"What's in those glasses? The pink stuff."

"Strawberry Smush. My dad's specialty. Started out as something he made for Wendy, then he tried a few in here and they're popular. Like to taste one?"

"Yes, please," she said and smiled at the way he slung bottled water between his fingers and held the pink thing in the same hand while he got napkins for both of them, and a spoon for Vivian.

When he put everything on the table, she giggled. "Do you feel like you're in the Gingerbread House?"

"No . . . Yes, tonight I feel like that," he said. "Left alone with the goodies."

He must mean the food and drinks. No, he didn't, he didn't do subtlety too well, but he was letting her know he liked being here with her.

8

Spike sat down beside Vivian and unscrewed the cap from his water. With every move he felt self-conscious. He felt her eyes on him, and he'd have to be dead not to know there was a good-size spark between them just waiting to be ignited.

Neither of them said a word until Spike couldn't stand it anymore and asked, "How about a sandwich?"

Vivian caught up her spoon and dipped it into the Smush, a concoction that resembled a strawberry mousse. She let that spoonful dissolve, almost with a popping sensation, in her mouth. "Can I have a raincheck on the sandwich until after I finish this? Maybe I'll be hungrier for one then. This pops in your mouth. Like it's carbonated."

"Made with 7-Up. The sandwich is yours

anytime you want it. Just got in a fresh supply of boudin rouge — best sausage in the world and not available on every street corner."

Vivian giggled and wrinkled her nose as the next spoonful of Strawberry Smush went down. Then she put her spoon in the saucer beneath the thick, dimple-glass parfait glass and anchored her hands between her knees.

Spike swallowed more water and waited.

"I don't know what came over me this evening," Vivian said. "This morning. Unless it was you."

He wiped any hint of a smile from his face. "I can be an overbearing man . . . Why would you come here because I'm overbearing? Not that you said that was it, only I do know about my faults and —"

"You're right. You can be overbearing but only when you think it's for the best. At least, that's how I see it so far. You have to think I've lost my mind. Apart from last night, we've met maybe half a dozen times and drunk a cup of coffee together — seems like I'm takin' a lot for granted."

"Nine times and I saw you the last time you visited your uncle at Rosebank and you went into Toussaint — three times," he told her. "Had coffee together twice and walked along the bayou when I met you comin' out of church that Sunday. I liked that. Only thing wrong was that I wanted to hold your hand and I couldn't. Then I wanted to kiss you, and I sure as hell couldn't."

"You could have tried," she said and turned her face away, amazed at her own boldness.

Spike got a fresh taste of arousal. At this rate he'd have a permanent zipper mark on his Pride of the South. He grinned at his own little joke, but the pressure didn't ease. They might as well be locked in a lovers' embrace for the connection he felt to her — maybe not quite that, but just thinking about it was its own prize.

"You are gorgeous, y'know," Vivian said, turning to face him again. "Look at you." She looked at him and he found he was short of breath. No woman had ever looked at him quite that way, studying his face minutely, spending extra time on his mouth until she leaned a little closer and her own lips parted. "And I like you, that's a good reason to come see you."

"You're embarrassing me," he told her. "But don't let that stop you."

She smiled, a quirky smile, and inclined her head to take in his body. He was grateful he remained what Madge Pollard, Cyrus's bright-eyed assistant, called lean and mean — only with enough bulk to make a girl weak at the knees. "Do you lift weights?" Vivian asked. "Live on some sort of chemicals with Gatoraid chasers? I don't think chests just come like that."

He controlled an urge to sweep her on top of the table and sit with his chair pushed back, making sure he hadn't missed anything about her — or as little as he could do that with her clothes on. "I do a lot of physical work," he told her and shrugged. "And I like to run. Oh, what the hell, I might as well fess up to it all. We've got an old Nautilus at the station and I love that thing."

"Worth every second," she said, her voice somewhat lower. She pointed an index finger at him, made circles with it, looked into his eyes, back at his chest, and slowly set her fingertip on one of his pecs. Vivian poked, quite definitely poked, and made an "ooh" shape with her mouth. "You've been eating your spinach."

He sent up thanks that she managed to keep things light enough to stop him from inviting her to join him anywhere, as long as he was inside her.

"Your face got to me the first time I saw it," Spike said, and Vivian saw a wicked glitter in his eyes. So this was to be tit for tat.

"You've got cheekbones that don't quit and your eyes aren't just green, they're green-green and when you close them, you've got more black eyelashes than one woman should have. They curve against your face, and flicker because you're always thinking about something. And your skin is so white. Black hair and white skin. Is your skin the same all over?"

Her eyes flashed at him. "That's a secret."

"I like secrets. They turn me on. Sometimes I can't quit until I find them out."

Her left hand rested on the table and he covered it with his right. She was cool, almost too cool. Their eyes met and she smiled at him, a conspiratorial smile. Spike turned up the corners of his mouth and made himself keep on looking at her, but something had changed in him and he couldn't afford that change. He wasn't going to be able to put Vivian Patin out of his mind easily. At this moment he doubted he would ever forget the way she looked at him now.

He could not have a woman in his life — other than casually. He already knew it didn't work. Vivian wasn't the kind of woman a man tried to get close to — with no strings attached.

She turned her hand over beneath his so

that their palms touched and their fingertips rested together. He played back and forth, softly, and saw her shiver again but not, he thought, out of fear or because she was cold — not this time.

"This may not be the best timing," he said, "but what happened with the fire your father died in?"

She nodded and bent low enough over their joined hands to ensure her face wasn't visible. "Chez Charlotte — that was my parents' restaurant. Burned to the ground. The fire started in the kitchens and that's where my father was found."

Spike knew he must listen quietly and not try to prompt her with his own questions.

She kept her face down but curled her fingers into his palm and made light rubbing motions that tickled vaguely. "My dad was a calm man — unless he lost his temper, and he did do that regularly. But he was alone there. Something I don't get, and neither does Mama. All alone and cooking. They say he must have been and that he probably set the stove on fire."

Spike picked up her hand and held it between both of his. Her fingers were long but disappeared inside his own. "What did the local experts decide?"

"Accident," she said.

"You don't sound as if you believe that."

"No. And less now with Louis's death. Poor man. We have to find what was taken from his briefcase. He became marked by it, whatever it is, I'm sure of that."

"We," Spike felt mean but it had to be said. "This is a job for the professionals, Vivian. I won't be one of them, you already know that. And Errol Bonine and his squad won't allow you to interfere. They'll do the askin' and tell you no more than they have to."

"He — Bonine asked me questions for two hours."

"I know. I was in the house, remember? What kind of questions did he ask?" He shouldn't interfere but didn't feel any remorse.

"Dumb questions. And the same ones over and over — when he wasn't *resting his eyes*. Where was I from? Why would I want to live at Rosebank? Was I in some sort of trouble in New Orleans? Why aren't I married? Was I ever married? Don't I like men?"

"Ass," Spike said with feeling. How Errol had risen as far as he had would always be a mystery — maybe. "Don't you worry about him. He's doing what he thinks he's supposed to do, only he's forgotten most of what that is. You just keep calm and don't let him rile you."

Vivian decided that Deputy Sheriff Spike Devol didn't know exactly what, or who, he was dealing with yet. He'd learn in time. If Vivian had her way, he'd learn everything there was to learn about her. She took a forgotten breath and felt a wash of hopelessness. Spike might be interested in an affair, a short, hot affair, but nothing more unless she was mistaken. That wouldn't be enough for her — tantalizing as it seemed.

"What kind of record does Detective Bonine have?" she asked. "For solving crimes, I mean?"

"Lousy, but that doesn't seem to cramp his style. I'm talking out of school but I'd say the detective lives very well for what I know he earns and the possibility is that not solving some cases pays well. I don't know if your case falls into that category, but don't expect any speedy answers. It's likely to drag on, then fade away."

"I've got to find the connection between my father's death and what happened yesterday. Uncle Guy only changed his will almost literally on his deathbed. Dad died a few weeks after Uncle Guy. The insurance wasn't nearly enough and my mother took a terrible financial hit. And that was on top of being brokenhearted over Dad's death."

"Stinking luck," Spike said.

"As things stand we don't have any choice but to make Rosebank work. There's enough money to creep along for a while and nothing more. We can't really continue with the renovations until we're more solvent again. We have to move so slowly when we need to go fast."

She drummed her fingers and he wondered if she was deciding whether to go on.

"In Uncle Guy's will there was a strange reference to having faith, that he had taken care of all eventualities and all the Patins would have to do was use their minds if their eyes were to see the truth."

She had all of Spike's attention.

"Louis said he was bringing good news. What would you make out of that?"

Careful. "I'd probably make some of the same guesses you're making. But I wouldn't get in the way of the law."

Her determined concentration on the table didn't fool him. The lady could become hard to handle because she wouldn't take directions easily unless they made a lot of sense to her.

"The connection has to be found." She sounded stubborn.

"If there is one." He slid his rump forward

in his chair and carried her fingertips to his mouth. "Heed what I say and don't meddle. Your life is too important to risk. I won't let you lose it over money."

Her startled eyes rose to his face.

Absently, Spike kissed the very tips of her fingers, ran his tongue across them. Vivian said, "I like you doing that. It makes me dizzy."

"Actually this is a bad idea," he said, speaking deliberately as if he were discussing the boudin rouge, only with less enthusiasm.

"Is it?"

She was an enigma, and irresistible. His voice might sound cool but what he felt was anything but cool. He'd better back off.

"How about you?" she asked. "Tell me something about you and what you want."

"I want a better life for Wendy," he said and Vivian wouldn't allow herself to remark that he was holding her hand too tightly. "She's fine now, but she'll need more and I'll give it to her. She's always going to feel loved and it'll never mean anything to her that her mother . . . left. Wendy will go to college. She'll get whatever opportunities it takes to get her to her full potential."

"I know you'll make sure of that."

The flashlight on the floor cast uplights

over his face. His gleaming eyes held a far-away expression.

"And you?" she asked. "What do you want for yourself?"

He looked at her and there was nothing faraway about him now. Spike studied only her face and for so long Vivian could scarcely bear the wait. Finally the corners of his mouth tipped up and he said, "I want you. It's wrong for me to say it, but it's true. Already I feel I've known you forever and I want to know you better. But it couldn't work out. Even if you'd have me, we'd have to sneak around to be together."

"Because you're afraid I'd hurt you, or Wendy. It's Wendy you worry about most and I like you for that. But are you really thinking about the whole picture, or just about sex?"

His eyes never left her face and he didn't flinch. "I need that, too. I want that, too. But I'd settle for kissing you — for now. Just to see how we like it. You probably wouldn't want that when I have nothing else to offer you."

Vivian looked at their joined hands and inched them toward her. He stopped her, kissed her palm, pressed it against his neck and leaned slowly closer.

She heard his breathing, focused on the

distinct contours of his mouth. He stopped moving toward her and she almost panicked at the thought that he might not kiss her.

His eyes closed. His lips found hers in a soft, careful kiss. She heard their mouths part, but almost at once he drew the tip of his tongue across her lips and nipped lightly. They shifted their faces, noses bumping gently. Vivian felt his features, the beard stubble, feathered her fingers over his brows, his closed eyes.

Spike maneuvered her to face him, pulled her forward until her knees were between his thighs. He held her head and stroked the corners of her mouth. Vivian pressed her mouth into his, passed her tongue over the smooth insides while his thumbs at the corners of her lips, rubbing, aroused her.

He heard her pant, felt her tongue meet his and shifted on the chair. The little white tank top had wriggled up and when he sought her waist he found a bared midriff. With each touch, she moaned, and he moaned with her. He found the indentation in her spine, between her hips, slid a hand beneath her jeans and held her smooth bottom, let his fingers graze the dip between the cheeks.

And Vivian rubbed him, his neck and shoulders, his sides, across his chest. She pinched his flat nipples and he thought he'd lose the last vestige of his control. Abandoning his mouth for his chest, she trailed her tongue over his skin, gradually lowered her head and sucked a dozen places on his belly.

Vivian didn't want to think about anything but the way he felt, and the way she felt with him. His abdomen, tight and inflexible, tasted salty. The sensation that came when he slipped her tank top from one shoulder stopped her breath. He bent over and kissed her there. His hands passed from her ribs to the sides of her breasts. And she burned, her nipples, deep in her womb, between her legs where flesh turned hard and erogenous. It swelled, throbbed.

In one swift motion, Spike pulled her from her chair and astride his thighs and, as she'd known must happen, he stopped kissing her. He held her in strong arms, such strong arms she couldn't catch her breath.

Beneath her, she felt his erection. He wanted her as much as she wanted him. He pushed the distended ridge behind his zipper against her center. "Spike?"

"This is going to sound crazy," he said against her face, rocking her, dipping his tongue rapidly into her mouth and, always, breathing like a suffocating man. "I want you so bad it hurts."

"I want you," she told him. It was too late for pride.

"Vivian, I don't just want sex with you." He gave a short laugh. "Not that I don't need that enough to make me want to take you no matter what the cost might be. But if I can't have all of you, all the time, I'm not going to do something that'll mean you'll walk the other way if you see me coming."

She pushed a hand between them and massaged the hard length of him.

Spike captured her wrist. For moments he closed her hand even harder over him and let his head drop back.

Just as quickly, he pulled her hand from him.

"I'd never walk away from you," she said, leaning on him, pressing her face into his shoulder. "Not unless you told me to."

They came together in a frenzied burst. He kissed her wildly and didn't confine himself to her mouth. Rocking her on top of his distended penis, he pulled her top above her breasts, held his tongue between his teeth while he narrowed his eyes to look at her. Beads of sweat broke out on his brow and upper lip.

Vivian couldn't stand waiting. She thrust herself toward him and he buried his face between her breasts. His mouth, settling over a nipple, pulled a cry from her and she moved him to the other breast. She put her feet on the floor either side of him and stood, pushing his head back while she tried to get closer and closer.

Spike unzipped her jeans and slid his fingers inside her panties. Her hips jerked against him. He'd just about lost it all. Even knowing he should stop, not because he didn't want her but because common sense told him to, he still couldn't bring himself to leave her on the brink.

Seconds passed in silence while he licked her breasts, flicked the tip of his tongue over her nipples — and got serious about his finger action. He longed to kiss her down there and finish the job with his mouth. Even if he'd decided to go for it, Vivian let him know it was too late. She curved forward over him, wrapped her arms around his head and held him hard against her, and came in a burst of convulsive thrusts.

Already she tore at his zipper. Why did this have to be a decision, he wondered. He needed her now. They needed each other. "Not now, *cher*," he murmured, holding her hand away. *He had to hold on, get through this.* "Not here."

"I like it here."

So did he, as long as she was with him.

"Spike, I'll never, never turn away from you."

"I'd rather not have to remind you of that promise," he said, and stood up, moving her to his side and zipping his pants. Blood pounded in his head, and elsewhere. He willed his drive for sex to calm down. "Maybe we'll get lucky and we'll become what? Appropriate? I'm following you home to make sure you get safely inside."

9

"The only identifiable prints on the phone are yours. And that jackass Devol's, of course. But since I figure he'd have fixed the thing if he was worried about it, I'm reckonin' he's probably clean, him."

Vivian swallowed several times but her mouth remained dry. Detective Bonine had set himself up in Uncle Guy's old office in the south wing, apparently oblivious to the dust that layered everything and swirled in a slice of sunlight through velvet-draped windows. He shifted papers on the rosewood desk, sending more murky clouds into the air, and didn't even sneeze.

Vivian sneezed.

So did Gary Legrain, whose very tall body all but reclined in an orange velvet chair with skeins of bright beads knotted on each leg.

She met his gray eyes but he showed no emotion. However, from the moment he'd arrived before nine that morning, she'd liked him and been grateful he was at Rosebank. He'd offered, without pressure, to act as Charlotte and Vivian's attorney if they wanted him, at least until they decided what to do about permanent representation. They assured him they wanted and needed him.

"Did you read my clients their rights last night?" Legrain asked in his rumbly voice.

Bonine slammed a bronze pineapple paperweight on top of a file. "I've told them they aren't suspects."

"That wasn't my question."

"Well you got the answer I decided to give you," Bonine said. "You still aren't a suspect, Ms. Patin, but I'd like to read you your rights just the same. Better for both of us." He whipped out a card and recited the Miranda in a rapid monotone as if he saw nothing wrong with having taken advantage the previous evening.

"You recordin' this?" Legrain asked innocently, scanning jammed bookcases at the same time.

Bonine's face had turned its signature shade of puce. The shaft of sun lighted a muzzy reddish halo around his grizzled head and Vivian got a fleeting vision of horns on top. Last night and early this formerly wonderful morning had not left her in the mood for sleep. Now she was exhausted and the horned mirage of Bonine made her giggle before wisdom clicked on.

"You're bein' warned, you," Bonine said. "There's nothin' funny about the situation here, or your part in it, Ms. Patin. You may not find me, or what could happen to you so funny in a while."

"Intimidating witnesses —"

"Shut you mouth, Legrain," Bonine said and Vivian didn't need someone else to warn her the man was melting down. "Much more out of you and I'll have you removed."

"On what grounds?" Legrain asked in a reasonable voice which wasn't likely to calm Bonine. "Where's the recorder?"

"On the grounds that you're a pain in the ass." Bonine got up and fussed around in boxes he'd had brought in until he produced the necessary recording equipment and switched it on. He gave his name, Vivian's, and the time and date in bored tones then added Gary Legrain's presence as an afterthought. "You gonna let me get on with my business now?" he asked.

Legrain levered himself out of his chair

and commenced to take long, slow strides around the room. He made the mistake of pulling one of the orange velvet drapes aside to get a better view of the courtyard and stables. Vivian lost count of the number of times he sneezed amid clouds of pungent dust.

"Are you done interruptin' this interrogation?" Bonine asked when the sneezing stopped. He went on without waiting for a reply, "Ms. Patin, isn't it true that you and your mama got money troubles?"

Vivian's temper rose. She looked at her lawyer but he continued his round of the room and didn't seem interested in the question. "We do," she said. Honesty paid in the end — or mostly it did — even if she was caught off balance by the question.

Gary Legrain stopped his pacing and sat on the corner of the desk — on the same side as Bonine. Vivian figured he had to be close to seven feet tall and he looked in good shape. He wore his dishwater-blond hair short and was more tanned than any other lawyer she remembered. He appeared to stare into the distance, much to the detective's ire.

"You comfy enough, Legrain?" Bonine asked. "You through sneezin' and tryin' to mess with my train of thought, you?"

"You've got the floor," Legrain said.

"So here you are with this place. It needs to be condemned or repaired —"

"It does not need to be condemned," Vivian told him, even though she knew she was being baited.

"As I was sayin'," Bonine continued, "you got a notion to do this place up and run some sort of rooming house."

Either he was trying to make her angry or he was operating with minus gray cells. Neither possibility encouraged Vivian. She didn't need a mean-spirited troublemaker or a mental midget with power.

"A hotel," she told him, turning up the corners of her mouth. "My parents were in the restaurant business and I've been in hotel management for —"

"I didn't ask for a life history," Bonine said. "I know all that. You wanna open a hotel then." A sneer didn't improve the arrangement of his belligerent features.

"We'll start small," she said, as if she hadn't picked up on his attitude. "A few rooms and a restaurant."

Bonine pushed back in his chair and hauled his feet onto the desk. "This whole place needs work."

"Don't I know it?" Vivian actually enjoyed hiding behind her innocent eyes.

"You got the money?"

Legrain said, "Where are you going with this?"

"You'll see, you," the detective said. "You got the money, Ms. Patin?"

She shook her head and managed to find bubbles of tears.

"Yeah," Bonine said with satisfaction. "I'd say you were in a big bind. How long have you known Devol?"

"Are you going to make some connections anytime soon, Detective?" Legrain's profile had turned hard. He narrowed his eyes.

Bonine ignored him. "How long?"

"We met a couple of years back, maybe longer," Vivian said. "We used to talk whenever I was here visiting my uncle." *And this morning we did more than talk.*

"We'll come back to that. You told me Louis Martin was bringin' good news. You told me what he said, but I don't necessarily read it the way you did. Maybe it was bad news. Perhaps there was something in the briefcase you didn't want anyone to see — some question about the ownership of Rosebank, maybe. Did he threaten you, want money or something?"

"The detective is way out of line," Legrain said. He snapped out his words and stood up. "I suggest you back off and rethink how

117

you want to pursue this, Bonine."

"Save it for the prosecutor, Legrain. You don't get to make suggestions to me. Devol would do anything to get back at me for whatever he's decided I've done to him. He'd be on the front line to help someone make a fool of me." He creaked sideways in the chair to peer at the recorder. "Will you look at that? Damn cheap equipment quit." One heavy finger plunked down on a button and Vivian realized he was turning it on, not off. When had it stopped recording?

Confused, she lost her battle to keep on seeming unfazed. "Spike had nothing to do with any of this. He didn't know you'd be the one to come."

"He knew," Bonine declared.

"Are you suggesting Devol's an accessory?" Legrain asked. "If so, that's a pretty flamboyant accusation."

Bonine gave a smile that flared his nostrils. "I'm not suggestin' anythin', me. Just doin' my job."

"Apparently the priest saw —"

"What he does or doesn't say he saw is between him and me at this point. I'm an analytical man, me. Time of death doesn't have to mean a thing in a case like this."

Tapping at the door startled Vivian. Legrain raised his eyebrows. Bonine's

118

frown wiped out his eyelids.

Vivian said, "Come in."

Madge Pollard, Cyrus's right hand, she who kept St. Cécil's — and Cyrus — running, trotted into the room with four cups on a tray, and a guileless smile on her lips. "Break time," she said, or just about sang. "From what Cyrus, and now Charlotte have told me, not one of you is taking care of yourself. How will you think your way through this tragedy if you don't give your brains a good slap now and then."

Bonine was exercising male viewing rights. Madge's cream shirt and tan pants were demure enough, but she had the kind of figure that would turn a Kevlar jumpsuit into sexy gear.

"Put it there," Bonine said, referring to the tray and pointing at the desk. He actually tilted his head to watch Madge do as he asked.

"Cream and sugar?" Madge asked. "I'll be mother."

Vivian clamped her lips together. Nothing Madge did would surprise her, but the ditzy brunette act could become a party piece.

"Cream, no sugar, please," Legrain said and his interested grin let Vivian know he hadn't missed Madge's charms, either.

Black curly hair, chin length, bounced

with each move of Madge's head and the deep intelligence in her dark eyes made them even more appealing. Vivian didn't think an interruption by Gil the gardener would have been as well received.

Once the men held their coffee, Madge handed a cup to Vivian and picked up one for herself. "We've got tea." She smiled all around. "Hot tea. Cools you down. Isn't that what we say, Vivian? Stops you from feeling wiggly." Another innocent grin. "I hate it when the heat makes you wiggly, don't you?"

Affirmative mumbles followed, and the clearing of throats, and a certain gleam in eyes that probably envisioned Madge feeling "wiggly."

Vivian stared at Madge in disbelief. Who would have expected someone else to spout Mama's tea and body temperature wisdom?

Madge had burst into the room to be a Good Samaritan and try to spring Vivian, but Madge was also having a great time with her act.

"I heard that about hot tea," Bonine said. He'd gotten up. "I need coffee for that brain slap you talked about. Very apt. But I'll remember to try the tea later."

What was she, Vivian wondered, yesterday's grits? Her own appeal had been remarked on more than a time or two, yet Bonine treated her like a cottonmouth. Spike, he was the reason. Bonine really hated him. She thought of the detective's earlier insinuations and pressed a hand into her jumpy stomach. It would be better for Spike Devol if he kept his distance from her — not that she expected Bonine to give up the notion that his old enemy had masterminded a potential coup, or assisted the mastermind. Things like this didn't happen to Vivian Patin.

"I don't think there's a need to continue the discussion now, do you?" Gary Legrain said to Bonine, who blinked a few times and gave a sharp shake of his head.

Slap it some more. Vivian had an irreverent vision of the detective's brain ricocheting inside his skull.

Madge inhaled sharply, audibly, and said, "Oh, ya, ya, I was so taken with the company I forgot to remind you of your appointment this afternoon, Vivian. Your mama asked me to."

Appointment? "Thank you." Vivian felt herself turning red. She wasn't a comfortable liar.

"I told you to be available at all times," Bonine said. "I told you that early this mornin'."

Madge put her arm beneath Vivian's. "Some appointments can't be ignored, can they?" She smiled encouragement.

"What kind of appointment?" Bonine asked. "Who are you seeing — Devol?"

"No," Vivian said.

Instead of concentrating on catching a killer, Bonine had turned Louis's death into a reason for a vendetta. Gary Legrain's pinched expression could mean he was thinking the same thing. Since he was taking Louis's death hard, that wouldn't be a pleasing idea.

Madge hung on her arm. "Now, Detective, you know there are some things a girl can't discuss around men."

Vivian wanted some of whatever Madge had swallowed before coming into the office.

Legrain actually seemed a bit flustered but Bonine's curiosity made his head jerk forward and his mustache twitch.

He opened his mouth to speak but Madge cut him off. "Private things," she said, her voice conspiratorial. "Do you know Reb Girard?"

"The lady doc in Toussaint?"

"Uh-huh. The very one. I understand she's real helpful in delicate times. She's guided a lot of women through similar situations. And, of course, she's a wonderful doctor. I've always thought women doctors were better at some things. They have smaller hands."

Vivian looked at Madge aghast.

10

"Hey there, Cyrus." Spike let the bubble-gum pink door to All Tarted Up, Flakiest Pastry in Town, close with enough of a bang to set the bell to jangling. "Just thought of a way to increase business, Jilly. Hold a contest to rename the bakery. Offer a good prize to the winning entry, like all the day-old bread you can carry."

Jilly Gable and her brother Joe owned the bakery and café. They'd come up with the current name to "make the place more sexy," poker-faced Jilly told anyone who asked.

"Sure," she said from behind a counter. "Not much of a prize when everything gets sold the day it's made, though. Maybe we could offer a tour of the Sheriffs office in-stead. That should take five minutes. And you could throw in some of that mud you call coffee."

Cyrus watched the two of them idly. For a while there it had seemed they might have something going, but whatever that was didn't last long. They'd come out of it even stronger friends than they were before, though, which said a lot for their characters and made Cyrus feel good.

"Join me," he said to Spike. "I had a nosy visitor a few hours ago. Our detective friend from last night. I'd decided the man didn't do mornings but he fooled me." Errol Bonine had turned up at the rectory at 8:30, to the consternation of Lil Dupre who didn't take kindly to interruptions in her carefully crafted routine. Since Lil had moved into the housekeeper position, which she considered the most prized and important job around, Lil had turned from a whiner who did good work into a tyrant, who still did good work.

For Spike, mention of Cyrus being questioned again interfered with the good mood his encounter with Vivian had left behind.

"Go sit down," Jilly said. "I'll bring your coffee and a fresh one for Father. It's comin' up on lunchtime too so I'll fix you something ahead of the rush." Her startling hazel eyes made you take a second look everytime. The eyes, the tawny skin and long, brown, blond-streaked hair.

She called to Samie Machin, the extra assistant who had been added in the past year since Joe Gable's law practice had grown and made it impossible for him to help out at all. "Two extra specials for Father Cyrus and Spike, please Samie."

Spike sat opposite Cyrus and said, "Ever feel like you're waitin' for the shit to hit the fan?"

Cyrus smiled faintly. "The way we're feelin' right now, you mean?"

"Yeah." Spike tossed his hat on the seat of the chair beside him and ran a hand through his short hair. "So Errol dropped in at the rectory? Did you know him before last night?"

"Never set eyes on him. Looked him up. He was baptized at St. Cécil's but he probably lives in Iberia now."

Spike grunted. "I don't see Errol Bonine as a churchgoing man."

He realized his mistake before Cyrus said, "You being an expert on churchgoing men."

Spike knew when to keep his mouth shut.

"He has pretty narrow interests," Cyrus said. "Mostly you, then you and Vivian Patin. I had to be the one to talk about passing poor Louis Martin when I was leaving Rosebank earlier in the day. He seemed to have forgotten."

126

If Errol didn't get his act together this was going to be an unsolved crime. "But he talked about it once you raised the subject?" Spike said. "What theories does he have — if he told you?"

"He told me he didn't think it made a whole lot of difference. In his words, 'what happened, happened.' The detective gets right to the point. He isn't putting himself out to find every angle. Gives a whole new meanin' to putting your trust in the Lord."

Spike didn't feel like laughing.

The shop bell rang again and kept on trembling. Doll Hibbs, who ran the Majestic Hotel, came in with Wazoo, their one permanent boarder, and Bill Green. Bill was Toussaint's leading Realtor. He was Toussaint's only Realtor.

Doll, whose moods were unpredictable, gave Spike an almost coy wave and said, "Good mornin' to you, Father," to Cyrus. Wazoo inclined her head at Spike but ignored Cyrus, and Bill Green joined the men while the two women claimed chairs at opposite ends of a table for eight near the windows.

"For a semi-wide spot in the road," Bill said, "this place gets more than its share of trouble." He raised his voice to say, "Hi, Jilly. Cup of coffee and one of those famous meat pies of yours, please."

Fresh-faced Samie Machin hustled from the kitchen to put plates in front of Spike and Cyrus. The smell of fried onions caught Cyrus by surprise.

"Eat 'em and weep," Jilly said, laughing. "We mixed cooked and uncooked to keep 'em crunchy. Jilly burgers. First time on the menu."

"These are tortillas," Cyrus said.

"You try saying Jilly quesadillas more'n a time or two."

"I'll stay with the meat pie," Bill Green said, screwing up tearing eyes. "I deal with the public."

"I don't know how any of you can eat today," Wazoo's high voice cut across the café. "A man hardly cold in our own backyard. All that blood and cut-up flesh. I'd surely faint if a plate of meat was put in front of me."

Cyrus's mouth twitched. He laughed, grabbed his napkin and pretended to be coughing, then gave up and managed to subside into bursts of chuckles. Spike, with his back to the women, didn't help a thing by rolling up his eyes in a parody of death.

"We're gonna be sorry Guy Patin's kin moved into Rosebank," Doll said. Her sunny episodes had a habit of not staying around long. "See if I'm not right. Too bad that house isn't a whole lot farther away. There's talk about what happened there yesterday and none of it's good."

Spike turned sideways in his chair. Everything about Doll was unremarkable, except her gift for understatement and her mean spirit. Pale gray eyes, light brown hair — long, straight and secured at the nape with a rubber band — average height and weight.

"Generally there isn't much good to say about murder," Spike said. "Best not to listen to gossip though. Even better not to spread it."

Bill said, "Amen," and went to the counter to get his coffee and meat pie.

"It's not gossip that it was those women's lawyer got himself killed," Doll said, sounding stubborn. "And that Vivian supposedly found him, or so she says."

"How do you know . . ." Spike glanced into Wazoo's smug face and shut his mouth.

Doll was undeterred. "Guy Patin was leavin' the place to some sort of charity. We all knew that. So how come those women moved in and started changin' things? Just maybe the lawyer —" she gave her attention to Jilly "— maybe he come to say they jumped the gun or somethin'. Could be they just *thought* Rosebank was theirs, or wanted it to be, and the lawyer was bringin' the will to prove they had no right."

"Now, Doll," Cyrus said in a more even voice than Spike could have mustered. "The dead lawyer didn't represent Guy Patin as far as I know. Speculations can be dangerous."

"Troublemaking can be dangerous, you mean," Spike said under his breath.

"I don't hold with speculatin' myself," Doll said. "I can't reveal my sources but I trust 'em. You wouldn't be wanting me to say anything about a certain someone, Spike Devol, but if you've got the sense you were born with you won't get too close to mud. It rubs off."

Four workmen in white overalls saved Spike from saying something he'd regret. The men took their time ordering food to go and talked loudly among themselves.

"What's she suggesting?" Bill asked, keeping his voice down while leaning forward to shrug out of his light blue seersucker jacket and hook it over the back of his chair. "I've met both of the ladies from Rosebank. Very nice they are, too. The young one's something to look at." Bill's tie was the next to go. He believed in wearing a suit to work every day but the temperature soared outside, and inside the air-conditioning couldn't keep up with the heat from the kitchen.

"Good people, too," Cyrus said, blessedly giving Spike a chance to think.

The workers filed out and Doll pointed at their retreating backs. "Working for that lovely Mrs. Susan Hurst," she said. "Too bad those Patin women don't have her money. They'd get their *hotel* put together a whole lot quicker. Have you ever heard such nonsense? A hotel in that fine old house?"

Doll paused for breath but she hadn't finished. "Mrs. Hurst isn't too pleased, I can tell you. She and her husband — and that beautiful daughter of hers, Olympia — they move in and call their home Serenity, only to have people come next door talkin' about a restaurant, not just for hotel guests but for anyone who wanders in. And who will they get to stay there, that's what I want to know. If folks want a comfortable, reliable place to stay, they know where to come." She crossed her arms.

"Doll's right, her," Wazoo said. "I'm the one who knows, too. I live at the Majestic. And my customers tell me how at home they feel, too."

Doll hissed for Wazoo to be quiet. The Hibbs were careful not to admit that they had a medium/palm, tarot and tea leaf reader in residence. Spike figured they were afraid some folks might not like the idea of staying in a hotel where what went bump in the night might not always be the head of a bed.

"I reckon it's time I got on," Spike said. He liked most things about small towns except the way some folks couldn't mind their own business. "Is Madge at the rectory?"

Cyrus, apparently speechless over a simple question, was the last thing Spike expected. The man stared at him, then looked away. "Madge," he said. "Oh, Madge. No, she had some errands to run. Said she didn't know how long she'd be."

Spike stood up but didn't go anywhere. Reb Girard, Dr. Reb Girard, that was, had arrived with her apricot poodle, Gaston, under her arm. Curls of Reb's red hair had worked free of the topknot she wore while she was at her surgery on Conch Street. Spike smiled at the sight of her. Marc Girard and Reb O'Brien had married just before last Christmas. Marc must be right for her, lucky devil. Happiness sparked in her very green eyes and six months pregnant looked wonderful on her.

"You can't see this dog, of course, no one can," she said to Jilly, "but forgive me for bringin' Gaston in. It's too hot to leave him in the car."

Gaston decided to growl. He craned his neck to look around Reb's arm and bare his teeth. His shiny brown eyes fixed on Wazoo.

Reb ordered lemonade and turned to smile at Cyrus and Spike. She nodded at Bill who looked at her with more appreciation than Cyrus liked to see. An ex-Marine, Bill was around forty and divorced — and lonely. He needed a woman in his life and, although he might be ordinary to look at, he kept himself fit and it showed. He had a nice home in a cottage behind the local book-shop, and a good business. He should be a good catch for someone nice who would be an anchor in his life.

"Sit down," Spike told Reb. "Get a load off . . . just sit down and I'll bring the lemonade. It's too hot for a woman in your condition to be walking around. The extra weight is a stress. Your ankles will swell." He'd looked at her slim feet beneath the long, loose cream shift she wore before a desire to disappear hit him. He couldn't have said the things he just said, he couldn't have.

Without a hint of either annoyance or amusement, Reb thanked him and took the seat he'd left. Jilly wasn't as kind. She made her already big eyes huge, and her eyebrows all but disappeared into her hair. Cyrus folded and refolded his napkin and didn't look at anyone.

"Reb," Spike said, "that sounded —"

"Hush," she told him, reaching out to take his hand and give it a squeeze. She lowered her voice to a whisper. "I wouldn't change a thing about you. Silver tongues are a dime a dozen. I understand there's someone else who's pretty impressed with you, too."

He swallowed air. Reb had to be talking about Vivian and there was nothing to talk about. Okay, so there was something to talk about after last night but he and Vivian were the only ones who knew about that.

"Follow your heart," Reb said. "You deserve someone special and this is your big chance." She pulled him down until she could speak into his ear. "I'll do everything I can to help, but some things are up to you. Don't wait. Women need to feel right about these things."

What exactly was she talking about? Spike said, "Yeah, well . . . I'll get on now."

Gaston growled again and Wazoo let out a little scream. When she had everyone's attention, she pointed a long finger, coated with the same powdered sugar that somehow clung to her eyelashes, frosted her black hair and tinted her normally sallow face white. "He's lookin' at me, him," she said of Gaston. The sugar had come from the donut she held in her other hand. "He's tryin' to say how he wants somethin' from me."

"Probably your donut," Jilly said without any expression at all and cracked up her clientele. "Hello, Thea," she said to a gray-haired woman who came in and joined Doll and Wazoo. Thea cleaned and helped out around Rosebank.

Cyrus couldn't find it in him to be amused anymore. Madge might think him oblivious to a lot of things but she was wrong. Just because he didn't always say a whole lot didn't mean he missed much. All the banter in the world wouldn't cover up the growing dread he felt. Unrest stirred the air, the kind of unrest he'd had the misfortune to feel before in this town.

"You okay?" Spike murmured to him.

"Are you?"

Spike shook his head slightly.

They'd been through bad times in the past and had barely managed to deal with the murderer of four women and a man without even more loss of life. Over a year had passed since the crimes were solved and Cyrus had become complacent about peace in Toussaint. He met Spike's gaze again and something there suggested their thoughts weren't so different.

After Detective Bonine left the rectory, Madge had grilled Cyrus on what had been said, then she'd insisted on going to Rosebank to see if she could help Charlotte and Vivian. There could still be danger at that house. He didn't worry so much about Madge driving deserted roads now that she had an almost new car and he made sure it was kept in tip-top condition, but it wasn't only on lonely roads that evil struck.

"I'd better go, too," he said, deciding to visit Rosebank himself.

Bill finished his coffee. "Samie Machin has me looking for a house. Her husband's overseas in special ops but he's due on leave in a few weeks and she wants some properties to show him. I'll stay put until I can have a word with her."

Cyrus joined Spike to walk out — and bumped into Madge on her way in. He grinned and would have hugged her, but the gentle warning in her eyes and his own caution stopped him in time.

Madge said, "I persuaded Vivian to come into town with me. She needs a break. We're going to sit outside. Say hi to her when you go by."

Before Cyrus could respond, Spike left without a word. He went outside to a table where Vivian Patin was settling into a chair with her little dog peering from the top of a straw bag she settled on her lap.

11

"Good mornin'. Or good afternoon now, I guess. Looks like Jilly's gettin' overrun."

Vivian looked up into Spike's blue eyes. He'd come from the pastry shop and hadn't put on his hat, probably because he had some of those old-world manners a lot of Southern men were born with.

"It's one o'clock already," she said, feeling inane. What exactly did you say to a man you'd almost made love with only hours ago?

"How are you feelin'?"

Fortunately, the blush she was working on could be mistaken for reaction to the heat. "Terrific. How about you?" *Liar.* Hopeless pretty much covered what she felt.

Spike looked at the ground. His hair was short, but very thick and the sun glinted on the ends it had bleached. "I've felt better,

Vivian," he said. "Too much on my mind, I reckon."

Disappointment tightened her skin. "Don't let me keep you," she said. A woman could hope and she had hoped he'd say something to steady her.

"Too much getting in the way of the only thing I want to think about." He met her eyes again, very directly, and her spirits rose, she couldn't stop them when Spike looked at her as if he couldn't get enough of . . . looking at her. "I'm not having much luck keeping my thoughts on track. Seems someone's been messin' with my mind."

"Funny you should say that." It didn't take so much to resurrect her natural courage. "My own mind's been messy lately. The difference between you and me is I could come to like it that way."

He leaned forward to spread his fingers on the white enameled table and braced his weight on tanned forearms corded with tight muscle and sprinkled with hair bleached by the same sun that got his hair, but darker than you'd expect at the root, dark like the hair on his body.

Vivian stroked Boa in her basket and tried to settle down.

She wasn't right for him, Spike thought, any more than he was right for her, but he

139

sure wanted it to be otherwise. "I understand Bonine was over to ask more questions," he said. He couldn't manage clever conversation right now but neither could he wave and walk on. "He went to St. Cécil's first."

She kept her head bowed over the dog. "Madge told me." Vivian's hair slid forward, smooth and black, to frame her pale face. "She didn't tell me what the detective wanted, though."

The cool yellow dress she wore was belted at the waist. It was hard to keep his eyes off her body.

"It's hot for Boa," he said to give himself some breathing room. "Wait right there."

Vivian didn't try to stop him from leaving her to go back into the shop. She'd have to be a fool not to know it was too soon for anything but sex to be causing the minefield between them, the one they'd already shown they were foolhardy enough to cross. So far they hadn't stepped on any explosives, but if they kept wading through that field something was going to get tripped.

"Emergency supplies, Boa."

Spike returned and Vivian did her best to ignore the women who sat inside by the window pretending, pathetically, not to stare.

Spike poured water from a plastic glass

into a saucer and put it on the table. Apparently he'd decided he was irresistible to dogs, even small, feisty dogs who weren't keen on men.

A Land Rover pulled into the shade of a dogwood tree at the edge of the sidewalk and right in front of All Tarted Up. The dark-haired man who got out, jangling keys in his palm, was the type who got noticed.

"Hi, Marc," Spike said. "How you holding up?"

The man shook his head slowly but gave a wide smile when he said, "The final months are the hardest."

Spike introduced Vivian to Marc Girard, Dr. Reb's tanned, black-eyed husband. "He pretends he's working out there at Clouds End," Spike said. "Bein' an architect. Doodling more likely."

"And taking care of Reb," Marc said. "Time to take that woman home. I don't like her walking around in this heat." He lost the smile and studied Vivian. "I heard what happened at Rosebank yesterday — and about that ass Bonine. I'm sorry for your trouble. Let us know if we can do anything." He clapped a hand on Spike's shoulder and went into the shop.

Spike watched Marc go, then he scratched Boa's head and carefully lifted her little body from the basket.

"Spike! Watch out."

The man took no notice of Vivian and set Boa on the table where she went straight for the water, scowling at Spike each time she paused for breath.

"Dogs don't belong on the table."

"My friend, Dr. Reb, taught me how dogs have less germs than people."

"That doesn't extend to the feet they walk through . . . through everything on." She felt eyes through the window again and her spine straightened. Looking directly into Thea's face, Vivian smiled — and Thea smiled back. The woman did her job at Rosebank enthusiastically and often mentioned how glad she was for the chance. She'd probably known Doll Hibbs for years and was used to the woman's rude curiosity.

Behaving as if having the town's law officer hover over her and her dog was nothing out of the ordinary could be the best way to go. Vivian waved at Thea who waved back and grinned. Wazoo waved, too, and Vivian wondered why the woman had chosen to dust her face and hair with white powder.

Boa was on her second helping of water and actually paused to lick drops from Spike's fingers.

Vivian watched the man turn his hand

this way and that and got a tingling sensation in her limbs. The slightest thing about him heated her up. She glanced at his face. Spike held the tip of his tongue between his teeth while he smiled at the dog. Vivian stifled a groan and looked away. He had a mouth she'd never forget, not the way it looked, or the way it felt.

"I'm not much for audiences," he said, inclining his head toward the bakery window. "How about taking a walk with me?"

She breathed in air too warm to expand her lungs. "Why would we take a walk together?"

"You aren't helping me out here, Vivian."

"You're a strong type. You don't need help, least of all from a woman — a woman in trouble no less."

What did they call those things, Spike mused. Pheromones? That was it, Vivian's pheromones and his own did something happy together.

"Afternoon, Spike." Ellie Byron walked by. Ellie owned Hungry Eyes, a bookstore and café with two apartments above it, one of which Samie Machin called home. The cottage Bill leased stood in a sizeable enclosed garden behind the building.

"Afternoon, Ellie," Spike said. "You met

143

Vivian Patin and her pit bull, Boa?"

Ellie stopped and seemed edgy before she held her hand out to Boa who turned her back. "You're out at Rosebank," Ellie said to Vivian. "I love that house. Your uncle Guy was a lovely man."

Vivian nodded and shaded her eyes to see Ellie better.

"I did a few book searches for him and took stuff out there when I got it in. A really kind, good man. He knew so much about so many things — particularly antiques. But he'd dealt in them for years when he was younger. He used to call me up and tell me he'd *cleaned* out some books and I could have them. That usually meant he'd decided to part with one or two of the thousands he had. And then I had to hang on to them for a while to make sure he didn't change his mind." She clucked her tongue. "You don't need me to tell you about your own uncle."

"I loved him," Vivian said. "When I was a kid, coming to Rosebank was like getting into Aladdin's cave. He gave me the run of the house. 'Take an apple with you,' he always said when I took off around the place after breakfast. It's huge, did you realize that?"

"Oh, I surely did . . . Well, will you listen to me, forgetting myself." She held out a hand. "Ellie Byron. Hungry Eyes at the other end of the square belongs to me. Books and gifts, mostly books — new and used. And the iced tea is always free. There's a little café, too. That's not free." She smiled and laughter in her eyes transformed her serious expression.

"My kind of place," Vivian said, liking this woman but wishing she could be alone with Spike again. "You weren't always there, though."

"About two years now," Ellie said. "The place used to be Connie and Lorna's Eye For Books. For the first year I managed the shop, then Connie and Lorna moved to Rayne to open a Mardi Gras costume business. That's when I bought them out."

"I'll visit you," Vivian promised.

The afternoon felt airless but there was enough of a cross current to move Ellie's short brown curls. When she smiled she looked even younger than she probably was. A pretty woman with a voluptuous body under the loose gauze dress she wore. Ellie's bright blue eyes were the only jarring note. Beautiful, faintly upswept eyes — too old in their depths and wistful even when she laughed.

She cleared her throat and fidgeted. "You're having a hard time," she said. "I can only imagine what you've been through with your father's death and now this thing that happened at Rosebank. I'm very sorry."

Vivian glanced briefly at Spike. "Thank you, you're kind."

"See you at the shop one day, then," Ellie said. She hovered as if she had more to say, but then she walked on. "Good to meet you. Bye, Spike."

Spike and Vivian said, "Bye," in unison and as soon as Ellie was out of earshot, Spike told Vivian, "We need to talk but not here."

"Where?" she asked, her heart pounding in her throat.

"Do you have your own car or did Madge —"

"I brought my own. It's parked near your station. Madge said that's where smart people park because it's safe."

He didn't comment on that. "Leave it there. Walk to my car with me. If we go to the office someone will hear about it and some folks will come to the wrong conclusions."

"Are you embarrassed to be seen with me?" she asked him. "Or afraid of guilt by association?"

He held her arm and helped her to her feet. The way he looked at her made Vivian

146

squirm and his hard fingers ground the bones in her forearm.

"What is it with you?" he said. "Are you trying to goad me? I'm afraid of very little, and you don't qualify at all. And embarrassed to be seen with you? Hell, I'm not wasting my breath on that. Common sense is never a bad idea though, *cher.* Toussaint, birthplace of gossip. And that's about the way it is, so for your sake I don't want anyone getting the wrong idea. Like I'm questioning you officially."

"The inevitable?"

"Almost inevitable. Some could already be linking our names. If they get serious about it because we give them reasons, that will not be a good thing. Walk."

Spike handed Vivian her basket and swept Boa under his arm. She figured a dog attack wouldn't be long in coming and could be ugly — and when Spike Devol blamed Boa for biting him, Vivian would tell him she had witnesses to the fact that he'd been warned the animal could be hostile.

A man's firm hand at her waist felt better than it ought to. This man's hand felt fantastic.

They walked down one side of the town square — which had a triangle of grass decorated with painted gnomes, stone animals

147

and plastic flamingoes at its center. Santa and his sleigh were kept permanently ready to be illuminated for the holidays.

By the time they reached Spike's official Ford, Vivian could see her van in the distance.

Spike opened the passenger door for her and closed it once she was inside. Her ducked head, the way she frowned through the windshield made him look around expecting to see something or someone nasty. Not a thing. He checked her out again and shook his head. Boa had wriggled around until she could rest her head on his shoulder and he figured the boss wasn't believing what she was seeing.

"Daddy! Daddy!"

Wendy's voice surprised him and he swung toward the buildings. She ran down the steps of the gaudy Majestic Hotel and leaped into his free arm. "Hey, sweets, where's your gramps?" he said and barely stopped himself from asking who was taking care of business.

"He's talkin' to Mr. Hibbs. He let me sit on the steps as long as I ran back inside if anyone came. I saw Wally, too. He said I was a baby. He's eleven, you know. But he let me see Nolan. Oh, Daddy, you bought us a dog. You said you wouldn't, but you did."

Spike's daughter bubbled and smiled, and scratched between Boa's ears with small, slightly grubby fingers.

The subject had to be changed until he could think of the best way to get out of the dog thing. "You couldn't have seen Nolan," he told her. "Nolan went to tarantula heaven."

"This is Nolan two. That doesn't mean he's Nolan, too, just that he's another Nolan. He's got cute legs. They're all fuzzy."

Spike kissed her nose, hugged her tight, and thought as he so often did that he was one lucky man.

Inside the car Vivian watched with a smile on her lips and tears in her eyes. And she felt like a complete outsider. The little girl had to be Wendy. Pretty small for five, Vivian thought, not that she was an expert. Straight, tow-colored braids stuck out from the sides of her head, and an impishly up-turned, freckle-spattered nose balanced a pair of pink glasses with round lenses. Thin arms and legs. Wendy was the kind of waiflike child Vivian invariably had an urge to gather up and care for.

Spike talked to Wendy as if no one else existed on earth. He sat her comfortably on a forearm and she held on tight with both arms around his neck. Bows at the ends of her pigtails matched the fabric in a blue floral dress she wore tied with a sash around the waist. The dress seemed old-fashioned but well-cared-for and whoever combed her hair had practiced.

Vivian had passed the Majestic a few times but never really saw it clearly until now. Thea had told her how Doll Hibbs figured the place was all the hotel the area needed.

Lime green walls and a lilac-colored, gold cross-hatched dome on top of a tower at one side made for a lot of visual interest.

"You've got a prisoner in your car, Daddy," Wendy whispered in Spike's ear, her sunny smile giving way to a frown. "Is she dangerous?"

"Oh, yeah — what am I sayin', of course she's not dangerous, and she's not a prisoner. That's Miz Vivian Patin. Remember that big house where we went to pick roses one time? Rosebank? Vivian and her mother live there now."

"Why is she in your car?"

Five-year-olds could have one-track minds. "I'm going to drive her to her vehicle. This is her dog, Boa."

The frown grew ferocious. "Why are you carrying the dog, Daddy? Is the lady hurt? Can't she carry her dog? He's very small."

"She," Spike said automatically. He needed a smooth retreat from the brink of disaster. The worst thing he could do would be to make too much out of this. "Vivian's a nice lady. I know she'll let you pet her dog if you ask nicely."

"Why are you carrying the dog, Daddy?" Now the tone was stubborn and behind the owlish lenses, Wendy's hazel eyes were worried.

"Just bein' polite and helpful," he said, feeling foolish. He did the only thing he could think of to do and approached the passenger window on the Ford. Vivian rolled it down. "Vivian, this is my daughter, Wendy. Wendy, say hello to Miz Patin."

"Vivian. Call me Vivian, Wendy. You have the cutest pigtails."

Wendy reverted to her hair-tugging, pouty act and didn't answer.

"Did you meet my dog, Boa?" Vivian got out of the car. "She's a Chihuahua but she thinks she's a lion. D'you know what I mean?"

Wendy regarded Boa, reached to stroke the dog and received a lick on the mouth with a giggle. "Lions don't kiss people," Wendy said. "I don't think she wants to be a lion."

Spike met Vivian's eyes over his daughter's head. "My father's here," he said, indicating the Majestic. "Come on in and meet him — and Gator Hibbs."

He could see how much she wanted to refuse, and how she argued herself into giving a nod and going up the hotel steps past the colored whirligigs Doll stuck in planters on either side of the door. It would be easy enough to let her off the hook, but she might as well see how different their lives were.

Inside the vestibule they were confronted with rose-covered stained glass in the interior door. Spike reached around Vivian to turn the handle and let them in. Immediately, Wendy wriggled from his arms and ran across the shabby lobby to the room where hotel guests were invited to sit and watch television in the evenings.

Vivian saw there were people in the room Wendy had disappeared into and turned away blindly, walking straight into Spike's chest. Boa whined.

"Hey, hey," Spike said quietly. "Nothing fearsome here. Just inconvenient. We'll have that talk soon, just as soon as we deal with my dad. I warn you, he's unconventional."

"Give Boa to me. They'll have one less thing to wonder about."

He handed over the dog. Little, showy dogs weren't his thing, or they never had been.

Wendy dashed back and took her father's

hand to drag him with her into a room papered with more roses, these climbing brown lattices. Cabbage rose chintz covered sagging chairs and two couches. Wendy didn't smile at Vivian and Spike decided he'd be chatting with his girl later. She knew better than to be rude.

His father and Gator Hibbs had got to their feet when they saw Vivian. Gator wore his customary T-shirt, baggy overalls, and ingenuous grin. He wiped his palms on his pants. Good old Homer did what only he could do so well, he got rid of any expression at all.

Vivian stood up tall and met Gator Hibbs's eyes. He pushed a sweat-stained Achafalaya Gold Casino baseball cap far back on his head. He nodded and hovered, probably waiting for someone to say he could put his round rear back in the chair.

A tall man who could be in his seventies eased forward from the windowsill where he'd been sitting. His hair was still thick and peppered the way blond hair did when it was time to turn gray. A thin face, clean-shaven, and eyes a darker shade of blue than Spike's gave the impression that Homer Devol was sharp. Vivian could see the lines of the son's face in the father's — but no trace of the optimism she saw in Spike's expression from time to time, or any hint of his knock-'em-dead smile.

"You must be Spike's dad," she said, extending a hand. "You've got your hands full with the business and a little girl to care for — but Wendy sure is cute."

"Wendy's no trouble. Never was. Never will be to me." He took his time to shake her hand.

Strike one.

"I'm Vivian Patin, Guy Patin's niece. My mother and I moved into Rosebank."

"I know who you are," Homer said. "Reckon just about everyone for miles around does."

She was proud of her smile and her nonchalance. "And to think some people go looking for fame," she said. "I like a quiet life myself, not that Mama and I have a choice until this horrible thing is finished with."

"Who's keepin' shop, Pops?" Spike asked. The cold tone of his voice startled Vivian.

Homer's still sharp chin came up. "Ozaire. Said he was glad to do it, just like he usually does. I'm gonna give him a reel he's had his eye on."

Spike's hands dropped to his sides and he made fists. "You left Ozaire Dupre at our place? The opposition?"

"You never used to mind." Homer shrugged. "You gotta trust people. Ozaire's honest."

"Sure he's honest. He's probably making an honest effort to sabotage my crawfish boiler. And while we're talking about dumbass things to do — Wendy alone on the stoop qualifies, damn it all."

Homer colored and looked away and Vivian felt terrible for both men.

"Hey Pops," Spike said, raising his palms. "Sorry for sounding off. I've got a lot on my mind."

"I can see that," Homer said, looking at Vivian. "Better concentrate, boy. I hear that Errol Bonine's on your case again. I don't want to be visitin' your beat-up body in the hospital again."

Spike set his jaw. "Did Claude's order get picked up?"

"Sure," Homer said. "The woman came from the houseboat in her pirogue. Never could figure why a man like Claude would live in the swamps the way he does, him bein' clever and all."

"He pays promptly," Spike said, still grim. "Most of those bayou folks are good business."

Mumbling incoherently, Gator slid from the room and his feet could be heard

155

clumping up the stairs.

From the corner of his eye, Spike saw Wendy start chewing the skin around her fingernails, something she only did when her beloved Gramps and Daddy were on the outs. He made himself relax. Later he'd deal with his father. Now he was under the gun with other things. "I'll behave myself, Pop," he said and grinned at Wendy. "Tell Gramps I can be good if I try."

Wendy giggled.

Homer looked at his pocket watch. "Watch yourself on the steps, Miz Patin. Spike, maybe you better come on out to the place and make sure Ozaire hasn't gotten up to anything."

Burning, Vivian turned on her heel but didn't make it past Spike who stepped in front of her. "I'll leave that to you, Pops. Nobody's tougher than you are. Vivian and I will take Wendy with us to the rectory."

Vivian didn't want to be in the middle of this.

"Run up and say goodbye to Wally," Spike told Wendy. "Tell him he should come over to the station and show me his new Nolan."

The child went silently. Spike resented that she'd witnessed hard feelings, not that it was the first time by too many.

"No need to take her," Homer said. He

rolled in his lips. "You know I go off sometimes. Bad habit."

"Forget it, Pops. Wendy enjoys Lil Dupre. She can help her in the kitchen while we see to some business with Cyrus." He stared at his father. "You've been around me enough to know how a murder has a way of taking over everything."

12

"They're still over there at Rosebank, Daddy dear. How long do you suppose it'll be before someone decides asking us a few questions wasn't enough. They could decide to check out the inside of Serenity House?"

Dr. Morgan Link held on to the side of the new pool Susan had built for him inside an elegant white marble pool house. Olympia Hurst plagued him daily. He'd expected her to show up here. Calling her mother's second husband "daddy" while she came on to him appeared to give her a perverse thrill.

He wiped water from his eyes but made sure he didn't look at her. "If I were a policeman, I would search any properties near the crime scene if I could get the warrants. That's not always easy unless there's a real good reason."

"And that wouldn't bother you?"

"Why should it?" He pushed off the wall and began swimming a length of the pool in an easy backstroke.

She laughed and shouted after him, "You don't think the little secret would come out before you and Mama were ready?"

It wouldn't come out unless someone talked out of school. He'd have to make sure that didn't happen.

The strength he felt in his limbs, the perfect tone of his entire body, satisfied him. Only one thing could make this swim more perfect. He reached the far wall, flipped over and started back. Olympia wanted him as much as he wanted her — even if their reasons were the smallest amount different.

Perhaps he should shock the little tease and pull her in here with him. He'd seen her enter the bathhouse in a gauzy white halter top and tiny shorts. She loved to flaunt herself whenever she could get him alone.

She felt safe baiting him, goading him . . . letting him know she hated the man who took her father's place, even though she couldn't stay away from him.

He heard her laughter bounce from the slick and soaring walls. Best not to react. She had no self-discipline and she was like a bitch in heat, wiggling her pretty heart-shaped ass almost in his face, making sure he got the scent of her. So far he'd managed not to touch her.

She hated him but she hated her mother more. She would let poor Susan spend a fortune trying to turn her into Miss Southern Belle yet her ultimate fantasy was to fuck her own mother's husband. The supreme betrayal. Olympia knew Susan wanted the contest win for herself, to give her another reason to brag. The girl felt the expenses were coming out of her own inheritance. And the excesses Susan showered on Morgan ate more chunks of money the girl wanted for herself. After all, her father had earned it and Susan was only supposed to safeguard it for Olympia, or that's the way she saw it.

"Look at that, Morgan," Olympia shouted. "Something's come up, but I'm sure you've already noticed that." Her laughter scaled high. "What a waste. And here I am, ready to help you — and me, Morgan."

How had this become so complicated? He *had* married Susan for her money, mainly. That wouldn't surprise anyone. All they'd have to do was look at the two of them to figure it out. But he hadn't planned on the daughter being a vindictive, sex-starved nymphomaniac. Quite the combination, there. "How could you possibly help any-thing?" he asked Olympia, pushing close to the wall and continuing to float on his back. Let her look at the tent pole his dick had become. Let her squirm and salivate.

She dropped to kneel on the tiled edge, pressed her breasts together with her arms, made sure he could see inside her top. If he sat beside her he'd be looking at her nipples. "I could help a lot," she said and stretched flat on her stomach. "That can't be comfortable and it's certainly a waste."

He knew what she wanted to do. Perverted little cocksucker. She wasn't ready for the finish yet, oh no, O-lym-pi-a didn't intend to get him all the way inside her unless and until it suited her crooked plans.

"Come closer," she whispered, and the whisper ricocheted about the crystalline palace Susan Hurst had built for her husband.

"Why should I?" he said. He slipped a hand inside his trunks to fondle himself.

"I can do that so much better than you," she said. "Poor baby, that's what you get for marrying an older woman. You learn to take care of your own needs. Is the money still worth it, Daddy dear?"

Now and again he felt sorry for her — a little sorry. One day when she pushed too far, and had too much to lose by striking back at him, he'd tell her it was too bad she couldn't study her mother's mastery of the art of sex because Susan was a master and she could teach a lot to a willing hedonist in training.

"Are you ignoring me?" Olympia whined through pouty lips. Blond and with her mother's fine bones and soft features, when she looked at him like that, with that child-behind-a-woman's-beautiful-face impression she pulled off so well, he reminded himself how dangerous she could be.

He splashed water and she squealed. When she swung to sit on the edge with her feet trailing in the water, her soaked and transparent halter didn't hide a thing. He never tired of perfect breasts.

"Olympia," he said, tiring of the un-requited ache she caused. "Perhaps you need some therapy, someone knowledge-able to listen to your fantasies."

"Someone like you, our resident psychol-ogist?" She parted the halter at its plunging V and peeled it apart. "Talk to me, doctor. Tell me what's wrong with me and what would make it better."

"Playing with other children, I should think," he told her and looked at her breasts, naked, and all too tempting in their wet sling. He made sure she knew he was staring at them. "That doesn't look comfortable. Big girls need all the support they can get."

"All the support this girl needs is you, Morgan. We've been handed a prize. There's time to collect it, but not too much time."

"There isn't a 'we' and I haven't been handed anything," he told her, furious at the way she made light of heavy things. "I saw an opportunity and figured out how to use it. But either I make all the right moves from now on or 'we' will kiss goodbye to a lot of dreams, yours and mine."

"Don't threaten me," she said and took the top all the way off. She hopped to her feet and shucked her shorts. "I'm not the killing type, remember? You, on the other hand —"

"Shut the fuck up. Never say anything like that again." Anger aroused him even more and Olympia, her weight on one foot, running her hands over her body and panting each time she sank fingers between her legs, brought him to the brink.

Without warning she jumped into the pool.

Morgan swung his feet down and trod water, careful to keep some distance between them.

"Is Vivian Patin your type?" she asked.

He frowned at her and said, "Where did that come from? I don't know her."

"Do you think she's sexy?"

"No." What was one more little lie between friends?

"Will it bother you if they pin the murder on her?"

He must not forget, even for a moment, that Olympia would always put herself first. "You're letting your mind stray," he told her.

Grinning, she shot forward, twined her arms around his neck and gripped his waist with her legs. "My mind isn't straying. I still know what I want."

Her tongue entered his mouth before their lips met. What followed wasn't so much a kiss as a feeding frenzy before she flipped onto her back and scissored her legs about his neck. With her feet and ankles secure, she spread her knees.

He could, Morgan decided, use her sex addiction to bind her to him — until he didn't want her around anymore. And it wasn't a hardship to play her game.

With his mouth planted exactly where Olympia wanted it to be and his tongue doing rapid pushups, he pulled and shook her nipples. She came quickly and he used the echoes of her spasms to bring her to climax twice more in rapid succession.

With her eyes closed, she pushed away from him, moved her arms slowly while her legs trailed.

Morgan didn't realize what she was up to until she was already in motion, propelling herself beneath the water and yanking down his trunks. She popped up for air and gave him a mock snarl. When she gave him a backward push, he obliged by letting his legs float to the surface.

She mouthed, "oh, my," and slid her lips over him.

The concept of getting a blow job from a woman who hated him only deepened his pleasure. Yes . . . yes . . . yes. She was so willing; why not make this a habit?

He exploded and thrashed at the water while he emptied.

Olympia didn't swallow. He smiled at that thought.

"I knew you'd like that," she said when his breathing evened out.

"*That* was just the hors d'oeuvres," he said, calculating every word. "How about the rest of the meal?"

She paddled to the edge of the pool again and pulled her clothes, or what passed for her clothes, into the water. "Wouldn't want

Mama to wander in and see those out there with us in here."

Earlier they'd visited the rectory at St. Cécil's in Toussaint, intending to impress Father Cyrus with their neighborly concern for the Patins. The priest had been out and after doing some groundwork with Lil Dupre, the housekeeper, Morgan had returned home with Olympia. Susan had remained in Toussaint to see Bill Green about a piece of vacant land adjacent to Serenity House. He would join her there when she called. He didn't remind Olympia that she was only fantasizing danger because it aroused her.

"She's got to go, y'know," Olympia said, bouncing in the water. "You and I will make the best team ever, perfect partners while we grieve. It's too bad we'll never be able to marry."

"A shame," he said, anxious to leave and get into Toussaint. "But don't get distracted. Nothing gets done out of order."

"How come you get to decide the order?" she said. "What if I want to switch things around?"

He had her by the throat before he could stop himself. Then he didn't want to. "If I go down because you interfere, I'll take you with me."

Her eyes were wide and she grappled with his hands. "You're frightening me. Stop it."

Morgan squeezed a little tighter and gave her a shake. "You stop it. Repeat after me — one move at a time."

"One move at a time," she murmured.

"And only Morgan's moves *when* he's ready to make them."

"And only Morgan's moves when he's ready to make them."

He nodded at her and eased his grip, placed his thumbs, side by side, on her chin. "And what's our first, our biggest priority?"

Olympia's mouth trembled. "To make sure Rosebank never becomes a hotel."

13

Saturdays were Cyrus's favorite days, even this one when he'd confronted another dose of Errol Bonine's sleazy arrogance and witnessed how little his parishioners took his anti-gossip homilies to heart. On Saturdays he got away with wearing an old shirt and jeans to do whatever needed to be done around the parish. Things that didn't have to fall under Ozaire's control.

The morning and part of the afternoon had already been used up but there were a lot of daylight hours left.

Knowing Madge was in the house didn't hurt his mood. She'd decided to follow him back to the rectory and catch up on some of the paperwork she'd left when she went to Rosebank. Even though she wasn't supposed to work past noon on a Saturday, and any Saturday work was optional, he hadn't found the backbone to tell her she should go home.

He didn't dwell on his motives, just accepted that when she was nearby he felt as happy as he ever expected to feel.

This afternoon showed little sign of last night's torrents. Earlier in the day steam from the ground mixed with thick mist over the bayou and the trees had seemed rooted in a layer of clouds. Heat still rose in quivering waves but the mist and steam were gone. Bees hovered and darted in the bed of wildflowers Cyrus had planted on the bayou side of the rectory. He shaded his eyes from the sun and cast a satisfied eye over the white church that sat, surrounded by glittering tombs and green grass, on the opposite side of Bonanza Alley from the rectory. A low, white fence surrounded both pieces of property.

Ozaire Dupre's rusted blue truck bumped to a halt beside the church fence and Ozaire, Lil's husband, meandered along a path leading to his shed near the church. Short and thick, Ozaire might give the impression he didn't have the energy to scratch his nose but he was the strongest man Cyrus had ever met, apart from his predecessor, William.

Cyrus didn't want to think of the people

he'd lost since he'd been at St. Cécil's, some of them good, some of them plain old wicked. And he didn't want to think about the scenes at Rosebank yesterday. Some might laugh and say that a murder was a murder, but experience had taught him that some unnatural deaths were more significant than others. He thought the murder of Louis Martin could turn out to be real significant.

From the path that ran alongside the rectory on the Bonanza Alley side came Wally Hibbs. The boy didn't change much and at almost twelve he was as rangy as ever. His brown hair fell over his brow and he fastened hazel eyes on Cyrus with the delighted look he assumed whenever his benefactor came into sight.

During school time, like now, he could only come around on Saturday and Sunday, but in summer he was there most days. It was Cyrus who made sure that Wally, the son of Doll and Gator Hibbs, proprietors of the Majestic Hotel, got the help he needed with his homework, and that he had someone to talk to.

"You tendin' them Oribel flowers, you?" Wally shouted. "Or you diggin' them up. Ma calls 'em weeds. Jilly thinks they're the prettiest things she ever saw. 'Cept for they set 'round the Fuglies way they do."

"I like my Fuglies," Cyrus lied about the primitive bronze sculpture of five cavorting two-dimensional figures in the middle of the lawn, surrounded by what Wally called "Oribel" wildflowers. Oribel Scully had been Lil's predecessor and she had gifted the piece of sculpture to the parish, but the slender-stemmed show of oranges and blues, white, red, lavender and yellow celebrated something other than her generosity. They reminded Cyrus of life and how precious it was.

"Spike brought that pretty lady from Rosebank to the Majestic," Wally said. He sat, cross-legged, on the grass and Cyrus noticed the boy settled a white plastic box by his feet. Holes punched in the box made Cyrus suspicious that he knew what was inside. "Vivian Patin she's called. Wendy Devol was there, too. She's okay for a baby. Homer brought her over to visit with Dad. From what I heard, they were talkin' about how the Patins are outsiders and Spike's makin' a fool of himself with Miz Vivian. Homer's bellyaching about how Spike's aiming too high and Wendy will get hurt all over again when Miz Vivian moves on."

Wally made a sudden, swift move and

caught a cricket which he slipped into the white box.

"Reckon there could have been a dust-up when Spike showed up with Miz Vivian," he said. "Weren't there any time at all when Wendy came up to say they was leavin'. I thought they was comin' here. Guess they already left."

"Must have changed their minds," Cyrus told him. "Probably decided to take Wendy home first — if they're coming at all."

To hide any giveaway expressions, Cyrus returned his attention to the flowers. Spike had him worried. Homer could just be right about a relationship between his son and Vivian being a poor idea. But Cyrus was worried about more than that and he needed to talk to Spike alone. Remarks had been made at Jilly's that left him with suspicions he'd like to forget, but he had a job to do, a duty, and for all his failings, he took his responsibilities seriously.

"Stuff's happenin' again, isn't it?" Wally asked in the hushed and hoarse voice that became less audible the more unsettled he was. "Not just that killing. Other stuff. I can feel it. That Miz Vivian didn't kill no one, but they're tryin' to say she did and there's plenty willing to believe it. I reckon that detective just wants to have someone to blame and move on."

Cyrus tossed weeds into an old cardboard box from Ron Guidry's Louisiana Lightning hot sauce before he looked at Wally. "You do a lot of thinking. A lot of working things out. Our job is to try not to interfere or give opinions, Wally. But I think you're right and we may eventually have to do something. Meanwhile, watch out for yourself. What's in the box?"

Wally smiled his one-sided smile. "A buddy."

"Doesn't have hairy legs, does he?"

"Yup." Wally nodded and grinned. "Nolan Two. I like having him around."

Cyrus had hoped Wally's need to prove he was different had worn off. Maybe it never would, at least not until he was grown and could make his own decisions.

The back door to the house opened and Wendy Devol ran from the kitchen, her braids flapping behind her. She went toward Wally who didn't look unhappy about the little girl's attention.

Next came Vivian carrying her little dog, with Spike behind her.

Cyrus shaded his eyes to watch them. She was lovely, would be even more lovely without the anxiety that tightened her expression. Vivian looked over her shoulder at

Spike who settled a hand on the back of her neck. When she faced Cyrus again, her brilliant smile didn't need an explanation. These two were wading in deep with each other, just as Cyrus had feared.

He didn't remember Spike ever looking at anyone the way he looked at Vivian Patin. He hid the exposed need quickly enough but something almost more dangerous remained; Spike wasn't just falling, he'd already fallen for this woman. Cyrus looked down at the flowers. His own experiences with passion would stay pure and safe as long as his faith was never tested too harshly.

Cyrus dropped the trowel he'd been using and stood up. A rush of sensation had constricted his lungs. He was capable of feeling another kind of passion, had already felt it and fought it on too many occasions. The gentle, exhilarating warmth of human love was denied him by his own decision.

Service, that was his mission, and he would use service to keep him from stumbling so badly he couldn't recover.

"Lil's in the kitchen putting groceries away," Spike said. "Looks as if she's laying in stores for the whole winter. She's in a good mood."

Cyrus sighed. "That's probably bad

news." He raised his face to the almost too-blue sky and said, "God forgive me for my mean spirit."

"You're only sayin' the truth," Wally said, sounding disturbed. "You're never mean. Lil only gets cheerful when she's been mixin' somethin' up."

Spike frowned in the direction of Wally and Wendy. Cyrus could almost hear him wondering if he could trust Wally to look after the little girl. "Vivian and I would like to talk some things over with you," he said to Cyrus, still repeatedly returning his attention to the kids.

"Wally," Cyrus said, giving his sidekick a significant glance. "Take Wendy upstairs to my sitting room. I expect she'd enjoy the books and you might even want to watch a cartoon." He didn't suppose he should suggest television to a boy, but none of them would feel safe leaving Wally and Wendy out here.

Wally said, "Okay," with a lot of enthusiasm and once Wendy got a smile of approval from her father she bobbed up and ran for the house, her arms swinging in circles like miniwindmills. Boa made a close third, scrambling from Vivian's arms and taking off after the kids. "We'll take care of her," Wally shouted.

"Look at that," Vivian said. "My faithful friend deserts me for children. Never fails."

"Under the tree?" Cyrus asked, indicating a white-painted bench beneath an oak. "I don't think we'll get past Lil too easily if we try going to my office."

"The bench is fine," Spike said and put a hand at Vivian's waist while he walked with her.

Spike touched her, the tip of his fingers curling in then spreading, as if she belonged to him, and nothing about her response suggested she didn't like it. Cyrus smelled disaster in the making — if it hadn't already been made.

Vivian sat in the middle of the bench and patted the slats on either side of her, expecting the men to join her. They remained standing and before her eyes they both traded smiles for frowns. Even the atmosphere changed.

Men. If a situation was bad, or might be bad, they made it worse with their efforts to strike the right attitude and take charge.

"We were coming right over after I picked up Wendy from the Majestic," Spike said. "Got a call. Domestic violence, or so the dispatcher said. Nothin' more'n a lot of cryin' and threatenin'. Two kids with a kid of their own. Married a year and scared stiff about money and how to bring up the little one."

Spike shook his head. "Their parents didn't approve of the marriage so they don't have anyone to turn to . . . or they didn't." Spike smiled and Vivian had to smile with him. He could look like a gleeful, overgrown boy. "They called and spoke to Madge while I was still at their apartment. She's got them coming over to see you after nine o'clock mass tomorrow."

Cyrus said, "Good, good," in a distracted manner. He repeatedly looked from Vivian to Spike.

Spike cleared his throat and glanced at Vivian. Typical. When it got right down to it and the problem was his own rather than someone else's, the man wasn't so ready to deal with it.

"Madge said you knew Bonine was coming directly to Rosebank after talking to you," Vivian told Cyrus. For a woman who hadn't had much sleep, she felt jumpy with energy. She wanted to move around, get things done. "Gary Legrain, Louis's associate, showed up very early this morning, thank goodness. He's acting for Mom and me so he sat in on the interview."

She felt Spike frowning at her and tilted her head sideways, trying to see his face in shadows cast by the oak. "What's the matter with you?" she said. "Why are you looking at me like that?"

"You didn't tell me about Legrain, or the interrogation."

"I haven't had a chance yet," she told him, starting to stew. "You know I couldn't talk about things like this in front of Wendy."

"You should have found a way to take me aside. I need any information exactly when you get it, not hours later."

"Spike," Cyrus said mildly, his thick dark lashes lowered a little over blue-green eyes. "Calm down, huh? You're not being fair to Vivian."

"Not fair?" Spike stopped speaking with his lips parted and his expression passed from angry to mortified. He stuttered slightly when he said, "Maybe. If that's true, I'm sorry. None of my damn business, anyway."

Vivian felt like slapping him. "So you say." Unfortunately what he said was true but she intended to change that. "You're in this case up to your neck. Errol Bonine's got his net strung between trees just waiting for you to pass that way, then he'll cut the rope and you'll be hanging right where he wants you."

Cyrus and Spike gave each other that

man-to-man glance again and Vivian took deep breaths to keep her cool.

"Aren't you going to ask what I mean by that?"

"Sure," Spike said in a voice guaranteed to make her doubt he intended to take a word she said seriously.

"No," Vivian said and stood up. "I've got a question to ask first. And if you two insist on standing over me — like you weren't already twice as big — I'll have to stand, too."

"Don't be ornery with me," Spike said and kicked at the grass with the toe of a brown boot. "The last thing I want to do is make you mad."

She managed to avoid rolling her eyes. Cyrus sat down on one end of the bench and stretched out his long legs.

"What did your father mean when he said he didn't want to visit your broken body in the hospital again?" she asked Spike.

Damn Homer's big mouth anyway, Spike thought. There wasn't any harm in him but sometimes he just didn't think. "I had an accident in New Iberia. I was a detective." And his bitterness showed. "Just one of those things."

"What things?"

From the interest Cyrus was taking, Vivian could tell this was news to him also.

179

"There was a problem with some guys. Three guys. I'd been stakin' them out for weeks and couldn't seem to get enough on 'em to take 'em down."

"Why was that?" she asked.

"Vivian, don't you ever stop askin' questions?"

"Not after what your dad said this afternoon, and now this explanation. Homer meant you're in danger again. He thinks Bonine was behind what happened to you."

"What makes you think that?"

"Was he?"

Spike pushed his hat low over his eyes. "He swore he knew nothing about it. And the gov'nor believed him so I had to as well. Didn't matter because I was kicked out for not being a team player." He gave a short laugh. "I learned from all that. I used to think I was the maverick who would set the world on fire. Now I'm grateful to have any kind of job in the law and I know I'm going nowhere."

Vivian moved closer to him until her toes, bare in strappy sandals, touched one of his boots. She looked up at him, way up at him. "If there's one thing I can't stand it's a loser."

He raised a brow and became expressionless.

"I don't mean you're a loser," she said in a hurry. "I just mean you've been knocked around — and I know that creepy Bonine was behind it — and all you have to do is start believing in yourself again. We're going to make hash out of that man and feed it to pigs."

Cyrus found a Kleenex and blew his nose. "Something in the air," he said. "This has been the worst year for allergies."

"*You*," Spike said to Vivian in a menacing tone, "will keep your nice nose out of my business. This isn't a party game. For God's sake, Cyrus, tell the woman there's a killer on the loose out there and she's not to do anything stupid."

Very suddenly Cyrus got to his feet and called, "Madge, why are you sitting over there?"

Responding from her seat on the top step outside the kitchen, she raised her voice and said, "I'll wait till you're through. I don't want to interrupt."

"You couldn't interrupt," Cyrus told her. "Come join us."

Vivian met Spike's eyes but he looked sad and lowered them at once.

"Lil's poured iced tea for us," Madge said. "Any takers?"

They all chorused "yes," and Madge disappeared back into the kitchen to reappear with a tray and head in their direction.

"She's so pretty," Vivian said, appreciating the other woman's energetic walk and the way her clothes fit so well — and her hair bouncing about her shoulders.

"Yes," Cyrus said and this time Vivian avoided looking at Spike.

Madge reached them and held out the tray for each of them to take a glass of iced tea.

"Thanks," Vivian said. "Just in time to save you and me from the wiggles."

Madge looked at her uncertainly but Vivian pressed on. "I was so grateful you arrived in time to stop Detective Bonine from wiggling. I'm not sure I wouldn't have gotten sick."

That pulled a grin out of Madge. "Do you know why the detective is so angry, Spike?"

"Uh-huh. Me. He hates my guts. We used to work together and he was afraid I'd upstage him, or get in the way of whatever he had going," he finished darkly. He winced and said, "Forget I said that, please. I know better."

"Do you want to explain all that wiggling?" Cyrus asked.

"Oh, that," Madge said innocently. "Just a

girls' joke, right, Vivian?"

"Yup."

Apparently unconcerned about grass stains, Madge sat on the ground with her feet crossed in front of her. She fell silent but fidgeted, turning her glass around and around and making patterns in the condensation on the outside.

At last she said, "Barging in on the interview was unforgivable. I'm sorry."

Vivian choked on her tea and swatted at some flying insect intent on a divebomb attack. "Well, I'm not sorry. Bonine would have had me there for hours. If you weren't sexy enough to distract him, goodness knows where he could have gone with his questioning. He'd already scared me. But one look at you and he got all cuddly."

Cyrus looked right at Madge but let his eyes slide away and Vivian wished, again, that she could learn to censure her mouth.

"Sometimes," Madge said, "I get completely carried away. Usually when I kind of get into something I've got to pull off. Do you know what I mean?"

Vivian had been trying to forget Madge's wild words in front of Legrain and Bonine. "I know," she said.

"The first idea you figure will shut people up doesn't even connect with your brain before it slops out of your mouth."

"Oh, yeah," Vivian said with feeling. "Done that one too many times."

"I don't think anyone read much into it," Madge said. "Probably just thought I was blathering on."

Vivian prayed that it would be true. "Don't worry about it."

The men were quiet and watchful and when conversation faded, Spike said, "You're talking in code. Are you gonna crack it for us?"

Madge looked panicky but Vivian giggled and kept on giggling until Madge joined in. When they collected themselves, Vivian said, "You'll find out when the time is right," while she fervently hoped no one noticed or repeated the not very subtle hints Madge had delivered at Rosebank.

Vivian edged closer to Spike, but faced the opposite way. Two heron swept in to land on a bleached cypress tree barely showing above the surface of the bayou. Vivian tried to concentrate on the birds and their freedom to come and go, but there was too much more to say here and all of it was bad.

She needed to feel Spike's warmth, his strength. And she didn't think she cared what anyone else thought. He could be the one to re-

buff her if he wanted to. She slid her left arm beneath his right one and held on. Spike still faced the others while Vivian looked toward the bayou.

He rubbed her forearm and she wanted to kiss him. He might only be trying to give her courage, but still he didn't care who saw him around her.

"Hang in there," he said. "Dealing with bullies takes time to learn. I think you're doing great."

"This is what Bonine wants to make people believe," she told him. "He believes I killed Louis and you helped me because you hate him and you've been looking for a way to make him look bad."

"*Bullshit.*" Spike said through his teeth. "Crazy. He's lost what mind he ever had."

"My prints are all over everything. I ruined any hope of lifting footprints from the ground and messed up the rest of the evidence. The only prints on the telephone were mine and yours — and Louis's, I guess. I took it from inside of his briefcase. Of course I shouldn't have done that but I wasn't thinking rationally. He thinks Louis was really bringing bad news, probably that Rosebank didn't really belong to us, according to him. And Bonine decided there was something to that effect in the briefcase and I stole it."

"Ass," Spike said, glaring into the distance.

"Take heart," Vivian said. "He told me you'd have gotten rid of your prints if you were worried about them. He only thinks you're covering for me. Lucky you."

"Don't take Bonine seriously, y'hear," Spike said. He didn't like the way Cyrus and Madge were looking anywhere but at him and Vivian. "He's not interested in you."

"I know what he's interested in. Don't sell me short, Spike, I may get down, but I also get up again when I've got to get on with it." She pulled her arm from beneath his and turned around. "Listen up."

Cyrus and Madge paid attention immediately. "Enough pussyfooting around. I've got one major mess on my hands. We already knew there were those who didn't want us here. Between trying to make big decisions, like how many rooms to finish before opening, and how we'll make the grounds inviting enough to camouflage how most of Rosebank will still be under repair for a long time — and hitting walls everytime we try to get the money worked out — we've had plenty on our minds."

She had their full attention. "Now we add the tragedy of Louis's death, and the fact that there's a crazy killer running around out there. We have just about nothing going for us except guts, but we've got plenty of those.

"Everyone means well and I love you for it. Without all of you, I don't know what we'd do. But —" she gave long looks to Cyrus and Spike "— don't talk down to me or treat me like the little woman. Some of us really don't like that."

"Amen," Madge said and Cyrus's head whipped around. Vivian decided it wouldn't hurt Madge to get tougher around here.

Spike shoved his hands deep in his pockets and slouched, the brim of his hat so low over his face it all but touched his nose. If there was one thing she couldn't stand, it was a sulking man.

"That detective intends to get you," she told him. "That's old news. I just don't know if you're taking it seriously enough. He wants you as an accessory to murder."

"You read too many crime books," he said, infuriating her. "I don't need anyone to watch my back for me."

Arrogant son of a bitch. "Well I do," she said and instantly regretted her renegade tongue.

All eyes were on her.

Spike shifted his weight. He continued to

look stubborn and closed. She guessed they really hadn't known each other long enough for her to understand the man and maybe she never would.

Vivian felt her mood shift. She had a sudden desire to be outrageous, something she still hadn't learned to control. She reached up and knocked his Stetson forward so that it fell. And she caught it before Spike could. He shook his head, but smiled faintly.

"You've got to watch yourself with the ladies," Cyrus said. "Didn't your mama tell you how unpredictable they are?"

"Crazy, you mean? Nope. My mama didn't tell me much of anything."

Little by little the pieces of Spike Devol came out. If Vivian had to guess she'd say talking about himself was unnatural but something had knocked him off his guard.

"I don't find it admirable when men put women down because they don't know how else to keep on feeling superior," Madge said and gave Cyrus the benefit of her considerable talent for staring people down.

He smiled at her.

Madge didn't smile back.

From what Vivian had been told, Madge was known to be direct but it could be that today would be remembered as the day she climbed all the way out of her envelope.

Spike kept on scuffing at the grass and Vivian had a notion to stand on his boots. She made sure she did no such thing. "Spike," she said, breaking an awkward silence. "I want you to work the case at Rosebank."

She had the sensation she was all alone out here and talking into a void. Not one word did any of them say.

"I trust you —"

"What are you thinkin'?" he said. "You know — and I would like to do it — but you know I can't. Not unless you can get that place moved over the line into St. Martin."

Vivian decided not to jump on that one. "I've worked it all out," she told him. "There's nothing to stop you from doing some private work when you can, is there?"

He said, "No," in the slow manner of a man who felt himself backing into a corner.

"Good. Then will you work for me?"

Spike became aware of bees droning, and how much hotter it was getting. Madge hummed and Cyrus joined in. The tune could be "A Good Man Is Hard To Find," but he couldn't concentrate well enough to be sure.

Vivian watched his face and when he couldn't stand either the rustling quiet, or not looking back at her, he met her eyes and felt himself taking a nosedive. She leaned slightly toward him and repeatedly wetted her lips. *Concentrate, Devol.* Didn't she get it that if Bonine was pissed at him now, having Spike pop up around every corner saying, "I'm Vivian's P.I." was going to start a war? He wanted to take her in his arms and soothe her, and tell her she could lean on him, but he wouldn't work for her.

"Spike?" she said. "Will you do it? Please."

Aw, hell. "You mean you want me to moonlight as a P.I. for you?"

"Yes." She spoke in a whisper. "A private investigator . . . and bodyguard."

14

Cyrus led the way into Lil Dupre's fragrant-smelling kitchen. Either Lil chose to ignore the strained atmosphere or was too tied up with her own agenda to care. She didn't greet them.

Cyrus decided it was time he had those private words with Spike and he didn't look forward to the event. "Spike, if you could spare me a little time? We'll go back to my office."

He couldn't understand the glare he got from Madge, or the damp sheen that sprang into Vivian's green, green eyes. Truly, he did not get women. Oh, sure, what was he thinking of? Spike hadn't responded to the request for him to investigate at Rosebank. In fact he'd come into the rectory without a word. Being spurned tended to make females resort to crying. He didn't like to see it, though, especially not when Vivian had been through so much.

"Father Payne, there you are at last," Lil Dupre said as if noticing him for the first time. She stopped still, halfway up a kitchen ladder and with a bag of cornmeal in each hand.

"How are you today, Lil?" Cyrus said. The official address didn't bode well.

"I'm as well as any woman can expect to be when there's a killer on the loose. I wouldn't think there's a woman for miles around who feels safe."

"The victim was a man," Cyrus pointed out mildly. "Not that it's any less of a tragedy."

"The *first* victim," Lil said, depositing the cornmeal on a shelf and turning around. She didn't climb down from the ladder. "If he *was* the first victim. And who's to say the next one won't be a woman? For all you know that madman killed the lawyer to throw us all off the track."

Spike offered Lil his hand and she held it to climb daintily to the floor and stand with her yellow high-top sneakers planted apart. A short, wiry woman with symmetrical rows of manufactured sausage-shaped curls circling her head, she gave her knight a coy smile. "I always feel safer

192

just knowin' you're around, you," she said. "I surely can't imagine what we'd do without you."

Spike said, "Thank you," and disentangled his hand. "Cyrus and I have some talking to do so we're hoping we can leave these ladies in your care."

Lil wasn't so easily distracted. "I think it's a cryin' shame the way you trained up them two assistant deputies and they transferred from under your nose."

"That's the way things happen. I'm glad they're getting a chance at advancement."

"Sometimes you're too sweet for your own good, you. Now all you got is that Lori who don't never say a word."

Spike glanced at Cyrus as if for help. "Lori is going to make a fine sheriff one day. She's shy is all, and not used to making small talk. Next time you see her Lil, give me a hand and be extra nice to her. Ask her about her horse. I think that's about all the company she's got."

Cyrus screwed up his eyes. He was still waiting for a response from Madge or Vivian and he didn't have much longer to wait.

"Madge," Vivian said. She stood straighter and ran her fingers through her shiny black hair. "You've worked long enough on a Saturday. Would you like to come back to Rosebank with me and look at some of the rooms we've started renovating? Things are pretty much at a standstill for the moment but we'll get going again. I'd like any ideas you have."

Madge said, "You bet. I'll get my purse."

"Did you have lunch yet?" Lil asked the women.

They shook their heads.

Lil didn't look either of them in the eyes. "You'll be that Vivian Patin."

Vivian said, "Yes, pleased to meet you," although she wasn't sure that was truthful.

"Well, I was hoping you'd eat with me," Lil said. "I made me some boulette and they full of crawfish. Went light on the onion on account of it hurts my eyes to peel them things. They get to me even if I cut 'em under water."

"I'm jealous," Cyrus said. "Enjoy yourselves."

"There's plenty of food, only you're too busy to eat it," Lil said, putting fresh fruit in a bowl. "I had visitors while you were in town. They waited a bit in case you come back but then they give up. Never could understand why folks in the same family insist on usin' different names."

Vivian crossed her arms and concentrated

hard, hoping Lil would clear up her meaning.

"Dr. Link, Susan Hurst, Olympia Hurst. Now why wouldn't a woman take her husband's name, I ask you?"

"It's common enough practice for a woman to keep her name," Cyrus said.

"Not around here though, Lil, right?" Spike gave her another smile and Vivian decided he was almost too good at charming women. "We're old-fashioned types."

"We surely are," she said, puffing up her chest and looking pleased. "They wanted you, Father. If you'll forgive me, Miz Vivian, I just have to tell Father what happened. They wanted your opinion on how they could help the Patins. Neighborly, that's what they are. Of course, they're concerned about the murder right next door. And they're very social so they don't want any hint of something sordid getting to their friends."

Vivian kept quiet but her temples pounded.

"The Patins are penniless," Lil said. "Or so Susan told me. She said it's pathetic how they have big plans and no way of carrying them out. Dr. Link didn't think anything would come of it anyway. He can't imagine people wanting to stay in a run-down dump like that — especially when it gets around about the murder."

Vivian felt sick. She avoided looking at anyone, but Madge squeezed her arm and whispered in her ear, "Let her gabble on if you can stand it. We might want to hear everything she's got to say."

A glance at Spike found him trying to telegraph a message to her and Vivian thought it might be pretty close to Madge's. With a nod, she slid into a chair at the big oak table in the window.

"Why did you say these people wanted to see me?" Cyrus asked, also playing along, but not looking happy about it. Vivian was afraid he'd get a giant case of conscience and stop Lil from having her say.

"I told you. To ask your opinion and to tell you some of what's happened to them. They aren't sure how to deal with stopping the Patins from trying to get their hotel going." Lil's brow puckered and her eyes slid toward Vivian. "Like Susan said, it isn't like those women want to have a hotel, they just want a way to make a living. And someone should help them figure out they can't handle what they tryin' to handle."

"It isn't Dr. Link or Susan Hurst's place to interfere," Cyrus said and Vivian noted he deliberately avoided looking in her direction.

"Oh, they wouldn't do anything they shouldn't," Lil said. "And a lot of what I'm saying is what I think they meant not what they said. But you can see how bad this is for them. They want to be kind to their neighbors but they don't want their own plans ruined. Dr. Link said they'll do whatever they have to do to get rid of the Patins."

"Get rid of the Patins?" Spike said slowly. "Did they mention how they'd go about that?"

"Well, maybe they didn't say exactly that. Get rid of the nuisance is probably closer. They're going to ask you if you think lending them money would help. I think that's real decent of them." This time Vivian got a significant glance from the woman.

Vivian pressed her lips together and swallowed. She should consider herself lucky to hear all this. At least she and Mama would know what they were up against with the neighbors.

Lil scanned her audience with avid eyes. "Do you know there's an awful detective in charge of this case and he even asked Dr. Link and Susan questions. And the daughter. Can you believe it? Good upstanding people like that?"

"Pretty hard to figure," Spike said. Vivian's eyes were downcast and color slashed high on her cheeks. He wanted to stop this but the investigator in him had to be sure he didn't switch off any useful information. Vivian had to understand the importance of that.

"Um . . . The detective kind of suggested he thought Miz Vivian killed her own lawyer because he disappointed her over something." Lil looked at the floor. "You need to know all this Miz Patin. And accordin' to what Olympia Hurst said, that Detective Bonine thinks you were involved, Spike. I told her to watch her tongue 'cause that couldn't be, but she's the kind who doesn't care what she says."

Vivian had an elbow on the table and she held tightly curled fingers against her mouth.

"I appreciate your confidence," Spike said when nobody had spoken for a long time.

Lil ducked her head to focus her bright eyes on Vivian. "I thought you should know everythin', too." She marched to the refrigerator and took out a jug of iced tea. Selecting a tall glass, she filled it and plunked it in front of Vivian. "Now, let's us have us some boulette and Madge can help us get acquainted."

Spike didn't want to leave Vivian. "Look," he said to Cyrus. "There's something I want to say to Vivian — alone. Give me a few minutes and I'll be right in. Okay if we use your office, Madge?"

Madge nodded and told them to make themselves comfortable. She'd start on the boulette.

"Follow me," Spike said to Vivian and wished he didn't sound so gruff. He half expected her to ignore him, but she got up and walked behind him past walls papered with flights of ducks, to the sitting room Madge used as a second office. She usually worked at a desk in Cyrus's study.

On the way past the bottom of the stairs, Wally and Wendy could be heard laughing upstairs in the counseling room where Cyrus kept a TV.

They went into Madge's hideaway and Spike closed the door. Madge's music system was still on and there was no mistaking the washboard, fiddle and accordion sound of the zydeco she loved. Everyone knew Madge was an enthusiast.

"We'd better keep this short," Vivian said, crossing well-worn gray carpet to stand beside a desk. "Cyrus is waiting on you. And I need to put distance between myself and Lil while I have a chance to think about all she said. I'm not sure she wanted to help me. Maybe she enjoyed watching my reaction." The only window was high in the outside wall, but an overstuffed red chair and two more covered in a red floral chintz made the room cozy.

"Maybe," Spike said. "But I hated what you listened to, informative as it was. It's all crazy. Do you truly believe there is some provision for the upkeep of Rosebank?"

She nodded. "I told you I do and so does Mama." What proof did she have outside what a dead man had said? But he had said it and he'd been in a position to know. Uncle Guy had enjoyed his little jokes and she was certain that once he decided his brother needed Rosebank more than the preservation society did, he'd devised some clever plan to make sure his beloved house could be kept up.

"I think there is, too," Spike told her. "I think Louis died for it."

"But if there's a trust or something, I don't see how anyone else could claim it."

"No," Spike said. "Neither do I. Which makes me wonder if what we should be lookin' for is somethin' other than money."

Vivian shook her head. She put her hands behind her on the desk and gave a little jump to seat herself on top. She swung her feet and the full skirt of her yellow dress rippled about her calves. "I start imagining treasure maps and midnight searches," she told him.

Spike screwed up his eyes and fell silent.

They remained where they were, looking at each other, and Vivian grew apprehensive about what else he might say.

"I like you in that yellow," Spike said. "I like you in anything, really — and most of all, in just about nothing."

He embarrassed her and she didn't answer.

"There's something we've got to straighten out," he said and muscles jumped in his lean cheeks.

Vivian slipped to stand on the floor again, crossed her arms and held her elbows. Ever so slightly, she swayed to the music.

"You like to dance?" he asked.

"I've never had much spare time but I like it when I can."

"Like me." He walked around her and came to a stop in front of her. With his hands on her arms, he swayed to the music and she swayed with him. "No spare time."

His smile was speculative and he pulled her closer until he could put his arms around her and rest his chin on top of her head. And they kept on swaying.

"We can't stay here," she said. "It will look suspicious."

The phone rang and a button flashed red. Almost at once the call was picked up elsewhere in the house.

"I've never worried much about what other people think," Spike said.

Vivian giggled and bowed her forehead to his chest. Spike held her even tighter and moved, letting her know he was no stranger to dancing.

As abruptly as he'd started, he stopped, stood still and studied her face. "I saw you cry out there."

"I don't cry."

"Fibber. You cried when you thought Cyrus and I were going off to talk on our own."

"No, I didn't."

"You did. I'd like to think that was because you didn't want me to go, but I think it was something more. I hadn't answered your question and you were hurt."

Vivian raised her chin. "We shouldn't be here like this."

"You've already made that point and I disagree. It's a fine idea. The only better one would be for us to know we were alone and would stay that way as long as we wanted." With that his face set. He took two steps backward, dropped into the red chair and pulled her off balance until she fell into his lap.

Hot all over, she pushed her hands down to propel herself to her feet again. Her hands were on his penis. She looked into his face. She wasn't the only one who was hot around here. Vivian pulled her hands from their very intimate position.

"Are you always erect?" Vivian said and hid her face, mortified at what she'd said.

Spike didn't laugh. He pried her hands from her face. "No I'm not, but it seems to happen a lot since I met you. Do you want to know what I've got to say to you?"

"I'm not sure I do."

His gaze rested on her mouth and she returned the favor. They closed the space between them and rested their lips, skin to skin, tip of tongue to tip of tongue.

Vivian opened her mouth wider and Spike followed her lead. He put a breath of distance between them and she saw how his eyes were glazed. Once more he closed the gap and his eyelids lowered. Back and forth he glided his mouth over hers, back and forth, back and forth.

The heat built, the sweet tension. Spike stroked one of her shins, took his hand beneath the full hem of her dress and continued up her thigh. He shifted her, pulled her legs over one arm of the chair and cradled her head on his shoulder.

The hand on her thigh passed over her hip and around to her bottom.

And still he kissed her, sipping at her lips, breathing harshly, adjusting her until her head fell farther back and they attacked each other's mouths, flesh crushing flesh.

This was all about sex, nothing but sex. They hardly knew each other. Vivian turned her face from him and when she resisted his efforts to find her mouth again, Spike ran his tongue around the folds of her ear and nuzzled her neck. "Come on, Vivian," he said. "Loosen up."

Loosen up and give him what he wanted, and expected to get? She twisted rapidly and scrambled away from him. She'd been the one to follow him to his home and incite him, but they were going much too fast.

What she didn't expect was exactly what he did. Spike came after her, backed her to a wall. Tearing away had only excited him more. His eyes, the searing fervor there, shook her.

"What is it?" he asked. "You already showed me we're on the same page. You want me and I want you."

She couldn't argue with him because it

was true. "I'm nervous," she said honestly.

"Shh," he told her. "You don't have to be nervous when I'm with you." He leaned against her and his weight felt better than it should. "I like knowing your legs are bare under that dress." He looked openly at her breasts and she was grateful he didn't remark on her not wearing a bra. Her nipples stung and she breathed harder, wanting to be naked and to have him touch her all over.

"It's going to be good with us," he told her, pressing a heavy thigh between her legs.

He played with the shoulders of her crossover bodice and pulled them down a little. "Beautiful," he murmured, settling his mouth on the place where her right breast began its swell. "So beautiful." And he used his thumbnails and the texture of the yellow fabric to tease her into forcing herself harder against his fingers.

Any restraint she'd felt vanished. Vivian worked buttons free by touch and passed her hands inside his shirt. Warm, supple skin over muscle and bone. She braced herself on his shoulders and kissed whatever parts of his chest she could reach. Rocking back and forth on his thigh drove her wild. She pressed a hand into his belly and worked down until she could cup the bulge inside his pants and claw a cry from him.

Spike had agile fingers. It took him little effort to reach her nipples inside the dress and pinch just hard enough to bring her back arching away from the wall. She squeezed him and the wildness she felt in him provoked her. For an instant she released him and pushed the dress aside to reveal her breasts, and Spike grabbed her wrists and held them on either side of her head. His kisses were on whatever bare skin he could find. He fastened his mouth on a nipple, grasped both of her wrists in one hand and reached down to pull her skirts up to her waist.

He was almost savage, but Vivian felt just as primitive. Tiny flashes of caution were quickly extinguished. She unzipped his pants and found her way to engorged flesh. Spike removed his leg from hers and stroked over her panties, between her legs, and she didn't care that he'd know how wet she was, how much she wanted him.

"Spike." It was Cyrus's voice that hailed him from outside Madge's office.

Vivian jumped and clung to Spike. "Not now," Vivian whispered.

He smiled at her but his teeth gritted.

"Spike, sorry to interrupt but something's happened."

"Yeah," Spike said. "Coming."

But he kissed Vivian again and kept his lips on first one breast, then the other, until the very last second before she eased the dress back into place.

Vivian buttoned his shirt, zipped his pants, but kept right on feeling him until he dragged her hand away and gathered her up in his arms.

"Is it enough for you?" she asked. "The heat and the promise, but then nothing, no completion."

"Real soon I'll show you the answer to that," he told her. "In the meantime, if anyone asks why I wanted to talk to you alone, don't tell 'em the truth. They don't need to know I'm going to die by inches until I can bury my interested party so deep in you we may both die happy."

"That's what I *don't* tell them," Vivian said and her skin felt raw all over. The sensitive and hidden parts of her hurt with the wanting.

"Uh-huh." He helped her up and made sure they were both respectable. "Tell them we had to discuss the terms of my employment as your bodyguard."

She blinked. "You're going to do it? You'll look into the things Bonine isn't bothering with."

"Fortunately I just happen to have my P.I. license from a period when Detective Bonine managed to make sure I didn't have a job with the department. I've kept it up." He settled his hands on the sides of her face. "I'll keep you safe. And I'll keep you happy. We'll have lots of time to make it really good between us."

"What exactly does that mean?" She'd never been good at stopping her thoughts before they reached her mouth.

Spike shrugged. "Does it need an explanation? We're going to have accommodations to make and it looks like that'll be easy."

Vivian cooled off fast. "It'll be easy for us to have sex because you'll be around Rosebank?"

He caught her by the waist. "You pointed out that what we've had isn't enough. We can't be alone at my place because of Homer and Wendy. I want to be with you, Vivian. We can get lost together at Rosebank."

"And you'll guard my body." She felt sick, and foolish, and cheap.

"Sounds good to me."

He was *oblivious*. "Casual sex always sounds good to men, doesn't it? I've embarrassed myself."

Finally some of the confidence went out of his eyes. He frowned and reached for her. "I don't understand you, *cher*, but I'm not going to lose you now."

Vivian evaded him and walked out of the room.

15

Vivian walked toward Cyrus with an expression he could only describe as desolate. He noted that her hair was mussed.

She nodded at him.

"I'll only take a few minutes of Spike's time," he said.

Vivian shrugged with a surprised look that didn't quite come off. "Why should that matter to me?"

Something matters to you very much. "Charlotte called and wants you to call her back. No hurry, she says." If Spike had hurt Vivian he would be reminded that Cyrus wasn't always the even-tempered man he appeared. "I had an idea about Louis. I'll tell you when I'm finished here."

She mumbled something that could have been, "yes," but he wasn't sure.

Spike didn't appear from Madge's room

so Cyrus stuck his head around the door. With his hands sunk deep in his pockets and his back to Cyrus, Spike evidently found Madge's bookshelves engrossing.

Cyrus shut the door behind him and Spike looked over his shoulder.

"What did you do to Vivian?" Cyrus asked.

That got him a short, mirthless laugh and the original view of the back of Spike's head.

"I don't know her well yet, but she seemed very unhappy to me. I'll repeat the question. What did you do to Vivian? Or say?"

Spike ran the fingers of both hands into his hair. "I'm hopeless. I don't know why, but I am. Somehow or other I offended her. Now I don't want to talk about it. I want to be alone to figure this out, if any man can figure out what goes on in a woman's mind."

"Were the two of you . . ."

Spike swung around. "Are you asking me if we — ?" He shrugged.

"I wouldn't do that." So what had he been asking? And why couldn't he just sit the pair of them down and have a civilized conversation about a very sensitive subject.

He couldn't. That was it.

"Be grateful you don't have to deal with this garbage," Spike said. "They're nuts. Freakin' nuts. All of 'em. What did I say wrong, that's what I want to know?"

"Repeat it and I'll see if I can figure out what annoyed her."

"Repeat it?" Spike's voice rose to a squeak. "Are you freakin' nuts, too? I'm going to tell you what I said to a woman . . . You think I'll repeat what I just said to a woman who matters to me?"

"How much does she matter to you?"

Spike squirmed. Yes, Cyrus could definitely describe the movements Spike made as squirming. He drew up his big shoulders. "She matters. Maybe a lot." He pointed at Cyrus. "But she's nuts."

Cyrus didn't know what to say next. "I had two calls while you were in here. By the way, the others in the kitchen figured out there was something going on between the two of you. I could see it in their faces."

"Two calls?" Spike turned red and got pale under his tan by turns.

"Bill Green says he wants to make some suggestions about how to help the Patins out."

"I thought I heard you say people shouldn't interfere in their affairs."

"That was different. Those people who came here talked about getting rid of Charlotte and Vivian just to make sure there wouldn't be a hotel next door.

212

"Bill's talkin' about helping them get on their feet, get started. I think we should discuss it with him."

"He's horny," Spike said.

Cyrus managed to clean any expression from his face but he laughed inside. Later, when Spike had a chance to go over this conversation alone, he'd wish he could rework a lot of it.

"Did you hear what I said?" Spike asked. "Did you see the way he looked at Reb Girard. She's married and six months pregnant for crying out loud."

"She looks lovely. Relaxed, the way a pregnant woman is when she knows her mate is committed." It wasn't a real subtle approach, but it was something.

"Marc and Reb have it together," Spike said. "We're talkin' about Bill Green and what we both saw him do. He looked as if he'd like to jump her bones. Sorry."

Cyrus didn't even want to think about Bill's reaction to Reb when they'd all been at Jilly's. He considered before saying, "You're seeing things that aren't there. I'm pretty good at picking up on anything like that and I didn't notice." Might he be forgiven for his lie of convenience.

He didn't like the quizzical way Spike raised his eyebrows.

"What?" Cyrus said. "What is it? Why the look?"

"You pick up on those things easily, do you? You feel that charge of sex in the air? Geez, I don't know how you do it. Whaddaya do, pack your balls in ice every night?"

Cyrus wasn't amused. "Bill will be over later. And I want you to remember he's a good-hearted man who didn't want a divorce but wasn't given any choice. Also, he's only a man, just like all men — except he also knows what it's like to be in combat and get decorated for valor."

He wasn't sure Spike was buying a word. "Am I out of line if I say a man's mind isn't always in gear when he looks at an attractive woman? Don't *you* ever look first, react, and think later?"

"You're right," Spike said, spreading his hands and letting them drop to his sides. "Sometimes I get carried away. I can't believe what I said to you. I apologize. I'm not myself."

"Forget it. And don't say a word to Marc about the way Bill looked at Reb. He puts on a good front but he worries about her doing too much while she's pregnant. A hint that some guy looked his wife over might just give him a focus for the frustration he can't do a thing about. Marc's used to being in control and this one is out of his hands. It doesn't help that he won't let go of looking for his sister."

One of society's dropouts, Amy Girard hadn't been heard of in a year. "I think he takes that as it comes now. Hey, Cyrus, I want to seriously apologize for talking to you the way I did."

"We've got more important things to discuss. I don't want to talk about this to anyone who can't keep their own counsel, but the other call I got was from Charlotte Patin. Gil Mayes, their gardener, didn't go home last night. The man's seventy-two and arthritic. He works as long as he can and goes right back to his place. It was his brother who called. He lives in the other side of a duplex Gil owns in Loreauville."

Spike passed a hand around the back of his neck. "People change their habits. Happens all the time. Maybe he went to visit friends, or he could have a lady friend somewhere. He doesn't have to tell his brother everything."

"Spike," Cyrus said. "Gil's pottin' shed at Rosebank is wide open. He's very particular about locking it before he leaves because he propagates stuff in there."

"He forgot," Spike said. "People do that, too."

"If you say so. He also forgot to take his car with him."

16

"They can't find Gil Mayes," Ozaire Dupre told Homer Devol, sliding a tiny, expensive cell phone back into a jeans pocket. "That was Lil. They got a call at the rectory couple hours ago. Lil say Father still shut away with Madge and Spike . . . and that Vivian Patin."

Homer had got back to the store by the middle of the afternoon, but Ozaire had stuck around. Having him to help out sometimes eased the load, but of late he had taken to hanging out at the store whenever Spike wasn't there and Homer didn't like it much. The other man behaved as if the two of them were friends, which they were not and never would be. Ozaire had his finger in every pie for miles around and considered it his due to skim the cream off the top of anything that made money. Like fish boiling and party barbecuing.

"You don't got enough help around here," Ozaire said when Homer failed to pick up on the gossip from Lil. "I got more time to spare. How about I do the bayou traffic for you? I could run those orders out easy and save you all kinds of time."

The man never quit working the angles. "We got that under control. But thanks for the offer. Ain't you got duties at the church? One of these days they gonna find someone who really wants that job."

"Never you mind about that, I got everythin' under control." Ozaire's shaven head gleamed and his black eyes narrowed to slits. "You hear what I say to you before? You better be listenin' because this could be bad news for you."

Homer continued slicing meat for tomorrow's sandwiches. "I'm listening to you." But he would not be giving Ozaire the satisfaction of hearing him admit that Spike's involvement with the Patin girl, and with the trouble at Rosebank, had Homer on edge.

"I don't know what you're suggestin'," he said. "Gil Mayes is missing? Can't imagine how that would be. But if it is, why is it anything to do with Spike? You don't like my boy and you're mixin' things up for no good reason."

Ozaire looked wounded. "You know

218

better than that. I've always liked Spike. All's I want is to help you out in your time of trouble. The police already suggested Spike had somethin' to do with what happened to that lawyer. Made himself some sort of after-the-fact alibi. If Gil's bought the farm now and they figure this is related to the other one, it'll only get worse for your boy."

"I don't know where you get your ideas." But Homer didn't like hearing them. "Spike don't have a thing to do with whatever happens at Rosebank."

"Spike's hangin' out with Vivian Patin." Ozaire hitched at his jeans. "Or by all accounts, he is. Lil says you could cut the air between 'em with a knife. Wonder she don't get shocked when she walks near 'em, she says. Some thinks they only just met but me, I know they been circling the landing strip ever since she came here for good."

"It's not my place to criticize another man's wife, but Lil should zip her lip," Homer said. "A couple of young sparks can take an interest in each other without nosy folks makin' somethin' of it."

The T-shirt Ozaire wore sparkled, it was so white. All but around the neck where his head just about rested on his shoulders and a ring of sweat darkened the fabric. "She might not look like her, but Vivian Patin reminds me of that Precious Depew. Another one of them women with a way of windin' a man around her little finger."

Finally too angry to keep quiet, Homer slapped down a block of cheese and leaned toward Ozaire. "You mad? Precious Depew is servin' time for kidnapping and that husband of hers is away for a long time. Chauncy Depew is a small-time hoodlum who finally did enough to get himself noticed. Never did have no good examples, Precious, with her mother bein' crazy and all."

"Yep," Ozaire said, showing no sign of offense. "Crazy Oribel," he said of Cyrus's former housekeeper. "Did she go off the deep end or what? Wouldn't be surprised to see Precious back in Toussaint and makin' trouble one of these days, though. Chauncy, too. He's mean enough to keep popping through his own slime and starting over again."

"*Ozaire,*" Homer said, blood pounding at his temples. "You just suggested Vivian Patin, who hasn't done a thing wrong as far as either of us know, is a sex-crazed kidnapper like Precious Depew. Start thinkin' and keep your mouth shut while you do."

A sly twitch completely closed Ozaire's left eye. "If Spike had to go away for a while, you'd have your hands full."

There was no keeping a conversation on track with Ozaire. But Homer had all the practice he needed in hiding his thoughts. "Now why would Spike go away? He likes it here and he's got a job to do — and Wendy to bring up."

"You not foolin' me you dumb," Ozaire said. "You know what I'm talking about and it isn't takin' a vacation or movin' to another town. I'm talkin' about spending time at a government hotel."

He paused to check Homer's reaction before going on. "And speakin' of Wendy, that's somethin' else you might want to think about. Who's putting that little girl first, apart from you? She's already had enough bad stuff. Lil says she's lookin' after her at the rectory now on account of Spike's gone off and left her. Someone took a bunch of cash from the office at the ice plant. Now they just about got a riot on their hands out there 'cause everyone blame everyone else."

A shade of violet gray crept into the early evening sky. The spots were already on outside the garage and over the pumps. Homer switched on the multi-colored lights around the store roof. They glowed inside plastic Chinese lanterns and were Wendy's favorites.

His instinct was to close up and go get her but Homer knew better than to interfere with Spike's handling of his daughter. If the little one was at the rectory, she was safe, no matter how much fuss Lil made about being put out.

"Father's gone to Rosebank with that Vivian. Madge is along, too. Father and Madge spend too much time together, or so Lil thinks, and she's in a position to know."

"That's not respectful talk," Homer said. "People should learn to mind their own business."

Ozaire shrugged. "If Wendy's papa goes off the deep end, too, she'll need you even more. You'll have to make sure she gets what she needs. I heard about some child service of some kind what takes kids away if they don't think they in a good place."

The bell for the pumps went off and Homer gave silent thanks for the interruption. He wasn't a violent man but Ozaire pushed too far. In a fistfight Ozaire Dupre would win, but just hitting him would feel good.

Homer leaned to see who was at the pumps. He and Spike ran a pay and pump operation controlled from the store. A motorcycle cop had dismounted and was talking on his radio. From the bike it looked like the man was from Iberia. The officer finished talking and came in the direction of the store.

"Here come trouble," Ozaire said in a low drone. "You don't deserve this after all you done for your family."

"Can it," Homer said, an instant before the officer came in, his impressive leather boots creaking. He didn't bother to remove either his wraparound, bug-eyed black sunglasses, or his helmet. His gauntlets were clasped under one arm. " 'Evenin', Officer. What can I do for you?"

A brawny hand slapped money on the counter. "Gas."

Homer figured he could compete with Chatty Cathy. He rang up the amount, dealt with the pump and put the receipt beside the man's fist on the counter.

"Spike Devol's place."

It wasn't a question so Homer just stood there with his arms crossed over his chest.

"Obstructin' the law's a bad idea," the officer said. "I asked you a question."

Homer weighed just how far he wanted to go with making this punk's life difficult. "I thought you was just remarkin'," he said. No point in mixing things up when it could make things tougher for Spike. "Homer Devol," he said, sticking out a hand.

"Spike's my son and this is his place."

Rather than shake Homer's hand, Barker, as his nameplate announced, stuck his right thumb in his belt. "Where is he?"

Homer felt Ozaire's excitement. Maybe he'd hit him anyway. Even if the satisfaction was short-lived, it would be worth it.

"Where —"

"Workin'." Homer cut Barker off. "Job's never done for a small-town deputy with one assistant. Call the office. There's always someone on the switchboard."

"This is personal."

"Oh, you're friends." Homer could handle a little thin ice.

"Personal," Barker said. "Between him and another jurisdiction. They want him in for questioning and there's a pissed-off detective who isn't takin' much more from him. If you know where he is — and we both know you do — you'll do both of you a favor by giving me the information."

Homer shook his head and caught Ozaire's eye. Give the man his due, he was loyal enough and managed to look confused and out of it for Barker's benefit.

"You won't tell me where he is?" Barker said, creaking louder. Everything from the leather strap across his body to his belt, holster, boots and probably things Homer hadn't thought about, creaked as if the man was expanding inside his clothes.

"I don't know where that boy is," Homer said, trying a smile. "If you got kids you know you can't keep track of 'em even when they're young. How am I supposed to figure out where a grown son is? He's a busy man, I tell you. I'd help you, but I can't." He couldn't on account of he wouldn't.

Barker shifted very slowly but Homer braced himself to look down the barrel of a gun. The motorcycle cop pulled on his gauntlets. "You better hope I don't find out you're deliberately holding back information." He turned for the door.

"You'll need your receipt," Homer said, holding it out.

Barker took it from him gently enough to send a dart of cold up Homer's back. Damn that kid of his anyway.

With Ozaire at his elbow, Homer watched while the cop filled his cycle then went through his little rituals of checking this and that, hitching this and that and, finally, kicking off the stand.

"Reminds me of a few of them baseball players at the plate," Ozaire said. "Spit three times, hitch your jock, kick the dirt twice, hitch the jock again and cross yourself."

Homer smiled at that.

"Look," Ozaire said. "I know you think I'm only out for myself, but it ain't true. We gotta stick together, us natives. We gotta look out for one another. You still gonna argue Spike's not in any trouble? That boy may be white as driven snow, but someone's out to get him."

Like that was news? "Spike can handle himself."

"But he could be set up," Ozaire said, his face all puckered. "That might get worked out in the end but it's gonna take time. I reckon that Errol Bonine — he's a detective Spike worked with in —"

"I know who Errol Bonine is." Homer didn't add, *crooked cop taking graft to look the other way.*

"Yeah, well, there's no love lost between those two and word has it Bonine thinks Spike's interferin' in the Rosebank case on account of he's having a thing with the Patin girl. But it's more than that. Bonine's workin' on provin' she killed the lawyer and Spike's tryin' to help her cover."

Homer finished wrapping a batch of pastrami sandwiches and stacked them in a refrigerated case before saying, "That's the second time you told me more or less the same thing."

"I could help you out, Homer. You not so young anymore."

"You neither." Homer wondered how many others around Toussaint had heard Ozaire and Lil Dupre's speculations about Spike and the Patin girl. Just about everyone in town he'd guess.

"I'm strong, me," Ozaire said. "Constitution of an ox, Dr. Reb say. You and me could make a team, my friend. I'd put some money into this place. I got money, me. That's between you and me. Suits my purpose to have folks think I'm poor. You gonna need help. I feel it in my bones."

Homer slammed the case shut, washed his hands, reached for his hat — taking his time over every move. "Gotta check around the place. I'll be lockin' the store while I do it."

"Time like this, you shouldn't be out there on your own," Ozaire said promptly and fell in with Homer on his evening rounds.

Strolling, Homer looked at the pumps, then slid open the doors to the garage.

"You don't do no repair work out here anymore," Ozaire remarked.

"Never have since we've had the place. If someone's in trouble we give 'em a tow to the repair shop in town." He was wishing he'd had his wits about him enough to stay out of the garage while Ozaire was around.

Too late.

Spike's truck with the boiler and the big barbecues for catering backyard parties, took up a good portion of the space and Homer could imagine his son's reaction if he could see Ozaire openly sizing up the rig.

"I gotta admit it's nice," Ozaire said. "Nothin' but the best quality."

"Spike doesn't mess around when it comes to business."

"No, he only messes around —" Ozaire laughed his neighing laugh and slapped his knees. He shook with mirth at his own wit and pointed a finger at Homer. "You know. The other kind of messin' around."

"You got any particular point to make before you go?" Homer asked.

"I told you what I heard about Spike for your own good," Ozaire said, sobering. "You gotta make plans for the future and since he's not around much now — it's not too soon to get on with it. I got me plenty of help with the boilin'. Man can't do everythin' himself."

Homer pretended he didn't get Ozaire's drift.

"Wouldn't be no trouble for me to take on your rig, too. I be more'n fair with splittin' the profits. O'course, you'd deal with maintenance and gas. Only other thing you'd need to do is give me your contact list to work off."

Maybe he should get himself a pair of those bug-eyed police specs, Homer thought. Might camouflage whatever made him look like a fool to folks like Ozaire Dupre.

"How come you work at the church?" Homer said. "Man of your means and business expertise don't need to mow between tombs."

"Contacts," Ozaire said, sobering. "People trust you when you're with the Church. And I meet everyone coming and going."

Settling his hat low on his forehead, Homer raised his head to look at Ozaire from under the brim. "If you're patient, I can see them new babies comin' into the world, growin' up and maybe thinkin' you're okay. But I should think the revenue from the ones goin' the other way would be about as high as anythin' you'll ever make trickin' us out of part of our business."

17

"I've tried to talk him out of it," Charlotte Patin said, "but Gary insists he wants to stay here nights and commute to New Orleans."

Gary Legrain and Charlotte stood side by side in Guy Patin's office where they'd been going through drawers. A lamp with a monkey balanced on a pineapple for a base rested at the very edge of the desk top to give more light.

Several of the bookcases were hinged and could be opened to reveal concealed filing cabinets and cupboards. The spaces stood open.

"You're a nice man," Vivian said. "But you don't have to do that. We'll be fine." And despite the tension between them she still had Spike to do anything that needed to be done in the way of security around here.

Cyrus and Madge remained just inside

the office door, each of them behaving as if they weren't taking any interest in the conversation.

"I've refused to be denied," Gary said, his gray eyes smiling. He had a way of looking at her for a little too long and with too much interest. "So I'll be stickin' around. But I promise I won't get underfoot. It's for my peace of mind, Vivian. And I owe it to poor Louis who would have done the same thing in my place." He indicated the desk with its open drawers. "This is probably a useless exercise, but we're starting to go through every piece of paper we can find to see if there's anythin' here about the additional inheritance Louis spoke of. He was excited, you know. Said you weren't goin' to have to worry anymore."

Vivian spread a hand over the front of her neck. She smiled but felt again the terrible disappointment that came with Louis's death and the disappearance of whatever he'd intended to show them. Guilt plagued her. She should only think about the tragedy of Louis's death and the urgency to find Gil.

She, Madge and Cyrus, and Boa, who shot away into the house the moment the door was open, had arrived on the estate more than half an hour earlier. Spike expected to catch up with them unless the ice plant complaint turned into a bigger mess than expected.

Again an officer manned the main gates to the estate and yellow crime scene tape decorated both sides of the driveway. The grounds were overrun by deputies from the Iberia Parish Sheriffs Department and volunteers who were searching through the undergrowth.

Detective Frank Wiley had seen them and reported that the search for Gil Mayes had widened but brought no leads. He'd warned them to be ready for more questions.

At least Louis's car had been removed.

"That lovely green and gold room in the east wing, the one with its own sitting room and bathroom, should do nicely for Gary," Charlotte said. "It's a bit shabby-opulent but comfortable, and the plumbing works."

Charlotte's relaxed manner relieved Vivian, but even though she liked Gary, she didn't want him to stay — not when she wasn't sure how Spike would take it.

Spike and his opinions mattered to her, maybe too much.

"It's a lovely suite of rooms," she said. "But you don't need to stay here, Gary. We're fine."

He looked down at her from his considerable height. A good-looking, intelligent face. "I know you're fine," he said evenly. "I just wanted to keep an eye on you. But I understand if you'd rather not have a stranger hanging around. All you have to do is call the offices in the Quarter and I can be down here in a couple of hours."

"*Vivian.*" Truly, there were times when Charlotte didn't understand her daughter or her manners. "I've already thanked Gary for being so kind and I, for one, will be hurt and disappointed if he doesn't stay."

Gary looked uncomfortable.

Without meeting her mother's eyes, Vivian said, "Forgive me, Gary. I have this thing about not putting people out. We need you here so I hope you'll stay."

"And you will, won't you?" Charlotte said, smiling at Gary and nodding.

Gary considered before saying, "Yes, I will. All of this is going to come clear. It's early days but when the case is personal, the waiting is harder. Tomorrow I'm going to assign a member of our staff to search David Patin's files, and see if your husband may have had any dealings with Louis that we're not aware of, Charlotte." He looked apologetic. "That's unlikely but we can't assume anything in a situation like this." He indicated three triple file cabinets revealed by the open bookcases. "Those are going to

take time. Supposedly they're filled with re-
search for a book Mr. Patin was writing but
who's to say there's nothing of interest
there?"

Alone with Vivian, Cyrus thought about
what he wanted to tell her. She was the one
most likely to keep ego out of giving him an
honest reaction.

"Madge will get a look at more of the
house," Vivian said. Charlotte had invited
Madge along when she took Gary to the east
wing. "Has she ever been married?"

"No," Cyrus said. He shouldn't feel any
reaction at all to that question, but he did.
One day the answer would change and he'd
react to that, too.

"Why does she live in Rayne? Wouldn't it
be easier if she was closer to St. Cécil's? She
could . . . no, I don't suppose it would be a
good idea for her to live at the rectory even
though there's so much room. They say you
shouldn't live where you work." She turned
the corners of her mouth down. "Oops, you
live where you work."

"That's different," he told her. The subject had to be changed. "I don't know how
much time we've got but I wanted to run a
couple of things by you. Has Spike said anything about actual findings at the scene of

Louis's death? Anything about the body?"

"Nothing," Vivian said. "I don't know if he has any way of finding those things out."

"I wouldn't be surprised if Spike had ways of doing a lot of things we'd never even guess at." Spike had been in law enforcement in the area for some years. He must have contacts. "Did you think Louis had put up a fight?"

It was a warm night but Vivian shivered. "Well, I don't guess so. I hadn't thought about it. No. It was like he sat there, the person opened the door and cut his throat then Louis fell sideways."

"The killer was left-handed," Cyrus said. There were plenty of pros looking at the case and they'd say they didn't need him to move a single gray cell on the issue, but he sometimes wondered if those people got jaded and stopped noticing things, or caring as much.

"You saw the body?" Vivian picked up a brass monkey paperweight from the desk. "I guess you must have. I can see it when I close my eyes. Sometimes it wakes me up."

"They let me go to him when I was on my way out. I told them I didn't know if he'd have wanted a blessing but it couldn't do any harm. That's when I figured Louis didn't put up a fight. Nothing. I didn't even see any wounds on his hands like he'd gone after the knife."

Three deliberately separated taps on the open door announced Spike's arrival. He'd rolled up his sleeves and unbuttoned his shirt almost to his waist. Weariness hovered on his face. "You missed your calling," he said to Cyrus. "Criminal investigation needs you. Did you figure out a reason why Louis didn't fight?"

"Because the killer had a gun on him," Cyrus and Spike said in unison. Cyrus smiled and continued, "From the way it looked, with Louis's face pointing up, and the wound deepest on the right side of his neck and fading away just past the wind-pipe, I'd say the gun was in the man's right hand and shoved into Louis while his throat was cut."

Spike nodded and looked grim. "That's my take, too."

"I was asking Vivian if you'd heard anything from the Iberia people."

Spike gave a lopsided mirthless smile. "They wouldn't comment if a truck was about to hit me. I take that back. They'd probably keep me too distracted to notice the truck. Bonine should be here, lazy bastard. He's doing his usual number, not putting himself out anymore than he has to."

"Why can't they find Gil?" Vivian said, even though she didn't expect an answer. "Where would he go without his car? Do they think he's been murdered too? They do, don't they?"

Spike stretched a hand toward her and, after a brief glance at Cyrus, Vivian took hold of that big, warm, workworn hand and felt comforted.

He pulled her beside him and her eyes were on a level with his collarbones, with the toned muscle in his tanned chest. A little flip, a little tensing hit low in Vivian's tummy and she looked at the floor.

Spike squeezed Vivian's fingers and he said, "At any other time I'd be thinkin' Gil just walked off for some personal reason. But we've had one murder here, so jumping to conclusions about Gil is human nature."

"Louis's body was left in his car," she said, looking up at him, at the beard shadow on his jaw. A red mark, turning purple, hid just beneath his chin. Dried blood clung to a cut behind his ear. "What happened to you? Spike, you're cut and there's a bruise."

"Ice plant," he said, rolling his eyes at Cyrus. "Those guys were really going at it. Everyone blaming everyone else. Poor Zeb Dalcour, he's still the manager out there, he's tearin' his hair out. I ended up not charging anyone because I couldn't even find out how much was supposed to be missing. They didn't know, they just *thought* there'd been a theft."

"Please God they were mistaken," Cyrus said, smiling a little.

"But one of them hit you," Vivian said, outraged. "Tell me who it was and I'll go say what I think about it. Worm."

"The worm was me," Spike said. He grimaced and ran a hand around his neck. "I slipped and fell — hit myself on a pillar. Wow did I feel dumb."

"Oh," Vivian said, trying to frown and look sympathetic.

"Go ahead and laugh," Spike told her. "Cruel woman. But back to the topic on the table. I think Louis was left in his car because that's where he was killed and he was a big man — not so easy to move. Speculatin' about Gil doesn't feel so hot but it wouldn't be hard to lift him and take him away altogether."

"Is Spike your real name?" Vivian asked and felt ridiculous.

He didn't rush to answer.

"Forget I asked," she said. "The thought just popped into my head. It's none of my business. Maybe you're into sharp implements."

"Vivian!" Cyrus said.

"Sorry. Again. I was just trying to loosen things up."

"Saul Paul Ike," Spike said. "After my father's father and my mother's father and someone or other's favorite statesman. You can call me Spike."

Vivian caught Cyrus's innocent expression and wanted to giggle. She didn't. "I like the name Saul. It's very strong. Paul, too — sort of a feeling name. I wouldn't think anyone would need to know about the Ike." She cleared her throat and rushed on, "But Ike is distinguished. You don't meet too many Ikes, do you, Cyrus?"

"A teacher read off the whole name in the classroom one time," Spike said, gruff. "I was stuck with the teasin' till I got bigger and meaner than a lot of guys in school. Bye-bye, Ike, hello, Spike. Now, *end* of subject."

"I still think it's really unusual . . ." Vivian patted a pocket in her dress until she found a tissue. "Louis's car was kind of wedged in. Do you think someone guided him there like that?"

"Yes," Spike said. "Put the pots of laurel where the vehicle was found, then closed the driveway side off with more laurel afterward. Too bad they don't have usable tire tracks because of all the rain. Not even the ones from Louis's vehicle — if that mattered but it doesn't really. I wanted to ask how far they've looked for signs that another car was parked somewhere. Whoever did this had to drive in."

Cyrus rocked onto the balls of his feet. "Yes, and he wouldn't want to go far carrying a body. If there is another body, of course, which I pray there isn't."

"The detective's going to come here, I just know he is," Vivian said. Spike had made no move to release her hand and she had no intention of doing so. "He doesn't like me and I don't know why because he doesn't know me."

"You're convenient and you're a friend of mine," Spike said. "He wants a scapegoat. He doesn't really think you've done anything wrong. But as long as he can center on you and take potshots at me, he doesn't have to do too much else. By the time they have to say you had nothing to do with it, the trail will be cold and Errol won't shed any tears. One more unsolved case for which he'll have dozens of excuses. And you will be a part of one of them, *cher*, you and all the evidence he insists you ruined."

"I don't care," Vivian told him and absolutely meant it. "I just want this to be over so we can get on with our lives."

She saw Spike's speculative expression but made sure her own was blank. Either they were heading somewhere together or a whole lot of misery lay ahead.

"Louis had been here a lot," Cyrus said. "And the way to the front of the house from the main gates is obvious."

"Yeah," Spike said. "So how did he get lured off track? He must have been waved in there and given some story about the main drive being closed farther on. That took guts, timing and luck."

"Luck for sure," Cyrus said. "I walked right past only minutes before. If I'd been a few minutes later . . ."

Vivian didn't want to dwell on that thought. "Those potted laurels." She stared into space. "Where did they come from?"

"With you two around I'll be out of a job pretty soon," Spike said, nodding. "We're going to have to hit it off with someone low on Bonine's feeding chain. Don't worry about it."

"You like taking charge, don't you?" Vivian asked. "I mean —"

"I know what you mean." Spike's mouth came together in a hard line.

"I think I'll see if I can get some coffee in the kitchen," Cyrus said.

Spike almost told him he wasn't subtle.

Cyrus looked from one of their faces to the other. "Take your time. I have some calls to make and I expect Madge will slow things down with Charlotte and Gary. She'll want to look into every room along the way." He turned and walked out, shutting the door behind him.

"Are we being left alone because Cyrus thinks we want to be?" Vivian asked.

"Something like that. What did he mean about your mother and Madge and Gary Legrain?" He didn't miss Vivian's loud swallow.

"Spike, my mouth is too quick. Then I say things other people take wrong. I like it that you're strong-minded."

"Do you?" He wondered if she'd really thought that through.

She walked away from him very deliberately and ran her fingers over the tops of furniture checking for dust. "Thea and the crew she found are doing a great job. Last night everything in here was covered with dust." She made the mistake of giving one of the green velvet drapes a shake. It slipped free of a painted gilt monkey wearing a red hat, screwed to the wall and with one of its paws curled to restrain the curtain. Vivian got a fresh whirl of fine debris to make them both sneeze.

"If you don't like the question, you change the subject," he told her.

At that Vivian returned and stood in front of him. "I do like your strength. I'm also strong-willed and it isn't always easy for two people like us to be together."

"There aren't any rules to cover any two people who happen to have some traits in common. I like you just the way you are." He paused long enough to watch her decide he'd complimented her. "You didn't say why Charlotte's taking Legrain and Madge to some suite."

"Madge hasn't seen any of the house. It's an interesting place. Could be very beautiful if we get it in shape," she said.

"Pineapples, monkeys, palm trees and all."

"Yes," Vivian said, grinning. "And pineapples and ruby-eyed, probably red glass-eyed, sultans. I want to keep Uncle Guy's exotic vision for Rosebank. Brought back to what it must have looked like fifteen years ago it'll be spectacular. If we can ever afford to do anything at all with the place."

"Madge told me quite a bit of work's been done and you want to finish a few rooms so you've got money coming in to carry on with," Spike said.

"Yes, that's the plan but even that takes a

fair amount to do. And we have to update the kitchens and bring them up to code. Until the real restaurant and a second kitchen is built in the conservatory, we intend to use one of the big rooms in the south wing as a dining room. There's a lot to work with, but a lot to be done, too."

"So Charlotte's conducting a house tour."

Vivian had never been a good liar. "Sort of."

Spike rubbed the back of her hand. "What's up? Can't be so bad you don't want to tell me."

"They went to see a suite in the east wing. For Gary. He's going to stay here for a day or two so he can look through all the papers here and see if he can find anything to help with whatever Louis wanted us to know about."

Spike breathed in and let the air out very slowly. "Why does he have to stay here to do that? Why does he have to do it at all? Your uncle did his business with Louis, he wouldn't leave that kind of thing floating around here. It would be in New Orleans like whatever Louis was bringing here had been."

Vivian stared into his eyes until they blurred. "The briefcase wasn't latched," she said, feeling far away. "Louis's. That could have been because something was taken out of it before he was killed. Couldn't it?"

"Maybe," Spike said. He was busier thinking about Gary Legrain hanging out here at night. "Yeah, I guess. Or maybe it was already open because he'd been using it and he hadn't closed it yet."

"He wouldn't have a reason to have it open when he was just going to carry it in here."

"That's not a certainty, Vivian, but it could be." *A lot of things could be and I want you at a safe distance.* "We should join Cyrus. Can I trust you to keep your cell turned on if I take a little trip tomorrow?"

Vivian gave him a sharp look with those green eyes of hers and bowed her head. Black hair slid forward, hiding her face.

"Now what?" he asked her.

"Nothing."

There was some book about the difference between the way men and women communicated, maybe he should try reading it. "*Cher,* would you please cut me a little slack here? I already got a tongue lashin' from Homer for leavin' Wendy at the rectory so long. He'd been over there and picked her up, which is what he wanted to do, but giving me a hard time adds to his pleasure." He'd appeal to her gentler nature.

"It's been a very long day and a half for all of us and I might just feel sorta skinny around the edges of my nerves."

"Cute," she said, clearly. "Always the cute comment to smooth things over."

"Hoo, *Mama,* you're testing me."

She shook back her hair and scowled at him. "First you sugarcoat an order for me to hang around with my cell phone in my tiny, trembling hand. Then you talk about taking a trip but don't say where, when or why. You Tarzan off to get the bananas, me Jane hiding in the tree house we don't have and waiting to be told what to do next."

"Kiss me," he said, tilting his head.

"Like hell."

Well, he'd known that request might not be a winner. "Let me kiss you, then."

She stomped back and forth. "No one kisses *anyone.* Got that? Why is it that men have such freakin' lousy timing?"

"Language, Vivian." If he told her this exchange lightened his tension she wouldn't give him a prize. "Okay, listen, I wasn't being secretive or bossy. And I didn't know I should have said anythin' different till you pointed it out. I'm going to New Orleans tomorrow."

"I see."

No, she didn't, but why shouldn't she . . . ?

246

"Would you come with me? I know how much you've got going around here, but if the two of us went we should be able to get through faster."

"Through what?"

"Make this easy on me, Vivian, make it easy, why don't you? You could just say whether or not you'll come, then go on with the third degree. I'm goin' to ask questions. About Louis Martin, and about your father. I want to stop by Martin, Martin and Martin and you could make it easier for me to get in."

Vivian put her hands to her cheeks. "You're going to do some P.I. work for me, too." She poked the tip of a finger into his vulnerable chest. "What a man you are. I'll come with you." Her voice softened at last and she smiled, faintly, sweetly up at him. Her eyes shone, her mouth — and he could already feel it on his — opened slightly and glistened, and he had only one thing in mind.

This was a big place, they'd figure something out.

Vivian slipped her arms under his and around his body. She stood just about as close as a woman could stand to a man.

He rested his cheek on top of her head and stroked her back. He could feel her through the dress, lean his erection against her pelvis. "I like being with you," he said, preparing to ease her head up and kiss her.

"Just hold me like this," Vivian said. "You don't know how rare it is to find a man who knows how to comfort a woman without trying to push her into something else. I . . . I like you for that, Spike Devol. Hug me, just hug me tight."

Spike put his chin on top of her head and did exactly what she asked. She spread warmth through his body, but she also turned him on so hard it hurt.

Funny how different men were from women. Hugging hadn't been what he had in mind — at least not as the entire event.

This blackmailer will not accept that he cannot control me. He is calling me again.

"I told you not to contact me anymore," I tell him.

He says, "You did well, but you're unpredictable. I can't afford your ego. Do you understand me?"

See how arrogant the man is, how sure of himself? He treats me like a child.

"It was you who made contact with me," I say because I will not let him forget the truth. "Guido told you our story. He trusted you to listen and give advice. You know what happened to him because I found out he'd talked. But you couldn't resist trying to use me. I didn't start this. What happens is on your shoulders."

"Not if you act alone. You were warned not to do anything unless I told you to." He speaks as if he doesn't hear me.

It feels good to laugh at him. "You should have stayed away," I tell him. "You wanted to use me, you threatened me so I would give you your own way. Now we are joined, you and I. Whatever I do, you might as well have done yourself. If you were capable of it. If I fall, you fall with me, only I shall not fall unless you betray me. I'm sure you won't do that."

"You've done your job I tell you. Leave the rest to me." His breathing is heavy.

"Do that and I might as well surrender to the authorities." I will have my way in this. "You cannot do what must be done, and I cannot stop until it is done."

"I'm begging you."

How soon he forgets how all of this began. "You threatened me with exposure if I didn't do as you asked. Now you can't stop what you started. I'm looking forward to the next one."

"For God's sake." He whispers like a frightened girl. "I promised you I would protect your secret and I will. Now back off."

"I enjoy killing women."

"What woman?" His throat clicks when he swallows. "No more killing."

"I will ask you again. How did you find

me? Who told you where I was?" The prob-
able answer makes me shiver with anticipation.

"You know I can't tell you that," he says,
predictably.

The coward is frightened. When he
thought he was in command he strutted
and postured. Now he whines because he
wasn't clever enough to see what might
happen if he actually got his way.

"There is someone I have not seen for
years," I tell him. "We both know his name.
If he knows where I am, if he was the one
who told you how to find me, he must
suffer for his betrayal of me — just as others
already have. Never forget what happened
to Guido. Now, you know who the woman
is. Pull yourself together. And pray we get
what we want."

"What we want?" He snorts. "I'm keeping
your secret, that's all."

Fool. "But you aren't thinking, as usual.
You have nothing to hold over me anymore. You're like me now, a wanted man
for as long as you live." My palm itches. I
need to hold the knife. "It's right for her to
die. She wants to interfere with the order
of things, and she sees too much."

"Meet me." His voice rises. "We have to
talk."

"I'll let you know when it's done," I tell him. "I'm not sure when, but not too long. First I will decide on the best time and place. You'll be the third to know."

"Who's the second?" Alarm makes him pant.

"I am, or perhaps she will be, depending on how you look at it. Later." I hang up. If he tries to call back, I won't answer.

She will fight me. I'll give her a chance to hit me, kick me, shout at me. Then she'll have to understand when we spend a little time together first. Violence and sex are perfect partners.

She'll be naked when they find her, her white skin decorated by my flawless work, and her blood. I promise I'll kiss her before I leave.

18

The third day

At the Majestic Hotel, L'Oiseau de Nuit stood outside an open door in a corridor painted pea green and carpeted in water-stained brown. Spike remembered, sort of, that the carpets used to have a large chrysanthemum pattern, but a leak in the roof had taken its toll.

"Why you bring him?" Wazoo said. The tip of a finger protruded from the ragged sleeve of her floor-length black lace coat and pointed steadily at Cyrus. "Pains my mind, him." She thrust out her palms and shook her hands, fending off poor Cyrus who had yet to take another step toward her.

"Calm down now, Wazoo," Spike said. When Wazoo's call came in, he and Cyrus had been eating together at All Tarted Up and discussing if and how to go forward with Bill Green's idea to help out the Patins.

"Father and I were havin' breakfast together when your request for help came in. I invited him along." He had to get out of here in time to meet up with Vivian and he counted on Cyrus to help him do that.

"Let's sit down somewhere," Cyrus suggested. "Spike's got to leave town but you know how he is, won't let a citizen down."

Wazoo blocked the entrance to her rooms. "Where you go, you?" she said to Spike. "There's trouble here. You needed."

Spike barely suppressed a groan. She was in one of her moods, which meant she wanted an audience and intended to be the one to decide when the performance was over.

"The longer we stand here, the less time I'll have to talk with you, Wazoo. The call I got said it was urgent I come here."

She shook back the bulk of her long, curly black hair, even pushed it from her face. Spike had not seen her so clearly until now.

Cyrus shifted and Spike guessed they were having similar thoughts. At this distance and without the tumble of hair over her features, Wazoo's age wasn't a mystery. Maybe thirty, but no more. And she was quite beautiful in a thin-faced, black-eyed way. Large eyes, exaggerated by heavy, dark green lines painted around them. Her hair shone and the curls had been brushed. Spike had never seen her take such trouble with herself before.

"You enter, you," she told Spike and hesitated, close to snarling at Cyrus. "And you. But L'Oiseau feel it if you try your powers."

The room they entered wasn't what Spike had expected. It had been turned into a sitting room for Wazoo and spartan took on a new meaning. He glanced at Cyrus who looked around with open curiosity, The only furniture was a black-lacquered chest inlaid with colored glass and surrounded by a ring of straight-back chairs. On the trunk rested a crystal ball that made Spike want to laugh. The word *hokey* came to mind. Small embroidered bags in two tidy stacks flanked the ball. Everything was clean.

"You don't come near, you," Wazoo said to Cyrus, curling her lip as if he disgusted her. "Spike, sit down." She swept a hand over the embroidered bags and said, "I read your cards?"

"I'll stand, thanks. Like I said, I've gotta leave."

"Like *I* say, where you goin'?"

He laughed at her impudence. "Not your business but if it'll speed this up any, I've got business in the Quarter."

A smile spread across her lips and she

rocked from foot to foot. "I know this. I have to test you to see if you honest with L'Oiseau."

"If you're psychic, or whatever," Cyrus said in his reasonable tone, "you shouldn't need tests to be sure Spike's telling the truth."

She ignored him. "I'm talkin' just to you, me," she told Spike. "You the golden one. Truth, and so sexy. Oh, yes, you a sexy truthful man."

Spike ran two fingers beneath his collar.

"All that tellin' the truth probably mean you suffer a lot in your life." She shook out her skirts and stood closer to Spike. Had he seen a glimpse of scarlet petticoat under the layers of black? She tilted her head and smiled up at him. "You and the Patin girl share your bodies yet?"

Spike missed a few beats before he found his voice. "What did you want to talk to me about?" Just the mention of making love with Vivian had a predictable result. He changed his mind and sat down after all.

"Now you," Wazoo said in a hoarse whisper, pointing at Cyrus again. "You a sexy man, too, but you hide."

"I think you've said enough on that subject," Cyrus told her.

"Why? Because the man of God put on

his collar and his thing fall off? I don't think so."

Spike pressed his lips together and frowned. Damn, she could be funny — as long as she wasn't talking about him.

"You're right," Cyrus said, so calm Spike would have taken his hat off to the man if he'd been wearing one. "I'd say the thing I have is right where it's supposed to be."

Wazoo laughed and slapped her knees. "And it works, too, I'm thinkin', me. You no mystery to me, God man. Not like to some others. You scared to put your thing in a woman on account of you got to be just a man then. Shout like a man, and cry out when you come, hold her breasts in you hands and kiss them sweet things, let her pump you out and leave you dry. Helpless. Like I say, just a man then and just a man mean you can't hide no more. You a sinner like the rest, then, and you human."

Astonished, Spike couldn't look at Cyrus. This woman's gall struck them both dumb, yet she had wisdom.

Cyrus's face stung as if she'd slapped him. When would it stop being his lot to have his commitment to the Church questioned? This exotic little woman wasn't a fool. She spoke to shock, but she spoke the truth. Stripped down to a few sentences, L'Oiseau set his mind and his struggles naked before him.

She gathered up her hair and held it on top of her head. With one hand a man could all but span her fragile neck. A pointed chin, a bowed, full mouth, shadows beneath high cheekbones. If he were free to do as he pleased, he'd ask her what she was hiding from and see how honest she might be with the roles switched.

"We different," L'Oiseau said. "But I could like you because you strong and brave."

"Thank you," Cyrus said, "and God bless you." He didn't expect any response.

Spike watched the crystal ball as if he saw something there — the truth? Cyrus wondered. Ah, the truth, whatever that was. He folded his arms tightly and prayed for this little woman with the troubled mind, and perhaps heart. Soon he must pray for himself.

Perhaps each human being needed a crystal ball, Cyrus thought, amused at the idea even as he chastised himself for such ideas.

"I know things," Wazoo said, sitting down on the gray carpet with her legs crossed. "Yes, I am psychic. I was born so, me. Once I didn't want it, but now I know I am sent here like this because there is work for me to do."

Cyrus and Spike made polite noises. Cyrus hadn't forgotten Wazoo arriving at Rosebank with a radio hidden on her person.

"Things happenin' in this town, and in certain other places I know, me. I see things."

"So you've told us," Spike said, checking his watch again. "How about telling us what they are quickly so we can go on our way."

"Can't hurry these matters. Need to do ceremony here and there first. Got to drive the evil out."

"Sheesh, an exorcism," Spike said, unable to contain himself any longer. "Go on."

"Miz Patin, she go with you to New Orleans?"

Spike planted his elbows on his knees and supported his head. He would keep his mouth shut from now on.

"I see," Wazoo said. "She do and you in a hurry. Maybe better to be slow. Get there late and stay somewhere. Drivin' when you tired is no good. Spend the night. One room cheaper than two. Dark night in strange place, two bodies so different. Mystery and discovery. If you ain't been with her then it's time. Readiness for sex is not a convention thing, not how long you know each other.

Your bodies tell you and should not be denied."

"Gotta go," Spike said, beginning to like her suggestions too much. "Come on Cyrus."

"You go you be sorry," she said and stretched out on her back on the carpet. "Something missing must be found. Maybe someone already got it. A guide to treasure, maybe? Worth to kill for, huh?"

"You're guessing," Spike said.

"But people die for treasure, yes?"

Reluctantly Spike said, "Sometimes."

"Vivian will be expectin' you," Cyrus reminded him.

"Yeah," Wazoo said. "She waitin'. She crazy 'bout you that one."

He surely hoped so. And he hoped he'd be able to do something about it.

"Keep me around," Wazoo said. She looked at Cyrus and said, absolutely serious, "You tell him I good woman, me. No malice. Only want to help."

Spike expected Cyrus to slide out of that one but he said, "We all need to be needed. I think Wazoo is a good woman."

Then Cyrus must see something in Wazoo that Spike did not see. Wazoo watched the priest with puzzled eyes.

"I try to talk to that ugly one, Bonine," she

said. "I don't think he know nothing but he bluffing. I ask if I can help him and he laugh in my face."

"So I was second choice?" Spike said, his tongue in a cheek.

"I mad with myself now. Should have started with you first."

"That's touching," Spike said. He got up. "Detective Bonine is a more formal man than I am. He's not so approachable."

"I drive evil spirits out of Rosebank, maybe Serenity House, out of Jilly's place, too."

"All Tarted Up?" Now she was completely losing him again.

"Uh-huh," she said. "All the people around go there. Leave evil behind. I already do work at your office, Spike, when you and that poor Lori out."

"Poor Lori?"

"She one woman with the job of six officers. You need better pay and so does Lori. And she need help."

"You know a great deal," Cyrus ventured. "But I think you want what's best for others."

She flapped a hand at him. "And I work on the girl with no past."

Spike felt blank.

"You know her," Wazoo said. "Ellie Byron at the bookshop. I know she good

261

but so sad. She go back maybe five year ago when she show up in Lafayette. Before then, nothing."

"You're giving me a headache," Spike told her with honesty. "Tomorrow I should have a little time. We can talk then."

"Too late," she said. "I tell you more. The woman at Serenity House, Susan Hurst. She who not take her husband name. She too busy on her own, do too many things. She here and there. There's a man. She visit him sometimes and she different when she leave his place."

"I don't think we'll touch that," Spike said.

"Wazoo," Cyrus said in his priestly voice. "I'd like you to come and visit me. You'll find I'm not a fearsome man and perhaps I can help you deal with these things you imagine."

"I expect people to say I make things up." She closed her eyes, disgusted, and said to Spike, "You deputize me. This an emergency. You deputize me and I work for you so no one else dies."

Spike looked straight ahead and hoped for guidance.

"You won't be sorry," Wazoo said. "I help stop the killing. Unless I make a mistake like two days ago."

"What mistake?" She had all of his attention now.

She pressed her lips together and poked fingers into her temples. "Nothing. I not mean that, me. I can help. I stay near you."

"I really appreciate your generous offer," Spike said, "but even if I'd been told to take on another deputy, it wouldn't have anything to do with the Rosebank murder. That's not in my jurisdiction." When would someone other than Errol Bonine finally accept that? "I'll admit to needin' more help in Toussaint but there's no money for it." He'd also admit to himself that he wouldn't rest easy unless he kept a watch on this woman.

"I want to help," Wazoo insisted. "I work for free. I worried for Vivian Patin, me. Find a way for me to be close there. I ask my friend, Ellie Byron, what she think and she tell me to ask and hope you not laugh."

"I'm not laughin'," Spike said, "but neither are you tellin' me everythin'."

"May I, Spike?" Cyrus asked and when he got the nod turned his attention back to Wazoo. "You're frightened. Let us help you."

"Nothin' frighten me," she insisted, sitting up again. "I have power. I offer to help you is all."

Spike met Cyrus's eyes and he wished

they could talk alone before this thing went any further.

"I tell you one thing," Wazoo said, her eyes glazing. "Gil Mayes don't leave Rosebank. I don't see exactly where he at yet. But I will." She closed her eyes and bowed her head.

Spike wanted to leave but something he couldn't put in words kept him there, waiting for her to finish.

"I see what I got to do," she said. "You take me to that house and make sure they accept me there. Charlotte and Vivian need help and I can do things."

"I don't know —"

"Maybe Gil still alive." Wazoo raised her chin. Her eyes were wide open and radiant. "I got to hurry."

19

Martin, Martin and Martin occupied quarters entered through an archway to a cool, leafy courtyard just off Chartres on Toulouse in the Quarter.

Vivian knew the place too well. The green wrought-iron gates that separated the hot and bustling street from the courtyard stood open. At night they would be locked to keep out both revelers and those who called the alleys and doorways of New Orleans home.

"Is this a good idea?" she asked Spike. "You never really explained what you hoped to find."

Dressed in a navy-blue shirt with buttoned-down collar and tan chinos, the man beside her seemed very different from the Toussaint lawman. He wore loafers. The shirt cuffs were turned back from wrists where hair picked up the afternoon sun. He looked at her with concern and she wondered if he were afraid she'd get in the way of his plans for the lawyers' offices.

She didn't expect him to hook one side of her hair behind her ear and she flinched at his touch. Spike eased her in front of him and settled his mouth on her forehead.

Vivian blinked. It wouldn't be hard to stand here, a little too hot, perhaps, aware of the pungent odors of old, mossy stones, stale booze and the sweet perfume of jasmine and ginger, and decide to forget about murder.

His hands were around her waist and she could feel the beat of his heart.

People brushed by, laughing, shouting, singing along with boom boxes, but Vivian didn't care. She slid her hands up his arms and across his shoulders. "Do we have any choices left?" she asked him. "Could we forget anythin' terrible happened and just hope it all works out without us doin' anything?"

"No. But I wish we could." Spike looked down into her face. He surely wished they could because he saw nothing but more danger and trouble ahead. "I didn't say I was hopin' to find something we can hold in our hands, *cher*. Or maybe I did but I didn't mean it quite the way it sounded. Like I told you, I don't buy Gary Legrain's talk about tryin' to find clues in Guy's records or somewhere around Rosebank. Legrain wants to keep you and Charlotte as clients because he figures you'll be worth it again once things iron out."

"I figured that," Vivian said. "But I do think he's kind. He wants to do the right things to help us."

Why, oh why? "Ooh, ya ya, I need to keep thinking straight." He tilted his head for another angle on her. "I . . . I want this to be over and I want to quit worrying about every little thing that comes into my head." He'd almost said he mistrusted Legrain's reasons for being quite so attentive, or rather, he had a good idea what some of them were and didn't like them. The man didn't look at Vivian as if he thought of her as nothing but a client.

"Do you think we should call this off today?" she asked.

"Uh-uh. Somethin's naggin' at me. Martin, Martin and Martin. No Legrain. He told me he'd been with the firm eight years. Wouldn't you think he'd be a partner by now?"

Her magenta blouse and white slacks showed off a body with the power to distract Spike. While she thought about his question, he made the mistake of studying her mouth. Then he began to feel it beneath his and deliberately looked over her head to distract himself.

"The other two Martins are Louis's sons," she said finally. "I've only met them socially. I never thought about whether or not Gary's a partner. Maybe he is and they haven't changed the nameplate over there."

"What about the letterhead?" He already knew the answer.

Vivian frowned. "I'm not sure. No, his name isn't on it but he's never had a reason to write to Mama as far as I know. Why would he before now? Anyway, he could have his own stationery."

Spike shrugged. They both knew otherwise. "Charlotte promised to call Gary after we left and let him know we'd be stopping by just to visit."

"She never said anything. I thought we'd just see if he was in and had a few minutes." She gave him a withering look. "You and Mama knew you ought to ask me what I thought before arranging that. You don't think twice about doing something behind a person's back."

"I didn't think of making a song and dance about it." He hadn't. "But now I think it was a real good idea since you look like you'd back out if you could."

"I still can. And that would mean you couldn't go snoopin' around in there either 'cause I'm your ticket in."

"Absolutely true," he said, although she was wrong if she really thought he wouldn't go in anyway. "Wouldn't want to push you into anythin'. After all, you only asked me to do the work you don't think Bonine will get to. But if you've changed your mind we might as well get along back."

Vivian looked at her feet and considered, if only for a second, landing him just a little kick to one of his solid shins. Instead, she did what she preferred to do anyway and gave him a good poke in the chest.

She shouldn't have done it. The moment he staggered backward, clutching a handful of his shirt, moaning, Vivian knew she should not have poked him.

"Stop it," she hissed. "You're making fools of both of us."

Apparently stumbling over his feet, he wove his way back, this time managing to seem drunk. Falling on her neck and hugging her tight enough to wind her he muttered in her ear, "Learn a lesson, sweet Vivian. If you say things you don't really mean, I'll call your bluff every time. Are we goin' home or goin' in? Your call. Of course,

I'll be sorry if you decide you don't want me workin' for you after all."

Vivian pushed him away, but she smiled and the rush of feeling to her throat was close to pure happiness. She loved being with this man. "I'm sorry for getting cold feet," she told him. "Everything feels so strange but I want you, Spike, you know I do."

Not a hint of humor remained in his expression. "Do you?"

Her tummy did odd things. "I meant I want you to keep on working for me." When he turned the corners of his mouth down she added, "You know how I feel about the other, but I'm confused. I know I've given you the impression I don't have any reservations and maybe I don't. Give me more time."

It had been worth taking the chance, Spike thought, shaking her shoulder gently. She might have fallen for it and given him the nod on the personal angle. Not that she'd exactly turned him down and the day wasn't over yet.

"Let's go in," she said. "I'm still not sure what you want to accomplish but, hey, I'll find out."

He wasn't about to make a big deal out of his having nothing but a hunch and a hunch that could be based in part on male possessiveness.

Vivian caught his sleeve and he stopped. "Something has bothered me about Louis's death, other than the horror of it. His sons didn't rush down to Rosebank. They haven't even made a call. I don't think that's normal."

"It's not." He was still getting accustomed to the thought of Louis's sons. "But families have different ways of dealing with crises."

The second floor entrance to Martin, Martin and Martin took them up a flight of iron steps to a gallery. On the ground floor, on either side of the archway, were the backs of an antique store and a gumbo shop on Toulouse. The shiny painted doors and bright windows of residences occupied the rest of the spaces. A stone dolphin spouted tinkling water in a small corner fountain.

"You think all this belongs to one owner?" Spike indicated the entire property surrounding them. "Probably leased out, huh?"

"I remember my daddy tellin' me the Martins owned the whole thing," Vivian said.

A short distance from the highly polished oak doors of the legal firm, two women sat at a round table, smoking and laughing. They spoke Cajun, which Vivian didn't understand enough to translate, but the way they eyed Spike did hint at their subject.

Spike's finger on the bell produced a harsh ringing from inside and a woman's voice over the intercom. "Yes?" One of those wordy types.

Spike announced them and they were buzzed in without any comment.

The discreetly lit interior felt rich and graceful. Vivian wondered if this building and its contents had been spared in the 1877 fire or if the Martins had accomplished a particularly perfect renovation and spent a fortune on antiques to fit the period.

A woman sat behind an old French desk and watched them approach. "I've let Mr. Legrain's assistant know you're here," she said, and Vivian decided she wasn't rude, but uptight. She glanced repeatedly over her shoulder. The loss of Louis must be a blow to the staff.

"Tate Barnes," said a blond woman in a big hurry who rushed toward them over oriental carpets and glowing wood floors. She shook hands with both of them. "I remember you, of course, Ms. Patin. Come with me to Mr. Legrain's waiting room. He's got unexpected visitors but I hope they won't be with him long." Like the receptionist, Tate Barnes showed nervousness.

Situated at the end of a long corridor, about at a corner of the building, Vivian figured, Gary's suite was more sparsely furnished than anything they'd seen so far, but no less tasteful.

"Mr. Legrain asked them to come," Tate whispered. "They never said they would. Just showed up. Do make yourselves comfortable."

Spike barely stopped himself from asking who "they" were.

Before he and Vivian could sit, the door to Gary's office opened a crack and from the way the highly polished brass handle wiggled there had to be someone holding the other end.

"I'll get back to you," a man's voice said, an angry man.

Whatever the response, Spike couldn't hear it.

Tate flitted about, straightening papers on her desk, glancing anxiously at her boss's office and then at Spike and Vivian.

"We don't know who the woman is, but if it's true my father left her a big chunk of his estate, we'll make sure she doesn't collect a penny," the man at the door announced. "I don't care what my father may have said, make sure you forget every word. You know who you work for now."

Spike felt sorry for Gary, who was almost certainly on the wrong end of this.

More inaudible conversation.

"This isn't the time, Gary. You know you don't have to worry about anythin' like that. You're fam'ly. You don't need a fancy title to prove how important you are around here. By the way, we'll want to be here when you interview any new hires. Gotta run."

Two men of average height emerged from Gary's office and left the door open. They were both thin, dark-haired and wore light-colored suits. So similar in appearance were they that Spike assumed they were twins. Each had piercing eyes and a wide mouth.

"Well, if it isn't Vivian Patin," one of them said, approaching her with an outstretched hand. "It's been too long. Terrible loss you and your mother have suffered, terrible."

Vivian shook his hand and said, "Thank you, Edward. I don't know what to say about Louis. Such a horrible shock. Are you hearing much from the police?"

Edward looked grave. "They seem to be making very little progress. How unfortunate that such a thing should happen on your doorstep."

"I'd rather not talk about it," Edward's

brother said sharply. "Talk accomplishes nothing and it's all too painful."

Spike noticed what set the men apart. This one's nose had obviously been broken more than once.

Vivian turned to Spike and gave an awkward little laugh. "Forgive me, Spike. This is Louis's son, Edward Martin, and this," she indicated the other man, "is George Martin, Edward's twin. They were frequent customers at Chez Charlotte."

Edward kissed his fingertips and said, "I mourn the loss of the best food in the Quarter."

Had Edward Martin commiserated with Charlotte and Vivian's "terrible loss" of David Patin, or only the restaurant? Spike found the pair overly aggressive.

"Well," George said, "we mustn't hold you up when you are obviously here to see Gary. Is he taking good care of you? You do know how much we value your loyalty to the firm?"

"I know." Vivian felt strange. She hadn't considered how she would feel when confronted by Louis's sons.

Gary stood at the threshold of his office now, his watchful gray eyes seriously measuring the scene in front of him.

The Martin brothers took their leave and

for many seconds after they left there was silence, then Gary said to Vivian and Spike, "How long were you out here?" He turned his attention to Tate. "Kindly wait elsewhere until I page you. I have no more appointments this afternoon. Please make sure I'm not disturbed."

As soon as she was gone, Gary reiterated his question about how long Spike and Vivian had been there.

"A few minutes," she told him.

Spike said, "Long enough to figure out that you and the Martin boys may be fam'ly as they put it, but I don't think you're buddies."

Gary turned on his heel. "Please come into my office."

When they'd followed him inside he closed the door. "Sit down." He waited while Vivian sat in a stiff-backed embroidered chair with gilt legs before he dropped onto a couch that looked to be the same sort of style but covered with different fabric. Spike took a second chair that matched Vivian's.

The seating area took up one side of an L-shaped room while Gary's office, including a red lacquer desk, filled the other. This was indeed a corner of the building. Of four tall, narrow windows, two would face Chartres while the other two probably looked out on

St. Peters Street, possibly with a view of St. Louis Cathedral. These were expensive digs.

"There's hot coffee," Gary said, starting to get up again, "or perhaps you'd prefer something stronger."

"No, thank you," Vivian said and Spike echoed her refusal.

"Charlotte called," Gary said. He constantly glanced around the room and the toe of one foot tapped up and down. "Glad you wanted to stop by." He gave Spike a less than "glad" stare.

"Spike was kind enough to give me a lift to New Orleans today," Vivian told him and hurried on to say, "he's got things to do here, too."

Spike could see that his presence was likely to muzzle anything useful Gary might have said to Vivian on her own. "Vivian," he said. "I can wait for you in Jackson Square if you and Gary would be more comfortable."

He saw panic in her eyes and almost swore aloud at his own stupidity. What was she supposed to say when it hadn't been her idea to come in the first place?

"No, no," she said, and to Gary, "Spike mostly only came today to give me a ride."

"Because her van is playing up," Spike added, not particularly proud of his ability to come up with a fast lie.

"Yes. And I want you to know each other better anyway," Vivian continued before turning a very attractive shade of pink. "I regard you as a friend, too, Gary."

Don't take it too far. "Vivian likes to think everyone gets along," Spike said.

"I don't have too many people to get along with," Gary said, "so why not? What did you two think you were hearing before the Martin brothers left this office?"

Spike figured he'd better make sure they didn't overplay their hand but saw an opportunity to align himself with Gary. "They like to make sure everyone knows who the senior partners are." That could be overplaying things anyway.

"Partners." Gary made a scoffing sound. "You might as well understand the way things are. Louis and I were the two working lawyers in the firm. Edward and George never practiced a day in their lives. Never even took the bar. But Louis lived in hope they would and, at least on paper, they were his partners. Greedy, spoiled . . ." He shook his head. "Excuse me. That was wrong of me."

"Surely they aren't senior to you," Spike said.

"Louis and I had an understanding," Gary said, squeezing at the corners of his eyes with a finger and thumb. "I was supposed to be made a partner. Only it never happened."

"Oh, how awful," Vivian told him, sitting forward, her expression concerned. "Was that what Edward meant when he told you —"

"Yes." Gary cut her off. "I'm not to worry because I'm part of the family. I'm supposed to believe they'll make it right. Meanwhile they've told me to look for another lawyer who will work under me although I can't make the hire on my own. Those two have to be around for any interviews."

"Leave," Spike said. "Set up on your own. You must have clients who would follow you."

"Do it," Vivian agreed.

"I've said too much. You didn't come to talk about my problems. I'll be fine."

"You're already *not* fine," said Vivian. "They're taking advantage of you."

Gary turned his head toward her. "You're perceptive, but I felt that about you from the first time we met. If I walk it'll be with what I've got in the bank but nothing else. Legally I have nothing else coming to me. And I had to sign a contract with a clause stating I wouldn't attempt to poach any Martin clients."

"That won't stop people from following you if they want to."

"That's true, but it also wouldn't stop the Martins from drumming up some charge about my work being inadequate or whatever it took to ruin my reputation."

"Why did you sit still for it?" Spike asked, and expected to be told to keep his questions to himself.

Gary looked at first one palm, then the other. "Don't blame you for asking. I never tested well and I finished in the lower third of my class at law school. I'd put myself through on loans and came out as a good lawyer in the making but with huge debts and what looked like an unimpressive school record. Louis thought I had potential and took me on. He gave me the chance nobody else would and said he'd make me a partner in time."

"And the time never came," Spike said.

"No. So I've got two choices — leave and risk everythin', or stay and hope the Martin boys need me enough for me to be able to force their hands."

"I don't see how they'd manage without you." Vivian crossed her legs and leaned forward earnestly. "Seriously, you're the one who knows everything."

Spike wanted to know the identity of the

woman the Martins had been talking about. He decided against asking now.

Vivian shook a finger at no one in particular. "With Louis gone, they own everything," she said slowly. "They don't look broken up by his death and they didn't even attempt to contact me when it happened."

If he'd dared, Spike would have told her not to pursue the thought.

Gary didn't meet her eyes, even though she turned to him. "What if Louis was getting tired of handing out money while they did nothing but enjoy themselves. There would be one way to make sure their daddy didn't hold the purse strings anymore."

"That's dangerous talk," Gary said. "And they won't get it all. Not quite. There is a friend of Louis's, a lady, to whom he made a bequest. I didn't deal with his will, but he told me that. I don't know who she is. Those two think they can stop her from getting it, but Louis was wily. They won't be able to do it."

Vivian stood up with enough force to almost knock her chair over.

He would not groan or tell her what to do or say, Spike warned himself, he would not.

"This is terrible," she said. "That woman's life could be in danger."

"Vivian," Gary said with a cautionary note in his voice.

She turned on him. "You're too generous for your own good. Who benefits from Louis's death?"

Spike had to at least try to stop this runaway train. "You're jumping to conclusions and they're too obvious," he told her. "Those two don't look like fools to me and if you could join those dots so quickly, don't you think anyone . . . well, I mean any of us could wonder about the Martins but we'd be wrong."

"Would we?" Gary also got to his feet, but sat down again. "I'm not myself. Of course we'd be wrong."

"They'd obviously have someone else do the dirty work," Vivian said, straightening her shoulders. "All we have to do now is find out who it was."

Spike cleared his throat. "Either way, nothing changes. We're still looking for the same killer."

20

Charlotte felt sorry for little Wendy Devol. The child balanced on the edge of an armchair seat in the receiving room, her feet crossed at the ankle and swinging many inches off the floor. She pressed the skirt of her green plaid dress between her knees with laced hands and gazed through round, pink-rimmed glasses at the high ceiling.

"Would you like some lemonade and cookies?" Charlotte asked. She smiled at Homer Devol, "If that's okay with you, of course."

Homer had continued to stand, hat in his hands, and quietly dignified with his tall, slender build and straight back. He looked at Wendy with his brow furrowed and she wiggled just a little while she watched him.

"We didn't intend to upset your schedule, ma'am," Homer said, his frown growing deeper. "Looks like Wendy would like what you offer. Like I told you on the phone, I think you and I should talk."

Charlotte decided Homer was awkwardly trying to signal that he wanted to say whatever he'd come to say without Wendy listening. "Thea's in the kitchen and I know she'd like company. Would you like to go out there, Wendy?"

Wendy nodded and slid to stand on the floor.

"I'll take her," Homer said quickly, then coughed. "I mean, to be honest I want to be sure it seems safe. I know Thea and she's a good woman, but things have happened here."

"I understand," Charlotte told him while her spine prickled. "Turn left out of this room and walk straight back." The search for Gil continued. There were still no leads at all on Louis's death, and she felt pretty scared herself.

Homer left his hat on a chair and held Wendy's hand to walk toward the kitchen. A very small five-year-old, Charlotte decided, watching tow-colored braids bounce in time with the child's skipping walk.

Had life ever been easy? Charlotte thought. Even a year before, when David had already started to be difficult to get along with, her world had been a dream compared to now. Her husband could have shared anything with her, even his financial mistakes, and they would have worked them through together. If he had told her everything maybe he'd still be alive.

Vivian didn't know everything that led up to David's death and Charlotte intended to keep it that way.

From her seat on one of the two gold damask-covered couches, she glanced from the black grand piano with gilded pineapples at the base of its legs, to gold-fringed red velvet drapes with swags of palm tree print satin above them. Even the white marble face of the fireplace sported carvings of pineapples, and cherubs with decidedly monkeylike features.

This place was both wonderful and a huge challenge. She couldn't disagree with Vivian's conviction that the eccentric decor was worth preserving, but she didn't have to love it.

Homer returned with two glasses of iced tea. "Thea wouldn't take a no on sendin' these in," he said. His eyes were dark blue and startling in a thin, very tanned face. There could never be a doubt that Spike Devol was this man's son.

She took a glass of tea from him. "Please sit down, Homer. You're a long way up there and I'll get a crick in my neck trying to talk to you." She smiled at him.

"Yes, ma'am," he said and took the chair Wendy had vacated.

Guy's grandfather clock ticked loudly. An exotic, grinning potentate popped rhythmically in and out of a crescent-shaped window in the clock face.

The ticking grew louder, or so it seemed.

Homer set his tea on a brass table, a heavy, beaten tray set atop palm fronds. "We got trouble on our hands," he said. "With our kids. I came to talk parent to parent, knowin' you want the best for your daughter. Same as I do for my son."

At a loss for the appropriate response, Charlotte made polite noises.

"Spike's a good man, the best. He's hardworkin', smart and honorable. And he's had to fight for everythin' he's got. I wasn't much help when he was a boy. I took him everywhere with me but we scraped along and it was my fault. I let my own troubles get in the way of doing the right thing for him. I could have settled down and made him a stable home, but I couldn't get the other out of my mind."

"I see," Charlotte said, touched by the man's openness and struck by how much he must care for Spike to talk this way to someone he didn't know. She doubted it came naturally.

"You don't see," Homer said without rancor. "Spike's mother decided she wanted somethin' different in her life and I told her to go with my blessin'. I should have tried harder to show her we could have a good life, then maybe she'd have stayed. I didn't try on account of stupid pride and my boy suffered. I'm a carpenter by trade. Could have made somethin' of that but I lost the wantin' somehow."

"I'm sorry," Charlotte said. She couldn't think of anything else to say.

"Anyhow. We've made our way and we're doin' well, but we're from different worlds, you and Vivian, Spike, Wendy and me. Don't get me wrong. Spike's good enough for anyone but he's had one bad marriage and I can't sit by and see him get all twisted up over another woman who's likely to get bored around places like this. Vivian's used to a lot more, but what you see in Spike is what you get — he isn't going to go back to school like he planned because he's got Wendy to consider."

Once more, Charlotte wasn't sure what to say. "Vivian and Spike aren't children. They have to make their own decisions." That was her best shot.

"It wouldn't work." Homer sounded stubborn. "Besides, it wouldn't be good for him to have folks talkin'."

Now Charlotte perked up. "Talking about what?"

Suddenly the iced tea appealed to Homer and he drank until he drained the glass. He took a clean white handkerchief from his pocket, unfolded it and wiped his mouth. "That was good," he said. "Thank you."

Charlotte continued to wait.

He swept one arm wide. "Aw, you know how folks are. They *talk*. They'd say Spike was gettin' above himself. Aimin' too high. And they'd talk about him gold digging. He thinks he can deal with all that now, but when it happens, he's going to get defensive, then he's going to get mad. That's bad stuff for Wendy. And it wouldn't be what Vivian would enjoy, either."

Laughing wouldn't be at all the thing to do. "Gold digging?" Charlotte said. "Homer, my husband and I didn't only lose all we had, our business, home, and everything we worked for. We — I'm still in debt and when I can't quite manage to feel optimistic, I get so down I'm convinced I'll never get out of the hole. This house is my only possible way to get back on my feet. Louis Martin arranged one loan for me but it's about gone and I don't have a way to get the real money it would take to make it happen for Rosebank. And I also lost my husband," she finished quietly.

"I know," Homer said. "Spike told me and I'm sorry for your loss. But folks see what they want to see. You've got all this around you, even if it isn't the way you want it yet. We've got a gas station and convenience store. And a mobile crawfish boilin' and barbecue outfit that's a lot of work and a lot of pain."

"I like Spike," Charlotte said. "He's straightforward and that's not so common. He probably gets that from his dad and I'm not tryin' to sweeten you up. I don't know if anything's likely to happen between them, but I can't interfere."

He crossed his arms and jutted his chin. "Likely to happen? What makes you think it hasn't already happened? They're off in New Orleans together today. Alone. Spike wasn't about to tell me what that was all about but I can guess."

She chuckled. "They're there on business. Spike's helping Vivian deal with some legal things. You men, you're all alike. You can't imagine that one of you doesn't have an ulterior motive for wanting to spend time with a woman."

"Can you?" He gave her a steady blue stare.

"*Yes,*" Charlotte said. "They like each other." But although she wouldn't admit it to Homer, she also figured Vivian and Spike were smitten.

"If you say so. Will you help me make sure they don't go beyond likin'?"

She studied the backs of her hands and unvarnished nails.

"Will you?" he pressed her.

"What if they could be good for each other?"

"You want to risk what will happen if they get in up to their necks then change their minds?"

She did see the way Homer's mind was working and how much of his concern came from prior experiences with women. "Vivian's had it with the city," she told him. "She wants to be here. She likes the small-town feeling — the isolation, even. I don't know what's likely to come of the two of them, but I'm not moved to interfere with anyone's chance for happiness."

"He finished college," Homer said as if distracted. "Wanted to go back for another one of those degrees and go into the FBI. Somethin' to do with computer crime."

"He's still got plenty of time to go back."

She was learning a lot and not disliking much of it.

Homer shook his head. "You don't understand. I know you love your girl and I love my boy. If you won't help me on account of you don't want your daughter takin' up with a man who's carryin' too much baggage and who'll make her want to fish in other waters when she gets tired of the routine, do it for Spike. He's not your concern, but I don't think you'd want him to go through what happened to him before."

Charlotte made up her mind what to say. "I'll join forces with you to keep a watch on our kids," she said. She couldn't just turn him away, even if she didn't agree with him. "And if I see anything I think we need to worry about, I'll tell you."

She got the stubborn jut of his chin again. He said, "You gonna tell the big mouths in Toussaint to mind their own business when they say Spike's above himself?"

Charlotte squared her shoulders. "I surely will if I ever hear it. That son of yours is any man's equal. Homer, this could pass. Let's just give them a chance and trust them. I know Vivian wouldn't do anything to hurt Spike or Wendy. And Spike's solid, I already believe that."

"And others will make sure it doesn't

work for them. Mark my words. That girl of yours is smart and beautiful. Someone with more to offer than Spike will come along —" he scrubbed at his face "— I'm not goin' to let my boy get hurt again."

The response Charlotte prepared to give wasn't likely to make peace between her and Homer, but Wendy ran into the room in time to interrupt. "That funny lady from Wally's hotel is here," she said. "In the kitchen with Thea. I came away 'cause I knew you'd want me to, Gramps."

"Wazoo, or whatever her name is?" Charlotte said.

"Must be," Homer said. "Now, Wendy, you've been listenin' to gossip. There's nothin' wrong with that little woman that wouldn't be cured by some kindness. I'd best get on, Miz Charlotte. Keep what I've said in mind."

"Oh, I will." It would be easier to discount his suggestions if he didn't show so many flashes of wisdom.

Wendy planted herself in front of Charlotte and said, "Your house is, is, is like in a movie. Rich people live here and there's important stuff all over. I like it."

"Then come back whenever you can," Charlotte said, choosing not to tell the child she was wrong about the "rich" bit.

Homer had his granddaughter's small hand enclosed in his own large, work-scarred one. "We're not the kind to push ourselves," he said. "Thank you for the tea."

Stubborn critter.

On the way toward the front door, Wendy swiveled to walk backward. "Thank you for the lemonade and cookies, ma'am."

"You are more welcome than you know."

Homer stopped at the door he'd opened and turned back. "I'm still a fair carpenter and I like the practice. If there's somethin' needs done here, just ask."

Homer had barely closed the door, leaving Charlotte with a strange tightness in her throat, when Wazoo tiptoed as far as the entrance to the room and tapped the doorjamb. "I'm sorry to interrupt, but I hope you talk to me."

What an afternoon. "Come on in," Charlotte said. "Wendy Devol said you were out there with Thea."

"We friends, now," Wazoo said. She actually looked less wild than usual and had tied her hair back with a red ribbon. "Thea, Doll Hibbs and me." She smiled, turning an already lovely face into a brilliant thing with flashing eyes. "Not much alike, huh? Sometimes that's good."

"Yes," Charlotte agreed, waiting for the real reason for this visit.

"I need a job, me," Wazoo said, all seriousness again. "Some folks don't like a psychic around and if that's you, I understand. But I know you lookin' for more help and I work hard. Do anythin'."

At a loss, Charlotte said, "But wouldn't that interfere with your other work?"

Wazoo's gaze didn't waver. "Business is bad. The hotel cost too much and I gotta move, but still I need a steady job."

She had, Charlotte noted, exchanged her jet-studded sandals for a pair of sneakers that did nothing for the outfit. But the sneakers were clean and practical.

"Gator and Doll will be disappointed," Charlotte said.

Wazoo shrugged. "They gettin' ready to rent to some students comin' to study somethin' to do with sugarcane. They make more money from them."

"You're saying you'll do anything?"

"Clean. Work in the gardens. Fix the cars — I'm good with cars, me. Help with painting or repairs. Anythin'. And I am reliable, me. Don't seem so if you don't understand me, but it true."

More money to go out, but there was no doubt she and Vivian were desperate for help. "Do you have references?"

Wazoo shook her head. "But people here will say Wazoo honest and kind. And they know I can work because I do odd jobs when I get them."

No references. "Okay, how about this. I'll give you a trial. Thea will tell you what she wants done and I'll be asking you to do things, too. Can you work for several bosses?"

Wazoo nodded and smiled like a happy child. "Oh, yes, oh, for sure. I start now?"

Charlotte prepared to tell her to wait for Monday, then wondered why any time should be wasted. "Okay, yes. Have you found a place to live? I hope you won't have to travel too far. Do you have transportation?"

"I got a van, me, but I can't afford to run it much. People say things. They say you thinkin' of rentin' just a few rooms to get started. Short-term rents they call 'em. What them gonna cost?"

"People" meant Thea. Vivian and Charlotte had discussed doing short-term rents but only between themselves and around this house. These freight trains kept barrelling through Charlotte's life. But why not rent Wazoo a room, at least until she proved it was a bad idea. "That might do very well.

You may have to move as the work is done. We'll work out the rent and we need to talk about your salary. What if you get the room and a smaller paycheck in exchange?"

Wazoo looked as if she'd won the state lottery and for a moment Charlotte was afraid the woman would kiss her, but Wazoo's eyes shifted away to the window and Charlotte turned her head to see Susan and Olympia Hurst passing on their way to the front door.

"I'll answer for you," Wazoo said, bubbling.

Charlotte thought to refuse the offer, but changed her mind. She didn't have to impress Susan and her offspring, unless it was with the Patin independence. "Thank you, Wazoo."

When Susan Hurst recovered from the evident shock of being greeted by Wazoo, she poked around the room. Charlotte wished she could leave at once.

Olympia Hurst was too old for her behavior. Dressed in a pink sundress that barely covered her panties and which laced at the top to reveal a good deal of her large breasts, she slid into a scarlet silk slipper chair and propped her hands behind her head.

"Olympia," Susan chided, in the process

of examining an old silver box with stones, or pieces of colored glass, studded in the top. "That's not ladylike. Sit up and pull your dress down. Really darling, you've got to learn what to do with that beautiful body of yours if you're going to reach your full potential."

Olympia yawned dramatically and flipped at her long, blond hair. "I know what to do with my body, thank you, Mama. Women of my age usually do. Ability in that direction doesn't usually fade until much later."

Susan ignored her and tried to open the box.

"It's locked," Charlotte said, amused. "Always has been but it doesn't look like a good place to hide treasure d'you think?"

"No," Susan agreed and quickly put the thing down. "Your brother-in-law was really into this jungle thing. He was ahead of the curve. I believe it's quite popular now. Not my style at all but I expect you're going to change things here."

"We have a lot of planning to do," Charlotte said, not about to discuss anything private with Susan.

"Is Vivian here?" Susan asked.

"No, she's out for the day. Did you want to talk to her? I'm sure she'll be here tomorrow."

"I was just makin' conversation."

"You know you saw her leave with that sexy Spike Devol," Olympia said. She'd decided to loosen the lacing on her dress. "Fess up. You're curious about whether they're getting it on."

"If you can't behave yourself," Susan said, "please leave. Go home and help Morgan."

"I offered, but Daddy dear said he's got paperwork to do and doesn't need me."

Charlotte didn't care for the secret smile that crossed Olympia's lips.

"Olympia's stressed," Susan said, dropping her red-streaked, brown hair forward, then throwing it back and shaking it into place. "She's got months of preparing for contests ahead of her and so much work keeping that figure gorgeous and choosing clothes and taking dance lessons. It goes on and on."

Olympia looked vacant.

"I came to talk to you, Charlotte."

Why not, everyone else had.

"Mama, I said I'd keep you company, but not if you're going to take so long," Olympia said, yawning again. "Just spit it out about the police."

"Oh, dear." Susan perched her jean-clad bottom on a chair. "Yes, the police. Morgan wouldn't approve of our being here, but I believe in complete honesty. It's the best way to get things done. The police searched our house." Her voice rose, she closed her eyes and pressed a hand to her bosom. "We actually had people in at the time and had to ask them to leave. Can you imagine our embarrassment?"

There had to be a point when a little pity would come her own way, Charlotte thought. "We've been dealing with a lot of that and it's not pleasant."

"Not *pleasant?*" Susan rolled her eyes and gave her hair another good shake. "Charlotte, we have to talk. Seriously. Would you have dinner with us tomorrow evening? You and Vivian — and her sheriff friend if that's what she'd like."

Olympia's laughter shot so high that Charlotte winced. "Oh, Mama," Olympia screeched, pointing a long forefinger. "You old spoof you. *If that's what she'd like.* It's what *you'd* like."

"Will you come?" Susan persisted, ignoring Olympia. "I'd regard it as a favor."

Charlotte said, "Yes, of course," partly to support Susan in the presence of her bratty daughter.

"Wonderful," Susan said.

"*Wonderful,*" Olympia echoed. "Make sure you warn Vivian she'd better make sure

Spike's pants stay zipped."

Susan walked to her daughter and slapped her face soundly. In the appalling silence that followed, Olympia glared hatred at her mother with dry eyes and didn't touch the welts forming on her skin.

"I apologize for my daughter and myself," Susan said. "I shouldn't have struck her. We'll have a good time tomorrow evening, I promise, and I hope we get serious businesses tended to. We must, Charlotte. There isn't a choice anymore."

"What do you mean?" Charlotte asked quietly. "I'm not aware of any business between us, serious or otherwise."

Susan stared at Olympia, clearly warning her not to interrupt. "Morgan and I don't want to take legal action against you for the trouble you're causing but we will if we must. We think that can be averted. You have needs and we have needs and we think they can complement each other. We believe it would make all of us happy if we bought Rosebank from you."

21

They'd decided to have lunch at the Court of Two Sisters. Vivian chose it for old times' sake, half hoping memories of a prior time there with a prior male interest would help remind her of the reasons she didn't really like men.

It wasn't working.

It hadn't had a chance to work once Spike walked into the place as if it were home away from home and Vivian had grown instantly jealous. Ridiculous. Of course the thought that he'd probably brought another woman there didn't make her jealous.

Yes, it did. She felt furious. He'd become quiet, pensive. Thinking about *her.* Who had it been, Jilly? Vivian didn't think so because Spike and Jilly were buddies and showed no sign of pining for each other romantically.

Vivian studied Spike covertly. He sat half-sideways in his chair with his arms crossed.

They were a pair, both pretending no ghosts hovered with them at the wobbly table balanced on uneven courtyard cobbles.

Vines climbed every concrete patched brick wall and metal arbor. Fountains ran softly and flashed the colors of pale gems in the sunshine. Birds knocked themselves out in the race for crumbs. Spicy scents, a jazz trio playing low enough to stay out of the way but not too low for a little foot tapping, blasts of color, purple, orange and white bougainvillea; a warm bath for the senses. Vivian glanced openly at Spike and he smiled, deepening those smile and squint lines around his impossibly blue eyes.

"This wouldn't be a bad moment to stop the clocks, huh?" he said.

Vivian looked at clear skies and said, "Stop the world, we'll get off here," but one thing was missing: peace in her heart. The thrill of wanting this man just about made up for that.

A sweet-faced black waiter with a web of gray spun over the tips of his hair poured more ice-cold water into their empty glasses. "A drink from the bar?" he asked.

"It ain't too late for the best mimosa in town."

"I'm delicate," Spike said, laughing. "I'll take an Abita. A good beer is about the best I can do this time of day."

Vivian had white wine.

They chose the buffet and she figured they were both looking to escape their thoughts and put off making more awkward conversation. They walked to loaded tables in the cool interior of the building.

Vivian was ready first and went back outside, finally starting to relax a little. Who wouldn't in a place like this?

She approached the table but stopped several feet away, her heart missing beats. The skin on her face tightened and she felt cold. Slowly, she went closer and stood motionless at her place, unable to sit, unable to as much as swallow. Her plate felt too heavy and her hands shook as if she might drop it.

Balanced across her silverware lay a single, long-stemmed white rose.

If her feet would move she'd probably run.

"Everything I like but shouldn't have," Spike said, arriving at the table. "Cyrus says he never met a bad crawfish étouffée. I say he's sawed off his tastebuds with all those peppers he sucks back. But this is going to

303

be a great one. Would you look at these boulette? Grown-up hush puppies my dad calls 'em."

At last he noticed she wasn't saying a word and still stood in front of her chair. "What is it, *cher?*" he said, frowning with concern.

She swallowed several times and pointed at the flower. "Do you think this is funny?"

Spike looked from her face to the rose. "Me?"

"Who else but you could have put this here?" She picked up the thorny stem and slid her plate onto the table.

"*Cher,* use your head and tell me when I could have put it there?" He looked in all directions, backed from the table to see areas hidden from some angles. He returned and said, "I was at the buffet with you. When could I have put the rose there? And why would I do a sick thing like that?"

He couldn't have and she was making a fool of herself. "I sound crazy. Of course you didn't do it. This is to frighten me, and the reason is because I'm on his radar, the man who killed Louis. I'm being warned. But I don't know if it's because he wants me to stop poking around or because he's going to kill me anyway and wants to terrify me some more first." She drank water to moisten her dry throat. "Who would have a grudge against me? As far as I know I don't have any enemies."

"It was put there to frighten both of us but we won't let it work. I keep turning things over in my mind, what little we have, and it doesn't amount to a hill o' beans. But I do know we can't let ourselves be lulled by the passage of time. That happens. The hours and days pass with no more events and you convince yourself things are safer. Vivian, I don't want you to panic. We already knew we had big trouble, and we pretty much know just how big."

"Bonine isn't doing a thing, is he?"

Leaning too heavily on a hunch that Errol's mob connections might not want him to solve the case could be a time waster. Errol had a history of just not wanting to be bothered. "He's lazy and he never forgives. He hates me and I'm involved with you. That means he hates you." He thought a bit. "Maybe I should stay away from you. Might be safer." Might also drive him mad if he couldn't do his damnedest to keep her safe.

"I could be a danger to you," Vivian told him. She wanted the whole mess to go away.

"Stay here," Spike said. "Promise you won't move."

Being told what to do usually made her

edgy but she'd do as he asked. Unfortunately, she didn't tell him so.

"Damn it!" he said, real low. "Don't waste time. Practice your independence when this is all over and it isn't likely to cost one or both of us our lives. Sit down and stay there."

He walked swiftly away, threaded his way between tables, and she saw what he intended to do. He went from waiter to waiter asking questions.

Vivian sat down and looked with distaste at the food on her plate.

When Spike returned, he slid onto his seat and drank some of his beer. "It was a boy. Came in and put the flower on the table then left. The waiter assumed I'd arranged it and didn't think anything of it. Flower sellers come in off the street all the time. The man says he wouldn't know the boy again."

"It's all hateful," Vivian whispered. "What have I done — or Mama — to make him set out to get us?"

"If I had to guess, I'd say there's only one clear reason for any of this. Want to take a guess?"

The colorful afternoon had grown dimmer in her eyes. "We're in the way."

"You could say that," he said. "I'd put it

more finely. You've got something someone else wants. Rosebank is slap bang in the middle of everything and that's where we need to concentrate our efforts."

His cell rang. He checked the readout and pressed a button. "Hey, Lori. Problems?" He listened, then said, "Hmm. Hmm. No. Just like I don't have any official rights in Detective Bonine's kingdom, he doesn't have any in mine. He sure as hell can't have access to my files. Did you tell him I was away for a few hours?"

Lori said in her wispy voice, "I think he already knew, sir. He's in the hall shoutin' at anyone he thinks will listen. Sheriff Dufrene stopped by and Bonine's giving him an earful about you."

Spike closed his eyes and shook his head. "Can you get Dufrene to the phone — without Bonine being in the area?"

"Sure thing."

In the dead time that followed, Spike covered the receiver and said, "My boss never drops by but he chooses today when I'm not there. And Bonine's hanging around kickin' up a ruckus. Yeah, hi, Sheriff. Sorry to miss you. I took a few hours off." He said, "Thank you," when Dufrene told him he deserved a break when he could get it.

"Bonine's been on my case forever."

"I know," Dufrene said. "Don't worry about it. He isn't making any points with me. But I" (Dufrene's "I" came out as a long "aah") "do wonder what bee he's got up his ass, apart from the obvious one. He don't like one thing about you. Is this all about the Patin case?"

"Yes, sir," Spike said. "Like I reported, I was there the night of that killing — visiting the ladies who live at Rosebank. Bonine decided I had something to do with the crime."

"Mad bastard. Don't forget, even for a moment, that this case isn't ours."

"Anything I do will be on my own time, Chief."

Dufrene grunted at that. "Yeah, well, I'll get rid of him, but check in with me tomorrow. I think we got to cover our asses on this one."

"Will do," Spike agreed and switched off the phone. "Shee-it. Excuse me. Forgot myself there. Bonine —"

"I think he's involved," Vivian cut in. "I think he's trying to use you to move any suspicion away from himself."

"Could be," Spike said. "Or he could just be actin' out the old grudge." He took the rose and placed it carefully beside his plate. "I'll get a plastic bag. I doubt if there'll be

308

any prints, but it's worth a try."

He looked at her wan face and his temper rose. "Eat somethin', okay? Just to please me. You need your strength."

"You sound like my mother," she said, but put a forkful of dirty rice into her mouth.

Spike grinned, then wrinkled his nose when his phone rang again. "Devol," he said into the mouthpiece.

This time it was Cyrus. "How's it goin'?"

Oh, great, they would never be left alone. "Could be better," he told him and explained the rose.

Cyrus didn't answer at once. "Petty," he said at last.

"That isn't the word I would have used," Spike said.

"Think about it," Cyrus said. "Theatrics. He couldn't resist taking the chance. But maybe we should be glad. This man's so in love with his own stage dressing he seems determined to run risks spreading it around."

"There is that."

"Vivian holding up?"

"Not as well as I'd like. She's a trouper, though — under the circumstances."

"I've got to talk to you about that some more," Cyrus said. "Have you given any more thought to what I said?"

Spike wished Vivian weren't hanging on his every word. "We're at the Court of Two Sisters on Royal and there's too much noise," he told Cyrus. "Let me move to a quieter spot." He smiled at Vivian, got up, and took himself off to a shady corner.

"You still there?" Cyrus asked. "Before I forget. Bill's idea of helping the Patins get some of their place opened up is taking off. People are comin' from everywhere to lend a hand. Wazoo's planning the biggest fete in history. And, hey, I got a call from Homer saying he'll do some carpentry."

Spike's mind did a blank act.

"You there?"

"Yeah. You took my breath away. My dad's a great carpenter but he hasn't so much as lifted a saw in ages. His heart seemed to go out of it. He could be a real help."

"He's in on it, and Bill of course. One of the things I like about him is he isn't all talk. Gary Legrain says he's got two left hands but he can use a paintbrush. Several ladies have volunteered to sew and clean. The thing's gathering steam the way these things do when you've got good people and a good cause. Ellie from Hungry Eyes says she's got time and Joe Gable volunteered to help outside — so did Marc Girard."

Spike smiled. "You're making me feel better."

"Between us we can get enough rooms spruced up and do the basics in a reasonable length of time. Then they can make a start and stop feeling so desperate."

"That's all great," Spike said, trying to come to terms with the idea that his father had offered help. "Is that the only reason you called me?"

"Two more. First, I spoke to you about the right order of things. People know about you and Vivian. For your souls and for — well, you know — you need to be doing something about the formalities. I don't want to push but I know you're an honorable man and you'll want to do the right thing."

It didn't take a great brain to figure out Cyrus was talking about . . . marriage! Aw, it was the priest talking because Spike and Vivian were spending time together, alone. Spike smiled at the thought. He looked at her from a distance and everything about her made him want what he couldn't have right here.

"Spike?"

"Yeah, yeah. Don't worry about it."

"Reb and Marc mentioned it, too. Reb said the months go by fast."

Spike scratched his forehead. "I appreciate their interest — I think."

"Well, moving on." Cyrus sounded relieved. "Second point. I've mentioned my sister Celina and her husband Jack. Jack Charbonnet has a lot of connections, some of which I probably wouldn't like. But he knows everyone and everything in New Orleans. I wondered if he could be helpful to you. Also, I'd like you to meet them. A brother can be proud of his only terrific relative, y'know."

"I'd love to meet them," Spike said although he didn't manage to sound enthusiastic. "Maybe the next time I'm here."

"I've been asking some questions about Martin, Martin and Martin," Cyrus went on. "Something screwy there. The sons are on the masthead but they never worked a day of their lives in the firm. In fact, as far as I can make out, they never worked a day anywhere in their lives. But they've got a reputation for throwing money around and being in on any shady deal that goes down. Nothing proved, though."

"Is that a fact?" Spike thought about the twin brothers.

"Fact," Cyrus said. "And they've got some sort of hate thing going for their father's girlfriend. They don't even know who she is but apparently the relationship was going strong when Louis died and they think he'd already changed his will to include her."

"I gathered a lot of this, but thanks, Cyrus. Have I ever said you make a great sidekick."

"No, but thanks. Jack and Celina expect you at their riverboat around six. She's the *Lucky Lady*. Take the Riverwalk. I thought that would give you and Vivian plenty of time to . . . ah, deal with business and pleasure. You two are a great pair."

Spike felt a foreign sensation. The tightening of bonds around him. Cyrus was determined to get him hitched to Vivian before the two of them even knew what they wanted. Why, Spike had no idea. "We respect each other as friends," he said, somewhat stiffly. He didn't tell Cyrus he'd rather not meet the Charbonnets today. In fact, he hadn't lost hope of spending time alone with Vivian.

"Uh-huh," Cyrus said as if what Spike said was difficult to believe. "Just remember there are times when women need extra consideration."

"I'll keep that in mind."

"Good. I'll let you go then." Cyrus's breathing was audible. "There has been one new development. Wazoo's got herself a job at Rosebank and she'll be living out there."

Spike pinched the bridge of his nose. He and Vivian had been out of town a few hours and things were turning upside down. "A job at Rosebank," he said. "Does Charlotte think they all need their palms read daily?"

Cyrus chuckled. "Evidently Wazoo has a lot of skills we didn't know about, including fixing equipment." He cleared his throat. "I was going to lose my nerve about saying this, but Charlotte's pretty upset. Susan Hurst went over there and said she and her husband refuse to accept the idea of a hotel next door so they want to make Charlotte an offer she can't refuse — for Rosebank."

At last Spike hung up and made his way back to the table. His meal had to be cold and his beer too warm. He sat down and drank the beer anyway. "News from home. Bonine's been trying to poke around in my office files. He's not getting away with it. Half the town is getting ready to work on your place and get you started in business." He held his bottom lip between his teeth. "But this afternoon's bulletin is that you and I are expected on a riverboat that belongs to Cyrus's sister and her husband, and Susan Hurst wants to buy Rosebank to stop you from turning it into a hotel."

22

"I'm not sure I can tell you much of anythin' you don't already know," Jack Charbonnet said. "Maybe we should go to our private quarters. We can be sure of not being interrupted there."

They sat, drinking champagne, in an intimate lounge on the second deck of the *Lucky Lady.* The ping and chime of slots, screams of excitement and groans of despair rang out steadily from the lower deck. Waitresses in short, fringed skirts and low-cut tops ran up and down wide stairs to load trays with drinks at the bar in the lounge.

"I like it here," Vivian said. She'd already come to terms with being in casual clothes while the rest of their company wore evening dress. "I've never been on a riverboat before, or in a casino." Nearby, patrons played keno with the aid of television screens and Vivian noted that some of them made her feel overdressed.

Jack's wife, Cyrus's sister, Celina, wrinkled her nose. "My husband knows this isn't my favorite place but he gets such a charge out of it I don't complain much." She had short, red curls and navy-blue eyes, and the kind of figure that turned men's heads. There was something of Cyrus in her eyes and they shared the same straightforward approach. She leaned closer to Vivian and said, "Jack's a hermit at heart. Don't you think people are attracted to opposites — from their own natures, I mean? Sometimes, anyway?"

"I think so," Vivian said.

"It's a good idea to keep an eye on who comes and goes here," Jack said, absolutely serious. He must have overheard Celina. "I'm the best one to do that. Not even the staff knows when I'll show up. That makes it tough on anyone who wants to take a personal interest in things while I'm not around. Some would like to skim the cream from the operation. I make sure they never get anything they can use against me."

"That's code for, we don't pay protection because of Jack's connections and what he knows," Celina said, and laughed. "I make him sound like a member of the family —

think Sopranos — but he's the gentlest man around." She slid closer to her husband on the banquette and he bent over her to kiss her quickly. The way his eyes lingered on Celina's made Vivian glance at Spike. He looked straight back and didn't hide the sexy hooding of his eyes.

"A friend of ours is joining us," Jack said. "He couldn't stand to be left out. We might as well give him a few minutes to get here or we'll have to start from the beginning."

Jack's Cajun background was very nice on him. His short, black hair curled the slightest bit and he had the kind of lean face and long, muscularly spare body guaranteed to please. He had eyes that hazel color, more green than hazel really, and he had a way of not blinking when he concentrated on someone. Vivian had seen him come from the outer deck and hold his beautiful wife's hand when she stepped over the raised threshold. Tall, broad-shouldered and lithe, he moved with languid grace Vivian decided was a cover for someone capable of speed and even deadly action if necessary.

Spike held her hand under the table. He spread her fingers on his thigh, surprising her, then turning her legs to water when her small finger encountered the bulge in his pants. He wasn't taking his eyes off her.

She smiled at him.

Spike watched her mouth and unconsciously curled his tongue over his upper lip.

If there was a way, they would be in each other's arms tonight. She contracted in pleasurable ways and in pleasurable places. The thoughts of darkness and skin on skin came too often now. She actually felt him inside her and sat upright with a start.

They hadn't made love, but still she imagined the smooth, moist stroke of his flesh within hers.

"Amelia wanted to be here," Celina said, startling Vivian. "She asked me to give you her regards. Her words, not mine. Comes of thinking she's an adult. She's eight and madly in love with her uncle Cyrus. I think she's convinced he's here and we're keeping him from her."

"Everyone loves Cyrus." Vivian smiled at the other woman. "Spike has a daughter, Wendy, she's five and sweet, but very grown up, too."

She felt Spike staring at her and glanced at him. His expression revealed nothing but made her uncomfortable.

"We can usually appease Amelia by saying she has to stay to help Tilly, that's our housekeeper, with her little brother but it almost didn't work tonight."

Spike liked meeting Cyrus's sister and Jack Charbonnet, who had the kind of worldliness about him that raised flags. They didn't have to be bad flags. Whatever the man's story might be, he'd lived, and seen more than most, Spike would bet money on that. He also figured they were circling, avoiding the real reason for this meeting.

A commotion rustled up from the lower decks. A man's voice gradually grew louder, and so did his laughter, until a full head of blond curls appeared. Compact, beautifully dressed in evening clothes, the whole package arrived — a man who exuded life and expected all eyes to turn in his direction. They did.

"This is Dwayne LeChat," Jack said quietly. And more loudly, "He and his partner own a successful . . . club. It's on Bourbon. Dwayne? Quit grandstanding and get over here. We've got folks for you to meet."

A pianist broke into a chorus of "Careless Love," and Dwayne flung back his head to laugh before bowing to the musician and going to put a bill in a brandy snifter. "He's playin' our song," he said, laughing over his shoulder at the rest of them. "Everyone in town knows Jean-Claude plays this for me."

He rushed over and kissed Celina soundly. She kissed and hugged him back before he took Jack in a bear hug.

"Vivian Patin and Spike Devol," Jack said, indicating his guests. "Good friends of Cyrus's from Toussaint."

"Cyrus?" Dwayne frowned a little and his intelligent brown eyes showed something other than the jovial clown he hid behind. "That sweet man. How is he? It's been too long since he came to see all of us and we worry. He's too good, you know, too vulnerable in a nasty world."

"He may be," Spike said, surprising himself. "He's a hard act to follow."

Dwayne shook his hand firmly and reached for Vivian's, which he took to his mouth for a brief kiss. He raised his brows.

"Vivian and her mother own Rosebank, a beautiful old home just over the line in Iberia — spitting distance from St. Martin," Spike said. "I'm the Deputy Sheriff in Toussaint — here as Vivian's friend," he added quickly.

Dwayne sat down. "And you've got trouble."

Vivian's lips parted but she didn't speak.

"We've got trouble," Spike agreed. "And you folks probably can't do a thing to help us but Cyrus thought you might have an idea about a couple of people who could be involved."

"Might, could," Jack said, not rudely but speculatively. He checked around and beckoned to a heavyset man, also in evening dress. What Jack said to the bouncer or bodyguard or whatever wasn't audible but the man stationed himself at the top of the stairs. "The Martin brothers," Jack said.

Spike didn't like this. Jack Charbonnet was a stranger to him, even if he'd married Cyrus's sister, but he'd already been briefed on why Spike and Vivian were in New Orleans. "Cyrus told you about the Martins?"

Jack regarded him without saying a word.

"Yes, the Martins," Vivian whispered, louder than if she'd spoken normally. "They're twins and —"

"I know all about them," Jack said. "You met them today. Tell me how that went, word for word."

"Did Cyrus tell you?" Spike asked with an eerie sensation that there was too much he didn't know about here. "He couldn't have told you about our meeting with the Martins. I . . ." No, the phone conversation they'd shared hadn't touched on any details of the visit to Louis's offices.

"Cyrus told me you were coming," Jack said. "He mentioned where you were going today and why — in general terms. I can't share sources with you, but my brother-in-law would tell you I can be trusted. Unless you're not comfortable with that, in which case let's enjoy the company. Have you eaten?"

Spike considered what the man had said, and what he had not said, and the possible ramifications of dealing with him. Jack Charbonnet hadn't asked to be involved and Spike would trust Cyrus with anyone's life any day of the week. He raised his brows at Vivian, who nodded. She read his mind; he could almost feel her understanding him.

"I'm comfortable," he told Jack. "Thanks for the food offer. You hungry, Vivian?" When she shook her head no, he said, "Neither am I. But thanks."

While Celina and Dwayne looked on, both of them apparently uncomfortable, Vivian let Spike fill Jack in on what had happened when they went to see Gary.

"Louis Martin was okay," Jack said after thinking awhile. "Lonely, I think. Although there were rumors about a woman in his life. He bought jewelry from a friend of mine. I read about his death — murder. A bad thing. One thing you can be sure of, his sons don't soil their hands. If they had anything to do with it, the talent was hired." He signaled the bartender. "If it was a hit, it doesn't sound like anything the Martins would sanction, though. Too messy. Too personal. But it's no secret they were waiting for their old man to pop off. Those two have holes in their pockets and a lot of expensive habits."

"We heard about the woman you mentioned," Spike said, watching Charbonnet's face carefully. "I understand she's in the will and the Martins want her out."

Jack said, "If she is, it's probably just as well no one knows who she is. She'd better keep it that way until the will's public. Harder for the Martin boys to interfere that way — if you understand what I mean by *interfere*."

Spike understood. What he didn't understand was where in hell Charbonnet could be getting his information.

"The sons know this person's probably getting a big bequest," Vivian said. "I heard them say something about it."

"But they didn't give her name, did they?" Jack asked.

Vivian frowned at Spike and shook her head slowly. "But Gary must know."

"He doesn't. No one does. Maybe it's time to find out."

"I may be able to help," Dwayne said. He

tapped the fingernails of one hand on the table before speaking to Jack. "You know the connection," he told him. "Meanwhile, would I be out of line suggestin' this sexy couple stay away from the Martin brothers?"

Spike absorbed the implications at the same time as he saw Vivian redden and take a big slug of her champagne.

"Spike," Jack said, "Dwayne and I go back a long way. We understand the way things go in New Orleans. If you're willin' to take advice, listen to our friend. The Martins could be bad news."

23

The late hour troubled Vivian. Her mother could get panicky. Vivian fished her cell from her purse and said, "I'm calling home to say we're okay. Mama's a worrier."

Spike didn't comment. He was driving the gray van he and Homer used for business pickups and deliveries.

Vivian didn't get past explaining where they were before Charlotte said, with too much satisfaction, "Why, you two young things just take your time. Best to come slowly when it's dark. It's gonna rain, too." She added a little tale, first about hiring Wazoo — which they would discuss later — then about Homer Devol stopping by with Wendy. When Vivian hung up, she couldn't quit smiling, or feeling warm inside.

Spike glanced at her, and glanced at her again. Just as Charlotte had said, it was dark and raindrops had indeed started slanting across the windshield. They were on U.S. 90 and vehicles ahead trailed shuddery pink ribbons from their taillights on the slick road. In those same lights she could see the rain bounce.

"What's funny?" Spike asked, his profile sharp in the glow from the dash. He turned her way again, briefly, and smiled.

She couldn't look away from him. "My mother," she told him. "She's funny. Told us to drive slowly because it's dark and she'd heard it's going to rain."

"That's funny?"

Men could be so literal. "Cute. Maybe I should have said cute."

He grunted.

She enjoyed the way the blond tips of his hair showed up in the darkness, and the shadowed grooves beside his mouth. Ooh, there were too many things about him that gave her sexy notions.

"I've got a surprise for you," she said and waited for another sidelong glance. "Guess who visited my mother today?"

He hummed and squinted as if in deep concentration.

Vivian looked at his right thigh and the way it flexed as he drove. Strong legs. Why was she so hooked on that? And the way his pants ruckled at the groin, and the fly didn't lay at all flat. She hid her smile this time. Spike wasn't only thinking about driving. Put that fly in the right perspective and you could test-drive off-road vehicles over it.

"Errol Bonine," he said suddenly.

"What d'you mean, Errol . . . Oh, you're guessing who visited Mama." Then she felt stupid. "Wrong."

"Couldn't have been Gary. We know where he was. *Cyrus?*"

"He did, but that's not who I'm talking about."

"Susan Hurst?"

"You're out of guesses," she said. "Homer and Wendy."

She'd give him points for neither hitting the breaks nor swerving. He also controlled his expression. "That right?" he said. "Why would he do a thing like that?"

"To be nice," Vivian said. "And ncighborly."

"We aren't neighbors."

She frowned at him and leaned closer until she could tweak his ear and take satisfaction in a loud "Ouch! Whaddayado that for?"

"Loosen up, Devol. Quit seein' ulterior motives where there aren't any. Homer volunteered to help out at Rosebank. He said he's good at carpentry and he'll be glad to do some jobs to help us open up as soon as possible. I don't like accepting favors, but when folks are being nice they make me feel good, welcome, I guess."

"My dad said he was good at carpentry." It was a statement. "He said that to your mother. Cyrus told me he'd offered, but not directly to Charlotte. The old fraud was great at it but he hasn't lifted a saw in ten years or more. Used to reckon he'd forgotten how when it served his purpose."

Vivian was still close enough to see him blink, swallow, pull in his bottom lip. "What purpose would that be?"

"Forget it," he said. "I gotta concentrate on the road."

She felt cross, and disappointed at his reactions. Without another word she crossed her arms and moved closer to the door, where she could look out into the darkness. They'd be passing the turnoff for Raceland soon. Still a long way from home.

Spike, suddenly taking a small off-ramp, pressed Vivian against the door, then tossed her the other way until he straightened the van out on a black road evidently from nowhere to nowhere. "Sorry about that," he said.

The rain fell harder.

"Where are we going?" she asked him. "Is this a shortcut?"

"Depends on where you're headed," he said. "It could be a shortcut to somewhere we can sit, uninterrupted, and talk a few things through. Since you seem determined to make conversation, let's get serious about it. Real serious."

She doubted if his tough words were intended to excite her, at least not in the way they were. Vivian kept quiet.

"Aren't you going to tell me you want to get along home? Tell me to quit frightening you?"

Did he want to frighten her? Well, that wasn't going to happen. "Why would I be frightened? I won't be frightened anywhere if I'm there with you." Let him think about what she meant.

"You ought to be smarter than that."

"What does that mean?" Sometimes she thought he spoke for effect.

"It means that I told the truth when I said I wanted us to talk alone."

Once more he made an abrupt turn, this time crossing the center of the road to make a left turn through dripping cypress trees and bumping over rough terrain until she saw the sheen of a bayou.

"This should be far enough for privacy,"

she said, hating to acknowledge a pinch of anxiety in her stomach.

"Soon will be. The other thing I thought we might get to is what's on top of your mind, and mine. I want to make love to you."

Vivian gasped. "Just like that? No finesse, no wooing, just *I want to make love to you.* Very romantic."

"Maybe not too romantic, but does the idea turn you on?"

Only enough to make her nipples stinging hard and her panties damp. "We'll have to see," she said, pressing her arms over her sensitive breasts. "Maybe you'll make me want to, maybe you won't." *Please make me want to. Revise that, I want to, I want to, but not like we're scratching some itch.*

His laughter didn't calm Vivian's jumpy nerves or stop goose bumps from racing over her skin.

The spirit she was known for made it difficult to keep her mouth shut for more than moments at a time. "This isn't like you. You're out of character — your character. Talking rough like you turned off the gentle side. Is that like gettin' courage out of a bottle for you? Kinda like bein' too drunk to watch your mouth?"

"Could be, or it could be I'm dealin' with

unfamiliar feelings. Laugh if you like, but I've wanted women before, just never the way I want you. Seems to disconnect my brain from my mouth."

"I won't say too much about talkin' with your . . ." What the hell, he was doing his best to shock her, this was her turn. *"Dick,"* she finished with a flourish before she wished she could disappear.

"Say it if that's what you think." Her language hadn't fazed him. "You'd be partly right, but only partly." He drove to the banks of Bayou Lafourche, stopped close enough to the edge for Vivian to look straight down at slow-running, rain-pocked waters. "This looks like a good place."

Carpets of water weeds slunk around worn-down cypress knees and, as she always did, Vivian wondered if alligators, in the company of a cottonmouth snake or two, skulked in the shadows. "How do you know your way around here so well?" she asked.

"I don't. Just lucky when it comes to finding beauty spots, I reckon."

"Maybe we shouldn't stop," she said. "It is pretty late."

"Say the word and we'll go."

"You're not fair."

He rested his head back and clicked his tongue. "You want me to beg you to stay?

Would that make you feel better about wanting to be here anyway?"

The tears that sprang to her eyes annoyed Vivian. She didn't understand why he talked of making love, then turned cold on her.

"Hey." He cupped her chin and turned her face toward him. "Are those tears I see shining there?"

"Don't be ridiculous."

"I'm sorry. When I'm unsure of myself I compensate with tough talk. It's often not pretty — like just then. I don't want to go. If you say you want to leave I'm gonna be one disappointed guy — and not only because I want to be inside you."

"Don't."

"Why not? It's true, I'm not sure I can get close enough to you to suit me."

Vivian kept her eyelids lowered and Spike didn't remove his hand from her face. "More tough talk," she said in a whisper. "Even if you do soften it up."

"It wasn't meant to be an insult." He stroked her cheek and rested his thumb at the corner of her mouth. "I like being with you, lovely Vivian. If I'm not with you, I'm figuring out how to get us together. Pretty talk doesn't come easy to me, but with you I could be going somewhere I never want to leave."

Pretty enough for me. "You wanted to discuss something."

"Yeah. The things that scare me."

She caught at his hand and kissed the backs of his fingers. "Nothing scares you."

"The hell it doesn't," he said.

"Tell me about it."

It was too easy for him to reverse the tables on her and do the finger kissing. She shuddered.

Seeing his face wasn't easy, but his eyes glinted, and so did his teeth, and she heard his breathing grow heavier.

"I'm fighting what you do to me," he said. "Since you showed up I haven't been the same. I can't afford to allow any woman to stir up what you do. You mess with my mind."

Without any warning, Spike opened his mouth against her neck.

"Don't do me any favors."

He stopped her from pulling away and only got more forceful when she pushed at his shoulders. "And don't you play hard to get. I know you don't mean it."

His breath turned hot, or was it her body?

"C'mon, give it up. This isn't a surprise for either of us. We came close before. If you don't want to relax, don't. I kind of like you fired up."

Tickling her skin with warm breath, he dragged his tongue to her ear and blew softly, nibbled the lobe, and resumed the trailing to the hollow of her throat. He kissed her there, softly, but his restraint didn't fool Vivian. His breaths got shorter and harder.

She made fists on his shoulders and tried her best not to respond. *Some hope.* With her fingers in his hair and her mouth on his forehead, she closed her eyes and tried to calm down. Holding him against her while he pressed his lips into the vale between her breasts wouldn't help. She took her own deep breath and knew she shouldn't have. Spike wasted no time before using his mouth on the swell of her breasts.

Talk first . . . and if something happened afterward it would be because they both wanted it to. "Spike, my mother's given Wazoo a job at Rosebank."

He stilled, turned a cheek to her breasts and rested his head there. "What did you just say?"

"I think you heard," she told him, smiling into the darkness while her heartbeat pummeled her eardrums.

"But you only said it to get my attention. Like you didn't already have it. Maybe you think your timing's cute. I think it stinks.

Anyway, Cyrus already mentioned this."

"Well, you didn't tell me about it. You could be right about my timing, though. I just don't want to forget the stuff I'm sure you'd want to know. If Cyrus told you on the phone when we were at lunch, he didn't have time to give you all the details. Wazoo went to Mama and said she'd do anything. She can't afford to live at the Majestic anymore and she's not making enough money. She's going to live at Rosebank free and draw a small additional salary. If she works hard — and works out — that's win-win."

"Live at Rosebank?" His pseudoweak voice didn't fool Vivian. "*Work?* You've lost your minds, both of you. Cyrus mentioned the live-in bit, too."

He made her just plain mad. "Then why keep actin' as if you're hearin' all this for the first time. Anyhow, sometimes, when you give people a chance, they change."

"I don't give . . . I don't want to talk about anything but bein' here with you." He looked at her face, pressed his cheek to hers. "I can't get enough of the feel of you."

"I thought you didn't do sweet talk."

"I don't." He drew back a little. "That was an accident."

"Talk, Spike. That's the main reason we're here."

"Oh, no, darlin', not the main reason, or not from what I'm feeling."

But he turned from her and sat straight in his seat. He sighed and clasped his hands behind his neck. "We've got to talk fast. This is killin' me."

Vivian sat on her hands. She wasn't sure she could keep them away from him if she didn't.

"I think hirin' Wazoo on is nuts and I should have told Cyrus as much," he said, "but we'll get to that later. Much later. You didn't tell the Charbonnets you'd like to meet their children."

Vivian blinked a few times. "No, I didn't. Neither did you. Why would I?"

"This is about you, not me. I wasn't going to suggest it to them unless you showed some interest."

She started to shake her head as if she could clear it, but sank into her seat instead and rested her knees on the dashboard. He was cooling her off and she missed the heat already.

"You don't show any interest in Wendy."

"What are you talkin' about?" She pushed out of her slouch and turned to face him. "Just what are you sayin'? The Charbonnet children were at home. It was gettin' late. Even if I'd thought of it, which I didn't, it wouldn't have been appropriate."

He wrinkled his nose and wouldn't look at her.

"And I have shown an interest in Wendy. I . . . she . . . *Why* am I defending myself about this? You're being irrational." She thought a moment. "If you're lookin' for a reason to end it with me, why did you come on to me just now?"

"Oh, no. Don't you go there, you," he said. "I told you before there were things we needed to discuss. Could be I should have said things I need to know about you."

"Let's go," she said. "Now. Before any real harm's done."

"I don't think so. Grown-ups look right at their issues."

"I don't have issues," Vivian told him. "You do."

"You're not keen on kids," he announced. "You've got your dog and you dote on it."

"*Her,*" Vivian said.

"Yeah. Kids are important to me."

She rubbed her face with both hands and rolled the window down an inch. "Leave Boa out of it. You don't make one bit of sense. Because a person loves a dog, they can't like kids? I like children a lot. I think Wendy's a doll but I don't know her yet and I haven't had a lot of practice with saying the right things to little girls."

"You don't have to worry about sayin' the right things. Be yourself. Kids know if you're a phony tryin' to make points." He didn't sound as if he particularly enjoyed what he was saying.

"Well, you've let me know I don't have to worry about being taken for a phony, then. I've let her lead the way, which is how I think it should be done." She felt like getting out of the van, but what would that prove when she wouldn't know how to get home? "I don't understand why you started on this."

"I want more children."

A very still place opened in Vivian's mind. No particularly constructive thoughts formed there. "The way you love Wendy, I'm not surprised."

"Am I wrong about you? Would you like your own children sometime? Maybe soon?"

Okay, so what did she say to that? What would make him ask such questions in this situation? "I hope to have children one day. I haven't had a reason to think about it."

"But you would like to?"

He was really serious about this stuff. "Yes, I would. One day."

"There's nothing like having your own kids. They love you because you belong to them and they belong to you. You can make them happy and secure or disappoint them sometimes. But they want to trust you so bad, and I think it's real hard to make them stop loving you."

The way he talked brought a lump to her throat. If she had the guts, she'd ask him if this was an offbeat way of saying he'd like her to be the mother of some children for him. She shouldn't even think about making fun of his feelings. How many men would take a woman aside to talk about how much he liked children.

No man in his right mind.

"You think I'm crazy," he said.

She started and laughed uncomfortably. "I do not. I think you're sweet and special. And lovable. I admit it's a shock to hear a man telling me he wants more children and explaining what they mean to him, but I like it." She did.

"Lovable? You think so?"

"I might. And it would be your fault for pressing my buttons."

"I'd like to press all kinds of things for you," he said. "And you could do the same for me."

Vivian caught her breath. "You change topics fast," she told him. "If you were a woman, you'd probably be accused of talking dirty, too."

"Life's short. Make love a lot," he said. "I don't believe in wasting time. And talking dirty can be a turn-on for some folks."

"Have I told you you're not subtle?"

"Yes, you have, but I already knew. At least when it comes to talkin' about things that matter to me." Spike slid a hand behind her neck and massaged the base of her head. "You're tense."

"Uh-huh."

"My fault for comin' on to you the way I did. I'd better fix that." The massage shifted to her shoulders, a kneading pressure that made her want to hang her head forward.

His hand slipped down her back until he reached her waist and tugged her blouse free of her pants. "Your skin's hot," he said when he played his fingertips around to her side and eased her to kneel on the seat. He moved her so effortlessly, she felt insubstantial and liked it. Tucking his hand beneath her bottom, he tipped her toward him over the console. "Put your arms around my neck," he said and she did as she was told.

"Didn't you just apologize for coming on strong?"

"No, *cher*, I just mentioned I had come on to you and said I needed to fix it. I think I meant, finish it."

She thought about the back of the van,

and immediately told herself off for wanting him so badly that she hated the console between them.

Then she couldn't focus on the console.

Had she been worrying about the console?

She needed to hang on to his neck tightly or she'd fall and might keep on falling forever. He turned sideways in his seat and kissed her. He had a lingering way with kissing, all careful attention to every tiny move. He kissed her as if he needed to eat her and her mouth was a great place to start. Swollen lips shouldn't feel so good.

Mr. Devol had special skills. His particular way of smoothing his hands over her bottom, of sliding long fingers between her legs from behind, of pressing, manipulating, could be a form of torture, or just plain magic. And he managed it all without taking his mouth from hers.

Vivian felt the start of a pulse, right where a pulse felt best, but she had enough reason to make sure she was only titillated, not satiated. She sat on her heels and made it impossible for Spike to keep on doing what he was doing.

"Mmm," he murmured. "A man loses one way of entertainin' himself, he finds another, *cher*." *Another* meant he took advantage of having her arms around his neck and her body stretched so that she couldn't protect vulnerable parts, and undid her blouse.

He shifted swiftly and slung her over his shoulder. While she laughed, he gripped her knees with one forearm, swept her legs over the console and wriggled her so that she lay more or less flat on the passenger seat.

"The circus," she panted. "You should join a circus."

A single long, blunt finger, landing on her lips, silenced Vivian. The faintest of air currents came through the window she'd cracked open, the occasional fractured drop of rain, even, but Spike had been right when he said her skin was hot. She'd burn up completely any minute now.

He held her down by the shoulders, under the blouse that wasn't covering anything anymore. Then gradually, while she saw his concentration, while he leaned over her a little, she forgot everything but his palms brushing her nipples, moving in circles, and bringing her bottom arching up each time a sweet sting darted through her. He filled his hands with her breasts and pushed them together. His head tilted back and he shook her flesh. All but falling on her, he sucked each nipple into his mouth, playing the tip of first one, then the other with his tongue, closing his teeth carefully, moving his face back and forth on her tender skin.

"Don't stop," she told him.

His answer was to drag off his shirt, roll it up and cushion her hips on that sneaky old console. On its way down, the zip on her pants sounded deafening. So did his. He concentrated hard while he did extraordinary things to render her naked but for the shirt still bound to her by the arms.

The moments he used to bury his face between her legs while he pulled her pants from the second foot made her thrash. "Ouch," she moaned, hitting her wrist on the dash. Then she just moaned. Next she pulled him away by his hair and he played her body like an inspired musician, hitting every note true and clear. She broke into a sweat, panted, tried to catch his hands.

Spike made it his turn to kneel on the seat, between her knees and then with her legs wrapped around his waist.

With his forearms beneath her, his hands at the back of her head, he entered her. Care lasted all of two strokes before he made a keening sound and drove them together. Vivian added her own impatient wildness to his, met him again and again for the few thrusts it took to reach that explosive, welcome little death.

The sound he made now was almost a sob, or was that her, Vivian wondered without caring.

"*Cher*," he murmured. "Darlin' woman. You are so beautiful and you make me feel I never want to move away — or I would if I didn't want to be on a soft bed with you. I don't want to wake up in the mornin' without you by my side."

"Hush," she said. This man who wasn't good with romance could sweet-talk babies to sleep anytime.

She opened her eyes. "I stopped taking my pills," she said, horrified at having forgotten. "I needed to come off them for a while."

He shimmied low enough to kiss her stomach and stroke his tongue into her navel.

Panic had never changed much of anything. "Spike —"

"I'm flattered," he said, laughter in his voice. "Guess I had you so distracted there were things you didn't notice. Nothin' to worry about, *cher*."

She relaxed and peered at him. He raised his face and she saw a very white smile in the gloom. "You're laughing at me," she said, although she wasn't serious.

"Just struck me you might think I'd decided to start one of those babies I talked about. Me, I'm not into trickin' like that."

"You're a bad man," she said, and felt herself quicken some more as he began his clever handwork all over again. "You love to tease."

"Hmm-hmm . . ."

He stopped moving, held completely still. "Hush," he whispered. "Do you hear anythin'?"

Vivian fought the urge to cover herself. She turned her head slightly to listen. Nothing. But then a faint rustle that didn't sound like wind or rain in the grass. She looked at Spike and nodded.

Carefully, he pulled her blouse over her and she buttoned it while he eased her back onto her side of the van and retrieved the rest of her clothes.

They didn't speak while she got her panties on and he pulled up his pants.

Spike didn't bother with his shirt. A film of sweat glistened on his shoulders and chest. "Keep your head down," he said while she was still working into her pants.

Harsh rapping on the back doors of the van stopped her heart. She pushed down a scream. "Don't get out," she begged, clutching at Spike's forearm. "You don't know what's out there. They could be armed."

He got the shoulder harness behind her and fastened the seat belt over her hips. For an instant he passed his fingers over her mouth in a silent order not to make a sound. He doubled her over and drew away.

Please don't leave me. Please don't go out there.

Whoever was torturing them knocked again, this time on the panel behind Spike's door.

Vivian heard the faintest noise when he turned the key a single notch in the ignition. Then a hiss reached her and she crammed her hands over her mouth so Spike wouldn't hear her retch. She'd roll up the window if she dared. Snakes liked abandoned vehicles and they weren't big enough in the brain department to figure this one was still occupied.

The hissing got louder.

"Shee-it," Spike said, not bothering to lower his voice. "Hold on."

He started the engine and gunned it. Immediately they listed to the right, the right at the front, just about exactly where Vivian sat.

"Lean my way," he said. "Do as I say. Now."

She tried, but couldn't do it. "We're slipping," she told him. "Going down the bank."

He eased back on the gas, then tried one more time to propel them forward and onto firm ground. Vivian felt the wheel grip and breathed through her mouth, daring to hope they'd make it out.

Cautiously, not taking his eyes off the windshield, Spike reached under his seat and produced a gun. He steered with his left hand and cradled the weapon in the crook of the elbow on the same side.

Vivian's instinct was to cover her face but that wouldn't help a thing and it surely wouldn't help Spike who didn't need to worry she was about to fall apart.

They stopped and once again the hissing sound came. Vivian had discarded all thought of snakes. This noise was wrong for that.

The van tilted forward and to the side and the angle increased slowly but definitely.

A mighty smash, on the back doors again, jolted Vivian. She took shaky breaths and saw Spike glance down at her. "There's a man out there, one man," he said. "I keep catching glimpses of his shadow. He only wants one thing, to scare us to death."

"He's already done that," Vivian whispered, her throat so dry the words hurt. "Why?"

"Probably just a powerless kook getting his jollies."

"Or someone warning us to stay away from some things. Like the Martins' business."

"Now you're guessing. We've gained some traction — now hold on tight. The ride out is going to be rocky with a slashed tire. We'll be driving on a rim."

The hissing. Of course. Air escaping the tire. "It's too dangerous," she muttered. "We'll have an accident."

The vehicle swayed and she found Spike's leg in the dark, held more tightly than she knew she should.

"An accident on the road, where we've got a chance of being seen, appeals more than getting stuck here with a loon. Fuck his creepy mind. I'll get him." The van swayed harder and harder. "He's not going to quit."

"But he'll knock us into the bayou. Drive, Spike."

He depressed the gas slowly, but might as well have saved his time. The right front wheel seemed to be spinning a deeper and deeper groove into mud and the crazy who tortured them rocked the van in earnest.

They slid sideways at least a foot and Vivian, pressed against the door, peered out of the window and looked directly at the shifting gleam of water. Spike was uphill from her now.

"I'm going to be sick," she said.

"You don't have time."

She crammed one fist into her stomach and grabbed blindly for something to hold on to with the other hand. She found the steering wheel and Spike cursed, not so quietly. He grabbed her hand and held it.

"Vivian," he said while they were thrown from side to side. With each bounce they tilted farther and farther over the water. "Vivian, he's trying to send us into the bayou and I think he's going to make it. If I try to get out and stop him, it'll happen fast and you'll be down there in the water alone, and if I don't get him before he gets me, he'll be waiting for you if you try to swim out."

"There are snakes in there. And alligators." She didn't want to wimp out on him.

Then it happened. The van half tipped, half slid down the bank.

Vivian screamed.

She felt Spike yanking her seat belt undone and he reached to roll her window all the way up. He was a big man and his weight finished them. With a screeching, tearing noise, the wheel rim jarred over embedded rocks, and the left-hand wheels parted company with the ground.

Vivian tried to twist toward Spike. He reached for her waist and hauled her against him, right before they landed against the door, his weight crushing Vivian. The vehicle hit the murky waters with a great slap.

"We're going down," Vivian shouted. "We'll drown."

"Not without a fight."

Second after agonizing second passed, filled with a roaring, sucking sound. Drops of water fell on Vivian's face. The van wasn't watertight. "It's coming in," she told Spike. "We've got to get out."

"Just hang on," he told her. "If we were alone we'd be out of here by now. Okay, that's what I hoped, we're righting a bit. Wait, then do exactly what I tell you."

With that, he hacked at the passenger window with the butt of his gun.

"It's not working." She sobbed and shook, struggled to keep a hold on his naked torso.

"Cool it," he told her, swinging a leg over her. He put all of his weight into kicking at the window. The glass parted company with the frame, but only enough to allow water to gush in. No way could they get out through the gap.

Vivian tried to stay calm. Hard things clattered across the floor of the van. Water poured in fast.

Spike twisted around and reached behind the seats. He scrabbled among objects that clanked. "There's gotta be something heavy enough," he said. "Maybe this."

She couldn't see what "this" was but it was long and curved and when Spike used it on the window like a battering ram, the glass shattered.

He didn't speak again. Grabbing Vivian, he pushed her through the empty window frame, pushed her against the blasting weight of water until she slithered out.

Almost instantly her head was above the water and on a level with the top of the van. Attempting to smother her coughs, expecting gunshots to explode around her, she fended off the floating water hyacinth that glided around her neck and shoulders.

She searched around, looking for Spike. Her shin cracked against a submerged tree trunk. Tears stung her eyes.

Spike should be right behind her.

Hands, closing on her ankles, punched her heart into her throat. She couldn't breathe. Something had happened to Spike. A brief vision of him, submerged and dead inside the car, froze her blood. Trying to hold on to the roof of the van was useless. Slowly her splayed fingers slipped. Slimy flotsam caressed her chin, then the lower part of her face. The man beneath the water, and she knew it was a man, felt for her arms and pulled them to her sides.

Help me, Spike. She cried out to him inside her head before she sank beneath the surface.

Water rushed into her nose, then into her mouth and down her throat when she tried to scream.

24

If she didn't drown or die of a heart attack, he might save them both.

The odds weren't great.

She'd think he was the enemy intent on killing her but there was no way to let her know otherwise.

Spike's lungs burned. He couldn't hold his breath much longer. Grabbing a handful of Vivian's hair, he pushed her back inside the Ford and up to the roof where an air pocket would keep them both safe, at least for a little longer. Clamping her there with his feet, he arched backward until his face broke the surface and he sucked in air. He wasted no time before slipping beneath the water again and lifting Vivian all the way into the vehicle before following her.

Water hyacinth decorated her streaming head. She pushed the trailing stuff aside and looked into his face. He was sure she'd instinctively realized it was him by now.

"Spike." She coughed and spat out water. "I thought you were dead. God help us. Is he up there waiting — seeing if we get out?"

"He may be up there watching but by now he's pretty sure he's done what he set out to do. Don't talk. There isn't much air."

Spike found the back pocket in his pants and fumbled with the button that closed it. In the end he tore the button off. He didn't expect it to work, but his cell phone was in there.

When he held it up, water ran from the seams.

"That won't do anything," Vivian said.

As if he didn't already know. He punched a button anyway and knew he was in luck, at least for now, when the light came on. He dialed 911 and gave praises when the woman who answered proved quick to understand the wild story he told. "On their way," he told Vivian, dialing again. "Cyrus? Where are you? Get here. Move it. We're breathing our last in Bayou Lafourche. Someone tried to murder us. We don't have much air — up against the roof."

The absolute silence that followed enraged Spike, before he thought about what he'd just told Cyrus.

"By the time you get this far, we'll be dead or with the local law."

Cyrus muttered something about making sure he knew how to find the local morgue.

"Very funny." Or it might be at some other time. "It'll probably be the Lafourche folks from Raceland who come. Find us there, or call and they'll tell you where we are." He switched off and wrestled the phone into his back pocket again before realizing that wasn't smart.

Spike thought he could hear sirens. Even if he wasn't imagining the sound, it was probably too early for them to be coming for Vivian and him, but he squeezed her arm as if he thought they were. She had guts but she wasn't made for this.

The sirens grew distinct and, finally, Spike could see reflections of rotating lights on the water. "They've come," he said, making to put her through the window again.

"Not this time," she told him. "You first, then hold my hand. Don't you dare let go of me."

"Giving orders again," he said. "Already."

Spike, trailing Vivian behind him, bobbed into a searchlight trained on the bayou and struggled through the mini-waves created by heavy rain, to the bank where more than one cop hauled them to muddy ground.

"We've got better things to do than rescue dummies who make out too close to the bayou," an officer drawled. "You might want to tone down the action in future — if you're anywhere near water. Must have been some wild stuff going on to rock the vehicle over."

Coughing, wringing water from the bottom of her blouse, Vivian said, "What's the matter? Are you jealous?" completely stealing anything Spike might have said. "Someone just tried to kill us. Get that van out of the water and you'll see what I mean. First he slashed a tire. Then he rocked us till we . . . You can see what happened."

"It went the way the lady says," Spike said, trying not to grin at the way the cops had turned to throat clearing and toe bouncing. "We're cold and damned wet. If you could get us somewhere we can dry off, we'd appreciate it."

The wardrobe available at the sheriff's department in Raceland would never make it at a New York fashion week, but Spike and Vivian were warm and dry.

"I can't let you two out of my sight," Cyrus said, floating his shockless Impala down U.S. 90 toward home. "Look at this weather. What would make you drive off the freeway and go down by the bayou like that?"

Spike hitched at jeans bunched around his waist with a belt and grunted. If Cyrus couldn't work that out . . . Well, of course he couldn't work it out but it was a dumb question anyway. The pants had to be a forty-inch waist and he'd had to roll them up at the bottom. He didn't want to think about the check shirt that billowed around him.

"Cyrus." Vivian sat between them on the front bench seat. She'd insisted this togetherness would keep them warm. "You know perfectly well what we were doin' by the bayou. You just want to hear us say it so you can count it as a confession of some sort."

Spike tried to sink lower. He'd swear a lot of what she said just came straight out of her mouth unchecked.

Vivian felt him scrunch down beside her and smiled tightly. Served him right for patronizing Cyrus with silence. Nothing shocked him and it was time Spike worked that out.

"We were, um, um, spoonin'," she said.

Cyrus chuckled. "I don't think I ever heard anyone but an old-timer say that. It's about time we brought you into the new century. Making out. Lip-locking — whatever. There's a bunch of terms they use now, I just tend to forget 'em. But they don't *spoon* and neither do you."

"We certainly could," Vivian said, sounding ferocious. "All we'd have to do is lie on our sides, one behind the other, real close and with our knees bent. Spike's knees up behind mine so I sort of sat in his lap. Or the other way around. That's not so popular. A man prefers a woman to sit in his lap. Makes him feel big."

Spike turned his face to the dark window and tried to count the lights they passed.

Cyrus struggled against grinning. "I'm not sure I knew that, Vivian. Thank you for explaining it to me. I expect that started way back when people needed combined body heat to stay warm when they were sleeping."

"Or not sleeping," Spike said. He couldn't help it. "A man who feels big may not be so interested in sleep. And people sure as hay-ell *do* still spoon. They just call it other things. Anyway, doin' that in the front seat of a van might present difficulties."

He'd managed to silence them and he sighed with satisfaction. Trouble lay ahead and it was time they concentrated on what they were going to do about it. Surreptitiously, he ran the knuckles of one hand up and down Vivian's arm. They could concentrate on the serious stuff, and on each other at the same time. He had only just begun to enjoy this woman.

Another pressing concern was where and how they could be together, alone — frequently.

"I like my new dress," she said. "It's soft. Makes it easier not to have any underwear when there's nothing rough on your skin — and no hard seams."

"Thank you for sharing that," Spike said. "I expect Cyrus appreciates it, too."

"I always appreciate knowing people are comfortable," the wily priest said. He kept his eyes on the road and repeatedly corrected for the bouncing, swaying motion of the station wagon. "Anything you two would like to discuss? Or announce?"

Vivian clamped her lips together. It was Spike's job to act like a man and wiggle out of this one.

"We've got a long list of things to think about," Spike said. If he didn't fear she'd deny it, he'd say they might be falling in love. Whatever that was. "We learned things in New Orleans that could have a lot to do with what happened to Louis, if we could only figure it all out."

"We will," Vivian said calmly.

"Sure," Spike said. "Then we have a

missing gardener, the murdered lawyer I already mentioned, questions about why there's criminal activity centered on Rosebank. And what could be the biggie and the root of all evil — what did Louis intend to reveal that would be valuable enough to snatch Charlotte and Vivian from the claws of financial disaster?"

"Almost forgot," Cyrus said. "Madge sent a flask along. Brandy. In the glove compartment, Spike."

"*Madge* sent it." Vivian shook her head. "That woman works too hard and too long. And she has to drive too far to get home. I still think she should either have a room at the rectory or . . . I just thought of it. We could do a room for her at Rosebank. She could have an apartment. It's time she abandoned Rayne, frog capital of the world, for something convenient. She could help choose the way the place is decorated and pick out the furniture she wants from around the house. There's plenty of it."

Spike found the brandy, opened the flask and poured some into the lid.

Cyrus didn't answer Vivian's suggestions and she felt funny for being so enthusiastic. "It was just an idea," she said.

"A good idea," Cyrus told her. "Generous. You might want to mention it to

Madge." He was quiet for a moment before saying, "It's time she was married and starting a family in a home of her own."

Only a fool would miss the wistfulness in his voice. Spike found Vivian's hand and squeezed. She was sure he felt what she did in Cyrus: his longing.

She accepted several sips of brandy from Spike. It felt warm and good going down.

"Will there be a full-scale investigation into what happened tonight?" Cyrus said. "That man wanted you dead. They must track him down."

"There are long fingers in this pie," Spike said. "I'd stake a lot on it. And it's all about money. I've got a feeling Charlotte and Vivian are right in the middle and that's where you'll find me. I have . . . I'm their bodyguard, so to speak."

"I feel better hearing you say that," Cyrus said. "Don't you need a license or something for that kind of work?"

Spike smirked, thinking of the things few people knew about him. "I've got a P.I. license. Got it after Bonine had me drummed out of Iberia and I needed an income. Kept it up. I can do anything I need to do and I've got anything I need to have, I make sure of that."

Vivian looked at him with fresh respect.

"You used to seem so quiet."

"I am quiet," he said. "You bring out the extrovert in me."

"Are you Catholic, Spike?" Cyrus said. "Vivian is, I know. Be easier if you were, too."

This time Vivian felt embarrassed. "There's nothing to make easier, Cyrus," she told him.

"Maybe not yet," he said, undaunted. "Best to be prepared, though."

"Bet you were a Boy Scout," Spike commented. "Darn good one, too. I guess you'd say I used to be a Catholic."

"I was never a Boy Scout," Cyrus told him. "You and I need another talk. This time I don't intend to let you put me off."

Great, Spike thought. He glanced sideways at Vivian and his heart turned. She looked so sad he longed to hug her.

"We're there," Cyrus said, bumping and bobbing down the road leading to Rosebank. "Charlotte knows there was an accident but you're both fine. I wanted to make sure she wasn't too shocked when she found out. She's stronger than I thought. All she said was that Spike would take care of you, Vivian."

At the entrance to Rosebank, the white stone, pineapple-topped posts shone in Cyrus's headlights.

"The law seems to have given up searching for Gil," Vivian said. "That amazes me."

"They're still looking," Spike said. "Other things come up and they have to spread themselves around. Gil will walk in one day, see if I'm not right."

"I surely hope you are," Vivian told him.

"What about his relatives?" Spike said. "They must be beside themselves."

"I thought his brother would come to the house, but he didn't. Mom and I have been over there but all he talks about is how long it takes to declare someone dead. He wants to move into Gil's duplex because it's bigger, then have his son move into the one he's using now."

"There's another brother, too," Cyrus told them. "If something has happened to Gil, there'll be a war there because brother three won't stand for being cut out of the property."

"Shit," Spike said with feeling. "Why do some people get ugly over stuff they never had a right to."

"If you ever figure that one out," Cyrus said, "I'd appreciate knowin'. Death brings out the worst in some. They see it as an opportunity."

Vivian pressed her hands to her face.

"Don't," she said. "Gil's probably alive. With a family like that I might run off just to get some attention."

Spike ducked his head to see the sky beyond the roof of the west wing. "Whooee, mama," Spike said. "Good thing it's rainin'. Looks like there's a bonfire goin' out back." He didn't feel as unconcerned as he'd made sure he sounded.

"New gardening crew," Cyrus told them. "Mrs. Hurst recommended them to Charlotte."

"And they already started?" Vivian gripped the dashboard with both hands. "We can't afford them. Anyway, they wouldn't be working now."

"The bonfire was goin' late this afternoon," Cyrus said. "Rain and all. I think they may have been encouraged by your neighbors to go the extra mile, Vivian. And from your mother's reaction I got the impression the men had been sent as a sort of gift from Susan Hurst. Charlotte didn't seem too sure what she should do about it."

Cyrus parked near the front steps.

If Spike hadn't got out quickly, he thought Vivian might have climbed right over him. "That fire's too big," she said, running the instant she hit the ground.

Passing her would have been easy but

Spike loped along beside her and Cyrus quickly caught up.

The scene they burst onto stopped their flight. A bonfire roared and in the jagged ring of light it cast, Charlotte and Wazoo yelled at three men in oilskins who were training hoses on the blaze. Garden hoses.

"It's gonna be okay," Spike said. "It's not goin' anywhere. I'm glad I'm not on the other end of your mama's tongue, Vivian. She's givin' them hell."

Shaking her head, Vivian marched on. "I'd say Wazoo's doing her bit."

Charlotte, her short, gray hair bright in the firelight, noticed the trio and threw her hands in the air. "Can you believe this?" she said when they got close enough. "There's plenty to burn and they asked beforehand, but I never thought of them pilin' everythin' on Gil's compost heap. He's going to be so mad."

"They thinkin' with they rear ends," Wazoo said, her grin showing just how much she was enjoying the fuss. "Or worse." She looked meaningfully at Vivian but ignored Spike and Cyrus.

One of the men left his hose to jog over. "It's dyin' down, ma'am," he said to Charlotte. "We lit it where we was told."

"Who told you to set a fire this close to the

building?" Charlotte said with no effort to sound reasonable. "The stables — the garage is right there and there's a lot of wood in the roof. And if there was a wind in the right direction you could have got the house itself. Who suggested it?"

"The man . . . A man. He said he worked for you. We were makin' the pile way back but he said this was where you wanted it."

Cyrus put an arm around Charlotte's shoulders. "Don't be so upset," he said.

Wazoo watched him as if she thought he might shed a skin.

"An older man?" Charlotte asked. "A bit bent over. Could it have been Gil, you think?" She looked at Vivian, then at Spike. "Please, God, let it be Gil."

"About so high," the gardener said, indicating an above average height for a man. "Can't say I remember much about him. Hey, either of you remember what the man looked like, the one who told us to burn here?"

"No," one man yelled.

"We were workin' hard," the other said. "Didn't notice what he looked like." The fire ceased to leap into the air but a great smoldering, flickering heap remained.

Spike wished he could be alone to ask questions. "You didn't notice? Had to be somethin' about him you remember."

All three heads shook slowly, The one who seemed to be in charge said, "Nothin'. Except he was sweatin' like a pig but he had on one of those thick hats. Wool. Pulled down so you could hardly see his face, but he wasn't no more than forties, I should think."

"Thank you," Charlotte said. "I don't know who spoke to you, or why, but I'm sure this wasn't your fault. I hope you'll keep coming."

"Sure will, ma'am," he said.

As soon as he moved off and picked up his hose again, Vivian said, "Mama —"

"No man like that workin' here, no way," Wazoo interrupted, hopping from sneaker to sneaker. "No, sir, no man like that at all. I'm seein' it, me, the shape. The way he walk and talk, him. He the killer. He still here."

My enemies are all around me. I watch their faces, see their fear. They don't know who I am, yet they think they are clever enough to beat me. That makes them more vulnerable.

What they don't understand is that they have no defense against me. When the moment comes there will be nothing they can do to save themselves. Meanwhile the game continues.

He, the one who believes he can control me, must also be removed. The only uncertainty is when?

Meanwhile circumstances force me to make a different move, but I shall relish it. This time I must be very patient and even more careful.

I have not changed my mind about that woman. She tests my tolerance.

25

The fourth day

Vivian had planned to visit Hungry Eyes and Ellie Byron at opening time that morning. Unfortunately she hadn't woken up until ten and then took half an hour to persuade her aching body into the shower.

She should be easy on herself. The ordeal in Bayou Lafourche would be enough to make anyone stiff and sore — and scared for some time.

Making love in the front seat of a van? Possibly that could stretch a few muscles and other things. Vivian parked on Toussaint's square, leaving herself about a block to walk to the bookshop. Making love with Spike, the way they'd made love, the sensations she wouldn't forget, were worth an aching back and sore legs. With Boa in her straw basket, she got out and walked to the shade of a big old sycamore tree.

Already the temperature soared and humidity with it.

She and Spike were in deep. Vivian didn't think she was jumping to conclusions in thinking they were both hooked. The future? She couldn't see one and that hurt so badly she felt sick.

She locked her green van. The words, *Rosebank Resort,* in black with gold shadowing had been added to the sides. Mama and Vivian had decided to take more visible steps toward establishing Rosebank's official image. They hadn't even hidden their pleasure when the van came back from the shop and they parked it where Susan Hurst could see if she wanted to look.

Susan and Morgan would make them an offer for Rosebank they couldn't refuse? The dinner at Serenity House was supposed to be tonight, but Vivian intended to do her best to scuttle it.

Hungry Eyes epitomized "quaint." Bow windows with stained-glass eyes on each small, square pane of glass had been added on either side of the front door. Similar panes in the door, without the eyes but with a row of books top and bottom, gave a "come in" feeling to the place.

Vivian could see round tables with blue chintz cloths inside the left window. Beyond stacks of books displayed on a wide shelf in the right window, she saw rows of book-shelves reaching far back into the store.

People sat at the tables. She recognized Dr. Reb Girard, Bill Green and Joe Gable, Jilly's brother, whose law offices were two doors away from Hungry Eyes.

"Miz Vivian?"

Wazoo's voice couldn't be mistaken. Vivian turned in time for the new Rosebank employee to catch up. "Hi, Wazoo. What are you doin' here? I didn't have a chance to talk with you today. Are you still enjoying working at Rosebank? There's so much to do, I'm afraid. We need lots more help but — well, I might as well be honest. We don't have the money to pay for much more help."

"I know so, me," Wazoo said. "You and Miz Charlotte savin' every penny for makin' the house nice. I think it beautiful already, me. The place Miz Charlotte give me? Ooh ya ya, that the sweetest room I ever see. But I guess you gotta do more stuff for visitors from big cities. They gonna come y'know. That house am so special. Even if it do need an exorcism."

Vivian sighed. "We don't believe in such things."

Today Wazoo wore a black dress that only

371

reached her calves, and hose with her tennis shoes. Nice legs. Her hair was in two explosive and long tails that fell from high up on either side of her head. She watched Vivian intently. "You afraid of what you don't know. I feel the spirits, me, and they gotta be put to rest. You can't have horny ghosts flittin' around ladies' bedrooms."

"*Wazoo.*" Laughter would feel good but it would also encourage Wazoo's outrageous chatter.

"On the other hand, Miz Vivian, you could cater to ladies who might get a real uplifted feeling out of some truly *spiritual* experiences." She grinned. "Might not say no to one or two of those myself. You could advertise *earth-moving satisfaction*. Mark my words —"

"Wazoo." Vivian said the name in the best schoolmarm voice she'd never had a reason to have. "You are irreverent. And don't forget that when you advertise, you have to deliver. Something tells me we'd be paying back a lot of reservations because of nonsatisfaction." She coughed, amused by the conversation.

"You gotta have rules. They guest ladies sleep nude with their ankles and wrists tied to the bedposts. And you got a fan right where it'll blow hard on them beggin' buds and tunnels o' love, Miz Vivian. Play the right kind of music, blindfold the customers, and pay someone to do a little somethin' with a feather here and there. Drip warmed-up oil real slow. Well, now, you might not even have to pay someone to do that. Could have candidates linin' up to work for free. Turn that fan on high, mind. Then you can just wait for them repeat customers at the door."

Stunned, but entertained, Vivian said, "I'm going to the bookstore. See you later."

"Why, I'm goin' the same place. Miz Ellie's gettin' me some new tarot cards. Now there's a girl who could use a little blowin' and pluckin'. That ain't baby fat under her dress. She's just got one womanly body. And don't think the men don't notice. You take a look at where Joe Gable's eyes are when he's around her. And I don't even think she knows."

Vivian hadn't met Joe Gable but he'd been pointed out to her and that was enough for her to notice he was better-looking than the average lawyer.

Wazoo trotted at her side. "That nice Mr. Legrain, he sure was mad when he find out what happen to you last night."

"I didn't stay up to talk to him about it," Vivian said. "He's already got his hands full without my problems."

"Sure," Wazoo said, opening the shop door. "But he sweet on you and he care about that." She wriggled her nose and her slim eyebrows rose. "I think the sheriff know that man's feelings, too, and I think he mad about it."

"Hush," Vivian told her, digesting Wazoo's remarks. "I hope Mama told you how we feel about gossip."

Wazoo flapped a hand from a loose wrist.

"Hi," Ellie Byron said from behind a glass case filled with pastries and sandwiches. "Vivian, I thought you would never come." Her oddly distant blue eyes were just as Vivian remembered them. Her short, brown curls shone in the sunlight. She wasn't quite real.

Vivian took in a sharp breath and went to the counter, returning greetings as she went. "Good mornin', almost good afternoon. I overslept. Don't ask me why."

"Because you get back from New Orleans real late. With that Spike Deeevol" (Wazoo's vowels were dragged out) "the pair of you lookin' like you wearing other people's clothes. And you was. Bein' pushed in Bayou Lafourche, in Spike's van, couldn't have done you no good."

Mesmerized, Vivian listened to this recital of her personal business and said, "Thank *you,* Wazoo."

"That's awful," Reb Girard said and that's when Vivian noticed Gaston on the floor under the table. "I want you down at Conch Street so I can examine you."

Gaston's bright brown eyes fastened on Boa's basket. The latter was smart enough to press herself into the bottom.

"I'm absolutely great," Vivian said. "It was really nasty at the time but we were so grateful to get out safely we felt better at once."

Black-haired, blue-eyed Joe Gable introduced himself and went on to ask, "How come you were down by the Bayou in all that rain last night? Late, too, from what's been said."

Everything said about small towns, or many of them, was true. News and personal details traveled a little too fast.

"I won't bore you with the details," she said, meeting his gaze.

Slithering across the floor on his belly, like a woolly apricot alligator, Gaston made his way to Vivian's feet and looked up into her face. He appeared to be smiling. With Boa and her basket held to her chest, Vivian hunkered down and scratched the poodle's head, heard a low growl and looked him straight in the eye. "I'm Vivian. You're Gaston. We're friends. Shake." She held out a hand. Gaston's eyebrows wiggled alternately before he sighed and closed his eyes.

Vivian wasn't fooled. She'd be watchful of him.

"Oh, wow." *Why hadn't she thought of it?* "Excuse me. I walked right in here with my dog and didn't think a thing of it."

"What dog?" Bill Green, the real-estate guy, asked. He shared a table with Olympia Hurst.

"She's in the bottom of this basket," Vivian said apologetically. "I'll have to come back another time — without her."

"What's that?" Bill, crisp and clean-cut in a tie and white shirt with the cuffs rolled back, indicated Gaston. "Doesn't look like a stuffed animal to me. Around here we figure a clean dog's as good as a clean person, right, Ellie?"

"Right. I love dogs. Occasionally Deputy Lori mumbles something about rules when Gaston's in here but Spike just gives him crumbs and generally acts silly with him. This is part of my home and I like dogs in it."

Reb, looking way more pregnant than she had even a week earlier, snapped her fingers at Gaston who ran and jumped onto what knee space Reb had available.

"I'd like a cup of black coffee," Vivian said. "No cream or sugar. Make it a mug. May I have pickles and gratons? If you have them?"

"You certainly may," Ellie said. Her movements were rapid and she had a way of glancing into the recesses of the shop, or through the front windows, as if she expected to see someone, and not just anyone. Ellie Byron expected a visitor, only Vivian wasn't sure she expected him or her to be friendly.

"Coffee for me, too, please," Wazoo said. "Did you tell everyone about the bonfire, Ellie?"

"I expect it did expensive damage," Olympia said but Vivian ignored the comment.

"We were talking about it when you came in. Bill says we've got things to discuss." Ellie winked at Wazoo.

"How would all of you know about the bonfire?" Vivian said, then looked at Wazoo.

"Okay," she said and shrugged. "I tell 'em. I call and tell 'em. We like to know when we needed around here."

"You want to gossip, you mean," Vivian said.

She turned from the counter in time to

see Joe Gable watching Ellie intently, a worried ruckle between his arched brows.

She already had enough troubles without courting other people's problems and her reason for being here would have to be dealt with as soon as she could find a way to speak with Ellie alone.

Hovering would only draw curiosity, so Vivian took her coffee, pickles and chips to Reb's table and was immediately asked to sit down. If Vivian weren't anxious, the interlude would be cozy. Inside the shop Ellie kept the temperature pleasant. Zydeco, played at a low volume, made the perfect background music. Handmade gifts were displayed on blue shelves that matched what could be seen of the table legs beneath the cloths. The chairs and their tied-on seat cushions also matched.

Vivian bought time by studying every inch of the place. The deep shop housed many more books than she had expected.

"The bonfire sounds terrifying," Dr. Reb said. "What would possess them to light it so close to the buildings?"

Vivian faced the table. "It happened fast. There wasn't time to be frightened." She bit the end off a whole pickle and followed it up with a strip of crispy pork cracklings.

"I heard some stranger pretended he

worked there," Bill said. He took a bite of a boudin sandwich as thick as an encyclopedia and had to chew his way through the sausage before saying, "Man the workmen never saw before told them to put the bonfire where they did."

"Just maybe he was the killer," Olympia said, smiling, her eyes bright with excitement. "The one who killed the lawyer. Did his head really fall off when you opened the car door?"

Vivian looked at her hands in her lap. "No, that's not true."

"I told 'bout that man, too, Miz Vivian," Wazoo said. She sat on a high stool at one end of the display case and held her coffee mug in both hands. "Maybe someone see this man and tell the po-lice. Maybe it's a clue."

"Maybe." Vivian hadn't the heart to tell Wazoo in front of her friends that she was compromising any clues. Since Wazoo responded slightly better to authority figures, Spike could deal with it later.

"Great coffee," Vivian said, wanting to change the subject. "If you started giving patients shots of this, Reb, you'd have a booming practice."

"I've got a booming practice," Reb said, and leaned across the table to say in a low voice, "and it would be a lucrative practice if anyone paid me in something other than eggs, chickens or fish."

Vivian smiled. She closed her eyes and sniffed the fragrant steam rising from her coffee before drinking some more.

"I can't take credit for the coffee," Ellie said. "I get it in pots from Jilly, and the pastries also come from her."

Vivian said, "Everything's good," with her eyes still closed.

"Are you sure you feel okay?" Reb said quietly. "Are you taking vitamins?"

"Every day," Vivian told her, puzzled.

"You don't get much nutrition from meals like that." Reb gave Vivian's plate an arch look. "Fat and pickles. It's important to take good care of yourself, especially at times like this. You've got too much stress to cope with."

Bill Green cleared his throat. As soon as all eyes were on him he said, "I don't have long so I should get this said quickly. I've gotta check in at my place out back and get to the office again. Wazoo let us know you'd be in, Vivian, and more people wanted to be here but you know how it is in the middle of the week."

Surely they hadn't gathered a committee to tell her they thought she and her mother

380

should give up on Rosebank.

"I'm here for Marc, really," Reb said. "He had to run into New Orleans but this will affect him more than me — obviously."

Olympia got up, said, "I'll be back" to Bill and hurried outside.

"Gary Legrain wants to be counted in," Bill said, "and Homer Devol, if you can believe that. Spike hasn't been officially asked but he will be and he'll want to do it. Ozaire Dupre, Joe here, Wazoo's going to be useful, Father Cyrus, a bunch of guys from the ice plant, Jilly, Gator Hibbs and the guy who bought the body shop. The list goes on. They all want to be in on it."

Vivian tried not to appear stupid but she had to ask, "In on what?"

Bill's wide grin made her like him even more. "We're going to get enough work done at Rosebank so you and Charlotte can get your business going. We figure eight or ten rooms and the dining room should be enough at first. Zeb Dalcour, the ice plant boss, he's gonna check the kitchens over because he knows about those things. Homer will lead a crew. Marc Girard already started roughing in some plans for adding bathrooms. He knows the house from when he was a kid. We've got it all worked out."

Vivian felt too overwhelmed to speak.

"Yeah," Wazoo said, "we got it. Ain't no way that Susan Hurst and her man get their hands on your place. She bad, that one. I'm settin' up the biggest fete you ever saw. Whole town's ready to celebrate — and buy stuff. All proceeds to Rosebank."

Vivian blinked and Reb reached across the table for her hand. "Don't be cross," she said. "There's no malice there."

"I don't mean no harm," Wazoo said in something close to a bashful tone. "I hear Mrs. Hurst tellin' about that to Miz Charlotte. And I didn't say it while that Olympia was here."

There would be no changing the habits of a lifetime. Wazoo would keep right on reporting their business, but perhaps it didn't matter. All of these people were used to discussing their lives. "It's okay," Vivian told Wazoo. "It's not important. But, Bill, I don't know what to say to you. I've never been at this end of so much generosity. We can't allow you to do it, any of you. You've all got your own lives to live."

Looking at his watch, Joe Gable stood. "I've got a client in a few minutes," he said. "Listen to me, Vivian, and keep an open mind. You've been in New Orleans during a hurricane. You know how folks help each other and stick together. They do the same

382

thing for all kinds of reasons every day. Take that way of thinkin' and multiply it a few times. That's Toussaint people, and the people in a lot of towns like ours." He glanced at Ellie and back to Vivian. "You'll hurt feelings if you refuse our help. And you'll wish you hadn't because you *need* that help. But you won't refuse, will you?"

The counselor knew how to back a woman into a corner. "I guess not, but I don't want anyone having a hard time keeping up with their own issues just because of us."

Bill said, "Joe's good at putting things into words. Things will start happening right away." He got up and excused himself to go to the guest house behind the shop.

Joe also left. Then Vivian caught sight of the dark Land Rover Marc Girard drove. It crawled to a stop in front of Hungry Eyes and Marc leaned across the passenger seat to look into the shop. Almost at once he appeared inside the door, which didn't have time to close before Spike walked in.

Spike tipped the brim of his hat to her and took it off. He didn't smile but the way he looked at her was intimate enough to braid her nerves.

"Uh-oh," Ellie said. "You're busted again, Dr. Reb."

Smiling, Reb held her hand out to her husband. "You caught me. I didn't think you'd be back from New Orleans so soon."

"I made sure I was," Marc said, and to Vivian, "I hope they explained how much we're lookin' forward to workin' on that great old house of yours. I'm going to need to spend some time there in the next couple of days, if that can be managed."

"Of course." She could barely swallow. "Come whenever you like, as long as you're sure you —"

"I'm very sure," Marc said and looked it.

The only presence Vivian could really feel was Spike's and he hadn't said a word since he arrived. He stood there, fiddling with the brim of his hat and looking fixedly at her. She loved his "at ease" stance, and everything else about him.

"Off we go, Reb," Marc said, keeping her hand in his while he hauled Gaston up and draped him over one shoulder. The dog literally put his nose in the air. If he'd purred, Vivian wouldn't have been surprised.

Reb stood up and Marc gave her a kiss that didn't qualify as a dutiful peck. Vivian knew her own smile was probably silly and didn't care.

"You were supposed to go straight home after two hours," Marc told Reb. "The heat's too much for you."

"I guess I didn't want to go if you weren't there," Reb told him softly.

Marc kissed her again, then, completely naturally, smoothed a hand over her belly, feeling, concentrating, then grinning when he must have felt a kick.

The slightest movement caught Vivian's attention. Spike watched the Girards as closely as she did. He watched with narrowed eyes and his mouth pressed shut. She saw him swallow hard and would have taken a bet that he was thinking of when Wendy was in the womb, and also wishing he had what Marc and Reb had.

The couple, with Gaston flopped over Marc's shoulder, said their goodbyes and left.

Vivian and Spike were virtually alone and silently watching each other. Ellie and Wazoo, talking loudly, had left the café to go to the back of the bookshop.

"They're leaving us alone," Spike said, and shrugged.

"You think so?" She tried not to look at his mouth, but lost the battle. "Thank you for being so supportive last night. I've got to thank Cyrus, too."

"Don't thank me," he said and reached for her arm. He pulled her between two book stacks. "I'm the lucky one. I'm feastin' on last night . . . before we went swimmin'. You surely look good enough to eat when you don't wear anything."

She wrinkled up her face at him and smoothed a hand over the front of his shirt. His heart beat hard and he felt wonderfully warm. "That's what I wanted to say to you," she told him. "You beat me to it."

"Thank you, ma'am. Anytime you want —"

Vivian put a finger on his mouth. "Keep your voice down or Wazoo will be spreadin' what you say all over. Spike, you wouldn't believe how many people are offering to help with some work at Rosebank."

"I heard." He looked pleased. "I'm in, too. I'd have to be or Homer would have something to say about it."

"We'd better be careful, Spike. People are talking about us."

"Let 'em talk. Unless you don't like the idea."

"I do like the idea, as long as you do. I thought you'd want everyone to think we were professional acquaintances."

He shook his head and put an arm around her. "This is hard," he said very quietly. "I came to tell you something. Then I've got to get going."

Her stomach flipped and she looked up into his face.

"I'm falling in love with you."

He said it, dropped his arm from her shoulders and strode out.

"Poof," she muttered. "Just like that. Here and gone." But she knew shock, of the best kind, made her babble. *I'm falling in love with you.* And he didn't even give her a chance to react.

"I gotta get back to work," Wazoo announced from somewhere behind Vivian. "Miz Charlotte wants me to look over all the sheets and towels and stuff and see if any of 'em are good enough. She says that'll take all afternoon but I work fast when I'm happy."

When she saw Vivian she said, "You comin', Miz Vivian?"

"Don't wait for me. Please tell my mother I won't be long."

Wazoo hummed as she left and, at last, Vivian and Ellie stood alone.

"I think you're liking it here," Ellie said. "I do, too. I never felt as at home anywhere else."

"I've been coming here for visits since I was a kid but I never expected to live here. I thought I'd always be in New Orleans."

"You still have family there?" Ellie asked.

"No. It's strange, but there isn't anyone.

My dad died there last year and we had money troubles afterwards. Or my mama did and it was the right time for me to be with her till she's on her feet."

"So you'll leave once the hotel is running?"

The question startled Vivian. She hadn't really thought about it. "I don't know." *I'm falling in love with you.*

"Till I found Toussaint, I used to think I'd never settle down anywhere. This is a long way from — just a long way, I guess." Ellie laughed, but only with her mouth.

"A long way from where?" Vivian asked.

"From where I grew up. Look, Vivian, I owe you an apology and that's too weak for what's happened. Guy Patin's books. That's why you came, isn't it?"

"Partly. I'd just like to look. I think it will make me feel closer to him. Uncle Guy loved his books. He was interested in so many things."

"They're sold."

"Oh." Disappointment hit hard enough to make her realize how much she'd been counting on seeing the books. "All of them?"

"Every one." Ellie slipped into a chair at one of the tables and put her face down on her hands. "I should have come to you and explained. When we talked outside Jilly's place I knew it should be right then. I was chicken because I couldn't figure out what I was going to say."

"It's not your fault," Vivian told her, awkwardly resting a hand on her shoulder. "You're in business to sell books, not to store them."

"You don't understand," Ellie said, her voice muffled. "One book wasn't for sale. It was in a silk bag and I was supposed to wait till you came looking for his books, then give it to you for Guy. He said you'd come for sure. I don't know why he was so sure."

"Neither do I," Vivian said.

Ellie raised her head. "I can't give it to you because it's gone. I noticed more than a month ago. Someone must have taken it."

26

Cyrus stood at the window in his office and watched Madge walk across the grass from where she'd parked her car on Bonanza Alley. It was almost three in the afternoon and he'd been looking out for her since morning mass was over and he'd finally dealt with all issues on the front burner.

He left his office and went out front to meet her. "Are you okay?" he asked.

She hesitated, shaded her eyes with a hand to look at him. "Just wonderful," she said and walked around him and into the rectory.

Cyrus frowned and shrugged. *Just wonderful* meant there was something really wrong, or it did when she said it that way. He didn't pretend to understand.

He entered his office behind her. "Another scorcher," he said.

"This is Toussaint, Louisiana, and it's September. Were you expecting snow today?"

"Ouch."

She went through the papers in his out box and didn't respond.

"Did you get any of my messages today?" he asked.

"All of them, probably."

He picked up a letter she dropped and handed it to her. "Are you feeling yourself? I guess you didn't feel so good this morning. Maybe you aren't ready to have come back yet."

"I'm as ready as I'm going to be." She wore a red shoulder bag and the strap slipped from her shoulder, landing solidly at her elbow. Madge flinched as if it had hurt. She tightened her mouth and continued looking at one sheet of paper after another.

Her black curly hair glistened. When she smiled, her eyes always shone and just looking at her warmed him. Madge wasn't smiling now but she looked nice in a sleeveless red blouse and dark blue slacks. The rectory never felt quite right without her there and efficiently going about her work.

They'd had a few disagreements in the years they'd worked together but Madge had put her concerns right out there. In the past she hadn't used silence to make a point.

Women needed to be complimented. His sister Celina had told him so when he'd had a girlfriend in high school. "You look quite nice today, Madge," he said, feeling more uncomfortable than he knew he should.

She glanced at him and instead of smiling because she was pleased, she blinked repeatedly and bowed her head again. Darn it all, anyway, why *did* they need to be told the obvious and why was it so easy to offend them? "Did I say something wrong?" he asked. Enlightenment, that's all he wanted.

Madge shook her head but he heard her mumble, *"quite nice."*

He just didn't get it. "I called after mass," he said.

"Yes, your first call was when you'd got back here and wanted to let me know you'd noticed I wasn't where you expected me to be. Then you called when I was actually late for work."

She went behind the desk and sat in his worn swivel chair before pulling today's mail in front of her.

She was angry, with him, but he couldn't imagine why.

"I called again after that, Madge."

"Several times," she said. "I heard you."

"You were screening calls? Who are you trying to avoid? Has someone been annoying you?" She thought she could take care of herself no matter what happened. He wanted her to be secure, not foolhardy. "I'll call Spike and ask him the best drill to get rid of this person. You should have told me before."

"Why?"

This time he got her full, dark-eyed attention. He couldn't be sure if she was angry or sad.

"Because you're smart, pretty, young, and you live alone. You aren't a match for anyone bigger and stronger."

"Garbage!"

The wall she'd put up between them began to annoy him. "I want you to be sensible. Tell me about this, please."

"I'll work late this evening and we'll count this morning as half a vacation day."

"*No*. You work too hard all the time. I won't allow you to use vacation time when you need a break. You earn that."

She got up slowly, hitched her bag back onto her shoulder and gathered papers and mail against her chest. "Do you know how much vacation I've taken this year?"

Cyrus thought about it. "No. You take

care of those things."

"Of course I do. And of course you don't know."

Okay, this baiting made him mad but she wouldn't do it if she weren't unhappy about something, something she considered his fault. One of the things he couldn't bear and wouldn't allow was for Madge to be upset.

He breathed deep, calmed his mind and said, "What's wrong, Madge? I can't do anything about it if you won't tell me."

She looked at him, stared him in the eye. Despite the tight way she held her mouth, he saw the faintest tremor.

He had no idea what to say.

"Why are you looking at me like that?" she said.

"I'm trying to think what to say next. How much vacation have you taken so far? I think it's time I gave you more."

"I haven't used any. Why would I? This is where the people I know hang out — around the church and rectory and in Toussaint. As you pointed out, I live alone. I come and go alone. Why would I want a vacation alone, too?"

"That's . . . Madge, it won't do. There's a really active singles group in the parish, but you know that. Why not —"

"Forgive me," she said, breaking eye contact. "I sounded petulant and selfish. We all have bad days. I'd better get on with this or I won't finish all this stuff before tomorrow's rolls in."

"Who's been annoying you on the phone?"

The door was open a couple of inches and Cyrus heard Spike's voice in the passage from the kitchens. Lil Dupre was talking to him. "People can't feel safe with a murderer runnin' around. Know what I think? Those Patins brought trouble with them. There's things they're not tellin' you so you won't look at them too hard."

"The crime didn't take place in this jurisdiction." Spike sounded less than his usual reasonable self. "That means the investigation isn't my job. But I don't think you've got a thing to worry about."

"You ain't found Gil. Now what's that about? Lettin' a man disappear and behavin' as if it's no big deal."

"The *Iberia* authorities are working on that. Working seriously. If you want more answers, I'll have to direct you to them."

"You want to think hard before you get into it with that Vivian. Oh, she's nice enough but she's a foreigner and she's been upsettin' things ever since she showed up here."

"Lil," Spike said, "Vivian Patin is a very

good woman and she's my friend."

Lil gave a loud "Hmph," and said, "You want to take notice of what people are sayin'. Word has it you're more than friends. When you test the taffy it sticks to your spoon, boy. Never put your spoon in till you're sure you'll want to keep tastin' the same flavor."

"You sure that's what you wanted to say?" Spike asked. "That's one ugly picture you're paintin'."

"Poor Spike," Madge murmured, wincing. "He's comin' to see you so I'll get out of your hair."

She switched the phones through to the room next door.

"I've asked you the same question several times," Cyrus said in a low voice. "Could you give me an answer, please?"

"Are Spike and Vivian safe?" Madge asked.

"You just heard Spike talkin'." A shaft of cold traveled up Cyrus's spine until the hair on his neck prickled. Madge, sweet, kind Madge, couldn't explain exactly what she was suffering over, but she was suffering and it was something to do with him. What if he couldn't put it right? "Of course they're safe."

Madge gave him that look again. *"Of course?"*

"You'd know if they weren't, Madge."

"I'd have known last night if you'd kept your word and called. It was a long night, by the way. I didn't want to call and be a nuisance, but you went off with nothing but a flask of brandy and *you said you'd contact me to keep me up to date.* For all I knew all three of you were lying dead somewhere."

"Knock, knock," Spike said, pushing the door open wider. "You got time to give a man some advice, Father?"

He stopped where he was, neither in nor out of Cyrus's office. The priest faced his assistant with a stunned expression on his face. Madge shook her head once, sharply, and turned the corners of her mouth down.

"I can come back," Spike said. "Looks like you two are real busy."

"Not at all," Madge said and walked past him. "We've covered everything."

A few seconds and the sitting room door closed quietly.

There was no appropriate comment to be made. "I was serious when I offered to come back later."

"It's not necessary. Spike, I told Madge I'd keep her up to speed with what went on after I left to find you and Vivian. Then I forgot."

"Uh-huh," was the best Spike could

manage. Cyrus and Madge would be confused to hear it, but they reminded him of a married couple with the standard communication problems. Her feelings were hurt and she'd convinced herself he didn't care enough to keep her in the forefront of his mind. He'd been broadsided and couldn't understand why she was making a fuss.

"Look," Spike said. "I'm going to take off."

"No, you're not. Perch somewhere." Cyrus's attention switched to a swarm of ruby-throated hummingbirds dive-bombing a feeder outside the window. "Do you understand women, 'cause I need help."

"Um — no man understands women. Some think they do but they're kidding themselves." He thought about that for a second. "Maybe I do understand them a bit better than some, now I think on it. Could be they want us to think they're more mysterious than they really are."

"They're a mystery to me." Cyrus sounded miserable.

"No, they aren't. I'm sure Madge didn't mean to, but she did the woman thing to you. You slipped up just once and she's putting a guilt trip on you. They never get it through their heads, women that is, that men have heavy stuff on their minds and can't always be wondering what the women in their lives want them to think about — or do. It's best not to react when they get upset, 'specially if they cry. They like to cry because they know, even before they're born, that the sight of a woman crying confuses the hell out of us. Sorry, Cyrus. Confuses the heck out of us."

"I said I'd call and let her know when all three of us were safe and on our way back. I should have done that."

"Yeah," Spike said. "Maybe you should have. They make a big deal out of things like that." They did if they felt possessive or responsible for a man.

"So I should do something to get me out of this jam?"

Spike felt sorry for him. "Good idea. Look, give her time to cool down, then go in there and apologize. And when you go out, buy her some flowers for her desk. She'd get a kick out of that. Do it to keep the peace. Women are real strange, Cyrus. I figure what they really want is to believe all a man thinks about is them. All the time. It's not selfish, it's just that they're not as sure of themselves as we are." He didn't like the strange look Cyrus gave him.

"Sometimes they'll say they kinda want this or that. Not that they absolutely must have it, just they kinda want it." He waggled his right hand to demonstrate that he meant women could be wishy-washy. "But if you don't read what they've really got in their minds, watch out. You're supposed to do that. Read their minds. And if you don't show up with the goods, they're gonna be convinced you don't love 'em. They are so complicated that way."

"I didn't realize you were such an expert," Cyrus said.

"Now I've figured out the mystery thing, there isn't so much to know. All their problems come from thinking we're just the same as them, that we think the way they do, and remember the smallest mistake we've made forever — the way they do."

Cyrus loosened his clerical collar and pulled it off.

"I came to see if you had some bright ideas on how to handle a woman," Spike said, "but I guess we're in the same boat. We don't really know, or not enough."

He closed his mouth and looked at Cyrus, wishing he'd had a brain transplant before coming here. They weren't in the same boat. They weren't even on the same ocean.

Cyrus smiled slightly. "Didn't you just tell me you're an expert on women?"

"Yeah, but Vivian's different."

"Ah."

"That was a dumb thing I said to you about the two of us being in the same boat," Spike said. "Our problems are different. Couldn't be more different. You just want peace in the valley with your assistant. I want to know what you think about a marriage between Vivian and me. Could it work? Should I drop the whole thing and back off? Did I do something asinine when I told her I was falling in love with her? That's what I've done."

"I can't make those decisions for you," Cyrus said. "Remember, I'm different from you. Are you falling in love with her?"

Damn, damn, damn.

"Are you?"

"I've already fallen, only I didn't tell her that exactly. I've been stuck on her since I saw her in town with Guy Patin the year before he died. I tried not to let it happen but each time we met it got worse . . . better, I guess."

Cyrus went to a plastic-covered, freestanding wardrobe and unzipped the front to take out a short-sleeved green shirt. "I'd have thought you'd have settled this before getting to the other." He exchanged his black garb for the shirt and a pair of jeans.

401

"Does she love you?"

The man had toned muscles. He was a big, good-looking son of a gun, and without the priest threads he *did* seem as human as Spike felt.

"I think she might," he said. *Before the other?* Cyrus had figured out they made love last night.

"Under the circumstances, this is all good. The two of you need to make sure you share some of the same goals, but don't drag it out too long."

He fastened his belt and said, "Excuse me," chuckling a little. "Should have mentioned I was goin' to change. I think I'll make some home visits."

Dismissed, Spike thought. Maybe he put too much pressure on the friendship. After all, he wasn't a churchgoing man and he probably ought to be if he wanted advice from Cyrus. "It's a good day for that," he said. "I'll see you around."

The intercom buzzed.

Cyrus held up a hand, indicated he wanted Spike to wait and pressed a button on the intercom. "Hey, Madge."

"Message from Bill Green," she said. "He said you'd promised to help on some project at Rosebank this afternoon. He says he understands if you don't have time to come but he thought he'd check."

Cyrus smacked the heel of his hand into his brow. "What is it with me? He only called an hour or so ago and I forgot about it."

"Too much on your mind," Spike said, and flinched. Cyrus would think he was suggesting a preoccupation with Madge.

"Cyrus," Madge said. "I'm sorry for being a bitch."

Cyrus blinked. Spike almost laughed aloud.

"Oh," Madge said. "I'm sorry. I've never said that before."

"Not to worry," Cyrus said. He didn't look sanctimonious, or smug, or as if he'd won a battle. In fact, he smiled and his features softened. The light returned to his eyes.

"Forget everything I said to you," Madge continued. "I don't know what came over me. I'm your employee and you don't owe me explanations about anything."

"Yes, I do," Cyrus said quickly. "I rely on you and I do owe you explanations. We'll talk about ground rules later. I'd better get going."

"I forgot to tell you I had a chat on the phone with Vivian," Madge said. "She and Charlotte want me to consider takin' rooms at their place. The price would be good and it would simplify my life."

Spike saw an extraordinary passage of expressions over Cyrus's features. He might as well not be there because Cyrus had forgotten him. Conflicted seemed a weak description for the struggle Spike watched in the man.

"Cyrus," Madge said, sounding uncertain. "My car will last longer if I don't have to drive as much and I can get rid of a lot of things I won't need. It would bring in some money."

Cyrus closed his eyes and pinched the bridge of his nose. "You need a raise. I'll see what I can do."

"Cyrus," Madge said sharply. "I'm sorry I mentioned moving. I thought you'd be pleased."

"I am pleased. If that's what you'd like to do, go for it," he told Madge. "It would be a good place to live." The priest gritted his teeth and forgot to control what he showed on his face. *Damn it all,* Spike thought. He wants her closer to him but he's scared of it at the same time. Cyrus had once made it clear that he was a man with a man's urges, but that his vocation came first.

What would it take to change Cyrus's priorities? Spike wondered, and thought about Madge.

"Y'know," he said, determined to make Cyrus feel better. "All a woman really wants is her own way. Trouble is, she wants her man to know what she wants without tellin' him."

Her man? Had he just said that to Father Cyrus?

27

Bill had decided the foul-smelling heap of debris left after the ill-fated bonfire should be moved. He said Charlotte and Vivian could see it from any window and every time they got a vehicle from the stables it would depress them. He, Cyrus and Spike would clear the pile and see about laying new grass in the entire area.

Spike, who had decided he could be contacted here as easily as anywhere else, worked with Cyrus and Bill, digging and filling two large wheelbarrows. To their surprise, Dr. Morgan Link from next door had shown up to wheel away one load after another to a spot outside the far end of a drained swimming pool. The pool, with a jungle theme fountain at its center, could be seen from the back terrace outside the south and east wings and would be beautiful when the pump was replaced and the interior cleaned. A job for the future, Vivian had told Spike.

"This stuff stinks," Bill said, rubbing his crewcut, tow-colored hair. "I mean, it *really* stinks."

Cyrus worked steadily. Sweat ran down the sides of his face and his forearms shone with moisture. "Compost," he muttered. "We need one of these at the rectory. Nothing like a good compost heap."

Morgan Link returned, dropped the wheelbarrow he'd just used and took hold of the full one immediately.

"Hey, Doc," Bill said. "Don't push it. Get some of that iced tea Mrs. Patin brought out."

Morgan considered. "Why not." He wore gloves to work in and despite the exertion, he still managed to appear cool. After removing his gloves, he poured four glasses of tea and handed them around. "Getting rid of this pile of junk was a good thought. Those two need something to lift their spirits."

"How's Susan?" Bill asked.

Morgan didn't look at him. "Well, thanks. Very busy with Olympia."

Bill snickered. "Plenty there to keep anyone busy."

Spike didn't like Bill's habit of sexualizing most references to women.

"Doctor," Bill said. "Is it true Charlotte might sell this place to you?"

Spike saw Morgan wonder where Bill had gotten his information. "Well, yes. At least, we hope she'll consider the offer we intend to make later. I don't think I'm talkin' out of school when I say there are big money worries here."

Cyrus kept on digging, throwing spadeful after spadeful into the barrows. Spike felt guilty and set down his glass.

The sun beat down, turning up the temperature notch by notch. Spike shaded his eyes to squint at the sky over roofs where heat waves hovered.

"Why would you want this place?" Bill asked. "In addition to Green Veil, I mean."

"Serenity House," Morgan corrected him. "We're people who understand gratitude. The world has been good to us and when we can, we like to find ways to pay back for that. Seeing these two nice women suffer for things that weren't of their making upsets us. We want to help out."

Spike thought, *bull*, but controlled his mouth.

"Admirable," Cyrus said. When he spoke to you, you expected a look straight in the eye. Instead of looking at Morgan at all, he concentrated on driving his spade into the singed compost.

Bill made no comment at all.

"These grounds show a lot of promise," Morgan continued. "We'll probably incorporate them into ours."

"And the house?" Spike said. Damn, he hated this man's assumption that he'd always get what he wanted.

Morgan frowned deeply. "We're not sure. Could be useful but it would have to be gutted."

Spike was grateful Vivian and Charlotte weren't listening to this. He wiped a forearm over his brow. He was assuming they'd have no interest in the offer for Link and Hurst to buy them out, but perhaps they'd be relieved to get rid of the place.

The kind of feeling that clamped his gut wasn't new, only the reason for it. If Vivian were to leave Rosebank, would that mean she'd drop out of his life? And how would he handle it if she did?

Vivian was nothing like Wendy's mother but he was still raw from the betrayal, and how did he know for sure it wouldn't happen again? How long did it take to trust again once someone had turned on you? He wasn't there yet, he knew that much.

Morgan took off with one of the wheelbarrows again while Cyrus, Bill and Spike kept on digging.

Cyrus spaded some of the compacted material down and started a minilandslide. He stood back and settled the point of his spade on the ground. While Spike watched him, puzzled, the man closed his eyes and crossed himself.

"What?" Spike said.

Shaking his head, Cyrus looked at him silently before continuing to dig.

"Hey, Cyrus," Spike said, leaning on his own spade. "If you weren't having a private vision just then, could ya share the moment?"

"Sometimes it's better to be patient."

Bill caught Spike's eye and raised his brows.

Spike heard an engine and looked over his shoulder. Vivian's green van approached. "Hey," she called through the window. Boa stood on her lap and surveyed the scene. "Didn't anyone tell you guys not to work too hard in the heat?"

"They did," Spike told her. "But it's always hot around here so if we followed that rule, nothing would ever get done. Now, who said that to me?"

"Spike," Cyrus said in a hoarse whisper.

"Yeah." Spike watched Vivian drive the van into the converted stables.

"Come here. Bill, give us a shout when Vivian comes this way."

"What is it?" Bill said, starting toward Cyrus.

"Stay there," Cyrus said. "Just until we head off Vivian."

"I couldn't head that woman off if I tried," Bill said, sounding impatient. He followed in Spike's footsteps until they stood beside Cyrus.

"Oh hell, it can't be." Bill wavered a little, then sat down hard on an upturned apple crate. His face had turned ashen.

"Don't use the shovel," Spike told Cyrus. He got down on his knees and carefully brushed dirt from a dead man's face.

28

"So the shit hit the fan," Susan Hurst said. She didn't share Morgan's careless attitude toward discovering the Patins' gardener dead in a compost heap. "I'd like to have seen that Detective Bonine taking Devol apart. That arrogant bastard deserves it." Spike Devol never took notice of her but she'd lay odds he'd start taking notice if she got him alone.

"It was ugly," Morgan called from the bathroom. The door was open to the bedroom and a haze of steam added to the humidity.

"I bet Devol didn't like looking the fool," she said. She loved this big room with its vast, white spindle bed, the white skin rugs on light wooden floors. The breeze through etched glass jalousies puffed at gauzy draperies. "Did he finally lose it? He can't be made entirely of stone, sugar. There's got to be somethin' real hot under all that stoic stuff."

"He didn't look embarrassed to me," Morgan said, appearing with a towel around his waist and his wet blond hair standing up in spikes. "I think he enjoyed getting a rise out of Bonine. Happens real easily, too. Bonine hates Spike's guts, you can see that."

"Know who I enjoy getting a rise out of?" Susan said in her most sultry, drawling tone.

"All kinds of people, honey," Morgan said. He took off the towel and rubbed at his hair.

She walked behind him and gave his hard butt a slap intended to hurt. "Only you, Morgan, you know that."

He grabbed for her, but the towel was still over his head and she was too fast for him. "You're asking for it," he said.

And I'll get it.

The orange satin camisole and matching G-string she wore were calculated to make her skin look warmer, and they worked. She slipped to the opposite side of the bed where a solid sheet of mirror covered one wall.

Susan didn't like clutter. Large, clear spaces pleased her and she considered her spare decorating style innovative. The only furniture in the bedroom was the bed. Double doors in one wall opened into a closet and dressing room almost as big as the bedroom.

In the mirror, she saw Morgan toss his wet towel into the bathroom. The exercise room she'd had built adjacent to the pool house didn't go to waste. Morgan's muscles rippled as he walked. His height was little more than average but he was tall enough for any woman, man enough for any woman.

And he was all hers.

"Come here," he said.

Susan smiled at him over her shoulder but stayed put. She looked fantastic. She'd gone to New Orleans to have the red highlights in her hair made more obvious and they picked up the light. When she shook her hair with her fingers, it bounced and shone.

"Do I have to come and get you?" Morgan asked.

Susan thought that would be just fine. Her nipples stood out, pushed against the camisole, and the satin was like glossy paint over the perfect shape of her breasts. Between the camisole and the all-but-nothing G-string, her small waist and flat stomach showed to advantage. A tiny triangle of the satin barely covered her pubic hair. Her hips were bigger than she wished they were but Morgan said he liked her ass just the way it was.

Susan did a handstand against the mirror. She visualized how she looked and smiled when she heard Morgan say, "Oh, God," not quite under his breath.

The camisole fell as far as the fullest part of her breasts but no farther.

"Come to bed," he said.

"Make me want to."

"If you don't do this my way, you'll wish you had."

She arced her curvy legs through the air and stood up.

Restraining himself excited Morgan. He liked to feel his cock grow harder until the skin seemed ready to split. Holding back was a sickness in some, a method of overwhelming a woman in others. He was in the second group. He hadn't been a fool to marry Susan, not in any way. Stinking rich, sexed up every second of the day, her preferences changed and he liked the challenge.

Maybe tonight would be one of those when he showed her who was really in control.

"Turn your back to me and bend over," he said. "Grip your toes."

She snickered, almost nervously, and ran her tongue over her lips. While he watched, she slid her hands over her body, pinched her nipples until they pushed out enough to make pegs for her short chemise to hang on.

"You're not doing as you're told." He liked seeing her round butt in the mirror and the way she tensed the cheeks together. "You're wet." She sure was. The tiny bit of satin where her legs came together, grew darker as he looked there.

She covered the area with a hand.

He took a step toward her and she took one back, twirled around and did another handstand against the mirror.

Susan liked kinky. Morgan wasn't averse to it but neither did he like to go to a lot of trouble. Going to his knees, he yanked the orange top until it covered her face, but sure as hell didn't cover her breasts. He liked big breasts and Susan didn't disappoint in that area either. Still on his knees, he sucked one nipple between his teeth and pinched the other.

"Ouch," she said, muffled. "Don't stop. Harder."

He closed his eyes and nipped. He nipped and squeezed till she gave a thin scream and her arms started to give out. "Let me help you," he said, landing her full length on the all-but-white wood floor, with her face in his lap. "You've got a big appetite. Seems like I ought to do something about that."

Her body shone slick with perspiration,

almost as slick as his. She turned over so that her slippery breasts rested on his thighs and, very slowly, closed her shiny pink lips over his penis. So slowly he couldn't keep his butt on his heels. He tipped his head to watch how she sank, millimeter by millimeter down his distended flesh. When she hit bottom, he had to be way in her throat but she could still nuzzle with her chin, and finger his tensed balls and start to move with long, firm strokes.

Morgan caught the camisole by the back seam and ripped it apart. He wanted to see her breasts bounce. "Do us both a favor," he told her. "I like it when you do that."

She didn't do as she was told. Morgan liked a woman to do as she was told now and again. Knowing she wouldn't stop what she was doing to him, slitting his eyes and gritting his teeth, he grabbed her right wrist and pushed her hand beneath the G-string. "Work those fingers," he said. "I want to see you struggle."

Susan stroked herself, pushed her fingers inside her, shuddering and fighting not to lose her hold on him, or her rhythm. And he got the bouncing he wanted.

The bouncing became a wild jiggle. Morgan's rear came up completely because he couldn't hold it down. Her slick skin, the rapid pumping of her hand on her own body, broke his control and he came.

Susan gulped and turned her head, wiped her mouth on his biceps, but she didn't stop dealing with her own business.

"Go for it," he whispered in her ear. "We've got more to do, but I wouldn't want you to miss a thing." Panting, springing into another erection, he pulled her hand away from her body and replaced it with his own. Seconds accomplished the results he wanted and she bucked like a crazed calf.

"Oh, baby," she muttered, falling forward onto a skin rug. "Baby, baby. This beats the hell out of dinner with the Patin women. I'm glad they're otherwise engaged."

Morgan said, "Oh, yeah," and half closed his eyes. *He imagined it was Vivian Patin clamped between his thighs and he slapped her lean bottom until the skin turned pink. She rested her cheek on the rug and her shiny black hair slid forward. Her tongue darted in and out of her mouth in a blatant fuck-me parody.*

He focused on Susan. He hadn't just had his first fantasy about dominating Vivian Patin. It was one of many. Her time would have to come.

"Don't move a muscle," he told his wife, and hopped to his feet. In the bathroom an animal-skin seat topped the white wicker

418

stool Susan used when she sat in front of a mirror to apply makeup. He caught it up and returned with it to the bedroom.

Susan's eyes were closed, but he saw the lashes flicker.

"Plenty of time to sleep later, pussy."

Her limp body amused him. He lifted her and draped her, facedown, over the stool. Then he sat on the floor and gave her the kind of tongue fuck that turned her feet into dangerous weapons. He moved in close, used her breasts as anchors, and sent her all the way to heaven.

"You're incredible." She panted and rested the whole weight of her upper body on his hands and forearms. "Who says married sex can't be a blast?"

"It might not be." He chuckled. "If the married couple weren't us."

"I'm so tired, Morgan. Can I lie down?"

He kissed her rear, one cheek at a time. "Mmm, not quite, my fucking friend." He laughed aloud and so did she. "One more little piece of fun and we'll curl up in that big, white bed."

Rotating her, he pulled open one of the drawers built into the side of the bed and drew out a long length of soft cord.

"No," she whined and tears actually stood out in her eyes. "I'm too tired."

"Stay with me," he said, giving her a quick kiss before pushing her backward over the stool and bending her like a delectable croquet hoop. Working rapidly, he used the cord to tie her wrists and ankles together. "You should see yourself, Susan. I could look at you for a long time. My bedtime snack. I'm gonna eat you all up."

She snickered and said, "You already did but you may kill me if you keep me here long. I'll suffocate." She laughed aloud and looked at herself in the mirror.

Morgan laughed with her. The weight of her breasts had only one way to go and she might have a point. He spread his legs and stood astride her belly.

"Morgan," she said faintly, her lips remaining parted.

"I'm just dealing with the aftermath of shock," he told her. "Death makes a man want to prove he's alive."

"You've proved it," she told him in a firmer voice, but she wasn't asking him to stop. "But do it again, just for the hell of it. Then we've got to talk."

He groaned. "How can you be practical at a time like this?"

"Because I've got a lot of money riding on this venture."

Hanging his head back, he breathed

through his mouth. "And I've just got a heavy load waiting to ride." He rubbed his testicles over her ribs, and guided the distended tip of his penis over her nipples, loving her thin scream and her helpless attempts to get closer to him.

Enough waiting. Although he enjoyed every second of the game.

Holding her shoulders, Morgan thrust inside her. He was renowned for the size of his cock, both its length and thickness, and Susan was stretched out with no way to move and absorb the shock of his entry.

First she shrieked, then she did her best to meet his every stroke. He had to support his weight on his legs and they shook from the effort. She made a keening noise punctuated with soft "oomphs" that made him think she'd take whatever he gave her for as long as he gave it.

Spent.

The reality almost surprised him. He'd ejaculated again and wanted only to lie down, but Susan was still moving beneath him.

"You two are good."

At the sound of Olympia's voice he jumped and Susan gasped. He looked sideways and directly into Olympia's eyes. She lay under the duvet on the bed with her head sticking out, so close he could have touched her.

"Get out," Susan shouted. "You're sick. You were born sick — just like your father. Out. Now."

Olympia's long, blond tresses slithered to fall down the side of the bed. "We've got things to talk about — in private. What better place than here?"

"Private?" Susan said. "You managed to walk in without us seeing you."

"I was already here. In the closet. Mama, I've got to applaud your taste. You married a stud and he knows how to use that wonderful dick."

"Untie me," Susan hissed to Morgan. "Now."

His mind had turned cold and clear, a useful trait he'd had since childhood. Moving with all the comfort he felt in his body, naked or otherwise, he undid the cord and helped Susan to his side. It was to his advantage that she not lose too much face in front of her daughter. Anyway, he kinda liked the game of cat and mouse between the two of them. After all, he was their piece of cheese and there were worse jobs.

Tilting up Susan's chin, he kissed her softly but passionately and while he did so, with Olympia looking on and probably fuming, he caressed his wife's body, stroked her breasts, rolled her nipples between his fingers. She turned toward him and wrapped her arms around his neck. Olympia would have a perfect sideways view of the two of them, naked and pressed together.

Olympia whistled.

Morgan smiled.

Susan looked smug.

The bedclothes rustled and Olympia wriggled free until she could stand up only inches from them.

Naked, but for a white lace ruff around her neck.

Susan went limp in Morgan's arms. She slumped against him and for an instant he thought she would pass out. "Get her out of here," she whispered. "Perverted little whore."

He whispered in her ear, "Name-calling's a mistake. She's obviously got problems we should try to help her with. Don't let her think she's hurt you."

The dig worked. Susan stood straight and thrust out her chest. "You know better than to play games you can't handle," she said to Olympia. "Run along — before we think up a punishment you won't like."

Olympia walked slowly behind Susan and

looped her hands around her mother's waist. Morgan watched the mirrored vision, fascinated at the spectacle of the girl nestling her breasts against Susan's back while she stroked her tummy and thighs.

He smiled reassuringly at Susan. This was something he'd thought could happen, also another of his fantasies, and he didn't want Susan to spoil it.

Susan looked straight at his chest. Her face flushed, then turned deep red when Olympia ground her hips into her mother's rear.

"That's enough," he said to Olympia, although he could have watched them for a long time. "Why not tell us why you really came, then leave us alone. We were getting ready for bed."

Olympia sputtered with laughter. She changed her position and stood between Morgan and Susan, slipped an arm around each of them and engineered a close embrace. Standing on tiptoe, she kissed Morgan, then her mother — on the lips. Susan immediately wiped her mouth with the back of a hand.

Olympia's tongue in Morgan's mouth meant he couldn't watch anymore, but the girl could use her tongue to suck a man all the way to his cock. The latter, resting against Susan's belly, responded and her face darkened with rage.

"I'm upset," Olympia said in a whiny little voice. "I need comfort from my mommy and daddy."

"Stop it," Susan snapped.

Olympia's hand passed from Morgan's back, over his buttocks and between his legs. He tried not to react but thrust against Susan's stomach anyway.

Big tears coursed down Olympia's cheeks. "I can hardly believe the police haven't come for us already," she said.

Morgan looked at her. "Come for us? What are you saying?"

"It's got to be all over the area that Mama's trying to buy Rosebank. She's drawn attention to us. People are bound to start making nasty connections and so are the police."

"Shut the *fuck* up," Susan shouted. "When we need your advice, we'll ask for it."

With difficulty, Morgan disentangled himself from the two women. "I'm going to the bathroom, then I'm going to bed. It's too late for this discussion."

The instant he closed the bathroom door, Susan climbed beneath the covers and pulled the sheet up to her neck. She pretended to be drifting asleep — until the bed sagged and Olympia climbed in with her.

Horrified, Susan tried to push her out, but ended up flat on her back with Olympia holding her wrists down on either side of her head. "Listen to me," Olympia whispered in a harsh voice. "I know all about you and your little *thing on the side*."

The rolling in Susan's stomach made her certain she'd vomit.

"I only want to share him," Olympia whispered. "Half for you and half for me."

"Get out." Susan spat in her face. "Go. Now. You're jealous and you're sick."

"And I'm powerful," Olympia said. "Do this my way and everything will be perfect. Be selfish and I'll make sure your secrets get out — yours and Morgan's. That wouldn't look so good for you, would it?"

29

The Iberia heat had taken charge — again. Bonine and nice Detective Wiley, with all the people who did their special jobs at times like this, and a bevy of foot soldiers, tromped about the grounds. Searchlights whitened the area between the west and south wings.

Errol Bonine hadn't been to any charm schools since the last time Vivian met him. Everyone in the house was a suspect until eliminated, and he said *"eliminated"* as if he meant *dead*.

Apart from a grunt, Gary Legrain hadn't said anything since he'd walked into the Rosebank kitchens, an hour previous. He'd dropped his briefcase on the floor and sat at the kitchen table with his head in his hands.

Seemed best to leave him that way.

Wazoo stood on the counter, cleaning out high cupboards.

Spike drank coffee with Cyrus, who had refused to leave after the grisly discovery of poor Gil's body.

It would have suited Vivian to be alone with Spike. Each time he looked at her she remembered what he'd told her at the bookshop. They had so much to say to each other.

Charlotte drank coffee, gazing straight ahead through the steam and not shifting her attention even when she upended the mug.

"Look at these," Wazoo said, holding an egg cup in one hand and salt and pepper shakers in the other. "Pineapples. Monkeys and pineapples. Mr. Guy Patin, he like they ever'where. Me, I even got monkeys with red eyes lookin' at me in the dark. They painted on the ceiling. Best room I ever had, me."

Spike wasn't sure he liked the idea of painted monkeys on any ceiling.

"Bonine's some kind of animal," Vivian said. Boa stood on a stool by the island with one paw raised and a wounded look in her bright, round eyes. Vivian covered the dog's ears. "A dumb animal, that is."

Jokes weren't going to work this evening. Not for Spike. "Bonine's a pain in the ass," he said.

428

"That's where he's a pain," Cyrus said, frowning and nodding his head. "The man comes around and restates the obvious."

"He said this couldn't be the same killer," Vivian said. "That makes me —"

"Panicky?" Spike suggested. "I don't blame you for being panicky, but don't be just because of what Bonine says. If this wasn't the same killer, I'll be amazed."

"Errol Bonine said these people who leave marks, like the rose and so on, keep doing the same thing to prove it was their . . . kill," Vivian finished in subdued tones.

Spike took her by the hand and seated her in a chair beside Gary. "And the signs were there. Time has passed, remember. Louis was a fresh kill — sorry. There were roses in that compost and one of them was probably deliberately left with Gil's body."

"But the kiss?" Vivian said. "I didn't —"

Spike shook his head slightly, signaling her to drop the topic. He still had a contact or two in Iberia and he'd already tapped one of them for some information on bloodred kisses — fresh or faded.

"Wazoo," Charlotte said. "I don't know how I managed without you. All you do is work. But I'm putting a stop to this day's work now and sending you off to get some relaxation."

"I'm not tired, me. I —"

"That's great, but I want you to stop workin'. I hear there's big doin's at Pappy's Dance Hall. The Swamp Doggies are playing like usual but they've got some group from New Orleans, too. Why don't you go over and have some fun. It's late but things will still be swingin'. Pappy's got a special on the menu, bread pudding Galatoire's style. And the gumbo's supposed to be somethin'."

Still standing on the counter, Wazoo faced the room and stood with her feet apart and her arms thrown wide, as if she were on the stage. She wiggled her fingers and sang out, "Poor crawfish ain't got no show, Frenchmen catch 'em and *gumbo*. Go all 'round the Frenchmen's beds, Don't find nuthin' but crawfish heads." She sidestepped in one direction then back in the other, slapping her feet like a clogger.

Cyrus and Spike clapped in time, but stopped at the disapproving expression on Charlotte's face. "We don't have any cause to celebrate," she said. "Please get down, Wazoo."

"You got it," Wazoo said, and landed nimbly on the kitchen floor. "I got the idea. We all go to Pappy's."

The silence that met her suggestion obviously gave her the message that she should keep her ideas to herself. She shrugged her shoulders up to her ears and backed out of the kitchens.

"Nervous energy," Charlotte said. "She's upset like the rest of us but she doesn't know how to be appropriate."

Cyrus scrubbed at his face. "This is unreal. The police don't have a thing yet. Or if they do, they aren't sayin'."

"I don't believe they've found any significant leads," Spike said. "But it could break real fast. That's the way things go a lot of times."

"No leads and no motives," Vivian said from the table.

"Yes, motives," Spike said at once. "Like I've already suggested, whatever Louis was bringing to you was what he died for. Gary's already said there had to be more in Louis's briefcase than the police found. Whatever's missing killed him. And it'll turn out Gil got in the way of the killer. They're going to place his death around the same time as Louis's."

"Sure of yourself, aren't you." Gary Legrain got up abruptly. He massaged the back of his neck. "And you're probably right. But what could have been worth two lives?"

"I just want whoever did it, caught," Vivian said.

"Don't we all?" Gary's breaking point had worked close to the surface. "I hope it's going to work for you and Charlotte to go into Toussaint tomorrow."

His question was met with silence.

"Louis's will is going to be read."

Spike watched reactions. "In Toussaint? Why?" Not that it was his business.

Everyone looked blank, as if they thought they hadn't really heard what Gary said or, at least, hadn't understood him.

"Louis made the arrangements himself before he died. Of course, I wasn't expecting this to roll around so soon. It'll be in Joe Gable's offices."

The silence continued until Vivian said, "Shouldn't you have told Bonine about this?"

"Louis kept his will private and that was his right and his business. He told me some of the broad strokes, but no details. It was his bank manager who let me know the will was drawn up by Gable — at Guy Patin's suggestion." Exhaustion etched gray shadows into Gary's face. He slid a folded piece of lined yellow paper from his shirt pocket. "It'll happen at ten in the morning. I already told you it would be at Joe Gable's.

The Martin twins will be there, and my-self — these are Louis's wishes — also Mrs. Angelica Doby and Charlotte and Vivian, And there should be a representative of the law agreed on by the majority." He looked at the paper again. "In case action is needed, the note says."

"Why us?" Vivian said suddenly, sharply, as the enormity of Gary's statements sank in. "I don't understand. And what does it mean, *in case action is needed?*"

Gary said, "If it's a problem for you to be there tomorrow, I'll ask for a later date."

"I just don't understand —"

"A later date is a good idea," Gary said. "That would give me time to see what I can find out ahead of time. This is as much of a surprise to me as it is to you."

"When Spike and I came to your office, you were talking to Louis's sons as if you knew all about the will," Vivian said.

"They were telling me the way things would be," Gary said. "They do that a lot. They were making assumptions about the will, which they assumed I had dealt with." The man looked chagrined at that.

"You didn't set them straight," Spike said. He raised a hand. "Don't take any notice of me. I'm talking out loud and not sayin' anythin' important."

"Are the Martins ready to be there?" Charlotte asked.

"Ready, and breathing fire," Gary said.

Vivian's stomach rolled. "And Mrs. Angelica . . ."

"Doby," Gary finished for her. "She says she can make it, but —"

"Tomorrow, then," Vivian said, looking at her mother who nodded agreement. "The sooner it's over, the better. The will's being read in Toussaint so it'll be fine if Spike's the law."

Gary shrugged. His gray eyes showed fatigue and his usually straight shoulders sagged. "If that's agreeable to everyone."

"Is it agreeable to you?" Cyrus said, surprising Vivian.

"Of course," Gary said at once. "Mrs. Doby said she'd leave the choice in my hands."

"Sounds like a majority to me," Cyrus said.

Gary frowned. "The Martins —"

"Excuse me," Vivian said. "I have to go to my room now." She left with Boa under her arm, feeling foolish and impetuous, but desperate to get away from more discussion of dead men, wills and angry sons. She didn't want to listen to what was bound to come soon, either: a discussion

434

about Louis's lady friend.

She climbed the stairs to the second floor. Now that Bill Green had taken charge of organizing work parties to get some rooms ready for guests, Vivian felt fresh hope, but Mama's pride seemed dented. She'd already found an opportunity to point out more repairs that must be made. And the subject of money, how little they had and that supplies would be costly, had come up.

Vivian's room looked out over the driveway and she already loved the view from her windows of the tree-lined sweep to the circular turnaround in front of the house. The only things to see out there now were the lights of official vehicles coming and going. What she was glad she couldn't actually see were the men, women and dogs searching.

In the morning, her favorite time to watch the light change over cultivated timber in one direction and flat rice fields and craw-fish farms in another, the renewed activity at Rosebank would be obvious and she dreaded that.

She dreaded the strange idea of being present for the reading of Louis's will just as much. When she and Spike had been with the Charbonnets on their riverboat, Jack hadn't been subtle about the Martin boys' reputations.

A thorough cleaning and some fresh white paint on the millwork were all Vivian had thought necessary to make her room perfect. It was the same one she'd used whenever she came to Rosebank. Uncle Guy had found the ebony four-poster with a carved canopy at a palace auction in Thailand.

A person had no excuse for boredom with a bed like that. She'd been finding new surprises in the carvings since she was a girl.

Boa licked her face and she squeezed the little dog until she wriggled free and took up her place on the embroidered tangerine-colored bedspread.

Vivian closed the shutters and the drapes. Light from colored-glass wall sconces in the shapes of scantily clad men and women didn't give much more than a muted glow.

She put on a nightie and bathrobe and prepared to go across the hall to shower.

From overhead came a bumping noise, as if something were being slid over an uneven wooden floor.

Vivian wrapped her robe more tightly around her. Apart from shaking out drapes covering the furniture, the rooms on the third floor hadn't been touched yet. No one slept in any of them, or had any reason to be up there.

She listened but heard nothing now.

A hot shower and a good night's sleep would settle her down. No, they wouldn't. Who was she trying to fool? She might feel a bit more relaxed but how could anyone settle down in this house?

Squeaking started, the sound of wood against wood? This time it didn't seem to come from the floorboards but it was definitely from the same room. And it went on for a couple of minutes, then stopped. Only seconds passed before it happened again, then again, and again. Vivian held her shaking hands beneath her crossed arms.

Someone must already be working up there. She'd been out a good deal during the day and with all the commotion over poor Gil, Mama had forgotten to mention it.

Working into the night?

Everyone who had offered help had work of their own to do, so why not at night? But tonight, when Bill had only announced his plans that morning?

Downstairs there were plenty of people who would help her check things out. And she'd feel like a jumpy fool for asking.

Murder had been committed in the grounds. But not today and the killer wouldn't be crazy enough to hang around.

Killers were always crazy at some level.

Take your shower and go to sleep.

Boa growled. Her lips were pulled back from her teeth and she stared fixedly upward.

Tiny hairs rose on Vivian's spine and her neck prickled. At the back of a drawer in a chest beside the bed lay a gun which had once belonged to David Patin. Her dad had taught Vivian how to load and shoot it, and made sure she knew to keep the ammunition separate from the weapon.

She'd never loaded it since the last time her father took her to a shooting range. But she hadn't forgotten how. She retrieved the gun and smoothly slid a clip home.

This is nuts. Her slippers were under the bed and she felt around with her left foot to find them.

Shivers shot up her leg and she pulled her foot back. People she trusted were downstairs. *"I think I heard something on the third floor and I'm afraid someone's under my bed."* Then they'd all think she was a wimp and maybe she was — just a bit of a wimp, anyway — but she'd deny that one to the death.

Eww, wrong connection.

Boa sat up, her ears moving back and

forth, and let out a single, pretty subdued bark. The sweet little thing must be picking up bad vibes from Vivian.

What she should really do was get over this need to withdraw and go back downstairs.

And if she did, it wouldn't be because she thought she could change the habits of a lifetime but because she was a chicken.

The squeaking started again, in short bursts this time. Vivian cocked her head, smiled, and began to chuckle. What would be so unusual about some sort of critters moving into available quarters?

She felt ridiculous. The exterminators would be called in the morning. Meanwhile, maybe she could scare the things to silence.

With her feet firmly inserted in her slippers and the gun in the pocket of her robe, Vivian left her room, retraced her steps to the staircase and climbed to the next floor. Boa hopped up behind her, snuffling. The dust was still bad in much of the house and there wasn't enough staff to keep up with it.

Most of the corridor lights were burned out. Vivian counted doors until she arrived at the room she thought was probably above hers.

The door stood partly open. She reached inside and felt around for the light switch.

Apart from clicks, moving it up and down produced nothing. A musty odor made her nostrils flare. Somehow the entire house had to be aired regularly.

Vivian stepped through the opening and cried out. She'd stubbed her toe on a brass doorstop that had been used to keep the door open. She bent to pick up the stop and smiled, couldn't help it. The episode began to feel like frames from an Alfred Hitchcock movie.

Inside the room, faint moonlight washed a bed, another four-poster with a wooden canopy, a freestanding wardrobe and white-draped shapes of other pieces of furniture. Vivian gave the door a push, opening it wide, and did her best to look around. She heard nothing, which probably meant any unwanted furry friends had skittered away, but she'd need to check for droppings. A lamp stood on a draped table in front of the window and she hurried to see if it had a working bulb.

It didn't.

At least she'd put her irrational fears to rest and could go and get some sleep.

When she turned back from the windows, a shadowy shape confronted Vivian. A woman in loose, pale clothes, her face indistinguishable in the almost darkness.

Vivian screamed. She screamed, and jumped so violently her legs buckled and she landed on her knees. With her face covered, she bent over, waiting for her pounding heart to explode. Breathing through her mouth, she struggled to calm down, and to find the courage to look up again.

Inch by inch she raised her face. The woman facing her across the room also knelt.

"Damn," she muttered. "Damn, damn, damn." The woman she saw was herself reflected in a mirror on the wardrobe door, a door which had swung open.

Shaky and exasperated, she stumbled to her feet. Time to get out of here and stop playing games with her own head.

What had caused the wardrobe door to open?

It happened. End of story.

But now she had to pass the open wardrobe to get to the door. One deep breath and she started forward, watching her reflection in the mirror as she went.

She reached the wardrobe.

"*Vivian?*" Her name, whispered, rushed to envelop her. Muscles in her neck and throat bunched and beat out a pulse of their own. She couldn't breathe.

The wardrobe door slammed shut. Vivian saw the looming outline of a man, his arms outstretched, his fingers reaching. She went for the gun in her pocket and wrenched it out. Her face flashed hot while the rest of her body felt frozen.

She threw herself at him and tried to shout for help, but her throat wouldn't move. He was no apparition. When she collided with him he was so solid she would have fallen back if he hadn't grasped her, one big hand like iron closing on her right wrist, the other around her waist, holding her in an embrace that stole her breath. He shook her wrist, worked his fingers over hers to release them from the gun. She closed her mind to the pain and locked her joints in place.

He cursed softly, pried her fingers apart, and she heard the gun hit the floor and slide.

She had feet.

Vivian kicked, sending pains through her toes inside soft slippers. And she used her left hand, her fingernails. He might kill her, but he'd be carrying enough of her DNA to convict him for it, and his would be on her.

"*Vivian.*" He shook her.

His face would never look the same when she'd finished with it.

"Vivian, it's Spike!"

30

Of all the crazy . . . She was scared out of her wits. Okay, he could buy that but what would make her mistake him for someone dangerous? Vivian had behaved as if she didn't know who he was.

"I'm not going to hurt you," he told her through his teeth. Now she was showing signs of collapsing, dammit. "Hold on, I don't want to trip. Where are the lights?" He lifted her and sat her on the edge of the bed. Dust didn't fly up in clouds so he guessed he should be grateful for that. "Now, stay put until you calm down."

He could hear her breath dragging in and out of her lungs.

"You don't even know me well enough to figure out who I am when you touch me — or hear my voice — or smell me, dammit? I could pick out your scent through manure."

She actually giggled.

"Pleased I can amuse you," he said. "Or is all this because you don't trust me? Is that it? What we've had is all about sex, but you aren't sure I'm not a killer playing both sides of the fence? If that's the case —"

"Shut up while you're *not* ahead, you idiot."

Okay, okay, he'd calm down and give her a chance to get over the shock she'd apparently suffered.

"How could you ask me questions like you just did?" she said. "You don't know why I acted like that. You're horrible. Mean. You say whatever comes into your head as long as it makes you feel like a big man."

Spike stood in front of her and shoved his hands into his pockets. When she was composed enough he'd point out that discovering she had a gun on him hadn't been a great sensation either.

"All about sex? You should be so lucky. You're supposed to be my friend." Her voice caught and she hunched over. "What are you doing sneaking around up here, anyway? On this floor? Are the others going to come here, too, for some reason? Boy, are you going to have some explaining to do. You thought it was funny to scare me out of my skin, didn't you?"

"That's enough, Vivian." She was shocked and he must not let his temper take over. "You left abruptly and it worried me. The rest of them aren't coming up here because they have no idea you aren't in your room. And they think I've gone outside to talk with Bonine and Wiley."

"You *lied* to my mother?"

"I didn't tell the truth to anyone in that kitchen. All I wanted to do was make sure you were okay. Know why?"

"No," she said.

"Want to know why?"

"No."

"That does it. You know damn well why. I don't know how you feel about me because you haven't told me. Maybe all this is giving me the answer now. I tried not to love you, but I couldn't do a thing about it in the end. I told you that today. Know what I'm spending my time worrying about now?"

"No." She sounded subdued.

"Your neighbors want to buy you out. If they do, you have nothing to keep you around here and you'll probably leave. That's what's making holes in my stomach."

"You make me so mad," she told him.

"How did you find me up here?"

"I make *you* mad? By . . . Boa was on her way down from this floor. I didn't have to be a rocket scientist to figure out you might be here, since you weren't in your room."

"How do you know which is my room?"

"Damn the woman," he said to the ceiling. "I try to come to her, to comfort her, and she gives *me* the third degree."

"How do you know what my feelings are? You think we'll sell Rosebank and I'll leave without looking back. Thanks for the confidence, but you're right, of course. I'm only ever interested in a little sex without strings." She got off the bed and before he guessed what she might do, slapped his face with an open hand — and started to cry.

Nothing he did or said was right.

She cried harder and turned her back on him.

Spike shut the door and stood behind her. He put his arms around her and kissed the back of her neck. She had been trembling when he touched her, now she shook even more.

"Neither of us is makin' any sense," he said quietly. "But we could. We could make a lot of sense right now."

"You're angry. You're trying not to sound it, but you are."

Yes, he was. Angry that the two of them could seem to have come so far only to arrive at an episode like this.

"You're not denying it." Vivian tried to pull his arms away but he wouldn't let her go. "You shouldn't be here."

"Why?"

"Because . . . You know why."

He knew. "Because you're afraid I'll try to make love to you?"

Once more she plucked at his hands. Her breasts rose and fell against his forearms. "That's what you want, isn't it?" she said. "You want some of that sex you think is the only reason I like being around you. Damn you, Spike Devol."

"And you don't want it?" He felt sweat on his forehead and between his shoulder blades. His heart pounded. And he was hot, inside and out.

"I never took you for a violent man, but I feel it in you now."

He closed his eyes. "I'm not violent. I've never been called that until now."

Vivian reached behind her and drove her fingertips into his thighs. "How wide is the line between passion and violence? There isn't a line, is there? It's all the same. Even

447

so-called gentle loving is a kind of violent thing."

Spike kissed the side of her neck this time, took nips at her skin and the lobe of her ear. Her crying turned into a shaky sighing, and the heat within him made his vision red behind his eyelids.

Her fingertips ran down until her hands were flat on his thighs, slid around as far as she could reach and urged him closer. Some things were beyond a man's control. Right now there was nothing he could do about his erection, the fact that she'd feel it all too well, or the truth that pounded through his body. Violence? Maybe. Passion? Oh, yeah.

"Spike."

Spinning her around, he brought his mouth down hard on hers. They shifted their faces, searching and reaching. He held her head and held her face wherever he wanted it to allow his entry into her mouth, and he made a demand with every tongue thrust.

"I'm goin' to take you," he told her. "Say you don't want it, now, or I'll believe we both want the same thing."

Vivian didn't tell him no, she couldn't. She had to have him. And she didn't attempt to unbutton his shirt but tore at it in-

448

stead. He pulled her hands away and trapped her against the bed with his legs. The shirt came off over his head and she kissed his broad, naked chest before he'd had time to free his arms.

He dragged off his belt.

She unzipped his pants and knew one reason why he was desperate to get out of his clothes. His penis strained and had to hurt in the confinement.

The fingers of one of his hands settling around her neck and the sensation that he locked his elbow and held her off weakened her knees. With his other hand he tore her robe open, and ripped her nightie from neck to hem.

Vivian wanted to cry out but once again had no voice. And she wanted him, all of him, and at his wildness she began to pulse between her legs, to burn, and tried to press her thighs together.

"Tell me," he said, confusing her. "Tell me if you feel anything for me." He didn't stop moving and was naked now. *"Tell me."*

"I do," she said. He'd bent over her breasts and pulled on a nipple with his lips and teeth. She grabbed his hair in both hands and held him against her. Spike covered her other breast and squeezed.

With his face buried beneath her jaw, he

slid his hands around her hips, gripped her bottom, parting the cheeks, and threw her backwards on the bed. She fell and he fell on top of her.

Spike's hands were all over her. Her flesh ached from her center, the desperation of her response to him spreading in searing waves.

He drove himself into her and she cried out from the invasion, the stretching, the shock. His sobs brought a lump to her throat. Again and again he withdrew until she thought he would leave her, but each time he penetrated her afresh, drove her farther across the bed.

Thin moonlight showed her his features, drawn as if in agony.

"I'm afraid," she whispered, raising her hips to meet his. "I'm afraid we won't be able to keep what we have."

He pounded into her and her climax broke. Almost at once, Spike cried out with his own release. They jerked together, clutching at as much as they could feel of each other.

Spike grew heavy and still atop her. He gathered her into his arms and held her tightly. "I can't believe you're here with me. But you are and we can keep whatever we want badly enough."

"Stay with me," she whispered. "I want you to stay a part of me."

He kissed her lips softly, licked the smooth skin just inside softly. "I want to be a part of you, *cher*. Whatever happens, you'll be with me for as long as I live."

"I'm frightened for us, Spike. But I love you."

31

The fifth day

"What's up?" Jilly Gable asked Madge. "You sick or somethin'? You look miserable."

Madge's feelings had always shown on her face. "Guess we all have glum days. This town doesn't feel like itself to me." She'd lost interest in her biscuits and gravy.

Jilly poured a cup of coffee for herself and joined Madge at her table. "Short rush this morning," she said. They were alone in the shop. Her blond-streaked brown hair had been cut to her shoulders and looked pretty and as superthick as it really was. "I know what you mean about things feelin' different. Everyone seems down. It's got to be the deaths at Rosebank upsettin' all of us."

As long as Madge could recall, Jilly had worn her hair almost to her waist. Even the idea of her getting it cut off could be another depressing thought. Beautiful as always, her gray-green eyes were a bit sad, Madge thought, and her pale coffee skin didn't glow the same as usual.

"Do you think that's what it is?" Jilly said.

"Yes. A couple more miles and Rosebank would be in St. Martin Parish. Green Veil, or Serenity House, or whatever they call it — same thing. And the folks there are pretty much a part of this town now. They change it because they're different. Not Charlotte and Vivian, really, but —"

"The other ones," Jilly finished for her. "You don't like them?"

Madge looked over her shoulder, half expecting to find Cyrus waiting for her answer, a frown on his face. She cleared her throat. "I don't know them but they have an attitude. They came to the rectory, y'know. Lil was the only one there and they started right in on how they thought the Patins needed help and they wanted to be the ones to help them. Then, the next thing we find out, Susan's talking about buying Rosebank. And I don't think that's because they want to help at all. I think they want the property, period."

Jilly nodded. "Whenever someone mentions Lil, I think about Oribel Scully and the awful Fuglies sculpture on the rectory lawn. No wonder that woman ended up in a sanitarium. She never could have been right but she sure ran that rectory tight."

"Hoo mama," Madge said, looking into the distance and seeing how things used to be when Oribel was around. "I heard Marc Girard's sister, Amy, intervened for leniency on Oribel's daughter's kidnapping sentence. That takes a big heart — tryin' to help a woman who did you wrong. We've had a couple of bad years around here."

"Now we got more trouble," Jilly said, deep shadows in her eyes.

Madge didn't like making her friend feel even worse by dragging up the past.

"I know Marc and Reb would like Amy to let them know where she is and come home, but she says she isn't ready," Jilly said. "Maybe she will be one day."

She drank coffee and smiled at Madge. "Wouldn't you like to know what Susan Hurst and Dr. Morgan are up to? I hear about how there's been a lot of renovation done to the house, but if I ask a question about specifics, I get turned off. It's almost like the people who worked out there were told not to talk about it."

"Yes, but who keeps a tight lip around here, even if they're told to?" Madge laughed. "Every secret that's told at eight in the morning is being talked about all over town by nine."

"Maybe they were paid to zip their lips," Jilly suggested.

Madge shivered. "That Olympia gives me the creeps. It's as if she doesn't hear anything that's said to her unless it's about Miss Southern Belle or how good she looks. Kinda like a talkin' doll." She looked at her watch. "I'm worried about Cyrus. He takes everybody's troubles on his shoulders. Young Wally Hibbs and that critter of his were over at the rectory first thing, just sittin' in Cyrus's office and not sayin' a thing. Cyrus is preoccupied all the time and he isn't eatin' enough. Between supportin' Spike and Vivian and tryin' to help out there, and dealin' with the altar society tryin' to get rid of poor Oribel's Fuglies, he hardly has any time. If he doesn't hurry up gettin' here, he won't even have time for coffee before heading over to Joe's."

"What's going on over there, anyway?" Jilly asked. "Joe mentioned having a big meeting this morning, but then he clammed up. Now you say Cyrus is going."

"Joe's reading a will." She'd better not reveal anything more. "Cyrus isn't going to hear the reading, just be around if he's needed."

Jilly frowned. "Why? You can't say stuff like that, then leave me hangin'."

"I shouldn't say. Cyrus would be mad."

"You really care what will or won't make Cyrus mad, don't you?" Jilly screwed up her face. "Forget that crack. He's your boss and you need to follow his wishes. After I close up this evenin' I'm takin' a box of his favorites over to the rectory. Marzipan tarts, best of the best at All Tarted Up, Flakiest Pastry in Town as far as he's concerned. I'll do up a few of those meat pies he loves, too. I need another batch so I can give a couple to Gaston. I swear those pies are the reason that dog's so smart. Even Reb says so now. Maybe I'll run some over to Rosebank for that little Boa girl. Yep, I'll just do that."

Madge knew Jilly had been half in love with Spike and that they'd both been down when things didn't work out. But trust Jilly to put all that aside and be nice to Vivian.

The pastry shop bell rang and Cyrus came in. One look at his face and Madge knew he wouldn't make her feel any better. "It's nine," she told him. "Lil said you didn't eat breakfast so you'd better have something here quickly before you have to go."

A smile transformed his handsome face. "What would I do without you taking care of me?" he said. "See how useless I am, Jilly?

456

Madge has to make sure I don't starve."

Jilly was on her feet and going behind the counter. Without looking at Cyrus she said, "I never met a man who didn't like to pretend he was helpless so he could get a woman to look after him. Guess you're like the rest. Human." Still, she didn't look at him, but Madge did and she regretted the vague confusion she saw in his face.

"Jilly's joshin' you, Cyrus. She knows you're capable of doin' everything for yourself."

He turned and gave her his full attention. "Am I?" he said, so serious she couldn't help but notice, yet again, how the corners of his mouth flipped up naturally. "I really don't think I am, Miz Madge. In fact, I think I'd be lost without you. It's a foolish man who doesn't give credit where it's due." He turned away again, sharply, and ordered scrambled eggs and toast.

Madge blinked back tears. She was the luckiest woman in the world to know Cyrus Payne, to work for him and to call him her friend.

The shop bell jangled again, this time because Ellie Byron and Bill Green came in. "You're here, Father Cyrus," Ellie said, panting as if she'd run all the way from Hungry Eyes. "Bill thought you would be.

Can I talk to you, please?"

Madge watched the way Cyrus patted her arm and smiled at her so that her tensed face relaxed. "Shall we sit in the window?" he asked.

"Well —"

"I've got to get over to Rosebank," Bill said. "Homer Devol and I are starting work on decorating guest rooms, so those ladies can get going with their renting. Homer can't get away for more than a couple of hours here and there so we've got to make the best of every minute." Bill wore an old pair of overalls and a green check shirt, open at the neck. A nice-looking man, Madge thought, even if he wouldn't stick out in a crowd — surely not if Cyrus were there.

"Thanks for knowing where Cyrus might be," Ellie said, and gave Bill a wave as he left. "He's a good man," she said.

"Coffee for you, Ellie?" Jilly called. "I always think it's nice to be waited on instead of waiting — now and again, anyway." She chuckled.

"Yes, please." Ellie raised her face to look at Cyrus. "I'd be happy talking with both you and Madge. If you didn't trust her, she wouldn't be where she is. That's good enough for me."

Once they were all seated, Ellie laced her

fingers on top of the table and leaned forward. She looked from Madge to Cyrus. "This wasn't a good idea. Runnin' to you. In fact it's a terrible idea. I probably imagined things and I'd best just run along back and get the shop opened."

Cyrus didn't have a strong measure of Ellie because she was a loner who kept pretty much to herself. What he did know about her, he liked. He'd learned to trust his instincts and his instincts told him this woman was good, if a little unhappy.

She braced her hands on the edge of the table, about to get up.

"I'm always like that when I've made up my mind to do something but then had too long to think about it," Madge said. "I feel silly. Usually I'm convinced my logic is faulty."

"Nothing you say will go beyond this table," Cyrus said. "Unless you want it to, of course."

"That's just it. I don't know what I want because I'm not sure I've got anything to say in the first place. I can be vague and misplace things. That's probably what I've done now."

Jilly brought Ellie's coffee, Cyrus's eggs and toast, and a plate of pastries. She left immediately. Jilly was one of those perfect

459

hosts who sensed when she should or shouldn't hover.

"Hang in here with us," Cyrus said to Ellie. "If there's something troubling you and we can help, then let us help. But I don't want to press you."

He stuck his fork into a large marzipan tart, conveniently set down to face him by Jilly, and transferred it to his plate — on top of the toast. "Marzipan tarts are my favorite things. I'll just have to do another lap around St. Cécil's grounds to work this off."

"Like you need to," Madge said. "Some things aren't fair. All I have to do is look at one of those things and I get another inch on my hips."

Cyrus smiled at her. He saw absolutely no sign of Madge putting on weight. "Have one of these pastries, Ellie." He wished he knew more about her. Perhaps he'd get closer to her now that she'd come to him for help.

"No, thank you," she said. "Do you ever put things where you're sure you'll re-member, then forget where that was?"

Madge laughed aloud and Cyrus chuckled himself. "I think Madge is laughing at me," he said. "She has one or two names she uses for that particular foible in her boss."

"So you do it." Ellie pointed at him but

appeared deeply involved in her own thoughts. "Oh, thank you for making me feel better. I won't trouble you any longer."

"Ellie," Madge said. "You're looking for any way to chicken out. You didn't go to Bill Green asking where he thought Cyrus might be just because you hoped Cyrus would admit he has brain farts."

Cyrus looked at her sharply. Ellie was already laughing and gripping her sides but Madge's face wore a wary expression since she was clearly waiting to see which way he'd go with his response.

She delighted him over and over again — and surprised him. "Is that so?" he asked her. "Nice turn of phrase. I'm writing a homily about making decisions based on whims. Brain farts could be useful."

"No, they couldn't," Madge said, trying not to laugh with the rest of them.

"I think someone's been getting into the shop at night and going through the books," Ellie said abruptly. She snatched up a Danish, looked at it, wrinkled her nose and put it down again.

Cyrus wasn't quite sure what to say.

"But it could be that I put things in different order than I think I do, though." She turned pink. "My stock is real big. It wouldn't be so hard to put books in the wrong place."

"Have you always done this?" Cyrus asked, knowing the answer.

"*No.*"Ellie's response was fierce. "I've always been able to go right to a book without . . ." She snapped her mouth shut and carefully took a nut from the top of the Danish. After examining all sides, she put it in her mouth and chewed.

"Is this your first bookshop?" Cyrus asked, and felt guilty for prying.

"No."

"How many times has this happened?" Madge asked.

"Three nights in a row. I was going to tell Spike but I feel so stupid. How do you prove a thing like this?"

With difficulty, Cyrus thought. "Couldn't it be that customers do it? Folks have a way of doing what's most convenient. Just the other day I was in the grocery store lookin' at the fruit — not a pretty sight, by the way. Anyway, this lady pushes her cart up in front of the pomegranates and gets all excited. Seems she really likes pomegranates. So she bags some up, then takes a box of cereal and a piece of fish, all rolled up in paper where it had been specially cut for her, and leaves 'em on the apples. They were next to the pomegranates. She smiled at me like that was the most normal thing in the world and said she couldn't afford all of it so she'd have the pomegranates instead of *those*. And off she goes."

Ellie squinted at him and waited, like there was something else to say.

"And?" Madge said. He could always rely on Madge to help him out if he lost the gist of something he was saying.

"Ah, careless people," he said with a sense of relief when he saw the route back to the point he'd set out to make. "They don't like to be bothered with goin' back and puttin' things they don't want where they came from."

Both women stared at him until he took his fork to the tart and concentrated on eating every tender crumb before moving on to his eggs.

Ellie cleared her throat. She ignored her coffee and drank water instead. "You're probably right. It's just that there's a kind of pattern. Each book I find out of place is on art of some kind, or it was until this morning. Oh, and I forgot to say it's never new books, only the secondhand and collectible ones. Rare clocks of the world. Valuable pottery and glass, the kind that sells for millions at auction. Paintings. Several of those. Tapestry. Rugs. Chinese antiques. On and on like that until this morning."

Cyrus thought it best to let her talk on her own timetable.

"This morning it was different," she whispered, glancing over her shoulder. "It made me think there could be something sinister about it. They didn't put the books back."

"Yes," Cyrus said.

"That is, if I didn't just miss them there last night and a customer had been considering buying one of them then changed his mind."

"Like the fish," Cyrus said.

"*Not* like the fish," Madge told him. "There weren't any pomegranates, just books and more books."

"Floor plans of well-known local houses," Ellie said. "It was published years ago by someone who lived in these parts. Left open on the table. And a county map. I ran to get Bill and see what he thought. I was lucky to catch him when he was leaving. It was his idea for me to ask you what to do, since I didn't want to make a fool of myself with Spike."

Cyrus kept the thought that there was probably nothing mysterious about any of this to himself. "Spike always says he wishes people would speak up when something doesn't sit right. Reckons it would save a lot of trouble down the road."

Ellie reached into the tote she'd been carrying and pulled out an oversized paperback book. "I guess this was what shook me." She set it on the table facing Madge and Cyrus. "And I'm only foolin' myself if I keep pretending I'm not scared. I never like much attention, but this is different again."

He read the title aloud: "*Tender Weapons, Living by the Knife.*"

Ellie took a picture of herself from her pocket. "This was between the pages," she said. "On top of an open page. There's a picture of an autopsy on a woman there. She was stabbed to death."

Ellie had been photographed by a lake and wearing a swimsuit. She smiled into the sunlight. And in the shadowy soft cleavage at the inner margin of her left breast, a hole had been made.

If Cyrus had to guess, he'd say that hole was made by the tip of a very sharp, very pointed knife. Someone had pushed it through the paper and turned it — around and around.

"And you thought *this* was somethin' you could ignore?" Cyrus said.

32

Charlotte and Vivian sat in Joe Gable's comfortable leather-and-brass waiting room. The only thing missing from the men's-club atmosphere was the smell of cigars.

Vivian felt anything but comfortable, and her mother looked ready for flight.

"I can't imagine why we're here, Mama," Vivian said, "but we don't have a thing to be awkward about."

"Of course you're right. I kind of wonder if there could be something Louis had of Guy's that he wanted to make sure we got back. They were close."

"Maybe."

Joe Gable's assistant had a desk right outside Joe's office door. Probably in her fifties, the lady had the kind of manner that put people at ease, or would put them at ease if that were possible. She smiled in their direction again and Vivian smiled back.

"We shouldn't have got here so early," Charlotte whispered. "Makes it look like we're eager or something."

Secretly, Vivian agreed, but there was no point in leaving and coming back at this point. "Settle down, Mama. There's only fifteen minutes to go. The others are bound to be here soon."

"You think Joe's already in his office?" Charlotte said.

"Joe's in," the assistant said before Vivian could try to give an answer she didn't know. "He's one of those early birds. Looks like someone else is coming now."

Spike passed the window, opened the door and came in. He looked only at Vivian.

Her heart bounced, and her stomach turned, and her legs wouldn't hold her if she tried to stand up, of that she was sure.

"Morning ladies," he said. "Guess we're all here for the same purpose."

"These are for you, Spike," the woman at the desk said, and gave him a brown sack with handles. "Ellie gave them to Joe."

"Books for the store," Spike said. "Thanks. I can't keep 'em in stock."

He sat beside Vivian on a low couch covered with soft, saddle-colored leather. "How are you, *cher?*"

She inclined her head ever so slightly in her mother's direction and shot him a warning stare. "I'm just fine, thank you, Spike. How're you?"

Spike made short, meaningful work of looking her over before staring into her eyes as if they were the only two people in the room. He slid sideways toward her and if he thought he was being subtle, he was so wrong. "Darlin'," he murmured into her ear, "if you don't think your mama knows about us, you are tellin' yourself stories. Or is it that you don't want to acknowledge there's anything between us?"

She rested her fingertips on his mouth, couldn't stop herself, and watched his lips part a fraction. "I hadn't thought about it," she told him. "I should have. Yes, I'm proud to have people know we're real good friends."

He wiggled his eyebrows and his so-blue eyes twinkled. "Real good friends, huh?"

"Hush," she told him, pretending to frown.

Charlotte said, "Mmm, mmm, this is one of those times when I'd like to scrunch up my nose and be somewhere else. Of course, you two have different feelings. You don't mind bein' here, but you'd probably as soon be somewhere private, together."

One of Spike's long, blunt fingers stroked up Vivian's cheekbone and tucked her hair behind her ear. His grin was far too satisfied. Vivian looked at her hands in her lap. "D'you think something terrible might happen here?" she asked him. "It isn't usual to have a member of the law present at these times."

"Nothing terrible is going to happen." His smile had disappeared. "I'll make sure of that."

The door opened again. Slammed open would be closer to the truth. "Friggin' hick towns," George Martin said to his brother Edward as they blew in. Beautifully cut dark suits had replaced the light ones they'd worn the last time Vivian saw them. "Did you see the greasy overalls on the guy at the hotel? Servin' breakfast in dirty work duds and wearin' a friggin' baseball cap."

Vivian couldn't imagine this duo staying at the Majestic, but she recognized Gator's description so they had obviously been there.

"Mornin', gentlemen," Spike said, getting to his feet. "Not the best of times."

George and Edward smiled at each other. Edward said, "Could be. Our father wouldn't want any mopin' around. He was all business and so are we. Sooner this is dealt with and we're on our way back to N'awlins, the better." Both of them ignored the hand Spike offered and didn't as much as acknowledge the presence of Charlotte and Vivian.

Vivian said "Good morning" anyway and earned herself grunts.

George Martin addressed Spike. "We don't know why someone like you would be here and you're not wanted. Clear out." His broken nose bone whitened.

Vivian was ready to defend and almost on her feet when Spike landed her back on the sofa and said, "I'm here at your late father's request. End of subject."

George came a step closer and opened his mouth to say more to Spike, but changed his mind and turned to Joe's assistant instead. "Mr. Gable in his office?" he asked.

"Yes sir." The lady at the desk sounded cool.

"We'll go on in, then," he said. "My brother and I, bein' the deceased's only kin, would like a word with his lawyer first."

Vivian thought, *I just bet you would.*

"Mr. Gable has his ways of doing things. Promptly at ten he'll be ready to start. He won't see anyone first."

"Did you hear what I said to you?" George asked, looming over the woman.

"We are the deceased's sons, his only living kin, and we want some words with his lawyer — alone and before the rest of these people go in there. Not that we know what they're doin' here anyways."

"Ditto," Vivian heard her mother mutter under her breath.

"So," Edward said to the woman. "We suggest you get your . . . Just trot in there and be quick about it."

"Hold it right there," Spike said, going to stand between the Martin twins and their victim. "I've got instructions on how this will go. Why not sit down quietly until we're told we can go in?"

Vivian could tell how much his restraint cost him.

"When we start taking orders from some small-town —"

"Mornin'." Gary Legrain came in with a pretty woman who could be Creole. Her features were fine and her skin the palest of polished gold. "I had to wait for Mrs. Angelica Doby to get here. I hope we haven't kept you waiting." Angelica might be in her late thirties but not a line showed on her face. Louis Martin could pick out beautiful women.

A chorus of "Mornin'" went up but the Martins didn't say a word. They only had eyes for the newcomer. Dressed in conservatively cut black clothes, she remained standing at Gary's side.

"You've got some explainin' to do, Legrain," Edward Martin said. "You never said a word about the will being anywhere but in our own offices."

"Wouldn't have been appropriate," Gary said, still looking tired. "And I didn't know where it was until Mr. Gable contacted me to be present today."

"Louis told you he had a will somewhere else and you didn't tell us?" Edward said.

"He was my boss," Gary said. "And he instructed me not to discuss his arrangements, not with anyone. He named you specifically. What would you have done?"

"Let it go for now," George said to Edward. "We'll take up the loyalty issue later."

Vivian said to Charlotte, very quietly, "Agatha Christie, eat your heart out. Maybe we could work all this into a new board game."

Charlotte didn't move a facial muscle when she muttered, "I've got the name already. *Who Gets The Money?*"

Vivian laughed and got herself center stage with an audience which, apart from Spike, looked irritated.

Joe opened his door. He was still shrug-

472

ging into his dark suit jacket and looked up at them with his almost painfully blue eyes. "Good morning. Come on in. I think we've got plenty of seats." His curly black hair just touched the collar of his white shirt. Joe Gable was . . . noticeable. Noticeable was an understatement.

Joe looked past all of them as they gathered in front of him. "Hey, Cyrus." He grinned and Vivian had the thought that some lucky woman would make it easy for him to catch her one day — when he was ready.

"I'll be making myself comfortable out here," Cyrus said. He wore his collar and his hair looked as if he'd been using it to exercise his fingers. The result was another "wow." The man and the mystery. Temptation out of reach maybe?

"Why the fuck is a priest here?" George Martin said. Even the appalled silence that followed didn't stop him. "There's nothing for you here. No weeping, sentimental survivors for you to comfort. No handouts in the offing. So why not run along?"

Cyrus's face lost all expression but the color along his cheekbones rose.

"*Pig,*" Vivian said, shocking herself. "Well, you are a pig, George Martin. You don't get it that there isn't anyone here who gives a darn about you and your brother and what you think. Apologize to Father Payne now."

"Vivian," Cyrus said quietly. "People are all different. There's only one like you, that's for sure. Let it go. We'll talk later."

"Like myself," Spike said with a cold fury he didn't try to hide, "Father Payne was asked to come along today."

Joe, as if trying to maintain his professional position but sensing he could have a big problem on his hands — like a fight — said, "Take your seats in my office, please. Thanks for coming, Cyrus. Joan will pour you some coffee."

The Martins strode past Joe, followed by Gary and Mrs. Doby. Vivian put a hand on her mother's shoulder and made to follow but Angelica Doby turned back. "Father," she said, her husky voice quite clear, "I'd surely appreciate it if you'd come along and sit with me. It would be a comfort."

"Christ!" Edward Martin spun around, his eyes rolling. "Does this have to turn into a melodrama? You heard what we said, lady, no *priests*."

Vivian looked at Spike who shook his head slowly.

"If Mrs. Doby would like Father present, he'll be present," Joe said. "Louis Martin provided for that eventuality, the same way he asked for a law officer to be here."

Angelica Doby went to Cyrus and tucked her hand under his arm.

"God," Edward Martin said, "let's get this three-ring circus on the road. We need to get back to the Quarter and sanity."

Charlotte and Vivian chuckled at the ridiculousness of the statement, but composed themselves quickly and moved forward to sit in Joe's cherry-paneled office.

As soon as Joe had closed the door and taken his place behind his desk Edward Martin said, "My brother and I request that we hear our father's will on our own. Our privacy should be put first. Whatever these people need to hear can be dealt with at another time."

Joe's lips parted a fraction. His face let everyone know he either didn't understand or didn't believe the request.

"You'll have folks warnin' off our prospective clients," Gary said to Edward. "They'll think you didn't go to law school after all. The deceased makes the rules here."

"We won't forget this," Edward said to him, leaning forward. "Changes will have to be made."

Gary shrugged. He looked like a man who

no longer cared about much.

Reading from an open file on his desk, Joe started into the standard preliminaries. The room grew still.

"Now, to the details," Joe said. "To Gary Legrain, the man I wish had been my son, I leave fifty-one percent of my corporation."

Vivian caught Gary's blank, shocked reaction, and the venom in the Martins' eyes.

"To my son, Edward Martin, I leave fifteen percent of my corporation. To my son, George Martin, I leave fifteen percent of my corporation."

Not a soul breathed in that room until George, his nose a bone-white ridge now, said, "Over my dead body, Legrain," and stood up, his fists balled.

Spike said, "Sit down, please, sir."

"Best let me get through this," Joe told the man. "So, going on. To Angelica Doby who nursed my wife as if she were her own kin and who has continued to keep my home and life running smoothly, I bequeath my New Orleans house and its furnishings."

"My God," George shouted. "That house is worth a fortune. And I hope 'furnishings' doesn't include artwork — not that we won't fight this and win. The old man couldn't have been in his right mind." He stared at Mrs. Doby. "Housekeeper? I bet.

Never saw her before in my life."

Edward had a restraining hand on his brother's arm when Gary said, "Mrs. Doby worked for your parents for ten years. How many of the household staff can you name, or would even recognize?"

"Shee-it," George said. "We got bettah things to do than hang around the folks. You grow and you move on."

"But you still expect to be taken care of," Gary said.

Angelica Doby was the one whose reaction interested Spike most. She bowed her head but he could see tears falling steadily onto the skirt of her dress. Cyrus rubbed her back and bent over her, talking softly.

"Touchin'," George said. "You nursed the wife, then moved on to lookin' after the husband. Disgustin'."

The woman raised her face and said with dignity, "You, sir, are disgustin'. I am a married woman and I love my husband. I loved Mr. Martin, too, but in a different way, because he appreciated everything a person did for him and never treated people who worked for him badly. Oh, he had his temper and he may have cared a bit too much about money, but that didn't matter to me."

"Mrs. Doby's disabled husband has lived

with her at Louis Martin's house for years," Cyrus said.

"Moving right along," Joe said, rustling a sheet of Louis's will. "$500,000 goes to Vivian Patin. I owe her."

Vivian frowned. She flushed and Spike saw her trying to figure out why Louis had thought he owed her something. For himself, Spike felt queasy. The figure was big and knowing Vivian, she'd build on it, build herself into a rich woman. And she'd take her mother with her. Rosebank would get off the ground very nicely.

With Charlotte's hand in hers, Vivian looked at her and a spark of cautious expectation passed between them.

"What did he owe you for?" Edward asked her nastily.

"There are a number of bequests to individuals and charities," Joe said, sounding like a man gasping toward the finish line. "I've made copies of these so you can all follow along."

He read off a list of gifts to people who had worked for Louis, and to a modest number of charities.

Joe paused to drink some water and clear his throat. "When we're done here, I hope you'll all join me in a drink to toast Louis Martin. He thought long and hard about this will and made some difficult decisions."

"Never mind toasts," Edward said. "By my figuring, there's still about nineteen or so percent unaccounted for."

Joe met Spike's eye with the faintest of signals. Something was coming and the attorney anticipated trouble.

"You're good with numbers," Joe said to Edward. "Louis Martin's final bequest is to Mrs. Charlotte Patin of whom he says, "Apart from my wife, Charlotte is the only woman I have ever loved and my love for her has only brought her pain. The remainder of my assets, both corporate and personal, go to Charlotte Patin."

33

Louis Martin had left a letter for Charlotte, and Joe Gable had found a private moment in the melee following the reading to give the envelope to her. She'd tucked it into her purse at once.

If she went to her room to read what Louis had written, Vivian, who knew Charlotte had the letter, would be justified in having suspicions about her mother.

"Mama," Vivian said, "I could use a glass of tea, how about you?"

"Sure." Brandy held more appeal but she'd only get sleepy. "Let's sit outside on the little gallery over the front door." The sound of distant hammering reached her. "Maybe not. Bill and Homer are working somewhere up there."

"If we sit out front on the terrace we should be able to avoid any of Bonine's people who happen along," Vivian said.

They'd parked in the driveway and gone into Rosebank through the front door. They didn't want to run into Errol Bonine.

"Mama, maybe you should go to bed. You look tired and I'm sure you want time on your own." Charlotte did look tired, but Vivian thought the letter she'd been given was responsible for that and Mama would want to read it alone.

"I'm going to sit out there and let you pour the tea. Thea would make a couple of sandwiches for us — or Wazoo if you can catch her. Viv, hiring that woman is the best whim I ever followed."

Vivian thought so, too, but lowered her voice to say, "You do know she's been seein' clients here?"

"I know," Charlotte said and smirked. "I'm thinkin' of lettin' her hang a special sign outside, how about that? How many hotels do you know of with resident mediums, or whatever Wazoo says she is?"

"You're wicked, you just love irritating the neighbors."

"That's something else we need to talk about," Charlotte said. "I know I'm probably irrational, but I'm suspicious of those people and they're starting to get in our way. Shoo, away with you and hurry back."

Charlotte loved to look at her daughter. Today she wore a long, gauzy dress, red poppies on a white ground, and as she walked toward the kitchen the skirt flipped out around her calves.

There couldn't be any benefit in waiting to look at the letter. Vivian would see her reading it and could ask questions if she liked. The dilemma was not knowing what Louis could possibly have had to write to her about.

Apart from my wife, Charlotte is the only woman I have ever loved.

How could he have loved her? They were acquaintances, maybe even friends in a way, but he'd never acted as other than a gentleman with her.

She would have to refuse the bequest and so would Vivian. With Gary getting fifty-one percent of the corporation, the Martin twins had no way of taking control from him. Anyway, what had been given to her wouldn't just go to the Martins, it would have to be divided up and . . . She just wanted to run this house as a hotel, with Vivian, and forget the headaches they faced now.

Arranging two white wood chaises in the shade of a bank of verbena laden with clusters of red berries, she made sure they

482

would be invisible unless someone came looking.

She sat down on the edge of a chaise and turned Louis's envelope over and over. He'd written her name there by hand.

Right now, at this very minute, those Martin twins would be talking about her as if she'd been their father's mistress. The horror of being speculated about like that sickened her.

When she opened the envelope her hands shook so badly she ripped the flap in several places.

The letter was handwritten, too.

Dear Charlotte:
You're reading this letter. That means I'm dead and there's no other way to put things right other than through the will you've heard read.

I have been wrong. More than wrong, but a man can want something so badly he'll do just about anything to get it. Or in my case, to try to get it. I know because that's what I did. Only I didn't plan for what happened, not for David to die.

Charlotte dropped the letter in her lap. Her vision blurred and when it cleared a little, her eyes settled on an ant with a long, skinny body. It scuttled along a crack in the concrete at the base of a wall, carrying some small prize to wherever its home happened to be.

She blinked, then continued to read:

I had nothing to do with the money trouble David got himself into. He talked to me about most things because we were friends. David was my friend, even though I hated him at the same time. He didn't tell me how bad things were until he'd borrowed from the wrong people and was in too deep to get out on his own.

That's when he came to me and I bailed him out.

He'd made some mistakes. We all do. But his were big, Charlotte, and he made them worse by trying impossible schemes. Times hadn't been so easy and business was down. You'll know about that.

What you don't know is he put money into a Mexican land venture — a lot of money because he needed a big return — and the whole project disappeared. It never existed in the first place. A scam, that's what it turned out to be and the people running it got away clean, and rich.

David had expected to start getting his payoffs from the venture within weeks, he counted on that and when he saw there wouldn't be any, his back was to the wall. He went through everything trying to catch up or at least keep going.

In the end he sold things, including the jewelry you had from your family. He said it was very old and although you didn't wear it, you wanted it for Vivian because she would. Only, Vivian wouldn't take it so you decided you'd leave it to her for when you'd gone.

He told me everything, and he was suffering, but he still had what I wanted. He had you.

"Mama?"

Charlotte heard Vivian's voice and felt her own tears at the same time. She hadn't known she'd been crying.

"Mama?"

"You brought the tea," Charlotte said, wiping at her face with the back of a hand and making much of pushing herself back into the chaise and putting her feet up. She held the letter tightly. "Thank you, *cher.*"

"Wazoo made sandwiches with soft shell

crab and some of that sauce they sell at Pappy's Dance Hall," Vivian said. She put the tray she carried on the other chaise, pulled a small iron table between the two and transferred the tray to it. "Have some tea, please."

Charlotte shook her head, no.

Vivian didn't press her, she didn't say anything. Instead she sat quietly in the other chaise.

I knew I probably didn't have a chance with you, but I thought if David looked bad enough for you to want comfort, I could be that comfort.

Charlotte grasped at the neck of her dress as if she'd breathe more easily somehow. Why hadn't David come to her and explained? They'd always shared everything.

I thought when David told you what he'd done, you'd leave him. What I couldn't stand was to think of him with you, and deceiving you when you should have had everything.

David came to me and I dealt with his debts. He had to be real careful but he started inching back very slowly.

That's when I called in the loan. I went

to Chez Charlotte on that night he died. It was after everything had closed. He invited me over himself. Said he'd made you go home to get some sleep but he was staying to get a jump on a catering job for the following day. He wanted to thank me for all I'd done for him. So I said I thought I'd stop by and have a drink with him.

He was the one who did the drinking. I talked and apologized and said how I had to have the money back. David just drank and said he understood.

When I left he was still drinking and I'd told him he should come clean to you. He said he would. Even when I was walking away I hated what I'd done and knew I'd most likely never have a chance with you. I could have helped him without any strings. He'd have paid me back in the end and I didn't need the money.

David was distraught, confused, and he was drunk. They said the fire was an accident and probably happened because David was drinking and passed out. But you know that.

I fell in love with you the day you first walked into my office. You never gave me any reason to hope and I never gave you a hint of what I felt. You don't deserve what I've done to you.

You and Vivian can't put what I've left you back into the corporation, I've made sure of that. So please admit that I owe you both more than money can pay for and do what would make David happy, make a new life.

With respect and love, neither of which you want from me,
Louis Martin

Charlotte cried and found she didn't want to stop. She sobbed. Poor, dear, foolish David.

"Mama, don't," Vivian said. "Whatever it says there, it's all in the past because the man's dead. If he was carrying some sort of torch for you then got murdered, it's so sad, but you mustn't think you're responsible for not being able to make him happier when he was alive."

Vivian, the logical one, only this time she had no idea what she was talking about. "I don't care anything for Louis Martin and I'm *glad* he's dead." She looked at Vivian and regretted shocking her. "I've got to think about it, but I think I should probably let you read this."

"Whatever you want," Vivian said while the sound of heavy feet got their attention.

Errol Bonine and Frank Wiley walked along the terrace toward them.

"I can't talk to them now," Charlotte said, desperate to get away.

"Good afternoon," Bonine said, and actually smiled. "We won't keep you long but there are one or two questions we'd like to ask."

Frank Wiley just smiled and said nothing. Despite the smile, Charlotte didn't think he was a happy man.

"This isn't a good time," Vivian said.

"You know what's going on around here as well as I do," Bonine said. "We can do this nicely, or we'll do it any way that gets the job done."

"How dare you," Vivian said with feeling.

"Hush," Charlotte told Vivian gently. "I'm fine. I'm feelin' better already." She wondered if she'd ever feel better.

"What made you feel bad, Miz Patin?" Bonine asked.

"Nothing," she said and knew the answer was lame.

"We could come back, Errol," Frank Wiley said. "There's no —"

"I make those decisions. We got an anonymous tip today, about a woman called Ellie Byron. You know her?"

Vivian said "Yes" before Charlotte even remembered where she'd seen Ellie Byron.

"Right answer," Bonine said. "We don't have a lot to say about her, in fact we don't have anything. Just wanted you to know we got the tip. You might want to stay away from that one because it sounds like she's sayin' things that don't make for no friend of yours."

Charlotte looked at Vivian who showed no more understanding of Bonine's comments than Charlotte had.

"Um, you don't need to worry your heads about that though," Wiley said, ignoring the fury in his partner's eyes. "Just something we're following up. These tips are a dime a dozen and the caller is probably someone with a grudge against Miz Patin."

"You heard what I told you," Bonine said directly to Charlotte and Vivian. "Now, when did Louis Martin tell you what he intended to do in his will?"

"He didn't." Charlotte sat up and put her feet on the ground. "What do you mean?"

Bonine held up both palms as if he was trying to calm her down. "Now, now, no need to overreact. We just wondered when you first found out that you were a major beneficiary of Mr. Martin's will. Must have been a great comfort to you, what with all your money troubles."

Vivian was on her feet. "I suppose if we were that kind of opportunistic people, *and* we'd known Louis was going to die, we might have been comforted. We aren't that kind of people and we had no way of knowing Louis would be murdered."

"You knew he was coming here that day." Bonine looked suddenly startled. "Frank, what are you thinking of? Take Miz Vivian away, please. I want to talk to her mother alone."

The sound of Vivian's cold laughter hurt Charlotte. "Why?" Vivian said. "Because you're hopin' we'll tell different stories if you separate us? Do you think there's anybody who doesn't know that's routine procedure? Except you, evidently."

Bonine's face turned its angry red.

"Seems like you have all kinds of mythical sources," Vivian continued. "And so-called tips that make no sense. And how do you know about Louis's will? Tell me that. You weren't there when it was read."

"We weren't, but others were," Bonine said with a sneer. "And you'd better hope we don't find out you did know about the provisions before the murder. Gary Legrain may have big problems, too."

My blackmailer is a moron. Yet again he is on the phone, ordering me about.

"Something has changed everything," he says.

I have no patience left. I shall tell him the complete truth. "Perhaps the picture has changed for you. For me it is the same. How do you stop a freight train with no brakes on a steep slope? If it's going downhill, with difficulty, friend. If it's already at the bottom, forget it."

He is crying in my ear, this man who ordered death to suit his plans. Crying because "something has changed everything."

"What changes," I say to him, "is that I can't take the time I prefer to take. Playing, planning the end, these are my pleasures, but you've taken them away from me. Not your fault, you say? It was your fault from the first words you spoke to me. Kill, you said, or else. So I killed and must kill again."

He still hopes to change my mind.

"Stop arguing, friend. Suffering takes all of your energy and you are going to suffer. You will pay for what I've done."

34

Homer, Wendy and Vivian, clustered on the old dock looking down, Spike assumed, at his boat. The boat he'd had four years and barely got to use himself. Homer took it around to make bayou deliveries.

He guessed this was just about the least likely scene he'd expected to walk in on today. Although, given that everything else that had come his way lately had knocked him off his horse, why should he be surprised at anything?

Wendy held Vivian's hand and bounced from foot to foot like she did when she was happy, and she looked up into Vivian's face as if she'd seen the sun.

Huh, well, he could relate to that feeling, but he'd be lying to himself if he pretended it didn't scare him to death to think of his little girl getting her heart all wrapped around a new mother figure, only to have it cut away if things didn't work out.

Homer separated himself from the woman and the little girl, touching the brim of his hat with that old-world courtliness of his, before turning to head for the house.

Spike stepped back from the kitchen window. He'd expected to walk in and find Homer and Wendy having an early dinner like they usually did when he wasn't going to be home. He'd even looked forward to having some of whatever they were eating. There were no signs that food had been cooked or eaten recently.

By the time Homer opened the screen door and walked in, Spike nestled a cold beer in his hand on top of the table, while he pored over the town's only newspaper.

"Hey, there, boy," Homer said, but as cheerful as it sounded on the surface, Spike sensed a touch of caution in his father's voice. "Thought you was on duty all evenin'. Oh, good, you got the books. We can finish Claude's order. I'm thinkin' of takin' a box of these along when I do the deliveries. See if I can work up a few impulse buys." He looked pleased with the idea.

"Sounds good." Spike rustled today's copy of the single section *Toussaint Trumpet*. "Things are quiet at the station. I decided to come home and look in on the two of you. Damn paper. Last week's news. Who gives a rat's ass if Ozaire Dupre catered the barbecue at the VFW."

"You do," Homer said. "Not that you've got time to be messin' with that stuff now. But you're right. That's old news. And you'd think that thing would be full of speculation about the murders."

"In the *Toussaint Trumpet*? Homer, you are losin' it. News, pure and simple, is what they advertise and the *pure* means purely Toussaint."

Homer shrugged. "Maybe that's as it should be."

"Yeah." Spike's mouth might be at work inside the house but three-quarters of his mind hovered around Vivian and Wendy. "I see we've got company."

Homer's head was in the refrigerator and he took his time pulling out eggs, sausage and a bunch of greens. "You talkin' about Miz Vivian?"

"Don't try the vague number on me, Homer. When did Vivian get here?"

"Hour or so ago."

"*An hour or so?* She must have come lookin' for me. Why didn't you get in touch?"

"We were talkin'. I was about to make contact when I walked in and found you here — pretendin' you was readin' the paper and drinkin' a beer, and not givin' a damn, when you're so doggone muddled up and mad you don't know which end is up."

Spike scooted his chair back and propped his feet on the table. His father gave them a meaningful stare, which Spike ignored. "Ever think you're gettin' too smart for your own good?" he said. "For your information I *was* reading the paper and drinkin' a beer, and I don't give a damn about anything."

"If you was a boy, I'd take the soap to your mouth." Homer snapped the words out. "You know I hate lyin', 'specially when there ain't no reason for it. You're in love with that girl out there and scared sick about it. What I don't understand is why. Sure, I've had my doubts, but only because I thought people might say you were a gold digger, but since the lady don't have no gold, just the prospects, I'm over it. You'd better get over it before you do something real dumb and lose her."

Spike let his head hang back and closed his eyes. "You've said more in a few minutes than I've heard you say in a decade. I thought you weren't keen on the idea of me havin' Vivian in my life. Now it's all the other way, but I guess women shouldn't be the only ones who can change their minds."

What would Homer have to say if he found out about the will reading that morning? Spike figured the answer could go either way because the old man had fallen under Vivian's spell. He liked her and it was written all over him. Too bad it couldn't be as simple as liking someone. They'd have to see.

"You do love her, don't you?" Homer said, breaking eggs in a bowl and taking up a wire whisk.

"That's personal."

"So you don't. Just as well. She's too much of a lady for you. Pity though when our little Wendy's taken a shine to her and they're getting along so well." He inclined his head to the windows. "They all right out there."

Spike welcomed the excuse to look and jumped when he did. Instead of being on the dock, Vivian and Wendy had walked most of the way back to the house and sat on a picnic table with their feet on a bench. They faced the bayou.

"Well?" Homer said.

"They look just fine to me." His belly contracted, and so did muscles in his throat. Close, side-by-side, Vivian and Wendy chattered; he could hear the faint murmur of it through the windows. And he hadn't seen

Wendy alone and at ease with a woman since . . . it hadn't happened with her mother, who left when Wendy was a baby, so he guessed he'd never really seen it. She leaned against Vivian and he saw the child's back move when she giggled. Vivian reached across to anchor the rubber band more securely around one of Wendy's braids.

"You don't look fine," Homer said.

Spike turned to him. "You're readin' too much into every word I say."

"You're probably right. And I'm probably readin' too much into all the words you're not sayin', too. Boy, I've spent some time around Vivian and Miz Charlotte and they don't come any better than those two women."

Rather than agree, which was all he could do with any honesty, Spike let his eyes wander past his father and bought time.

"What d'you think?" Homer said. "Should I make enough of this for four?"

"Hold dinner up for a bit," Spike told him and managed a smile. "Until I find out if Vivian wants to stay."

Homer cracked a rare grin.

Opening and closing the screen quietly, Spike stepped out onto the gallery. He regretted the idea of interrupting the intimacy between Vivian and Wendy, but his own selfish need to be with Vivian would win out and he knew it. Slowly, still stepping quietly, he walked toward the picnic table.

"Maybe she needs a baby brother," he heard Vivian say, and couldn't make himself keep on walking. "Children get lonely on their own sometimes."

"I know," Wendy said.

He couldn't believe Vivian would say something like that to Wendy.

"Well, I'll just have to talk to the right people about it and see what we can do."

Spike ran a hand under the back of his collar and his fingers came away damp. He wasn't hot, or he hadn't been. She meant she'd talk to him about having children? He didn't just smile, he grinned so wide his eyes began to close. He guessed he had nothing to worry about after all. Coming into all that money wasn't going to change her. In fact, it might be making her more sure of what she really wanted and if that was him, he might be able to stop being scared he'd lose her.

He went closer and said, "Hi, ladies. Nice afternoon."

Wendy swung around to look at him, and so did Vivian.

And his blood stopped moving through his veins, or so it felt. They were both so startlingly lovely with the sun at their backs and shining on their hair and lightly tanned skin.

Vivian said, "Hi," and smiled softly.

"Hi, Daddy," Wendy said, grinning and squirming around until her legs were all the way on the top of the table. "Look what Vivian brought for me."

He took a closer look. Wendy held the kind of doll he'd looked at in some New Orleans stores but never felt right about spending the money to buy. Golden curls, a sweet, pouty face, perfect hands and feet and covered up in frills and soft blankets. Now that he was near the table, he could see a wicker doll buggy, also decked out with ribbons and bows, standing on the other side.

"Isn't she a sweetie?" Wendy said, rocking the doll. "Vivian said it's a good thing I have trucks and trains and a two-wheeler bike, and that I play soccer and softball, but she says it's okay if I have general — gener —"

"Gender," Vivian said with a laugh.

"Yes." Wendy nodded seriously. "Gender toys."

"Gender-specific toys," Vivian suggested.

"Yep, those. It's all right if I have those, too, because boys and girls play with all kinds of toys now. I'm calling her Rosebud.

Will you come see what Boa did while we weren't lookin'?"

God help him, he was freezing up again and there was no reason. It was stupid to resent someone doing a nice thing for your kid. He followed Wendy's instructions and the direction in which she pointed until he could look down on Boa who had curled herself at the bottom of the buggy and appeared fast asleep.

"Look," Wendy said, leaping down and sliding her Rosebud under the covers in the buggy. "Boa likes this." She pushed the buggy over the grass, looking back every few seconds to make sure he was watching.

"You're furious," Vivian muttered. "It's written all over you. Oh, Spike, please don't spoil this for her. She's so happy and it made me happy to do it."

"I would never do anything to hurt her," he said and heard how stiff he sounded. "When she smiles like that I almost want to cry. It's a blessing and a curse to love so deeply." Let her wonder if he was only referring to his feelings for the child. A glance into her face let him know that's exactly what she was wondering about.

"I don't know what came over me," Vivian said. "Mama and I have had some strange dealings since we left you in

Toussaint. I need to talk to you about them but only when we can be alone. But when I had Mama settled in bed and resting, I wanted to see you more than anything else in the world so I set off. Then I thought about Wendy and I felt like I got bigger inside, like I wanted to show her I care about her and to make her happy."

She'd forgotten to swallow and coughed. The humidity had risen and her gauzy dress stuck to her back. "On the way here I remembered that shop that's in one of the houses before you get to Rosebank. It's called Comforts, and two sisters live there. They do well out of their shop because everything is either top quality, or top quality and handmade. The doll is really something and all dressed by hand, and the buggy was made by a local craftsperson. Love at first sight," she said. "I either had to get it for Wendy or for me, and I'm a bit old."

"I've never been able to give her things like that," Spike said.

Vivian was quiet, watching him.

"It doesn't hurt for her to have it, though. I'm glad. Thank you very much."

"Oh, please don't be so formal and stiff," Vivian said, her eyes filled with an appeal. "I don't have any children to buy things for."

"And now you've come into a little fortune, you can indulge an outlet that appeals to you. Money changes things."

Her mouth snapped shut and she turned her face from him.

Smart, Devol, damn your proud hide. "Forget I said that. Old habits die hard and I come from people who believe the man does the providin'."

"You can provide for me anytime."

He stared at her and couldn't close his mouth.

"I mean —"

"What do you mean, Vivian?"

"Nothin', just that I'm not some leftover suffragette. But I'll tell you one thing. The days are gone when a man has to get all bent out of shape because a woman believes she should do her share. And also, Mama and I haven't made up our minds about a thing. We're in a difficult position and I need your help. Your help, Spike, not the frozen shoulder because you come to stupid conclusions. I need you to be my friend — I don't trust anyone to be there for me the way I need you. If you want to throw all that back in my face, say so and I'll disappear."

Spike followed Wendy's progress with the buggy and its dolly, doggy load. "I'll be your friend for as long as you want me. It's only going to get sticky, really, really sticky, if you try to forget what we've had going between us. I want to take that dress off you right now and get you naked. I'm in the mood to love you tender, and love you wild. I'm not sure I can step back from that."

"*Spike.*"

"The thought sickens you."

"The thought makes me wet, you idiot, and distracted and if you touched my breasts right now, the pain would be incredible, and beautiful. Now stop it. You're taking advantage of my weaknesses."

He smiled, loving the gift she had for putting sexy stuff into words.

"I guess you don't have any personal reactions you could put into words for me," Vivian said. "Just so I don't feel like a forward woman working with an unwilling, maybe, participant."

"I don't have your way with words," he said, and noted that Wendy had started back. "But my buns ache, and my balls. Whoops, maybe I should have said testicles. My penis is downright painful and my gut is like a rock. My whole body is like a rock. And, if it's okay to mention it, you fill my heart and soul and I think, scary as it is, that it's love that does the filling."

"This is the strangest love affair, Spike."

"Oh, yeah? You admit we're having a love

affair. That's real progress."

She snorted. "I've already admitted it. More or less. Now hush up."

"Yes, ma'am. We've got work to do. I think I'm gonna need to enlist Cyrus — and even Madge. She's a gutsy girl and she'll do what has to be done. A lot happened today and I need to make decisions. By the way, Homer's smitten with you. Wants you to stay to dinner. How do you feel about that?"

"Hungry."

"I take it you're acceptin'. Good. Later when Homer's about his business and Wendy's asleep in bed, can we try to work some things through while I tell you my plan?"

"Wouldn't miss it. I'm stickin' to you, Spike. I need you. I think it's a good idea to bring in Cyrus — and Madge — but first we should go over a few things on our own."

He barely stopped himself from saying *Oh, yeah*. Wendy arrived, her cheeks pink and her eyes filled with light. "Boa's still asleep. He just wants to be a baby. Vivian said how it's difficult for kids to be all on their own so she's gonna see what she can do about it."

Spike held his breath.

"She's gonna talk to someone and see about getting a boy doll brother for Rosebud."

35

Olympia Hurst, Ellie decided, needed to be set free from her mother's ambitions. Ellie glanced at her from behind the counter and caught her, once again, lost in thought. When Olympia wasn't trying to either shock or impress, her expression became vulnerable.

When he'd dropped in earlier, poor Bill had made the mistake of sitting with her again and trying to make conversation, but whatever he'd said hadn't pleased Olympia and she had moved to another table. He'd shrugged at Ellie and grinned before making a fast getaway into the square.

Ellie couldn't help but wonder if an unhealthy rivalry between Susan Hurst and her daughter, at least on Olympia's side, accounted for Olympia's petulance around Bill. Susan and Bill seemed comfortable together — some said too comfortable although Ellie didn't see anything wrong with their friendship. But it could be that Olympia had a girlish crush on him and felt her mother was in the way.

For more than an hour Olympia had sat alone, staring. No other customers remained in the shop.

"Can I top up your coffee?" Ellie asked.

Olympia breathed deep through her nose and slowly focused. Before she had time to slap on another pout, an absent smile turned a beautiful face into pure sunshine.

Ellie took a coffeepot to Olympia's table. "Little more?" she said.

"Oh, no, thanks." Olympia checked her watch. "It's past closing time anyway. I'd better let you lock up."

Digging, she produced some bills from the pocket of her shorts and got up. "I need to pay for these, too." She had picked up several magazines, all of them on interiors and furniture.

"You're interested in houses?" Ellie said.

"I want to be an interior designer," she said. "If I ever get to do anything *I* want." The pout reappeared and the girl fiddled with the ends of her hair while she waited for her change.

Ellie locked the shop door behind Olympia and sighed at the prospect of another evening alone. Recently her old fear of the dark had come back and she dreaded the hours awake in her bed, straining to hear noises. During the day, logic told her the rustling, the sounds of breathing, were only in her head. Logic lost its comforting power once night fell and the time came to turn out the lights.

All day, since the discovery she'd made that morning, Ellie had kept busy and tried not to think about the sick way she'd been threatened. The memory of the defaced photo brought her fist to her chest. Muscles in her thighs ached.

Even before she became a teenager, Ellie had decided marriage wasn't for her but lately she'd wondered if it would be nice to have someone special in her life. Maybe. As long as special meant good. Ellie had seen too much of the other.

She pushed her hair away from her damp forehead. The shop was cool, but waking up bad feelings and breaking into a sweat went together.

Balanced on a shelf between jars of loose candies, a little radio filled some of the silence with Dr. John singing "Such A Night." Ellie sang along while she washed Olympia's mug and moved food into the refrigerator.

Outside, a deep quiet had fallen on the

deserted square as businesses closed. Joe Gable's army-green Jeep still stood under a twisted sycamore tree growing from a space in the sidewalk. Dust coated the vehicle.

Ellie liked Joe. He came in for coffee each day and she found she looked for him and his friendly banter. Joe went home to the place he shared with Jilly, but one day, and probably soon, he was bound to marry someone and move out.

Every female head turned at the sight of him. He would never look at her in that way, even if she wanted him to.

She didn't want him to, not really, he was just a convenient man to daydream about.

Her final duty before going up to the apartment was to replace unshelved books left on the table and chairs at the back of the store.

One day she'd have proper sliding ladders in the shop, but until she could afford them, a sturdy aluminum stepladder did the job and got plenty of use each day.

A slow, pinching roll in the pit of her stomach restarted the sweating. "Silly, silly," she told herself aloud. How long should it take a grown woman to bring baseless fears under control? Would she ever stop being scared of dark places where she couldn't see all the corners clearly? Places like the cup-

510

board she'd been into many hundreds of times for the ladder?

Spike told her she'd done the right thing in reporting about the books and the photo. He'd kept them to see if any fingerprints could be what he called "lifted" and told her to be "aware" at all times.

Aware? Every muscle in her body hurt from tension. She was never comfortable unless her back was where no one could get behind her.

The unshelved books could wait until the morning. And why not consider taking Ozaire up on his offer to find her a puppy? He said he had connections and could get her a good price on a German shepherd.

Under other circumstances she'd get a mutt, a stray, but a well-trained guard dog was what she had in mind. She smiled, thinking she felt more enthusiastic about most dogs than she did about almost all men.

Joe's Jeep passed the shop. Ellie had neither seen nor heard it until she glanced out and saw the rear of the vehicle passing out of sight.

The buildings at this end of the square emptied out entirely at night, except for when Bill was in the cottage behind the shop — which didn't change a thing for

Ellie — or Samie Machin came home to her apartment upstairs. Samie had a friend in town, another service wife and often spent nights with her.

Ozaire would be at the Rosebank fete tomorrow and Ellie would give him the go-ahead on the dog at once.

She had no place to go, no one to go to.

Self-pity wasted good time.

A door at the back of the café led to a vestibule with an exit to the yard that separated the main building from the cottage. Stairs to the upstairs apartments rose from the same area. Ellie went into the vestibule and locked the shop behind her. Bill and Samie used an entry from an alley beside the building when they were late.

Halfway up the stairs she heard the phone ring in her apartment and ran the rest of the way. She dashed in and snatched up the receiver. "Hello?"

A dial tone sounded. It shouldn't disappoint her so to miss a phone call. She waited, giving the caller time to leave a message on the machine. The red light started to flash and Ellie punched the button.

"Hi there, Ellie," a cheerful male voice said, "sorry to miss you. I was hoping you were free to spend the night with me."

The night? He must mean the evening.

The familiar voice wasn't completely clear and she couldn't think who it was, darn it.

"Call me back and let me know if you're in the mood for some fun."

How could she call him back if she didn't know who he was?

"You know the kind of fun I mean, but maybe I can help you make up your mind."

Ellie prickled all over.

"Don't turn chicken on me now. I can see your face and you're getting scared. You never have to be scared of me. All I want is to spend time with you and show you all the things you've been missing. Stop shaking now. There's no one but me to see you, so why bother?"

She shook her head. He couldn't see her, he'd just anticipated her reactions to what he said. "Don't listen. Turn it off," she said aloud.

But she couldn't follow her own orders.

"Energy is what it's all about," the voice went on. "Energy and pain — now don't go all shocked on me again. I'm going to help you make up for all the sex you haven't been getting. A woman with tits and an ass like yours can't be allowed to waste herself."

Ellie trembled. She had hurried into the apartment and grabbed the phone without turning on the lights or closing the front door.

"Relax. Call me. I'll be right over to fuck you to heaven. One thing, Ellie, if you tell anyone about this call, you'll suffer. I won't be half as gentle with you. This call can't be traced. I'm near you, Ellie. Do you like knives as much as I do?"

She tried to scream but couldn't make a noise. The message was over but the phone rang again and she picked up, praying it would be someone else.

Dead air. Silence, then the faint click of someone hanging up.

She dropped the handset. "Call Spike." The sound of her own voice, even though she panted, helped fill the silence.

"Number. What's his number?" This wasn't an emergency so she couldn't dial 911. "Where's my telephone book? Where is it?" She kept her leather-bound book on the table beside the phone but it wasn't there. "Put the light on, idiot. You're over-reacting."

"Is this what you're looking for, Ellie?" A man spoke from close behind her, and thrust her leather-bound book in front of her face. "Ah ah ah, don't turn around."

At last the swallowed scream let loose. Her eyes closed and she shuddered with the force of the terrible sound through her throat.

He was here with her; standing behind her in the semidarkness. He grabbed a handful of hair at the back of her neck and forced her head forward, twisted the hair until she dragged in sobbing breaths.

"Shut up, bitch."

The voice blurred. *He's speaking through something.*

Still using her hair, he pulled her upright and wrapped an arm around her waist. His breath was hot on her neck. "Forget calling the law. They already have suspicions about you."

"Let me go."

Again he tightened his grip on her hair, and again he shoved her head forward, shaking her while she cried out.

He walked with her doubled over, trod on her heels with each step until she yelped and hopped, trying to avoid the crushing sting in her ankles. With a final shove he cracked her shins into the couch, toppled her to kneel on the seat and landed her face on the back.

"Now listen to me carefully." He slid one knee on either side of hers, trapping her with his weight. "If you make the mistake of doubting what I say, you won't get a second chance to do as you're told. Understand?"

She gave a muffled "Yes."

"I won't forget what I promised you." He was erect and pressed himself into her bottom. "Mmm, mmm, a sweet ass. No, I won't forget."

Ellie retched. Her stomach heaved and her throat constricted.

The man laughed. "Getting overexcited? Don't vomit unless you want to drown. Tomorrow you'll go to the Rosebank fete and you'll smile. You will be happy, the life of the party. And you'll wait for a signal. Got it?"

"Yes."

"You will know when the signal comes. You will feel it and act at once. Spike will be near and you'll ask him, privately, to go with you because you have something to show him."

He wasn't going to kill her. No, he wanted her to do something for him. Laughter bubbled in her throat.

"Tell him things got out of hand. Take him to the pool. That's all you have to do." Tugging on her hair, he raised her face from the couch. "Do you understand?"

"Yes, but what will I say when we get there?"

"Nothing. You won't need to say a word."

Ellie sweated. The sickness would not pass. "Then what should I do?"

"You'll know what to do. You'll remember that I'll be watching you, even though you don't know who I am. You'll know that you must not mention me or this cozy meeting."

"But —"

He thumped her face on the couch again. "Do as you're told," he hissed in her ear. "Nothing more and nothing less. If you make contact with Spike Devol before the fete, I will have to make sure it's the last time you disobey me — or anyone."

36

"Does Homer always go out at night?" Vivian asked.

"Nope." *Like just about never.* "He does get together with his buddies now and then. He's probably like the dead man at the feast. What I don't understand is why he decided to stop by and see your mother — and take Wendy with him."

"Don't you?" Vivian raised her chin. "I think you do. I think Homer's decided I'm not so bad and he's figured out how close we are. He's giving us time on our own."

After supper Vivian had insisted on shooing Homer and Wendy away and doing the dishes. She stood at the sink, rinsing glasses and turning them upside down in a drainer.

"Homer doesn't believe in newfangled gadgets," Spike said. "Like dishwashers."

She felt his eyes on her back. "I'll have to make sure he sees a commercial one when we get it put in at Rosebank." The conversation might be light, but Vivian grew more tense with every word. Spike could as well be running his hands over her body.

"Stop that for a minute, will you?" he said. "I'll finish it up later."

Vivian looked at him and wiped her hands dry. "What's up?" He wasn't just being polite and she took her seat at the kitchen table again. When she crossed her legs, he watched, his lips pressed together.

From her ankles to her hips, hovering too long on her breasts and finally arriving at her eyes, he made a visual tour that dissolved her insides. "There's so much it's hard to know where to start," he said. "I've still got a connection or two in Iberia. I managed to find out something that was bugging me. The kisses."

"Gil didn't have one."

"He could have. Maybe it got messed up and faded is all. The mark on Louis wasn't made with blood. The murderer used a stamp — probably carved in a piece of cork — and shiny red lipstick."

"Why bother?" Vivian said. She locked eyes with Spike and saw a reflection of her own revelation. "More theatrics. The rose, the so-called kiss."

"Like he's trying to pretend he's something he's not," Spike said. "Making a profile to hide behind."

"The flower and the kiss are hokey," Vivian said. "Amateurish."

"Uh-huh, but the way the perp uses a knife is surgical. He's a pro. I think we're dealing with someone who's had a lot of practice . . . or a lot of training. Could be he's well-known in the business but hopes he'll be mistaken for a nonprofessional."

This was stuff Vivian expected to read about in the paper, not encounter in rural Louisiana. "Training makes it sound like you could be talking about someone from . . . I don't know, special forces? I can't imagine some guy covered in mud and wearing camouflage crawling around Rosebank."

He gave her a grim smile. "Have you seen anyone crawling around? No. But two people have died there, apparently in daylight. And there's no suspect in custody. Would it be so way out to think this was a professional job?"

"Like a hit?" Vivian said softly.

Spike rubbed his jaw. "Hell, I don't know, but anything's possible. What I wouldn't give to find that stamp."

"I bet." Hashing over the details sickened her. "I doubt if he's going to make that easy for you."

Spike looked sideways at her and his gaze flickered again. The atmosphere between them, still and tinder-dry, smoldered. "I have to make sure this guy doesn't kill again, Vivian. I only hope I can. It would be easy to decide both murders were part of an isolated incident and start to relax. But why only them? Why any of this? There could be another killing at any time." He shook his head. "And you and I didn't imagine being pushed into Bayou Lafourche. Then there's the Martin boys. They won't just go away. *Hell.*"

She pushed her hands across the table and Spike held her wrists tightly. "Ellie Byron had a nasty shock early this morning," he said.

Vivian sat straighter. "I was going to talk to you about Ellie and what Detective Bonine said about her. He warned me to stay away from her but didn't tell me why."

"Bastard," Spike said. "He was snoopin' around at the station, supposedly waiting for me, when Ellie turned up. I wasn't there so she poured out her story to Lori. He doesn't have a clue what it means but if

Errol can keep all of us away from her, he will."

"What happened?" Vivian asked, with the too familiar scrunching in her stomach again.

Spike's eyes were narrowed and he stroked his thumbs absently back and forth on her wrists. She jumped at the sensation. He gave her a lopsided smile and her own lips parted in response. Spike said, "Bonine doesn't have the right to step on my turf and start giving out orders. You've seen how he behaves when the shoe's on the other foot."

"Deal with that later," Vivian said, only too aware that Spike was doing the natural male thing and protecting his territory. "Ellie? What about her?"

Spike knew Vivian was right to make him concentrate, not that they weren't both aware of how the tension between them complicated that. His job was to keep people safe and now that there had been this incident with Ellie in Toussaint, the danger was no longer "somewhere else." "Fortunately Bill Green made her go to Cyrus — she wouldn't speak to me right off — and Cyrus took her to the station."

He told Vivian Ellie's whole story, sparing nothing, especially not the puncture made through her photographed body.

"It's so scary," Vivian said when he'd finished. The tale had shaken her. "Poor Ellie. I don't like thinking about her being there alone tonight after going through that. Why would someone do that? I wonder if it was something to do with my uncle's books." She told him a story of how Ellie and Guy Patin had been friends and finished by saying Ellie thought a book intended as a gift for Vivian had been stolen. He didn't make a big deal out of her not telling him earlier.

"There could be a connection, couldn't there?" she said. "Maps of the area with Ellie's photo. And a layout of the Rosebank estate? The house, you mean, or the grounds?"

"A lot of detail of the grounds?" He thought there must definitely be a connection. The big break could be coming and his job was to make sure it wasn't at Ellie Byron's expense.

"Lordy," Vivian said, with a sense of foreboding. "The *fete*. Wazoo's fete is supposed to be tomorrow? She and her friends have been busy arranging it so Mama and I wouldn't have any extra pressure. I keep forgetting about it. Did you?"

"Uh-huh." He surely had forgotten and it seemed to him that with the Patin women's new windfall, they wouldn't be needing raffles and dunk tanks in future. "That's a lousy idea right now. Anyway, Bonine and crew won't go for it."

"Apparently Bonine thinks it's a great idea and says he's going to drop in — with that poor Frank Wiley. Mama says word's out it's going to be a real extravaganza."

"In other words, Bonine thinks it's a fine idea to have scores of people destroying any last hope of finding useful evidence. He's never behaved as if he really wanted to solve this case."

Vivian was annoyed at herself for being too preoccupied to think about the fete. "It may be wisest to carry on tomorrow. Could be the best way to convince people what happened is under control — even if it isn't. Morgan and Susan should appreciate that. They hate living next to a crime scene."

"True," Spike agreed. "You might think folks wouldn't want to be at Rosebank after what's happened but I kind of think the ghoul factor will make sure there's a crowd. Do you know if Ellie will be there?"

"I'm sure she will."

"I'm going to make sure she's never alone." Damn it to hell that he'd be out of his jurisdiction again, and that he didn't have some trained people to use as off-duty eyes. With luck Cyrus would be there and Mark, Bill and Joe would keep their eyes open once they were asked. He'd even swallow his pride and have a word with Ozaire if necessary.

"I must get home and be with my mother." Vivian got up.

"Homer's there," Spike reminded her. "And Gary Legrain. I'd say Charlotte was real safe."

"This guy wasn't someone passing through," Vivian said. "He's under our noses, I only get more convinced that he is."

One of the many things he liked about Vivian was her logical mind. "That makes two of us." But he surely did like many things about Vivian. He'd like to take her apart and explore some of those right now.

She smiled at him but her features tightened. He saw the instant when a total, sexy awareness wiped the worry from her eyes. He couldn't breathe so regularly himself. Wildness hovered between them, barely in check. He narrowed his eyes and reacted to an erotic recoil. His thighs came together hard and he dreamed of being naked — with her.

"I don't know what's going to happen for us," she said breathlessly, coming to his side of the table. "But the fates were smiling when they sent me your way."

Vivian put her arms around his neck and kissed him, a sweet, maddeningly gentle kiss before she pressed her face against his neck.

Spike stroked back her hair and ran his hands over her shoulders. She smelled wonderful — and tasted wonderful. He took her by the waist and began to sit her on his lap but she pushed away. She smiled at him with anything but gentleness in her eyes. "If I sit there, we could get carried away." Slowly, she slid her hands from his neck, over his shoulders and down his arms. He caught hold of her hands but, still slowly, she pulled her fingers free. "I'm goin' to finish up the dishes and get home."

"I doubt it," he said in a low voice.

Tossing her hair from her face, she backed away. He forced himself to wait, to give her a few moments to feel in control.

Standing in front of the sink, Vivian dried dishes and reached over her head to put them away in cabinets. Spike enjoyed seeing her supple body stretch, and the way her dress skimmed higher over her hips.

He got up quietly. They'd lowered the blinds, so she wouldn't see his approaching reflection in the windows. Sneaking up behind her just as she lifted a pile of plates over her head, he reached around her and tweaked her nipples.

Vivian wobbled and said, "Don't do that. I'll drop these."

"Oh, I'd just advise you to concentrate on the plates. Those are Homer's favorites." Rocking his hips forward he settled the hardest part of his body between the cheeks of her lovely bottom and kissed her neck. She smelled warm and all woman. She smelled like dark places and wet skin, slipping and sliding.

By the time she'd managed to push the china on top of several other pieces, he'd delved under the neck of her dress, under her bra, and cupped her breasts. With his thumbs he made circles over the ends of her hardened nipples and she acted as if her legs would fail.

Rid of the dishes, she tried to swing around. Spike wouldn't let her. "I knew you could do it, *cher*," he said, holding her right where she was with her back to him and nibbling at an ear. "You are so talented."

"You cheat," she said, her voice husky. "You waited till I couldn't do anything to stop you and took advantage."

"And you hate it?" he said, pinching her nipples while her hips rocked back and forth. "Okay, I won't do that anymore. I'll

527

do this instead." And before she could make a move to stop him, he pulled her skirts up around her waist, leaned to keep her from moving and ducked to run his hands up the backs of her smooth thighs and over that rounded bottom. A white thong didn't cover a thing, as far as he could see. Spanning her ribs under the dress, slipping the bra undone so the weight of her breasts rested on his fingers, he kissed each cheek, turned his face, opened his mouth wide and felt his mind bathed in a muskiness that turned it dark and hot.

"Stop it, Spike!" She wiggled suddenly, violently. "What if Homer and Wendy walk in?"

"They won't. Homer knows I'll let you drive me over there, then the three of us will come back at the same time."

"Shut up and love me," she said. "My God, I want you."

For a slender woman, she had a lot of strength. He didn't try very hard to stop her from wrenching to face him. She clamped his face in her hands and kissed him like a madwoman, until he returned the attack.

He stumbled and they clutched at each other, slammed into the table and spun away. They reached a wall, not that he knew what wall. But the lights went out and he hadn't touched the switch. Vivian laughed deep in her throat. His shirt buttons parted company and she wrestled his belt undone.

"Whoa," he muttered, although he wouldn't change a thing.

He unzipped the back of her dress and pulled it from her shoulders. She shucked off the bra and managed to shimmy the whole mess down and kick it aside.

Vivian fastened her mouth on his and her hands shook so she couldn't manage his zipper. He did it for her but had a moment's anxiety that he might let everything go before he'd satisfied her.

"Wait," he muttered, tearing his lips from hers. He spun her slick body around and buried his face in her neck again. He stalled for time, even a second could mean everything. His butterfly touches on her breasts drove her wild. He pushed a knee between her thighs to steady her.

She leaned against him and rested the back of her head on his shoulder — and he pushed her breasts together while she moaned.

Sensations and instinct carried Vivian along. She raised her arms and locked her fingers around his neck. Her all-but-bare bottom pressed against his penis and it pressed back, thick and straining.

With the heel of one hand he smoothed hard down her belly and pushed his fingers between her legs. She breathed faster and faster and repeatedly dipped as if she would collapse. Spike smoothed deep with teasing strokes that flirted around the edges of where she really wanted to feel him. Restraint cost him plenty but he played on, occasionally closing his hand over her mound and applying pressure until she gasped and tried to make him move back to rub between distended lips.

He didn't make her wait much longer, he couldn't. He trembled with the strength it took to hold back. His fingers slid into place and he increased his speed until she arched back against him and climaxed. She hadn't completely stopped shuddering when she dragged his hand away and revolved in his arms again. With her frenzied help, he wrenched his pants down.

A weak light over the stove glistened on their skin.

Vivian looked down at him. She took him into both of her hands and massaged.

"No, Vivian," he whispered.

"Oh, yes," she said, but let him do the necessary while she held tight to his neck.

He barely got his hands on her waist before she hooked a knee over his hip. Spike tore her thong away and wrapped her legs around his waist. No time for finesse. He jerked himself inside her. The heat and urgency burned him up. Vivian rose and fell on him. They wrung each other out. And they hung together then, panting, Vivian crying in racking sobs he knew had nothing to do with being sad.

He wanted to lie down, and did slide down the wall, with Vivian in his arms, until he sat on the floor with her in his lap.

She rubbed her breasts against him. He started to quicken again and flicked the head of his penis over the swollen flesh between her legs.

From a great distance came the sound of the front doorbell.

Spike groaned and rested his face on Vivian's shoulder. "Who would come to that door? No one ever does."

"They can go away." She pushed back, knelt and took him into her mouth for a long, urgently sucking kiss.

The doorbell rang and this time it kept on ringing.

"Of all the bitchin' luck," Vivian said and Spike snickered at the language. Vivian didn't swear.

He reached for her but she dodged his hands and hopped up. She grabbed her clothes and started pulling them on. "I don't think they're going away. You might want to put something on."

"Ouch," he said, wincing. He'd stepped into his pants. "Look what you've started — all over again."

She looked and turned on the light to get a better view. "I see it," she said. "I want to be right back there."

Spike groaned, tucked in his shirt and got his belt fastened. Just as he'd expected, footsteps sounded on the gallery steps out back and someone rattled the screen door.

He ran his hands through his hair and saw Vivian shake hers. It had a way of falling into place beautifully. "Do up my bra, please," she said and he obliged. She slipped out of what was left of the thong and stuffed it quickly into her bag.

Spike opened the back door and looked out.

"Praise be," Cyrus said, yanking open the screen and herding Wazoo in front of him. "I've looked all over for you. Things are happening and you're the one to make decisions."

Wazoo scuttled into the kitchen and took herself off into a corner where she huddled and looked scared.

Cyrus closed the door behind him and took in the scene in the kitchen. He frowned and Spike felt his mind was being read.

"Hmm," Cyrus said. "I guess a whole bunch of things are happening. Remember that talk we kinda started, Spike?"

Spike hesitated before saying, "Yes."

"Good. We'd better get it finished. Soon."

37

Might make a man feel a little more respected if the should-be penitents didn't keep staring at each other with hot eyes. Cyrus took note of Vivian's flushed cheeks and swollen mouth — and of Spike's wrinkled uniform, and his equally well-used-looking mouth, and felt a wholly inappropriate irritation.

"I think I might as well talk to the two of you," Cyrus said. Vivian showed no sign of being anything other than a willing participant in what he'd interrupted. "Now, Wazoo, please don't cower."

"Miz Vivian, she gonna kill me," Wazoo said. "Then Miz Charlotte do the same t'ing."

"Wazoo," Vivian said. "How silly. You couldn't do anything to upset us more than a little. Oh, maybe you've called off the fete for tomorrow, if so, don't worry about it, we'll do it sometime in the future."

"I ain't called it off, me. It's going to be the biggest fete this place ever see and we gonna raise all kind of money to help out at Rosebank."

Cyrus glanced at Vivian who looked as uncomfortable as he'd expected. On the other hand, how easy could it be to say you'd inherited a fortune and didn't need help anymore? Well, he would never have to find out. St. Cécil's bumped along but there was never enough money.

Wazoo did the unthinkable. She cried, sat herself down on the floor and rocked.

Dealing with crying women was part of his duties, but it didn't get easier. "Now, Wazoo, this isn't goin' to be that bad. You know Miz Vivian is goin' to try to understand what you've done. She'll do the right thing even though she will be disappointed in you."

"*Cyrus,*" Vivian said, and he guessed that so far he wasn't doing too well with Wazoo.

"I won't have no home again, me." Wazoo's voice grew higher. "And I won't have my lovely job. I'll have to creep away into some swamp and live on rats too old to run away. My shoes'll wear out and nasty things will eat up my feet —"

"Wazoo," Vivian said sharply. "You're overdoing it."

"Not me, uh-uh." Wazoo shook her head hard enough to make Cyrus's neck ache just from watching. "I'm too bad. I'll have to go to prison first, of course, because you'll turn me in, you ain't got no choice. Criminal like me."

Spike went to Wazoo with the resigned manner of a man accustomed to sorting out problems of all kinds. "Up you come," he said, and lifted her by the shoulders. "Should I arrest you right now, or would you like to plead your case first?"

Cyrus couldn't hold back a grin but Vivian didn't look too happy. "That's enough of that," she told Spike. "Come and sit down, Wazoo."

Dragging her sneakers, Wazoo let Spike take her to a chair at the table. There she slumped, her face hidden in her hands. "I did it," she said. "I don't know what come over me, but I couldn't stop myself."

"*No.*" Vivian fell back against the refrigerator. "What is she saying?"

Maybe he just never would get the hang of women, Cyrus thought. "Hear her out," he said and noted that Spike wasn't smiling anymore either. "If God can forgive the offense, so can you two." He was getting angry.

"I should have come right out with it," Wazoo said. "But I had a whole lot of violence around when I was growin' up and it does things to you."

"I hate that," Vivian said, color returning to her face. "People who blame their own wrongdoing on what happened when they were children. Their parents were mean, or something, so they're mean." Her eyes glittered. "Or worse. Sooner or later a person has to be responsible for their own actions."

"Hush, *cher*," Spike said. "Start at the top, Wazoo, and let's have it."

"Start at the bottom, you mean," she muttered. "Ellie Byron's my friend. She treats me like I'm anyone else and there ain't many who would. So what do I do? I steal from her, me. She know I don't got the money for books but how I love the big, fancy ones with pictures of places and beautiful t'ings. She say I can borrow anything I want."

Cyrus had already heard the story but could feel how badly she needed to tell it again.

"It was the silk bag," Wazoo said, wiping at her eyes. "Yellow and orange and green and red stars all over it. And the shiny cord to close it, all gold and glittery. That's what made me notice. Me, I never seen a book kept safe in a bag like that, so I knew it was special. All I wanted to do was look at it. That was just before you come here, Miz Vivian, and I heard Ellie say she was fixin' to give it to you the first opportunity she got. So I borrowed it, only, Ellie was upstairs at the time and I left before I could tell her I was takin' the book for a little while."

Her eyes slid past each of them. "Oh, alligator poop. Who'm I tryin' to boondaddle? I was afraid she wouldn't want me to take somethin' that good so I sneaked off with it. Vivian's uncle Guy left it with Ellie. It was a present for you, Vivian. I should have given it back right away but I could tell what it was and what it meant, and I, well, I wanted to figure it all out and find that treasure for myself."

This, Cyrus hadn't heard. He smiled encouragement at Wazoo who had taken her tale into a make-believe realm. "It takes a strong spirit to be completely honest," he told her. "Thank you for being so open with us."

She glared at him, the old fire back in her expression. "Don't you do that God man stuff to me. If you're bad, you're bad, and I'm bad, me. I come to you because I reckon someone put a hex on you so you can't tell no one nothin' after it's bin told to you, that's all."

L'Oiseau de Nuit would take a special place in his personal memories. "That's fine," he told her. "And it was nice of you to agree to come here and tell Vivian and Spike. 'Specially since you only did it because you're sorry for me."

"Hah." Wazoo turned her face from him. "So you make me tell it again myself."

"As long as the book's safe," Vivian said, her arms crossed tightly about her. "I'm glad if you've had fun with it. But I really would like to have it back."

"That the t'ing," Wazoo said. "Someone stole it from me yesterday. Can you imagine the nerve of some people? Walked right into my room at Rosebank, where I got a right to guard my t'ings, and *stole* that book."

Vivian wouldn't appreciate a laughing priest when she'd just discovered something she wanted had been stolen from her . . . twice. "That's terrible," Cyrus said.

"Oh" was all Vivian said.

"You knew about this book?" Spike asked. He tilted his head and studied Vivian.

"Yes. Ellie told me, but I didn't know it had anything to do with what Wazoo calls treasure."

"Notes on some of them pages," Wazoo said. "They was short notes. Okay, they was only two notes. Well, two and a bit, 'cause there was a torn one, too. And your uncle drawed a sort of picture in one place — near a picture. Not *on* it. Near it. I think it's the treasure."

Vivian scuffed across the kitchen, and retraced her steps again. Her crestfallen expression only made Cyrus feel more helpless.

"Ah, Vivian," Spike said. "Is it so much of a deal now? I mean, how much do you and Charlotte —"

"Don't." She pointed her forefinger at him as if taking up position for a sword fight. "Don't you dare make presumptions about me. I thought you knew me better than that. What I need, and what my mother needs, is what was intended for us and what we'd feel okay acceptin'. The other is blood money, conscience money, and we don't want any part of it."

"Darn my mouth," Spike said. "I don't know what came over me. I do know you better than that, not that it's any of my business."

"Isn't it?"

Cyrus decided that any advice from him wouldn't be well received. He also decided these two were definitely in love.

Spike tapped the heel of a boot on the worn linoleum and reminded Cyrus of a very overgrown boy who hadn't been so good lately.

"Do it by the book," Wazoo said loudly and sat very straight as if expecting trouble. "That's what one of the notes said — the one what wasn't tore. I've got a good memory, me."

"Thanks," Vivian said. "And I would if I could."

"Check all your pineapples." Wazoo delivered this line in ringing tones.

Vivian frowned at Wazoo. "I beg your pardon?"

"The other note. *Check all your pineapples.*"

Cyrus was hearing all of this for the first time.

"That doesn't make any sense," Spike said.

"None," Vivian agreed. "Uncle Guy was a joker. I guess I should have expected him to lead me on a wild-goose chase if he could. Although I did think he intended to make sure Mama and I could keep the house up."

Laughter erupted from Wazoo in a high peal. "The goose that laid the golden egg," she said. "What else would he do but lead you . . . on . . . a wild . . . Well, no, he didn't. He did intend to provide for you. That man, he surely did. You got hundreds of pineapples, Miz Vivian. They all over that house. They carved on bedposts and chair legs and made out of bronze, and bone, and stone, and pottery, and painted gold and all manner of things. I know 'cause I been doin' my best to find one with that fancy egg in it."

"She's sick." Vivian got a glass of water and handed it to Wazoo. "It's okay, we'll take care of you."

"Uh-huh. That book was all about these dolled-up eggs made for some rich Russian people what got knocked off. Some Frenchman made 'em special, lots of 'em. Your uncle just had the one, but it's worth more money than you or me ever seen. Fabergé. That's the name of them. Your uncle drew a picture of the one he reckons is inside one of your pineapples. Leastwise, I think that's what he was tellin' you. He wasn't so much of an artist. But I know feet when I see em, ugly feet, too. This one had bumpy legs and ugly feet. And a tufty thing on top."

"A Fabergé egg," Vivian said with reverence. "A copy, I expect."

"Uh-uh. It come out of some passageway under a palace in Russia where it got lost for a long time. If it was like the picture next to the drawing, it was one of the ones made

542

real early, so it said. Someone died over it."

Vivian shivered. She took another chair at the kitchen table. "Come on, you two," she said to Spike and Cyrus. "Sit down with us. Seems to me we've got the perfect opportunity for our treasure hunt. With all this construction getting started again."

Morose, Wazoo said, "And all those people pokin' all over the place, prob'ly includin' whoever stole my book."

Vivian didn't correct her on the ownership issue.

"A map inside the book showed how the house is. I used that 'cause there was crosses on rooms and I found pineapple stuff all over 'em." Wazoo paused. "There was crosses on plenty of rooms. That map, one just the same, that's what the killer took from the lawyer's bag that day. I got good eyes, me. Couldn't see if he took anythin' else though."

"Wazoo," Spike said carefully, digesting what she was telling them, "what do you remember about the man . . . that man?"

She shrugged. "He wear one of them masks over his head so I don't see his face. Not too tall but big shoulders. Strong. And he move that knife so fast, all I see is a flash."

Spike glanced at Vivian — who flinched — and Cyrus.

"The other one, the one who said to start the fire where they did, he wore a mask, too, only he was taller."

"Taller," Cyrus said. "You mean there were *two* men in masks?"

"I told that," Wazoo said, sounding cross. "When the fire burnin' I tell that."

Two. "I didn't understand that's what you were suggesting," Spike said. "Wazoo, are you sure these men weren't pretty much the same height and weight?" he asked, thinking of the Martin brothers.

"Yes!" She glared at him. "I'm sure, me. I said what I saw and I saw it. They was different. It was the taller man who took Gil away. I recognized him when I see him again at the fire."

The Devols' house was old and creaked a lot. In the hush that followed Wazoo's curious comment, every board in the place made its presence known.

"Hoo mama," Wazoo wailed, freshly stricken. "I say it. Now I live in the swamp, for sure." She spoke to Vivian, "That night, the night when you found the lawyer, I should never have tried to cover it all up."

Now Cyrus was confused again. She hadn't mentioned anything about covering up the murder before. Or about seeing Gil taken away. "You saw Gil killed, too?"

She gave one of her ferocious shakes of the head. "No, I did not. I only see that other man take him away because he found him watchin' while the first one killed the lawyer. I don't know where he took Gil, but he surely did kill him later, didn't he?"

They nodded but couldn't look at one another.

"I'm greedy, me," Wazoo said in a small voice. "And I know that's not anybody else's fault, even if I have always been poor. I thought I'd finally found a way to get some money and make a start and I wasn't goin' to let no dead man in a fancy car stop me. I thought Gil would be okay." She scrubbed at her eyes and her wild black hair only made her white skin more luminous.

Spike got Cyrus's attention and shook his head. "Hold up, Wazoo." Spike was signaling that he couldn't let Wazoo go on without hearing a Miranda. "If you're gonna keep talkin' to us I'm going to have to read you your rights." He did so while her crying grew louder. "You need a lawyer."

"I don't want no lawyer. I don't need no lawyer. I can't afford no lawyer. How long will they lock me away for stealin' a book and not tellin' I seen a murder?"

38

"Okay, so either I put my job on the line and go along with this scheme of yours, or I'll lose the friendship of some people I really like." Spike was beaten. The day hadn't exactly been relaxing, and things had only gotten more strenuous later. He glanced at Vivian who was sitting with Wazoo, Cyrus and Madge in the upstairs sitting room at the rectory, and suffered a perverse hard-on.

The group mumbled what came out as, "S'right."

The face Vivian turned to him didn't help. A sleepy, tense, beautiful face that begged to rest on his pillow in the aftermath of making love again.

She smiled at him and he sank deeper in one of Cyrus's comfortable old chairs.

He'd called Homer and, after discovering that Gary Legrain had packed up and taken off for New Orleans right after he learned he'd just come into his own law firm, asked his dad to remain at Rosebank till he could get there. Wendy was being put into Vivian's bed and, so he was told, had suggested he not come for her until after tomorrow's fete.

Spike sighed. "Wazoo, I think if you're going to seek asylum with Father Cyrus until the morning, then hotfoot it over to Rosebank to make sure the fete's underway before you speak to Detective Bonine, I'd better be tied up and locked in a cupboard to stop me from doing my duty and taking you in now."

Vivian gave an explosive little laugh. "Just what I've always wanted to do to you. Promise you won't fight me?"

He met her eyes. "Would I fight you, *cher?*" His smile was for her alone. She felt its power and made herself look away.

"All the right notes," Wazoo announced, staring into space. "The torn note. That's what Mr. Patin wrote there. *All the right notes.*"

Uncle Guy had been a wonderful but an eccentric man. Vivian had loved him since she was old enough to know she loved anyone, but tonight she wished he hadn't had quite such a thing for riddles. "I'll think about that," she told Wazoo.

"There is something I think we've all forgotten," Madge said. She'd been quiet since they'd arrived, quiet and watchful. "Did anyone clear this fete with Detective Bonine? Are they going to want dozens of people tramping around the grounds at Rosebank?"

"I thought of that, me," Wazoo said. "I talk to that rude man but maybe I was wrong about him. He real nice to me this time and say the search at the house is over. Everythin' happen on the same day, they reckon — Louis and Gil — and now there ain't nothin' left to find."

Vivian wished she felt as sure of that.

"I guess that's good news then," Madge said. She shared a couch with Cyrus and he watched every word she spoke.

"Could have been random," Cyrus said, looking directly into her face. "A robbery gone bad. Someone passing through — apparently two of them working together — could have seen an opportunity to rob Louis but been interrupted by Gil — all without knowing Wazoo was watching. Now they're long gone."

"That would mean it's all over," Vivian said. "I'd be more than glad but it doesn't mean they don't have to find out what happened."

Spike raised a single eyebrow. "I'm still gettin' over the idea that there's nothing left to find at Rosebank. That's a crock and it won't wash."

The door opened and Lil, in curlers, stood there, panting from the exertion of climbing the stairs.

"You should have gone home hours ago," Cyrus said and Vivian figured he wasn't pleased that Lil knew exactly who was gathered there.

"Someone has to keep this place runnin'," Lil said with a pointed glare at Madge. "There's someone wants to see you, Father. A lady with a question. She come in one of them big, fancy cars with a man drivin' and wearing' one of them caps. Never saw her before and she says it's confidential. Wouldn't let me help her, that's for sure. Can I show her up?"

Cyrus got to his feet. "I'll go down."

The sight of Wally Hibbs with a large, lumpy sack over his shoulder silenced everyone. He went directly to Cyrus and stood on tiptoe to whisper in his ear.

"Okay," Cyrus said when the boy had finished talking. "Sit down and wait till I get back." He strode out with Lil behind him and his footsteps pounded down the stairs.

Wally took one look at Spike and immediately dropped his gaze.

The silence stretched.

At last Spike said, "So, what's in the sack, Wally?"

"Evidence," Wally said. Nolan Two hadn't made this trip and Wally, in a baggy brown T-shirt and cutoffs, looked wan, nervous, but at home in the rectory. He said, "Father Cyrus knows the right way to deal with these things."

Cyrus surprised them all by returning in only minutes. He went directly to a bar he kept locked and took out a bottle of brandy. He poured a measure into enough glasses for everyone present, except Wally. Wally got a glass of lemonade poured from a jug kept in a small refrigerator.

Madge helped Cyrus pass the drinks around.

"Take a good swallow," Cyrus ordered. "Our waters are muddied even more but this could be a good thing. I'd never have thought of this in a million years but it explains a lot. We just have to stop ourselves from jumping to conclusions."

Vivian shifted to the front of her seat, almost jumpy with wanting to know what he was talking about — now.

"It would be a mistake to start laying blame where it's very unlikely to belong," Cyrus said.

"Stop leading the audience and say what you've got to say," Spike said. "What's happened?"

"Have some more brandy," Cyrus said.

"Cyrus."

"Very well, but remember my warnings. The lady wanted directions. She had two business cards and said it was fine for me to keep one. I told her I wanted it in case someone asked for a referral. I know what you're going to think but don't jump to conclusions."

"Argh!" Madge said. "You've already told us that. Cyrus, give us that card or I'll take it from you."

That brought a round of chuckles.

Cyrus gave the card to Vivian, who was closest to him. She read, turned cold, and passed the card on.

It finished in Spike's hands and he whistled. "And you don't want us jumping to conclusions?" he said.

Madge fell against the back of the couch and blew into a fist. Her dark eyes fixed on some distant picture only she saw.

"I don't believe it, me," Wazoo said. "Not that man. Women, yes. Murder, no. There's a whole lot of woman trouble in this town, but not the other."

"What does that mean?" Vivian said. Her nerves sent up white flags. She'd had enough intrigue.

"Women," Wazoo said, unfazed. "We got sexy men. We got sexy women. What you think that means? And we got one mess what nobody wants to know about."

"Okay," Spike said. "What's all this about?"

"Uh-uh," Wazoo said. "I'm not tellin', me. I'm in enough trouble. Someone else in this town needs to talk about a married woman who likes to share her tail. Not me. I ain't talkin'."

"*What?*" Vivian left her seat to stand over Wazoo. "That's it. Please. Who are you talkin' about?"

"Spike told me not to gossip. God man told me not to gossip. I ain't gonna gossip. We found ourselves a killer, anyway."

Cyrus groaned. "What did I say about not jumping to conclusions?"

"What about my stuff?" Wally said in a loud voice. He hadn't seen the business card. "It stinks. I reckon it's got compost on it. I think someone dug it up from the heap at Rosebank. Whoever put it there thought it would burn up in the fire, but someone else took it away first. They put it where the bonfire dirt was dumped. Back of the pool." With that, he reached into the sack and pulled out several pieces of jagged wood. He fitted two lengths together. "See, it says Detour. I got another says Dead End. Somebody wanted them to burn up. Someone else wanted them to be found."

"You can't be sure of that," Madge said. "But it's a clever idea."

"He more than clever," Wazoo said. "They the signs that bad man stuck in them big tubs with laurel in them, the ones he dragged around."

Wally got up and marched in front of her. He turned one piece of the broken board over. "See," he said. "It was starting to burn."

Spike said, "Wally may be on to something. Is it okay if I take what you've found and have some tests run?"

"Yes," Wally said slowly. "Don't it make sense there's two of 'em. One who tried to get rid of the signs and one who wants to make sure we catch the first one? And the signs must've been put there after the cops searched or they'd have found 'em. It's one of them setups."

"Sign up that boy, Spike," Madge said. "Deputy Wally is ready for duty and you're shorthanded."

Wally blushed but looked pleased.

Spike held up the card Cyrus had taken from the woman. "So, what do we seem to have here?" He looked at Wally as if he might ask him to leave but Vivian saw him decide against sending the boy away. "Don't all speak at once."

Vivian immediately said, "A plastic surgery clinic for people who want the best and don't want to go home until everything's healed. Secretive people."

"Rich people," Madge said. "Probably famous."

Cyrus nodded. "The kind of people who don't expect murders to happen almost under their windows and draw attention."

"I thought Morgan Link might be a psychologist," Cyrus said. "Now we've really got a fresh mess on our hands."

"And Link lives right next door," Vivian said. "He wanders all over Rosebank whenever he likes. He probably knows it as well as we do. And neither he nor Susan ever said a word about opening an elite clinic. They must be desperate to get their hands on our place and make sure it never opens."

"Morgan Link wouldn't kill people at Rosebank if he were trying to avoid drawing attention," Cyrus said.

"Unless he just wanted an excuse to make

trouble and make sure Charlotte and Vivian couldn't go on." Madge spread a hand. "Who said killers are smart?"

"Wazoo," Spike said, "could the man you saw with Louis have been Morgan Link?"

She closed her eyes and hummed quietly. "Just a man in a mask." Her eyes opened wide. "Could be him. About the same size. Might be someone else."

Vivian didn't have time for the headache she fought. "A plastic surgeon has to be really good with knives."

A muffled scream, Wazoo's, stopped as abruptly as it started.

Spike stared thoughtfully at Wazoo, then said, "You can't go to Bonine and tell him anything yet. You understand me?"

Wazoo shrugged. "Never can tell what a man will do next. One minute he say if I don't give myself up, he could be in big trouble. Next minute, he orderin' me not to do what he said he wanted me to do before." She threw up her arms and swayed. "Sad, sad, a good-looking man, sexy as they come, and he losin' his mind. Maybe a devil or two in your brain, sexy man. Maybe we gotta call up some spirits to chase them devils out."

Spike bent and brought his nose close to Wazoo's. "And maybe you should start thinkin' about the possibility that someone could think you know too much. If it should happen that the wrong pair of ears hears about you bein' a witness to murder, someone with a lot to lose could find out what you know and decide to do somethin' about that. So, until our man — or woman — is in custody, you probably won't be saying a word to a soul."

39

"Looks like you'll have a fine day for your fete," Spike said. Vivian drove the Rosebank van and he looked ahead through the windshield. A tissue-thin moon played peekaboo between bands of red and orange clouds trailed across a royal-blue sky.

The fete wasn't hers, but Vivian let the comment pass. It was late and she was tense. They needed answers but weren't getting any. Spike's fear that people might get complacent just in time for another ghastly murder played repeatedly in her brain.

"What are you thinkin'?" Spike asked.

"D'you think Morgan did it?"

"I'm not ruling anyone out, but not likin' a man isn't a reason to convict him."

A big gathering of people at Rosebank, for the kind of bash that was touted as lasting all day and into the night, scared Vivian sick.

Anything could happen . . . or nothing. She locked her elbows and her palms were sweaty on the wheel.

"I take it you don't care if the weather's fine tomorrow," Spike said.

"Sorry, I didn't mean to ignore that. I've got a lot on my mind, just like you, and I'm worried something could go wrong tomorrow."

He rubbed the back of her neck and leaned to kiss her cheek. "I'm not going to lie and say you don't have a thing to be worried about, but I think we'll have things covered as best we can with a bunch of guys who don't represent the law in Iberia."

"You're a P.I.," she reminded him.

"I sure am." He laughed and she figured he was thinking the P.I. bit sounded weak.

"We haven't talked about payment."

The look he gave her ended that line of discussion.

"Cyrus, Joe, Bill and Marc are concerned citizens ready to come to our aid. Deputy Lori has to hold down the fort in Toussaint unfortunately, but I'm going to have a word with Ozaire. He's an ornery son of a snake, but he'd come through in a pinch. My dad's tougher than tacks —"

"So am I," she told him, irritated that he wasn't mentioning any able-bodied women.

"Have a word with Jilly. She'll be there sellin' pastries and coffee and if she could give us a hand, she would. She's no marshmallow."

Spike shifted and dropped against the back of his seat.

Vivian glanced at him. His eyes were fastened on the roof of the van and from what she could see of his face he was irritated. "What is it, now?" she asked. "Wasn't I supposed to say we have some women around who could be useful?"

"Of course you were. I had this sudden image of the motley army gathered on the front steps at Rosebank and I admit it was a, well, it was kind of a scary picture."

She laughed. "You'd feel better if they were all dressed in camouflage and toting machine guns or whatever."

"Vivian, Vivian." Ignoring the probability that she'd drive off the road, he got close again and kissed the corner of her mouth. "You've got a thing about camouflage. If you want the truth, I'd settle for a Ranger team or a few Navy SEALs. But if I can't have 'em, I'm satisfied with what I've got. And don't forget that the moment something happened, Big Bad Bonine would mount the attack."

He experimented with slipping the tip of

his tongue between her lips and dragging it slowly along her teeth to see just how badly he could distract her.

Vivian swerved off the road and braked hard, throwing him forward and while he was still grousing about irresponsible driving, she used his ears to anchor his face and kissed him soundly. When she pulled back for air, he was panting.

"Now," she told him. "*You* are irresponsible. Quit distracting me. We're expected at Rosebank."

He inclined his face so the dashboard lights cast the angles of his face in wicked line and shadow. "Do we have to go?"

Spike Devol didn't allow himself to be lighthearted often enough. She smoothed her hands over his chest, smiled when those very nice muscles contracted, and hooked her fingers under his belt. He also had nice muscles there. "You think we should park?" she said.

He rested his forehead on hers and sighed. "I know what I want to do, but it's not going to happen — right now. Okay, I'll go, but not willingly."

They were slow getting to the point where Vivian could drive away again, but they were almost there. She had rolled the windows down a little and within minutes the scent of roses crowded into the vehicle. She wasn't ready to forget the somber reminders the smell brought but neither could she hate the flowers or their richness.

She drove between the stone gateposts and along the winding alley of giant live oaks decorated with swaying Chinese lanterns. Wazoo must have a well-rehearsed crew at her command. Trailers, trucks and pieces of equipment for tomorrow were parked beside the drive. By tomorrow night a searchlight would be installed to bring more evening revelers. When she and Spike cleared the trees they saw that bunting had already been looped from branches surrounding the front lawns and strands of colored lights shivered in the breeze. Flashlights bobbed and shadowy figures hurried through lantern beams. Work continued.

"Homer and Ozaire are both boilin' crawfish and word's out there'll be a war on to prove whose got the best stuff. They're barbecuing, too, Mama said."

"Yeah," Spike said. He sounded disinterested and when she gave him another glance, she found his entire attention still trained on her. He smiled, probably to show her how sweet and harmless he was. She knew better.

"Here we go," she said, drawing up in front. "Into the next round. I never know what I'll find when I go through this front door. When I called Mama I told her that no way should she let Morgan Link in here. She's going to want to know why."

"Not a word until I say so," Spike told her, leaping to the ground and ushering her ahead of him up the front steps. Boxes of soft drinks stood like a fortification along the galleries and behind the soft drinks, barrels of beer had been stacked. He didn't comment but figured things could get overly cheerful the following day.

Vivian walked into Rosebank with Spike behind her and Boa came as if she had wheels, not legs. That was in the seconds before the wheels turned into wings and four pounds of dog leaped into her arms with enough force to drive her back a step.

"She's dangerous," Spike said and Boa scrambled up Vivian's chest and shoulder until she could glare at him. Vivian called out to her mother.

Charlotte trotted from the kitchens carrying a cordless phone. "You timed that very well. This is Jack Charbonnet from New Orleans for you, Spike. I didn't know he was Cyrus's brother-in-law." She said to Vivian, "What did you mean about Morgan?"

"Don't worry about it," Vivian whispered. "Spike will explain."

Mama raised her eyebrows and crossed her arms, but the next thing she said was, "Homer and I have had an interesting evening."

"I surely do remember you, Jack," Spike said into the receiver. "Vivian and I enjoyed visiting the riverboat."

"That so," he said, his brow puckered. "Did your source say he knew who got the payoff?"

Charlotte put her mouth to Vivian's ear and said, "I told Homer what you found out and we've been pineapple hunting. They're everywhere, and we aren't the only ones looking for them."

"Mama, don't overreact. What I didn't say on the phone is that Wazoo already admitted searching," Vivian said. "She told us because she felt guilty. She thinks we'll get rid of her and she'll go to prison." Vivian wanted to listen to Spike's conversation.

"Wazoo couldn't have done all the damage we found. It was done in a hurry, too, and they didn't try to cover up what they'd done. We've got damaged furniture everywhere in the north wing. We're going to have to find that egg. If we thought we needed money before, we need it more than ever now."

Vivian scratched Boa's back and got her neck washed in return. "How long ago do you think these other people started poking around?"

"Weeks," Charlotte said, throwing up her hands. "But how can that be? We've barely touched that wing. We're concentrating on this side."

"That wouldn't stop someone working here from going over there," Vivian pointed out. "Easiest thing in the world. And it means someone else knew about the egg before any of us — before Wazoo. Makes me feel creepy to think about it going on while we've been here."

Vivian saw Spike smile and her breath caught in her throat. He looked straight ahead and at nothing in particular but that bitter smile meant he saw ugly things in his mind. He said, "Thank you, Jack. I owe you. Bye," and gave the phone back to Charlotte.

Vivian caught the slight shake of his head and figured he didn't want her to ask any questions yet.

"I'd better get Wendy," he said.

Homer came down the stairs shaking his head. He'd arrived in time to hear what Spike just said. "She's sleepin', finally. Give her some time before you wake her up again." He addressed Charlotte, "If that's okay with you."

Mama didn't do cool too well. The grin would have given her away even without, "Don't anyone dare wake up that little angel. We won't hear of it, will we, Vivian? No, of course not. You see how Vivian and I wouldn't even allow you to wake that sweet child."

Homer looked at Charlotte as if she were not only the most admirable of women but definitely the one in charge of what would or would not happen to Wendy.

"I'll get along home, then," Homer said to Spike. "I reckon Charlotte will give you a place to stretch out till Wendy wakes up. See you tomorrow." He swept his hat from a chair by the front door and walked out into the night.

"I need my sleep, too," Charlotte said with a huge yawn. She pointed a finger at Vivian. "Whatever Wazoo may have done she already feels badly about, so don't you say another word to her about it. And that goes for you, too," she told Spike. "You just ask Father Cyrus about forgiveness. She got carried away and now she's sorry. Now, I'm going to sleep well knowing you're in the house. Make yourself comfortable wherever you like. Vivian will help you."

Off she went. Up the stairs with a whole lot of energy for a tired woman.

"Are you thinkin' what I'm thinkin'?" Spike said when the two of them were alone.

"I don't know what you're thinking," Vivian told him, "so how do I know if we're thinking the same thing?"

He caught hold of her wrist and led her into the small, circular sitting room at the entrance to the south wing.

Boa contrived to all but stand on Vivian's shoulder, all the better to show her teeth, all the way to her molars, to Spike. Fortunately Boa's coordination wasn't great. She put so much energy into baring her teeth that she overbalanced and fell to the floor. Vivian clucked and bent to pick her up but the dog shot away, out of the room, and her dashing feet made a scritch-scratch noise on the stairs. "I hope she doesn't wake Wendy," Vivian said.

"Not likely. That child goes out for the count. The Martins are out of circulation."

Vivian spread her hands. "What do you mean?"

He stood before a black marble fireplace, looking down on more carved pineapples, these with crowns of green enameled leaves. The things were set in straight rows and there must have been fifty of them, each on a separate tile.

"Louis was a smart guy, right?" Spike said.

"Very."

"Too bad his sons didn't inherit any of his brains. What interests us most is that they've been accused of paying graft. It's vague, no names, just tips to look around. But they're in custody for something really stupid."

Vivian moved beside him and waited.

"They hired some thickheaded parolee to break into Louis's house — Mrs. Angelica Doby's house now — and load all the artwork into a truck. They'd been told the Dobys would be away and the house locked up."

"But Angelica was there?" Vivian shuddered.

"She was away but the place is loaded with silent alarms. The guy dealt with the obvious stuff but never thought of a whole backup system." He snorted. "This is a loser I already know. Dante Cornelious. Small-time organized stuff. He was mixed up in a case here last year and the only reason he was paroled after a few months was because everything he set out to pull off, including knocking someone off, backfired."

"So he broke into Louis's house, then fingered George and Edward."

Spike rolled his eyes. "Listen to your language. You've been hanging out with the wrong people."

"Person." She corrected him. "And you can hope I never say anything worse than *fingered*. What does this mean?"

He met her eyes and she knew she looked hopeful. "I'm not sure, but I know what I'm praying for. This graft. If the Martin boys paid someone to kill their father it'll come out now. It wouldn't make it less ugly but it would mean we're in the clear."

"You think that's it?" she asked.

Spike hesitated long enough before saying "Yeah" to make her doubt he was being honest. She did think he'd like it to be true as much as she would.

"Spike," she said quietly, holding one of his forearms. "It could be all over. Couldn't we hold on to that thought? And still be vigilant, of course."

He smiled at her with the usual effect. Her womb turned liquid warm and her knees didn't feel too steady. "You've got it," he said. "We'll hold that thought."

They looked at each other. Vivian would never tire of seeing Spike and the thought unsettled her a lot. The case would be solved eventually. Then what? She couldn't quite accept that they'd walk off into the sunset together.

"There's a room next to mine — I mean, Wendy's — that you can use," she told him.

He reached for her other hand and rubbed his thumb back and forth over the knuckles. "Thank you, but I don't think I'll be sleeping tonight."

Vivian was instantly on alert. "Why? You think something's going to happen?"

He brought her fingers to his face and rested them against his cheek. "No. Other things will keep me awake."

She couldn't look away from him.

"If we drifted apart, I don't think I could take it," he said. "Danger puts people in another place. They cling together out of need. When it's all over, the closeness often goes away."

So they were thinking similar things. "And you think that's going to happen with us?"

His eyes were so dark they weren't blue anymore. "Things have changed a lot for you. Your life is going to be different. Hey —" He touched her mouth to stop her from protesting. "I know you haven't decided what it's all going to mean to you, but it isn't reasonable to think you'd want to keep on hanging around with a country deputy who works a couple of jobs — and has an old man and a daughter he's responsible for. And I wouldn't change the last two, by the way."

Vivian's stomach rolled and kept on rolling, but if he thought he'd sealed their fate — negatively — he was wrong. She was a fighter. "Instead of trying to get me to say something so you don't have to make any decisions, why don't you tell me what you want? If you want anything."

He caught her by the shoulders and his fingers dug in, not that she was complaining. "I don't even know where to start."

"My rule is to jump in as close to the end as possible without leaving anything out."

He bowed his head so she couldn't see his face. "I always say you're smart."

The only light in the room was a table lamp with a weak bulb. Since Spike stood in front, he all but blocked it and all they had was a muted glow. Vivian couldn't think of another body she'd rather look at. A slim man, nevertheless Spike was all muscle and the way his shoulders filled out his shirt and his torso tapered to his flat belly made a great view anytime. Since he was technically still on duty, he'd changed into a fresh uniform before leaving his place. She took hold of a button on his shirt. "What they said about the way women responded to men in uniform is so true." Except that she responded to him whatever he wore.

"Then I'll wear uniforms all the time," he said. "You're going to make me do the serious talking, aren't you?"

"I surely am."

"All this stuff is going to pass and there'll be you and me left to decide where we want to go, if anywhere."

"That's right," she told him, although she didn't like the way he handled his words.

"Whatever I do, I've got to consider Wendy's happiness."

She nodded. "Yes, you do. I wouldn't like you if you wanted it any other way."

"You live here and I live at my place. I don't know what you'd want to do about that."

"You're jumping the gun. Those things always work out. Anyway, Homer loves the business and he'd do a great job running it for you. He more or less does that now."

His next smile was brilliant and Vivian wondered what that was about. As quickly as he showed all those white teeth, he wiped the look from his face.

"You came here to help your mother get

this place off the ground. That's going to happen. I think it'll be the most successful hotel around."

She shoved away a fleeting thought about Morgan trying to get rid of them. Spike would have to get accustomed to Rosebank. "I agree with you and it's wonderful."

"What are your plans?" Spike asked. "Once your mother doesn't need you anymore."

Spike could make a woman real angry. Why didn't he just spit out what he wanted? "I like being needed," she told him. "I guess I'll just find someone else who could use a good partner."

He looked at the floor. "Makes sense."

Kicking him probably wouldn't help, but her throat burned, and her eyes. She couldn't do this all alone, supposing he wanted what she hoped for.

"Sometimes at night when I can't sleep, I go down by the bayou," he said. His thumb would soon be taking skin right off her knuckles. "I stand in the dark and listen. You can hear things movin' under the water, and the rustle of the hyacinth crowding together. Some nights you smell cedar. I love that. And the mist when it breaks apart and swirls around the tree trunks in the water. There's no other place in the world like this."

She could see it, feel it. "No. I've loved it here all my life."

"Have you?" He raised his face to study her. "But you'd rather live in the city."

"Who says?"

He didn't answer.

"Spike, I'm not going away anytime soon and I'll probably never live in New Orleans again. I'll always want to visit but I'll make sure I can do that."

He leaned back to get a better look at her. "Oh, God" was all he said before wrapping her in his arms and rocking her against him.

She held him tight and wished she could help him through whatever battle he fought.

"Do you think you could be happy living right here — in this area?"

She turned cold and goose bumps popped out. "Yes."

"You don't think you'd eventually tire of it and want to move on?"

"I don't think so."

He rocked her and rested his chin on top of her head. "It wouldn't be easy for me to get started somewhere else."

"You don't want to," she told him. "That would make it really hard. So why even think about it?"

"Because . . ." He held her away from him

and his hands shook on her shoulders. "You know why."

She would not do all the work. "Tell me, just in case I've got it wrong."

"Because I can't even think about not seeing you all the time. I don't think I'll ever be whole unless you're where I can get to you fast."

Spike didn't have a silver tongue but his words brought tears rushing to her eyes.

"I have nightmares where you're gone. You've left and I'm here, seeing you wherever I look, and feelin' so empty I don't know how to keep on livin'."

He was developing his word skills fast, and destroying her control in the process. "I wouldn't want to open my eyes again if we made a mess of this, Spike. I mean it."

"There you are, then." He gave a short laugh. "I guess we understand each other."

Taking him to that spare bedroom she'd mentioned and just lying wrapped in his arms would feel so good, but he was wrong, they weren't "there." "Tell me what you want," she asked him again.

Spike said, "Oh," and turned a shade of red under his tan. "Yeah, I should do that."

He walked away and parted the drapes on

nothing but darkness behind the building. When he turned around, he wasn't flushed anymore. She'd never seen him look more serious.

Spike came to her rapidly and shocked her by kneeling in front of her.

"Get up," she urged, laughing nervously. "What are you doing down there?"

Not a hint of a smile appeared. He took her hands in his and said, "I love you very much. Will you marry me? Please?"

"I will *not* cry," she said, bending over and pressing his face to her. "Yes, I'll marry you. Spike, I love you, too. And I love that we're here like this. It feels wonderful."

"Quickly?" he said.

"What?"

"Marry me quickly. I can't wait."

"Okay." Her chest was about to explode with happiness. "We'll talk to Cyrus."

Spike looked up at her and appeared panicked. "I haven't been inside a church in —"

"Doesn't matter." She hesitated. "When you were married the first time —"

"Vegas," he said. "And you're right. St. Cécil's it is, but it's got to be a real small wedding."

"You and me, Mom, Homer, Wendy and . . . Well, there would be a few people there."

"Wendy loves you," Spike said. "I think she'll be tickled when we tell her."

Vivian didn't want to break the bubble, not for a very long time, but she'd better show Spike where he could sleep and get some rest herself. They couldn't know what tomorrow might hold. She pulled Spike to his feet and they embraced while Vivian found she couldn't seem to concentrate on what she should do next.

Boa helped her focus by dashing into the room and threading in and out of their ankles.

"She's all wound up," Vivian said, reluctantly loosening her grip on Spike.

"That makes three of us."

Boa rushed for the door again, in time to leap into Wendy's arms. The child was wearing one of Vivian's pajama tops with the sleeves rolled way up, and her bare arms and legs seemed fragile. Her pigtails hadn't been taken down and odd pieces of hair stuck out. She'd put on her glasses and her eyes shone very large behind the lenses. Vivian figured if she held Boa as tightly as Wendy did, the dog would struggle away.

"Wendy," Spike said. He put an arm around Vivian. "We've got something pretty exciting to tell you."

"I know." Wendy's voice rose to a squeak and she kissed Boa's head over and over. "I was sittin' on the stairs, listenin'. I want to call Gramps and tell him I'm going to live with a dog."

40

The sixth day

Spike's cell phone rang at 5:00 a.m.

He fumbled to grab up the thing from his pocket before it woke Vivian. Too late. She'd been asleep with her head resting on folded arms on top of the kitchen table, but by the time he got the receiver to his ear, she blinked at him with heavy eyes.

"Yeah?" he said as quietly as possible.

"It's Cyrus."

Spike leaned back in his own chair on the side of the table opposite from Vivian. "D'you know what time it is?"

Cyrus cleared his throat. "I have to prepare for morning mass but I wanted to get to you and Vivian first. I've shirked my duty and I've got to fix that before I let more time pass. I know you're at Rosebank. Homer said so before he hung up on me."

"What's wrong?" Spike didn't feel tired

anymore. "What's happened?"

"I didn't call the house phone there because I didn't want to wake everyone."

"Good." He waited. Vivian sat upright pushing her hair away from her face.

"You're with Vivian, I expect."

Spike trapped the phone between ear and shoulder and crossed his arms. "Yes."

"Well . . . Yes, with Vivian. You know how much I think of both of you."

"We think a lot of you, too." He wasn't going to help Cyrus out, not at this time of day.

"I'll get right to the point, then."

Spike waited again.

"I said, I'll get right to the point," Cyrus told him.

"You do that."

"You and Vivian are special people, two of the best, and I only want what's good for you, what will make you happy. I'm losin' sleep over you."

It took restraint not to point out that Spike wasn't getting the sleep he wanted at the moment, either. "It's nice of you to care, but there isn't a thing for you to worry about. We're fine."

"Do you know the date for sure?"

Spike almost dropped the phone. "What? How do you know already?"

Cyrus sighed. "I've known a long time. The woman who works there, Thea, told Doll Hibbs and it eventually got back to Reb. She's feeling as bad as I do. Each time she starts talkin' about it to Vivian, she lets herself get distracted. We're both embarrassed to broach the subject but we care about you and want what's best."

Vivian got up and stood over Spike. He didn't blame her for being curious. "I don't see how you and Reb could have known anything weeks ago. Or Thea. Does everyone know?"

"Absolutely not. Thea and Doll swore to keep silent. That wasn't easy to pull off. That only leaves Reb. Even Madge doesn't know."

No way was Cyrus talking about a wedding. "You're going to have to be more direct," Spike said. Vivian ran her fingers through his hair and he smiled reassuringly up into her anxious face.

"The baby," Cyrus said. "Something was said at Rosebank about Vivian's condition and Thea overheard. Reb's worried because she doesn't think Vivian's seeing a doctor and it must have happened a while back, when we didn't realize you two had more than a casual thing going. I should have noticed how the two of you reacted to each other. Maybe I did in a way but I just can't remember thinkin' about it. I saw you at Jilly's together once and you were talkin' like you were havin' fun. I — well, I thought that was nice, nothing more."

Spike took the phone from his ear and looked at it, then he looked at Vivian again. "You aren't —" He shook his head. He actually stared at her middle before coming completely to his senses. "Of course you aren't expecting a baby. Where would he get that idea from?"

Vivian frowned, but only for an instant before she grinned and clamped both hands over her mouth.

He would never pretend to understand female reactions sometimes. Cyrus's muffled voice could still be heard.

"Whoever gave you the idea we're having a baby is wrong," Spike said, speaking into the phone once more. "Absolutely wrong and it's bizarre you ever got the idea. But you can do us a favor. Vivian and I are gettin' married. We'd surely appreciate it if you'd make the arrangements. It needs to be as soon as possible."

41

"Ozaire's chargin' a nickel less," Gator Hibbs said, leaning on the lowered tailgate of the pickup where Homer was hard at work over a bubbling cauldron of crawfish.

"Guess you'd best snap up that offer then," Homer told the man whose eyes watered in his round face from squinting up into the sun.

Gator chewed a toothpick from one side of his mouth to the other. From the back of a Ford 250 pickup parked beside Homer, a band Wazoo had brought in from New Orleans, "For free, 'cause we got ties," belted out "I Wish I Could Shimmy Like My Sister Kate." Despite there being an hour of morning left, dancers had already made sure a large patch of grass would have to be replaced.

"Cain't think," Gator bellowed. "Too much goin' on."

"Ozaire's undercuttin' my price," Homer yelled back. "You need to hotfoot it over there and get you some of his stuff."

"Rather have yours."

Homer tapped the price board again. "How much you want?"

"A nickel off," Gator said.

Homer turned his back to flip crabs on the barbecue and Gator wandered away.

To help out, and stop Wendy from running all over the place announcing that Vivian and Spike were getting married, Charlotte kept cooked crawfish and crab warm on a nearby table and enjoyed the novelty of selling food on paper plates. Ozaire's recent price cut was the second of the morning. The first had been only two cents but Homer insisted he wasn't playing the game. He'd stand on offering the best vittles.

She surveyed the crowd and figured it had to number a couple of hundred. They'd roped off the back of the house because Spike didn't figure they had enough people to keep a safety watch there.

With cars parked on a lot opposite Rosebank, the front grounds gave more than enough space, or so Wazoo insisted. Charlotte couldn't see a spare inch of ground anywhere but people seemed to like it that way.

She looked past the children's sack races run by Madge, with the aid of a clown on stilts, and saw Vivian with Spike, Cyrus, Joe Gable, and Marc and Reb Girard. They stood in the shade of some arrowwood bushes, except for Reb who sat in a lawn chair with Gaston. They all made a serious group and when Bill Green wandered up with an ice cream in hand, he soon lost his smile, too. Charlotte knew better than to try to find anything out in the middle of such chaos, but she wouldn't relax until she understood what was going on.

Wendy had finally quieted down after talking nonstop since they'd found Spike and Vivian dozing over coffee at the kitchen table that morning. Charlotte turned to say something to the girl, only to find her fast asleep on the blanket Vivian had spread for Boa. The dog and the child curled together in the shade of a golf umbrella.

"Hello, Charlotte."

At the sound of her name she spun around and looked up into Gary Legrain's face.

"I had to come," he said. "I wanted to see how you and Vivian were getting along."

"You left in a hurry," she told him. His anxious eyes softened her annoyance with him. "We've wondered about you."

He reached into his back pocket for his wallet and put down bills for a plate of crab. "Just realized I'm hungry," he said, smiling slightly. "I didn't think to eat before coming."

Charlotte didn't comment.

Gary put away several crabs, picked up a napkin and wiped his mouth. "The will shocked me. I had to get away for a little while and I also had to take stock of the firm and what it all means. Did you hear about the Martins?"

"Spike and Vivian told me. You weren't the only one shocked by Louis Martin's will."

He set down his plate and rubbed grease from his fingers. His eyes never left hers. "I know that. You understand that I don't believe there was anything between you and Louis, don't you?"

"Good, because there wasn't." She stiffened her back. "I loved my husband very much and I don't know if I'll ever stop missing him."

A flurry of customers arrived and Charlotte turned her attention to them.

"I'll take a wander around," Gary said. "If

it's okay, I'd like us to talk some more later."

Charlotte said, "Fine," and watched him walk off.

"I messed up, me," Wazoo shouted, although she also smiled widely. She wore one of her ankle-length black lace dresses with a long mantilla of the same lace trailing from a comb atop her head. She twirled as she ran by, and her flowing clothes twisted this way and that around her legs. "Listen up, all o' you. Wazoo forget a big event, real big. We gotta do it now." In one arm she carried a huge bouquet of flowers she must have bought — or appropriated — from tables in the driveway where the ladies of St. Cécil's Altar Society were selling them.

"Wazoo," Charlotte called after her, but got no response.

Around and around Wazoo sped until she finally captured enough attention to hush the crowd a little. "Now," she shouted. "It's time for some ceremony. Ain't no proper event without ceremony."

Ozaire marched forward with the megaphone he'd been using to hawk his wares and delivered a ringing announcement. "Listen up. This is me, Ozaire Dupre. I got the best crawfish and crabs around. Cheapest, too. Now give your attention to Miz Wazoo who's tryin' to have a ceremony." He handed the megaphone to her.

"Thank you, Ozaire."

Charlotte put her fingers in her ears to lessen the blast.

"It's late, but not too late. We're gonna have us the ribbon-cutting ceremony. Gimme a drumroll."

The drummer on the back of the Ford obligingly started a rumbling.

"Swamp Doggies." Wazoo pointed to the regular band from Pappy's Dancehall. "You play . . . that thing they do for the Pres-i-dent. Not too loud."

"Pomp and Circumstance," zydeco style, had men snatching off their baseball caps and slapping them over their hearts.

Charlotte noted that the dour gathering near the arrowwood bushes was actually smiling, and she smiled with them. Only Wazoo could create this kind of scene.

A huge circle of foam-topped water rose from the dunk tank. The tank was Joe Gable's contribution to the fun, even though he had Wally running it for him. Shrieks followed, ruining Wazoo's setup. She marched to the tank herself and laughter broke out when people saw it was Wally in the water.

Wazoo chided him loudly but he protested for everyone to hear, "I was just checkin' it out, Wazoo. It doesn't fall easy enough so I was fixin' it."

"The ribbon," Wazoo cried, giving Wally another scowl before she returned to the clearing she'd made in the crowd. One man held the end of a bolt of wide ribbon while Thea, looking bashful, pushed a sturdy stick through the middle of the reel and walked backward to unwind a long band of yellow satin.

"Now," Wazoo cried. "Dr. Link and Mrs. Hurst will do the honors."

Morgan, with Susan on his arm, came forward and took an impressively large pair of scissors from Wazoo. Charlotte couldn't help admiring the couple for the handsome picture they made. Susan wore all white and her diamond earrings sparkled in the sunlight. She looked pretty and young, and healthy. Morgan's relaxed stance and the way he looked at his wife made him more appealing than he'd ever seemed to Charlotte before.

"Say somethin' real meaningful," Wazoo said. She gave Susan the bouquet of flowers.

Morgan opened the scissors and said, "May each of us get what we deserve. I declare this fete open." And he cut the ribbon.

Spike and Cyrus stood on either side of Vivian. She caught each one of them by an upper arm and pulled until they bent close to listen to her.

"Did you see that?" she asked.

Both men said, "Yes," and she joined them in whispering, "Left-handed."

"I think I almost forgot about it," Vivian continued.

"Doesn't have to mean a thing," Cyrus pointed out. "Many people are left-handed."

"But many people aren't left-handed and adept with blades," Vivian said.

Shadow hid much of Spike's face. "I don't think the Martin boys hired Morgan Link to kill Louis, do you?"

"If they hired anyone at all," Vivian said, and when Spike looked at her she saw nothing too reassuring in his expression.

Spike filled the others in on Vivian's observation and all faces became grave. "I thought Bonine was going to be here," Marc Girard said. "Not that I expect any help from that quarter."

Joe pushed his hands deep in his pockets. "That man's a dud. It's like he's deliberately brushed two killings under the rug. He needs to be held accountable."

Spike and Vivian glanced at each other.

"You think something's going to happen today?" Reb made an automatic sweep of the grounds. "I don't think it will. Too public."

"I don't think anything else will happen at all," Bill said. "Ever. I think the killings were professional. Someone wanted Louis dead and poor old Gil got in the way. Now it's over."

Cyrus nodded agreement but Spike said, "If you remember, Vivian and I made an unscheduled landing in Bayou Lafourche. That had to be a warning, didn't it? For us to quit stickin' our noses into things. And that was after Louis died."

"I don't know." Bill narrowed his eyes. "You may have something there. When do you think you'll hear more from your Iberia source?"

A ball hit Cyrus in the middle and he trapped it against him, looking around for the culprit. Wearing a pleased expression, Madge jogged toward them. Cyrus lobbed the ball back and she caught it.

"To be honest," Spike said, "I may never hear another word."

"Shit," Bill said with a lot of feeling, then, "Sorry about that."

"You don't have to be," Reb told him. "This whole thing stinks."

Snickers apparently went over her head. "I've got to run out," Bill said. "Believe it or not I've got a couple coming in to look at that old theater. And before you ask what they think they want it for — they're talking about renovation and in time, putting on productions. I think they'll take one look at the place and take off running so I shouldn't be long. I'll be ready for a cold beer when I get back."

They shouted after him, promising to drink every drop before he could get any. Vivian saw Gary Legrain walking straight toward them and said, "Gary's back," under her breath.

"Nice of him," Spike said.

Grinning, Gary strolled up to them and said, "Hi. Some do going on here."

He got polite responses and stood among them as if he'd never left Rosebank without a word to anyone.

From close range, Madge sent the red ball back to Cyrus with enough force to buy her a solid "oomph." She followed it almost at once and he took her head in the crook of his arm while she yelped for mercy. He deposited her on the ground and went to his haunches beside her. "Wicked deeds never pay," he told her, keeping a hand on her neck. "Do you promise to reform?"

Spike and Vivian blocked the two of them from the others who couldn't have seen how the smile faded from Madge's lips and longing entered her dark eyes. Cyrus touched her hair, smoothed it lightly and jumped up, helping Madge to join him. "You did hear these two are getting married, didn't you?" he asked her.

Vivian winced.

"No," Madge said, smiling again. "I've been running the children's races. Nobody told me anything. Congratulations."

"And," Vivian said softly, "we've been able to put Cyrus's mind at rest about my fictitious pregnancy."

Madge stopped in the act of brushing grass clippings from her jeans. "Huh?"

Vivian winked at her. "Thea overheard some remark that made her think I was pregnant. She told Doll, who told Reb, who went to Cyrus for advice on how to help me."

"Oo, ya ya. That would be the remark I made to get you away from Bonine that day?"

"Uh-huh."

In barely more than a whisper, Madge said to Cyrus, "If you'd said something to me, the way you used to, I'd have explained." She looked at her watch. "Excuse me. Time for the egg-and-spoon race."

Vivian and Spike were silent, watching

Madge walk away and trying not to let Cyrus know they saw his confusion. Confusion and something close to anger. Vivian promised herself she'd push hard to have Madge move into Rosebank, then hope she could do something to help, like introduce Madge to a man who was both nice and available.

The egg-and-spoon race soon had them laughing. One toddler boy wrapped both pudgy hands around his egg and the bowl of a spoon and trotted toward the finish line with a huge pucker between his fair eyebrows. While turmoil raged around him and the field became steadily smaller, he kept on moving until he crossed the line first. He formed his own cheering squad but his parents and others were quick to join in, at which point the remaining contestants quit. Madge pronounced little Kirby the winner and the crowd laughed but demanded another race.

"That boy will go far," Joe said amid murmurs of agreement.

"Spike."

Ellie Byron had walked behind them and she tapped Spike's shoulder. When he turned to smile at her she said, "Would Vivian excuse you if I had you come with me for a few minutes?"

"Of course," Vivian said. "Did you bruise your forehead?" There were purplish marks there.

Ellie touched them and grimaced. "So silly," she said. "A book fell on me in the shop."

"Why don't we take Vivian with us?" Spike said. "We haven't had a chance to tell you our news."

"No," Ellie said. Her breathing was obvious and shallow. "This won't take long, Spike. Please."

Vivian swallowed. Something about Ellie frightened her. She gave Spike a little push. "Go on. I'll be here when you get back."

42

Almost everyone they saw had something to say and at least half an hour had passed before Spike and Ellie ducked under the rope that ran from a railing at the end of the gallery to a tree close to the boundary with Serenity House. Hand-lettered Private signs hung at intervals.

Spike expected to run into rule-breakers on the other side but, apart from two teenagers huddled together against a wall, didn't see any. "Can you tell me what's on your mind now?" he asked Ellie.

She looked at the ground and walked on.

He caught her by the arm and waited until she turned her face up to his. She didn't make a sound but tears ran down her cheeks.

"Ellie," he said gently. "Tell me. Let me help you now."

"I'm a coward," she told him. "I don't know what's happening, but please God I haven't put someone else at risk by saving myself."

Completely in the dark, Spike bowed his head to look at her more closely. She shook her arm free and took off, hurrying past the conservatory and toward the side of the north wing. He caught up with her and let her keep moving to the partially cleared but ruined gardens behind Rosebank.

"He told me to take you back here."

"And he is?"

She shook her head, whipping her curly hair back and forth. "I didn't see him. He came up behind me in the dark last night. My head . . . I don't want to talk about it."

"Well, you've done as he asked." There were situations in which pressing questions went nowhere. "Now what?"

"I don't know," she murmured and the tears flowed faster. "Why didn't I get in touch with you last night?"

"Do you want to tell me?"

"He threatened me. He would have killed me, I know he would."

Frustration made Spike's nerves crawl but he had to let her go at her own pace.

"He *would*." Ellie sounded as if she were trying to convince herself.

"It'll be okay," he told her, with no idea what he was talking about. "You were told to bring me back here. That's all?"

She put a hand over her mouth and looked past him. He glanced over his shoulder but saw nothing but the same scene from moments earlier: the gardens, pieces of equipment and the empty pool.

She spoke and Spike had to lean close to hear. "He said to take you to the pool."

Spike studied the pale stone rectangle more closely. At the far end, steps led down into the drained interior. Empty flower urns stood high at each corner.

"So we can go back now?" Ellie said.

He wanted to agree but figured he ought to take a closer look first. "Stay here," he told her and scrunched over weed-dotted gravel to the closest end of the pool.

Even through his hat, the sun beat on his head. His mouth grew dry and he thought about cold water — like the water that once filled the old Rosebank pool.

At the raised wall he stopped and squinted toward the opposite end. Small, wet pools glinted in the sunlight. He hadn't known they'd been testing the plumbing.

Bright pools, or narrow drizzles and drops, he guessed. In the glare they looked more like oil than water.

Planting a boot on the wall, he leaned over to see the shallow end.

The naked corpse, its hands tied behind its back, sprawled, chest down, where the poolside joined the bottom. The head rested on its side. A white rose bloom peeped coyly from beneath a shoulder. The obscene kiss shone sticky bright.

Shaded from the sun, blood didn't resemble oil at all.

43

He'd about had it with the real-estate business. Driving demanding slobs around, often because they were bored and it was cheap entertainment, sucked.

Well, Bill figured he'd be moving on shortly anyway.

The Bellevue Theater, a pink stucco building baking in the sun, opened onto deserted Crawfish Alley, a bleached, sandy little street without sidewalks. Opposite the old theater, paint peeled from a row of condemned shotgun houses. Other than his own dark gray BMW sedan, the only vehicle in sight was a rusted-out red pickup, not what the would-be theater owners were likely to drive.

The suckers were supposed to meet him there and he'd timed things so they'd show five minutes before him. Timing would be everything today.

Might as well open the doors and let in some air. The place would be a fry pan inside. The doors were double, arched and wide, with a broken lamp on either side. The box office had been shuttered for years. On boards weathered to paintless gray, layers of paste had petrified the withered fragments of playbills past.

The doors were already open. At least, the right one was cracked an inch or so. The key in Bill's pocket was supposed to be the only one. He pushed the door all the way open and a lance of blinding light spread over filthy carpet where the single color he could make out had once been red in a fleur-de-lis pattern.

Bill glanced back at the red pickup. Jerks looking for something or someone to break, and in the building to destroy before running away? Or his clients? Wouldn't be the first time by many that customers found a way to get inside some place before he got there.

The door could be warped and have opened on its own.

Flexing his hands, he stepped inside and stood against a wall. Old habits never died. The kind of habits he'd had to learn had kept him alive this long.

Dust instantly covered his shoes and billowed upward to spin in the light through the door. On the left stood the concession counter, covered with more thick, pale dust. A row of glasses, upside down, made an eerie sight sitting where they'd been left and strung together with skeins of cobwebs. The mirror behind the counter reflected wavery gray shapes in its grimy glass.

Bill turned, taking in the entire lobby. Sure it looked bad, but he didn't see any water damage. From the back of the ticket office he could see through the glass to where the cashier had sat. On the counter, beside a big brass till, were rolls of tickets and when he investigated he saw they'd been worth a dollar each.

He should suggest that his thespian enthusiasts could make a killing by turning the place into a haunted setup. If they still thought the play must go on, there were plenty of ghoulish productions they could run. Yeah, not a bad idea in a little town that could use a new draw.

In the mud-colored wall that separated the theater from the lobby were three brown baize doors with one tiny, oval window in each.

Bill approached the left one with caution and peered through the bubble glass. The smallest wash from the outside sun settled a faint rim along the back row of seats. He could see where the aisle started downward, but nothing more.

A sudden rumble had him ducking and covering his head. The noise rolled overhead and for an instant he wondered if it could be thunder.

Where the hell were his clients? He had to get back to the fete, the sooner the better.

He heard the rumble again and felt the building vibrate mildly.

If a couple of young toughs thought he was too old to deal with them, they were about to meet some painful truth. Bill pushed into the back of the theater, pulling a minute flashlight shaped like a credit card from his pocket. The device had a strong, directed beam but he wouldn't use it until he had to.

The sounds he heard came from the direction of the stage. Treading carefully, he walked slowly down the aisle, using his very acute hearing to separate the noise that was different from the creaks he expected in an old building.

More bumping came, and he heard a man laugh. That didn't sound like a kid. The prospective buyers had availed themselves of a weak lock to push their way in. Funny how few people understood trespass.

"Hey," he called out.

Silence followed before a man yelled "Hey" back. "We're looking for the fuse box back here. Should be in one of the wings."

Using the red beam of his flashlight now, Bill made his way to steps that led up to the stage and climbed to soiled boards that squealed at his every step. "Which side are you? Left or right? From where I'm standing?"

"Right. I see your light. We could sure use that."

Bill started for stage left but halted in his tracks. A whirring, a clanking, a whipping together of something overhead caused him to look up.

Just in time for a heavy gauge nylon net to cover and slam him to the ground. Winded, scrabbling with the netting, he tried to get out, but only became more and more twisted inside his cocoon.

"Help," he cried out, feeling foolish. "I think you touched the wrong thing. Help me get out of this." He tore at the mesh and felt the nylon strands cut into the palm of his right hand.

He felt but did not see someone move. Somewhere beyond his feet the man pulled on the nylon cords as if he were closing Bill inside like a big fish in a purse seine.

Sweat popped out, then it poured. His shirt stuck to him and his eyes stung. He'd dropped the flashlight.

"What do you want?" he asked. "Money? All I've got is what's in my wallet. My watch?" Wait till he was free, and he would be. He gritted his teeth and said, "Or is it the BMW? Say the word and the keys are yours." Long ago he'd been taught to decide what was worth fighting for.

"I've got money, and a watch, and a car." The man's laughter shocked Bill. He'd heard it before.

"Who are you?" he said, squirming. Danger was an old companion but still his stomach twisted.

"Don't you know me?" More laughter. "Don't you recognize my voice?"

Bill squeezed his eyes shut and said, "No. You're mixing me up with someone else." He wanted to believe it but he knew who had him in a net.

"Don't you wish. It's payback time, *Brizio*," the man sang out.

Bill struggled to stand up. He felt aware the way he'd learned to be when he faced a threat.

"Nothing to say, not even to your best friend?"

"I don't have friends, Ulisse. You are very stupid to come here like this. I've been merciful. I didn't track you down as most would have. You should have stayed gone. And you shouldn't have interfered. It was you, wasn't it? You killed the gardener and tried to draw attention to me."

A kick to his kidneys landed him in a gasping heap. He dragged air down an aching throat. "Bastard," he whispered. "You're going to pay. Don't forget who I am."

"I haven't forgotten anything about you, including the marks you murdered in certain places."

"They meant nothing to us. It was a game. We all agreed it was a good way to pass the time and we needed the money."

"Guido and I never did the killing. You did. We were stupid enough to go along. How do you like the net? Remember what fun you had using them?"

"Shut your fucking mouth. You made all this trouble. *You.*"

"But you'll pay for it," Ulisse said. "You've been set up and when you crawl out of here, if you do, you'll be charged with murder. It was unfortunate I had to kill the gardener, but we couldn't have him wandering around and seeing what you did to

605

the lawyer before I was ready to reel you in. Once he was dead it was pointless not to use him."

He continued in a droning voice. "Stupid move with the sheriff and the girl in Bayou Lafourche. If they'd died, you'd have brought New Orleans down on your head before it was over. And since you broke out of your little MO they wouldn't have thought it was the work of any serial killer."

"The bayou was supposed to be shallow there. They were supposed to climb out where I could finish them one after the other."

Ulisse sighed. "Only, you bungled it. I thought you were told to quit the killing. After all, the hit was supposed to be a one-time deal. You always were an over-achiever."

"You knew everything, didn't you? I wonder how? Have you been in touch with Guido's friend all along?" Bill surged upward and lunged at a darker confluence of shadows. The laughter came again and a fist smashed into the back of his head. "I did the fat old lawyer because *you* made it impossible for me to refuse when that other clown told me to. Thanks to you and Guido, he had everything on me and he used it to

606

blackmail me." He laughed despite himself. "Unfortunately for you, I turned the tables. I'm blackmailing him and to save himself he'll start singing about you."

"What a waste, I won't be here."

Ulisse kicked Bill's back, then moved swiftly to land a foot in his windpipe. He struggled to breathe and saw red behind his eyelids.

"You're the one they'll lock up forever," Ulisse said. "If they don't fry you."

Laughing caused pain but Bill laughed anyway. "They'll never suspect me. I've been with all the people here. They all like me. I even helped dig up the gardener."

"That must have been a kick in the balls for you. Nasty surprise, hmm?"

Bill smiled to himself. "It was a gift. Thank you very much. One more piece of evidence to show what a nice, helpful, trustworthy guy I am."

The knife sliced into his left shoulder and the back of his arm so rapidly he didn't realize what had happened until it was finished. "What are you doing?" He screamed, felt blood run around the arm, run from the shoulder across his back and down his chest. "Why?"

"For Sylvia and for Guido."

Bill thrashed. He grimaced against the

pain and threw himself around, trying to locate his enemy.

"We were friends," Ulisse said. "One for all and all for one, but you killed him with as little concern as when you stabbed those others. And you left him to die slowly. Sylvia . . . no, I won't talk about Sylvia."

"Our *leader* committed the ultimate sin. He turned into a saint who couldn't handle what had to happen to Sylvia, and went mewling to a stranger," Bill said.

"To someone who had been a close friend since he was a kid. Someone whose opinion he trusted and who he thought could help him decide what he should do. Who could have known he'd made a bad choice and the guy would save the information about you until it was useful to him?"

"Don't interrupt," Bill said. "You were the hater. What did that mean to you?"

"It meant I went along with what seemed like a prank at first and all I had to do was say nothing, move like a wolf, and keep telling you how much I hated. I didn't even know what I was supposed to hate. In the end I stayed in because it was too dangerous to get out. Guido learned that."

"You screwed my wife," Bill said, lunging upward again.

"Why didn't you kill me instead of Sylvia?" Ulisse said.

"She betrayed me."

Ulisse breathed loudly. "So did I."

"She was my wife. She belonged to me. She made promises she forgot when she let you fuck her. But I let you live and this is the thanks I get. How did you know where I was?"

"I've followed you ever since . . . ever since. When I was contacted to make a hit, I said I couldn't do it but I had a friend who could and he even lived close enough to where the victim would be to spit on the spot. Then I said who you were and he thought I was lying at first. Never underestimate the power of coincidence, asshole. And you didn't *let* me live. You couldn't find me — and I was right behind you all the time." He snorted. "The only way to make sure you didn't surprise me was to know where you were."

"We can talk this through," Bill said. "We can make it work for us. I know about something you've never heard of and it's worth millions."

"Whatever it is, it isn't worth anything to me. I don't need it. Not even the precious egg I've heard about. I loved Sylvia. You didn't. You treated her like a piece of garbage and thought she should hang around so you could walk on her some more. We're finished talking."

Ulisse knew about the egg? Bill's arm had turned numb. It felt heavy and cold, except for the hot blood that flowed. "I'm bleeding to death," he said and coughed, knowing he hadn't lost enough blood to be in danger yet.

"That's the whole idea. You're going to bleed to death and while you do, think of what you did to your wife — my lover. Like you said, you like to kill women. You have played with too many women, Brizio. The net is like a bag, isn't it? Tied tight. That one might as well be around your neck because it's going to finish you."

Bill lay on his side, semi-curled up and quiet as if he were failing. And he tried to work his knife from the sheath strapped to his calf. Thank God he was left-handed.

"I don't think you'll reach that knife," Ulisse said, singsong again. "I hate to say goodbye, but you'll get over it."

The man's blade struck again, this time stabbing into Bill's ass, once, twice, deep into the flesh.

He felt the bruising agony and faintly heard Ulisse leave, laughing softly as he went.

Bill passed out.

He came to, choking on dust. His right arm felt like granite and his rear end burned all the way to his bones.

The flashlight had to be there, somewhere. He searched as far as he could without moving. A hard object pressed into his thigh. He'd laugh at himself if he had the energy. Right there and he almost missed it. He managed to squeeze it and shoot a red beam around the area. He looked at his watch and could scarcely believe so little time had passed. What the beam passed over on the floor let him know he had to move, at once, and take charge of his condition if he didn't want to throw away everything he'd worked for. He'd lost a lot of blood. At first he'd had only revenge in mind, a plan to finger the guy who demanded the stuff from Louis Martin, but the stakes had grown far more interesting.

He located his knife and drew it out. With short, ripping slashes he cut through the mesh and struggled free. At the back of the Bellevue there was a broken-down fence. The fence and a narrow trail were all that lay between Bill and a wall behind the cottage he rented.

Cursing his slowness, cursing his foolishness, carelessness, he pushed through a side door from the auditorium and back into the glaring sunshine. Blood dripped from the fingers of his right hand and he knew it soaked his pants.

Deal with the bleeding. Deal with the pain. Finish the job and you're in the clear.

Limping, he made it to the fence and squeezed through a gap. Finally inside the compact cottage and standing in his bathroom, he stripped off his clothes, but there was something to be done before he showered and tried to stanch the blood with dressings and bandages.

Knowing how to deal with a crisis like this one had been part of what he and his "faithful friends" had taught themselves. He prepared rows of cocaine on the countertop beside the sink, but before he snorted, he found the morphine and administered the dose he knew he could handle, the dose he could rely on to work with the cocaine while it gave him the blast he needed.

Disaster supplies, he had. Showered, he stood in the stall until he'd managed to wrap the wounds tightly. Still naked, he climbed out and looked himself over in front of the mirror. He'd done a good job.

Clean clothes and back to the fete.

"Hey there, Bill," Vivian said. She had the little rat in her arms. He hadn't counted on that. He'd walked around the arrowwood bushes to avoid passing any of the others on his way to her. "You weren't long," she said. "Want that beer?"

"No thanks," he said, using every shred of resistance he had against the buzz in his brain, the colors that came and went before his eyes. He pressed his ears hard. Bees were buzzing in there.

"Do your ears hurt? Hey, we've got the doc right here, let's —"

"Please don't," he said. "I don't like to make a fuss and I'll be fine."

"Okay, but I'll be watching you."

Too cheerful, too sure of herself, too nosy. And she didn't look at him the way he liked a woman to do. It didn't matter. He was here to protect his alibi and he was doing a great job. Most men would still be spread out on that stage with their blood draining out. Not Bill Green. He'd live to chop Ulisse fine enough to make boudin.

"There's something going on," Vivian said. "A little while after you left, Ellie Byron asked Spike to go somewhere with her. Apparently it was to the back of the house. They're still there."

"Yeah."

"Bill?"

He turned his attention from the crowd

gyrating and merging into a single entity in front of him. "They're having a good time," he managed to say.

Vivian wasn't listening. Instead she looked down and when he followed her gaze he saw what the cocktail made sure he didn't feel. Blood ran from beneath his right sleeve and over his hand. While he watched, drops fell from the tips of his fingers.

Quickly, he pushed the hand into his pocket. With his left hand, he took hold of Vivian's and pulled her apart from the others.

"What's happened to you?" she asked. "You're really bleeding, Bill." She pushed out the words in worried little gasps. "Into the house. You need attention."

"You don't understand," he told her. "I hoped Spike would be here. Maybe I should go back there and find him."

"Ellie didn't want anyone else with them." She tucked the dog more firmly under her arm. It looked as if it would like to finish what Ulisse had started. She squeezed the animal and shushed her. "Spike wanted me to stay put and wait. But I'm getting Reb and taking you inside to see what you've done to yourself."

A red bird as big as an ostrich swooped in front of his face. Red bird that turned green, then yellow. The huge beak opened and a cottonmouth rolled out. The bird shook its feathers and drops of water flew, flew and turned into rainbow-colored confetti. *Bad ride,* he thought in his muzzy mind. When he tried to focus on Vivian she stretched and shrank and wouldn't keep still.

He shook his head. "You're right that something happened to me. I've been cut in several places. I think it was the killer, only, he blindfolded me and I didn't see him. He must have followed me to the theater. He thought I was dying and he left me there." Fuck it, he couldn't allow her to stay here and blow his cover.

Vivian turned white. "Let's find someone to take a message to Spike."

He put on a frightened expression. "I need the hospital." He swayed a little but clung tightly to Vivian's hand. "I was on my way but I stopped here to tell Spike about everything. I shouldn't have. I should have gone right to get help. Please, I don't like being the center of attention and I'm going to be if I don't get out of here. Will you drive me to the hospital? I trust you, Vivian."

She stared into his face until he feared she saw inside his head and knew what he was up to. "My car is in the old stables," she said. "Round back."

"Mine's in front of Serenity House. We could cut through there. Just drop me off at Emergency and I'll have someone contact you later. Tell Spike what I told you, but wait until you don't have an audience. We don't know enemies from friends around here."

Vivian backed away, past the bushes, pulling him with her. On the other side she said, "Can you hurry? Let me get an ambulance?"

"No! I can hurry," he told her. "I'm a strong man."

They made a run for the BMW.

44

"Look what I've done." Ellie didn't scream or cry, she simply looked matter-of-factly down on the body of Olympia Hurst and spoke in an even voice.

Spike knew shock when he saw it. He flipped on his radio and spoke into his collar mike. "This is Devol from Toussaint. Gimme Detective Bonine. Yeah? Where is he? No, you're right, you don't have to tell me a thing. How about Frank Wiley?" He said, "Sit down on that bench back there" to Ellie and she backed away slowly until she could do as she'd been told. "Detective Wiley? Frank? Thanks. Spike Devol here. I'm at Rosebank and we've got more trouble. Another body. You'll probably want to bring on the army."

He peered over the edge of the pool. Cloth had been stuffed in her mouth as a crude gag. Everyone had to be kept away and, much as he wanted to go down and take a closer look, he knew he'd make points by waiting for the Iberia folks and doing nothing to disturb evidence.

At the sound of footsteps on gravel, he spun around to see Wazoo, black garb flapping, speeding toward him. He motioned for her to go back but she kept on coming. Cyrus loped a step or two behind, looking exasperated.

"Something gone wrong," Wazoo said, and stopped beside Ellie so abruptly she might have had brakes on her shoes. "I felt it, me. I even bring this miserable God man with me and he don't want to come here nohow."

"Great," Spike muttered under his breath. "Wazoo, stay back. Go alert Marc, Bill, Joe, Ozaire, my dad and every other able-bodied man you can reach fast, and tell them not to allow anyone back here, and not to allow anyone to leave the property. Go!"

She went, skimming across the ground as fast as she'd come.

Cyrus got there, gave Ellie a sharp look and bent over the edge of the empty pool. For an instant he bowed his head, then he crossed himself and said, "May I go down there?"

"Not until the Iberia people get here. That'll be soon."

"Poor kid," Cyrus said. "Just a child still tryin' to grow up."

Spike intended to do what he wasn't supposed to do, ask Ellie some questions, but her blank face and empty eyes stopped him. Cyrus went to her and put a hand on her head. She looked up at him and he knelt to rest her head on his shoulder. "Be very quiet," he said, his voice gentle. "Be peaceful. You aren't alone here."

Spike decided he'd better do what he was always threatening to do and get lessons in woman handling from Cyrus one of these days.

On the other hand, what Cyrus did probably came naturally.

"I want to see her," Ellie said in a loud voice. She ignored Cyrus's attempt to stop her and joined Spike. "If I had called you last night this wouldn't have happened."

"We don't know that. We don't know when she died." From what he saw, he was pretty sure it hadn't been too long ago but Ellie didn't need to be told that.

Cyrus came to Ellie's other side. "Sentinels," he said. "Odd how one always feels responsible for protecting the dead."

"I didn't know what he'd do," Ellie said.

"But I knew it would be terrible. He said I'd know when to come for you, Spike. He cut my neck." She showed him a small wound under her hair at the back of her neck. "When I turned around I couldn't see anyone suspicious but I knew I was being told to go — and I thought someone else had probably died."

Later Ellie would need a lot of help.

Spike heard sirens and they drew closer. Lots of sirens. Wazoo burst from the side of the building again and raced to them. Reb, with Gaston trotting beside her, followed much more slowly.

Wazoo looked down at the carnage and soon Reb arrived to do the same. She shook her head and said, "Why would anyone do that to someone so beautiful and so needy? You'll have her mother on your hands shortly. She'll get wind of what's happened and you won't be able to stop her." With great care and ignoring Spike's protests, she climbed down some steps and onto the pool floor.

Ignoring any protests, Cyrus jumped down and stood beside her. She bent over Olympia's body and felt for a pulse, then continued going through the pointless routine that was her job to do.

Spike recognized Frank Wiley heading toward him with several pairs of officers. An ambulance bumped over the ground, stopped, and two women pulled a gurney and equipment from the back.

"We won't be needing that yet," Spike said. He called to Reb, "Anything to be done? The medics are here."

She shook her head slowly.

Wazoo paced back and forth, hugging herself and muttering. Each time she passed Ellie, she patted her.

The formerly silent place began to fill with official types, their paraphernalia and their hushed voices. Those hushed tones must be taught during training. It couldn't be that many of these people felt too much if they'd done the work for long.

Without warning, Wazoo sat on the edge of the pool, covered her face and began to say what sounded like prayers. Spells and incantations, Spike thought, were much more likely.

At a run, Marc came, his elbows pumping, looking in all directions with a horrified expression on his face.

"Reb's okay," Spike said. "She's helping out."

Marc's face went from white to red as his circulation kicked in again.

"No one else down there, please," Frank

Wiley said, all business but without Bonine's snide authority. "We'll take it from here."

Wazoo let out a moan. She stumbled to her feet, pointing downward, and visibly shaking.

"Wazoo?" Spike jogged, then ran to reach her. Her body trembled convulsively.

"The book," she said. "That came from my book."

He put an arm around her thin shoulders. "Hey, hey, friend, hush now. C'mon and sit with Ellie. She needs you."

"No." Wazoo threw off his arm. Her eyes seemed afire. "In her mouth. It's the bag that book was in."

She took hold of a handful of his shirt. "It's the treasure," she said. "She die for the treasure, her."

Wazoo wasn't making much sense.

Ellie approached. Close at Spike's side, she rested her head on his arm. Joe and Jilly, with Ozaire, watched the scene. More suits showed up.

Wally's presence didn't please him. The kid had just appeared but what he'd seen, he'd seen.

Spike gave Wazoo all the time she needed to calm down. There was nowhere he had to go. Charlotte came, and Homer, and he wondered how many cops were out front that they could keep the general public out.

Wazoo turned to him — on him — and with no warning beat his chest and shoulders with her fists. "Listen up, you." She shrieked and plucked at him. "That in her mouth am the bag what the book was in. The egg book. It in there when it got stole from me."

He clamped her against him to stop her from doing any real damage and looked at Ellie. "That's right, isn't it? The book was in a silk bag."

She nodded. "Yellow, orange and green. The one in her mouth."

"With red stars," Wazoo said, quieting slightly. "And a gold rope to close it."

"That's why you wanted the book," Spike said. "Or why it got your attention. Because of the bag. And because . . ." The sensation he had must be like getting a sandbag in the gut. "Vivian!"

Wazoo and Ellie stayed with him but he rotated, searching for Vivian. "Where is she?"

"She's with Bill Green," Wazoo said. "I seed them talkin'."

"Concentrate," he told her. "Think back. You said you heard Ellie talking to someone at the store about the book. Who was it?"

Wazoo shrugged. "Bill."

45

A second, less than a second, and he knew.

Cyrus came from behind him. "Spike?" His face loomed too close, his mouth stretched too wide. Spike heard him. The rest spun together.

Then everything broke free. His muscles worked. His heart beat hard and loud and he heard nothing else.

He took off, brushing people aside when they approached. The pounding of feet joined the roar of his heart. Others ran with him.

The bands were louder, bursting on him when he cleared the front of Rosebank. They must have been told to crank it up.

"Where are Vivian and Bill?" he said to anyone who might be listening.

"They by the bushes where you all was."

He hadn't noticed Wazoo keeping up with him.

In the center of the main lawn a huge barbecue had been set up and Dale Gautreax from the electrical contractors in town yelled, red-faced over the heat, about the best barbecued alligator in Louisiana.

Spike skirted the crowd that had gathered to watch. They seemed oblivious to the drama taking place.

He reached the bushes. But his gut had told him Vivian and Bill wouldn't be there.

He spun around. Marc, Cyrus, Joe, Gary, Homer, Madge, Ozaire and Charlotte were there, all staring at him, all expecting him to take command. Wally, on the dirt bike he was never without for long, rode back and forth with his snake box in a front basket.

"We don't know if they're on foot or if they've left by car," Spike said.

"Or if they've gone anywhere. Or they're wandering around in the crowd oblivious — or together at all," Cyrus pointed out.

"They together," Wazoo said. "I feel it."

"It was him," Spike said. "Bill Green all the time. He was everywhere, but how long have we known him? Not so long. He fitted in and we accepted him. Ellie was attacked in her apartment. He can get into that building anytime he likes. It's all too convenient and it all fits."

"And you could be dead wrong," Gary

pointed out. "We should go back to Wiley and let him take charge."

"*You* go back to Wiley," Spike said. "Until I've got Vivian, I'm following my gut. Homer, a search party needs to go through the grounds and the crowd. Get it organized. Wazoo, every room in the house. Would you go with her, Joe? Charlotte —" He made a move toward her, to reassure her, but she shook her head no. "Okay. Vivian's going to be okay. She has to be. Put in a 911 call. Wiley said he'd put guards on the gate. I'll hit them first."

"Wiley will get the news without me," Gary said. "I'm staying with you."

Between them they kept up repeated shouts of "Have you seen Vivian" rolling while they ran. The jam didn't help their progress.

The Swamp Doggies, dressed in signature mustard-colored suits, ambled down the driveway in the shadow of the live oaks, playing as they went and wandering back and forth, singing "We're Going To a Hookilau," with a spoken chorus of "Gator feed to you, boys."

Spike shouldered his way between them.

The officers at the entrance hadn't seen Vivian or Bill. They weren't allowing more people to enter the estate and no one could leave. Yellow tape vibrated between the gateposts. Already a grumbling, concerned gathering hovered around, wanting to know what was going on that they couldn't come in or go out.

"Someone better go back and tell Wiley anyway," Spike said, looking at Ozaire. "You go. Tell him we've got what could be a related disappearance — related to the current murder — and we need to search. Now. Tell him what we know so far."

Ozaire moved like a heavyweight sprinter.

"If I'm right," Spike said, "we may have minutes or hours. I'd put my money on the minutes."

"I saw Miz Vivian." Thea, pulling a red wagon piled high with packages of napkins, pushed her way to Spike. "I been to get these. Parked over there." She jerked her head toward the lot across the street. "Miz Vivian and Bill come out from there. That side by Serenity House."

Spike caught her by the hand. "Then what?"

"Miz Vivian, she carrying Boa and that dog squawkin' like a chicken."

"Where did they go?" Spike couldn't keep his voice down.

Marc said, "It's okay, Thea. Spike's anxious, is all. Did you see where Bill and Vivian went?"

Thea squared her shoulders. "This is what I see. They come out of there and they go to that fancy car of Bill's. Parked right there." She pointed a steady finger to the verge in front of Serenity House. "Somethin' happenin' because Miz Vivian set down Boa and do somethin' with Bill's hand. Bill, he didn't like that, but Miz Vivian doin' her thing. You know how she is."

Hurry, hurry. He met Cyrus's eyes and got a warning to lighten up. So he wouldn't get this done any faster by jumping all over Thea, but it was taking too long.

He waited.

Thea crossed her arms

"I'm getting my car," Madge said and took off for the parking lot.

"That's all," Thea said. "Me, I had to keep on pullin' this cart."

"How long ago?"

"I don't know. Few minutes, maybe."

Spike had parked his patrol car farther along the road and behind a hedge where any official Iberia eyes were unlikely to spot it. He went for it without stating his intent but Gary Legrain joined him while Cyrus went after Madge.

Marc threw himself into the back of Spike's vehicle the minute before he backed out.

"Darn it." Spike pointed ahead. "What the hell does Wally think he's doin'?"

"Using his head," Marc said. "Lookin' for the things we'll miss drivin'."

On his bike, Wally rode the shoulder, looking at the ground every inch of the way. When he saw Spike approaching he slammed his feet to the ground and waved his arms.

Spike cursed and slowed down, opened the passenger window. "Go back," he told him. That was before he saw Boa wedged into the bike basket beside Nolan Two's box. "Where —"

"Runnin' in the road," Wally said while the dog barked and growled. "There's blood back there."

Spike barely stopped himself from driving on without listening to the rest.

"Where they said Bill's car was. Blood on the road. I don't think they been gone long."

"Good kid," Marc said. "Keep on looking and call 911 with this if you see anything else." He tossed the boy a cell phone.

Spike shot forward, then made himself slow down and peer from side to side. "Watch the left," he finally told Marc. "Gary, take the Bayou side. Look for anything. Shit, where're the Iberia boys when I need 'em."

His answer came over the radio. The area crawled with reinforcements.

Spike's throat dried out until it all but suffocated him. He'd bitten his lips until they bled.

"Ahead," he said.

A motorcycle cop, parked on the side of the road, knelt on the other side of his bike.

Gary was ready when Spike lowered the window. "You looking for Vivian Patin and Bill Green, Officer?"

"Yeah. Got the word and saw the vehicle and license plate at the same time. Almost caught up. Son of a bitch ran me off the road."

"Man driving, woman passenger?" Spike said.

"Just the driver as far as I could see."

Bill Green killed Louis Martin. He'd said so.

Vivian tried to gauge how often his head fell forward and jerked up again. Either he'd already lost too much blood or he was high on something. "Let me drive," she said. "We need to get to Emergency and I'll be quicker."

"Shut up. You know I'm the one you and your raunchy sheriff friend have been looking for. And you know we're not going to any hospital."

She knew all right. And she knew she wouldn't get anywhere by crossing him. He'd already slammed her head into his lap when she showed signs of trying to signal a motorcycle cop.

In his left hand, clamped against the wheel, Bill held a knife. Each time Vivian glanced at it her gorge rose. A simple, businesslike steel knife with a narrow blade. Like a long scalpel. She thought of Morgan Link, who used scalpels, too, but not to kill anyone with. This knife of Bill's had carried the blood of dead men.

He intended it to carry Vivian's.

A panel truck with sheets of glass on either side traveled toward them.

"Signal them and you're dead," Bill said.

"Don't signal and I'm dead anyway." She blinked rapidly. She couldn't break down.

"Sooner or later you will be," he said, jolting his head up again. "Your choice."

She sat still when the truck passed. All he'd had to do was ask and she'd gone with him. But they were supposed to be friends. Bill was everyone's friend.

Their speed varied. Fast, but mostly a crawl. What were her chances of jumping out without getting the knife in her back?

"Why me?" she said. "I didn't know what you'd done."

"Let's get you into the house," he said in a silly voice supposed to sound like hers, she guessed. *"Shall I call an ambulance?* Fool woman. You saw the blood. You would have had everyone looking at me and I couldn't have that."

He liked puffing himself up. If she kept him talking she might get a chance to do something. "They wouldn't have figured out the truth. You've covered for yourself so well."

Bill's eyes were slitted.

It felt as if they'd been on the road for hours, but it was only minutes. They weren't that far from Rosebank yet.

"Someone else died today," he said. His head rolled. "Timing couldn't go wrong. Even with . . . even with what happened to me it was all working. But you had to be little Florence Nightingale."

"Who else died?" Vivian asked in a whisper.

"Knew more than she should because she snooped around. None of her business. Fool girl just like her fool mother."

Vivian couldn't form a word.

"Had to have sex with me because her mother did. Not that I minded." He sniggered and drool spilled from his lips. He shook his head. "Don't you try anything."

632

"I wouldn't, Bill." The only possible mother and daughter must be Susan and Olympia.

"I told the girl she had better tits, better ass, but her mother was better in bed. Made the kid mad."

Vivian breathed through her mouth. If she threw up he was likely to knife her right then and there.

"Wanted me to tell Susan we were finished and why. Because little Olympia and I were in love." His laugh didn't work properly and the car swerved off the road and back on again. "Told me she did it with her stepdad, too. Thought I'd be jealous. She's gone now, like you will be. They hate you. Afraid your . . ." His eyes closed.

Vivian looked at the keys in the ignition and shifted a little closer to him.

His lids opened heavily. "Susan and her hubby didn't want your cheap hotel putting off their rich clientele."

A swamp rabbit started across the road, followed by a second. They stopped and rose onto their hind legs.

"Watch out," Vivian said. *Now.* She went for the wheel and turned away from the trees and into the middle of the road. She'd take an accident there over the chance of being hidden in trees and brush with him.

"Bitch." He could scarcely get the word out. But he still had strength. He struggled but she held on, yanking to the left each time he pulled the car more or less level.

He was impaired. She'd keep reminding herself of that, keep on fighting.

She thought there were sirens, but then couldn't be sure. They probably wouldn't use them in case Bill did something awful when he heard them.

"Get — away — from me," he said. With his right elbow, he threw her off. Her head hit the window and her neck whipped back.

Blood from Bill's wounds smeared the inside of the car. It smelled sweet and sickly.

A moment was all she gave herself before attacking again. She threw herself at the wheel, reaching for the keys at the same time.

He gave her one short look and steel flashed.

Bill slit her forehead above her right eyebrow and the rush of blood into her eye was instant. She felt no pain, but neither could she see much.

The tires screeched and through the thumping pulse in her head she heard gravel churn. The car bumped forward, swung from side to side hitting hard objects as it went. She wiped away blood from her face with the back of a hand. Trees, they were hitting trees and running downhill.

An impact on the front left fender slammed them to a halt and the engine quit.

Vivian pulled on the door handle and it opened. She pushed and the door swung out. Clammy air flooded in. Her right foot met the ground at the same moment Bill threw himself across the console and on top of her.

She waited for the knife on her throat, but close in front of her she watched him open the glove box, remove a bag and manoeuver a needle until he could shoot something into a vein on his forearm.

The weight of him crushed her diaphragm and she struggled, beat about for more room.

He lay there and she thought he was dead or dying, until he shifted and hauled her from the car on his side, hauled her on her back through the cypress and the pond pine, the swags of moss turned to silver in the filtered sunlight.

It was hot and bugs swarmed.

He dropped her on boggy ground beside a live oak tree with branches dipping into Bayou Teche. Bill leaned on the trunk of the tree. She couldn't see him clearly, but she heard his rasping breath.

"You can still make it," she told him. "But you need a transfusion."

He retched and choked, but when she moved he kicked her flat again. "Pretty face you've got there," he said, swiping a hand repeatedly in front of his eyes. He muttered something else but she couldn't make it out.

Again he retched. This time he pitched forward onto his knees, but the knife still shone in his hand.

Vivian felt around for something hard and found a piece of wood. It wasn't big enough but it was hard. Blood soaked the back of his pants. She hadn't seen that before.

Rising up, she jumped over him, to his right side. She brought the wood down on his wounded shoulder and arm.

He screamed but didn't rear up as she expected. She hit him again. The wood didn't break apart and it was jagged. Again and again she beat on his shoulder.

Bill's screams turned into an endless wail.

Still wailing, he fought to his feet and tore at her wrist.

46

Spike wanted to drive with his foot to the floor but held his speed down to a lousy, crawling fifteen or twenty. Madge's car kept a steady distance behind him.

"They've lost us," Gary said. "They're probably miles away by now while we creep along like this."

"We aren't the only ones looking," Spike said. "I'm putting my money on Bill not wanting to go far with her. The longer they're together, the better the chance he'll get stopped."

"The way the motorcycle cop stopped him, you mean?" Gary said. "The guy didn't even think Vivian was in the car."

Spike hadn't missed what the cop told them and he didn't want to talk about it, but he said, "He didn't see her in the car. Doesn't mean she wasn't there."

The radio dispatcher came on. "Call just came in from a kid. Says to tell Spike Devol it's Wally. He knows where Vivian is. You need to turn around."

Spike rammed on the brakes and cursed when he looked in the rearview mirror. "Where? Gimme a coordinate." Madge was heading for his rear.

"Nothing scientific but it'll work," the dispatcher said. "Three posts that used to be white. Reflectors on 'em. About three miles north of Blanche Point Way. Bayou side of the road heading north. BMW went off road just past there. It's in trees. Subjects already out of the car by the time the kid got there. Says he hears them, though."

Madge stopped her car inches from the bumper of the patrol car. Spewing gravel, Spike spun a U-turn and sped back the way he'd come. He believed the fewer people mixing it up in a standoff, the better. He wouldn't have long before the Iberia crew were all over them.

Spike saw Wally before he saw the posts. Waving one arm, clinging to a struggling Boa with the other, he ran into the road to flag Spike down.

"Keep things quiet," Marc told the boy, jumping out before the car stopped completely. "Hold the dog's muzzle. If there's a chance of surprise, let's take it."

Wally already had a hand clamped around Boa's mouth and pointed into the trees where broken bushes and flattened grass showed the BMW's path. "I'll stay here," he said.

"Stop anyone from charging in," Spike told him, already on the move.

With Marc and Gary at his back, he crept in the direction of eerie keening sounds.

He saw Bill's car, nose into a wall of dense undergrowth, with both doors hanging open, and he saw the bayou through the trees. Then he saw Vivian and Bill and threw out his arms to stop the other two from going forward.

As well as moss, tangles of muscaline grape vines snarled the way, but the mess of vegetation also helped hide the advance as long as they stayed low.

Bill's were the howls they heard. He struggled with Vivian and Spike saw why she wasn't already dead. Bill had been wounded. Blood welled through his clothes at his right shoulder and arm and ran from the fingers on the same side. The arm hung useless. More blood soaked through the back of his pants.

He and Vivian fought over the knife Bill held in his good hand.

Gary rose out of his crouch but Spike shoved him back. He looked at Marc, and at Gary and signaled for them to wait. Then, on his stomach, he shifted rapidly over the ground, hat discarded, gun braced, the toes of his boots acting as propellers and rudder together and the rest of his body straining forward.

Instinct wanted him to rush Bill.

Cold odds told him that way led to a better chance that Vivian would be seriously injured or killed.

His face cleared the roots and branches. One thrust and he'd be in the open.

Vivian's silence — but for her labored breathing — amazed him. She poured her strength into holding the wrist with the knife in both of her hands.

And she was winning.

He freed his shoulders, gathered his legs beneath him, and threw himself. He'd take Vivian down with Bill but there wasn't a choice.

The impact shook her voice loose and she shouted. He got a grip on Bill Green's hand and weapon and all but tossed Vivian aside.

A man's roar erupted behind him. Another body scrambled over his, pressed his face down so that he couldn't see and he heard Bill's muffled yell, "Get back. I'll kill all of you."

Strong hands fastened on Spike's legs and pulled. He saw again, saw it was Marc who had freed him from Gary's weight. Gary had leaped on top of him to get at Bill. The knife rested feet from them, glinting, but Gary had a gun on Bill who didn't struggle anymore.

He did babble, and moan.

"Don't kill him," Spike shouted. "We've got him now."

"Spike?"

He glanced at Vivian. Her face and hair were smeared and clotted with blood. "Lie down," he told her. "Marc —"

"I'm okay," she told him.

Gary stayed where he was, stretched out on top of Bill, a gun held to his temple. He kicked the man's legs and pummelled his injured arm, even though Bill had quit fighting back.

Marc pressed a fist into Spike's back. "It's done," he said.

"Damn you," Bill said clearly. "You're too late, Legrain."

Gary abandoned the useless arm for the man's throat. "Move and you're dead."

"He's finished," Spike said, getting to his feet, but Gary didn't seem to hear. He pushed the gun into Bill's head and muttered in his ear.

Bill made a different sound. He cried.

"Okay." Gary's voice rose. "Okay. This is going to be done by the book. You'll get a lawyer. You don't have to say a word until you do."

Spike shook his head. People did the craziest things under pressure.

"Nothing," Gary said, squeezing Bill's throat harder. "Just shut up."

"He's lost it," Marc muttered.

"The gun," Spike said, then, "Gary, can you hear me? We've got him now. We need him alive. Just stay put and we'll take him. He'll get his rights read when it's time."

The two men rolled until Bill was on top of Gary.

"*Gary.*" All options were up. No way could Bill have turned them both over. Gary had done it deliberately. He intended to blow the man away and who would be able to argue how it really happened when the victim cut off any view of the weapon.

Spike put a bullet in Gary's leg just below the knee and prayed.

The scene blew apart.

Gary bellowed and went for his leg. Bill fell to the ground beside him and Spike, his weapon whipping back and forth, put himself between them.

"You're dead, sucker," Bill said to Gary. "You were from the start."

"Shut the *fuck* up." Gary panted, holding his leg. Marc had already picked up his gun.

"Medics are on the way." It was Cyrus who emerged from behind the live oak. He went directly to Vivian. "I kept them all out as long as I could but they'll be in now."

"You didn't need to do it, Gary," Bill said, sniggering, his head rolling from side to side on the slimy bayou bank. "Martin hated his sons as much as you did. You got what you wanted . . . Now you'll lose what you wanted."

Gary's pain silenced him but his eyes showed fury as well as agony.

"See." Bill coughed and tried to squint at Spike through swollen eyelids. "It's simple. He wouldn't work for the Martin boys and their old man never told him he wouldn't have to. Then Louis Martin made the mistake of crowing about treasure at Rosebank and how it was worth a fortune. He was going down to break the wonderful news to the two little ladies."

"He doesn't know anything," Gary said. "Take him in."

"You decided you'd make the treasure your consolation prize and knock off poor

643

old Louis at the same time — just to punish him for not loving you more than his boys."

Gary made a move toward Bill but his leg stopped him.

"He had something on me," Bill said. "From a long time ago. And then he needed what I do best."

"Kill people," Vivian said, her voice rising. "He killed them. He killed Olympia."

"*I killed lots of people,*" Bill said. He clamped his teeth together.

Spike heard the crashing of approaching feet through the trees and saw officers approach with weapons drawn.

"A friend of mine's fault, that's what it was," Bill said. "Guido got a conscience and told Gary boy about something I did years back. Doesn't matter now. Legrain thought he could blackmail me into getting his map for him. Well, I got it but he didn't. Pineapples and more pineapples and Gary's golden egg was supposed to be in one of them. Guy Patin must be up there laughing. Pineapples everywhere. All over his house. No eggs."

The arriving men fell silent.

"Kill Louis Martin and get me my map or I'll turn you in for what you did," Bill said, suddenly lucid. He raised his head. "That's what he told me. But he couldn't get me if I wouldn't go along, not without showing his own hand."

An Iberia officer approached and said, "We'll take them in now. You'll understand if we ask you to come in, too?"

"Sure," Spike said. He left Bill and Gary and went to kneel on the ground by Vivian. He took her face in his hands and kissed a bloody cheek.

"I'm okay," she said. "No, I'm not. I'm battered. I want to go home."

More Iberia uniforms tromped by.

"Hey," Cyrus said. "Look out there."

Spike followed his direction and saw a pirogue, swaying gently, a few yards from shore. "Not to worry," he called out. "Everything's all right here." It was the woman who lived on the houseboat with Claude. With the sun behind her, he couldn't see her face.

Standing in the shallow hull, she used her single paddle to bring the little wooden craft slowly closer.

The medics had arrived. They already had Bill on a gurney. Others worked on Gary's leg and one woman brought supplies toward Vivian.

"It's on the radio," the woman on the bayou said and her words carried clearly. "When I heard it I knew it was time I came.

That one, Bill Green he calls himself now, he murdered his wife, Sylvia. I know it all and I'll tell you."

With his arms around Vivian, Spike looked and listened.

"There were three of them, see," the woman said. "A kind of team. Bill, another man who called himself Guido — he killed him, too — and then there was Claude. He was known as Ulisse. They were young and stupid, but that one was all evil."

"Who is she?" Vivian whispered.

"I don't really know," Spike said. "Except she lives in a houseboat with Claude or Ulisse or whoever he was and comes to us for provisions."

"Thank you for coming to help, ma'am," one of the officers called. "We'd be glad to give you a ride to the office now."

"I'll make my own way along," she said.

"Will Claude come with you?" Spike asked.

She raised her head so the sun hit her face and he saw her smile. "My brother had to leave."

47

Three and a half weeks later

The feeling Vivian had today, right at this moment, would stay in her memory and her heart forever.

French doors stood open from Mama's favorite receiving room onto the front gallery. In the almost a month since the fete and what followed, and when the world had finally slowed down a little, work done at a wild pace had restored the room to its former bizarre glory.

The sun had begun to lower and shadows lengthened, but Vivian's closest people remained on the gallery and the front lawn. Not a big number, but enough. There had been more at St. Cécil's for the wedding and they'd have been welcome here, too, had they chosen to come, but they'd drifted away afterward, smiling, waving.

At last she had persuaded Spike to discard

his tie and unbutton the collar of his white shirt, but he wouldn't take off the jacket of his gray suit. Hours earlier, when she'd seen him waiting for her at the altar, tall, straight and so serious, tears had spilled and she hadn't tried to stop them. He had looked wonderful, but more than that, she had known his love for her was true and he wanted to marry her as much as she wanted him.

Cyrus had married them. Homer had stood at Spike's side and Charlotte had given Vivian away. Carrying Boa, Wendy had marched up the aisle first. *The best day ever.* Vivian wondered if she would ever think of it without wanting to cry with happiness.

Spike sat beside her on a swing decorated with white satin bows that fluttered in a late-afternoon breeze. She looked down at his hand, the strong fingers laced together with hers, and giggled.

"What?" he said, giving her one of his quizzical, just about too-blue stares.

"Look at us," she said. "Spike and Vivian Devol. When we first met I bet you never thought this would happen."

"Sure I did. Never doubted it for a moment."

"That's not true."

Wasn't it? "No, *cher.* I wanted it to happen but there surely did seem a lot of reasons why it never would." He was ready to take her away and have her to himself, but Charlotte and Homer, and the rest, still watched them covertly and he saw how they weren't quite prepared to let them go. And Wendy, dancing on the lawn with Joe Gable and Ellie Byron to the music of an ancient black guitar player with golden fingers, laughed and swung the skirts of her pretty green dress in a way that made him reluctant to break up the party. Vivian had curled Wendy's hair and it bobbed while she hopped and twirled.

"Look at you," Vivian said quietly. "Lovin' that child. It's so sweet to watch."

"I will love all of our children," he said, smiling at her.

She brought his hand to her mouth and looked up at him. "*All* of them?"

Spike narrowed his eyes on the alley of live oaks winding away toward the entrance. "Vivian, I talk a good story but I'm still not believin' this is happenin'."

When she grinned, she resembled a gleeful kid. "I'm just accepting it," she said.

Her green eyes sparkled. Above her eyebrow, makeup covered the healed wound Bill had inflicted. It barely showed. The layered skirts of her white cotton dress, yards of stuff she called eyelet, floated back and forth while Spike gently rocked the swing. The top of the dress was soft, with a tight belt of the same material. A froth of pale green lace showed from beneath the wide neckline from shoulder to shoulder.

And she'd married him, this lovely woman with enough guts to fuel an army. He hid a smile at the thought.

"What's funny?" she said at once.

"Mmm?" He looked down his nose at her. "I guess there's no foolin' you. I was thinkin' you're a tough cookie and I'd better watch my rear."

"I'll do that for you," she said, with absolute sincerity.

"I'd appreciate it."

"It's going to be hard to leave them today, isn't it?" She glanced around. "My mother looks more peaceful than she has since my father died. I think it's the right decision to use some of Louis's money to finish the renovations here, don't you?"

"You've asked me that before. Several times. I think it's right, partly because it's what the man would have wanted and partly because he was correct in thinking he ought to try to set some things straight. Vivian?" He made sure he had her full attention. "I'm going to manage to leave — with you — and not be too depressed about it."

If she admitted just how badly she wanted them to be alone, they might forget about being restrained. "I won't be depressed at all."

"Homer's goin' to be over here every day after we get back, y'know."

She knew what Spike meant. He'd agreed, at least until the hotel and restaurant were up and running, to bring Wendy to live at Rosebank while Homer ran their business. Later? Well, they hadn't tackled that too deeply yet but there wouldn't be room for all of them at his house.

Fresh dishes and trays arrived at the banquet table beneath a green-and-white marquee in front of the gallery. Cyrus, handsome Cyrus, led an amazingly enthusiastic line to fill up more plates. Marc filled two, one for himself and a second for Reb who sat sideways on another swing farther down the gallery. Poor Gaston's lap space had shrunk to nothing but he clung there on his beloved Reb just the same. Boa, who had decided Gaston made a fine plaything, waited beside the swing for the other dog to make the mistake of jumping down.

Today there had been no talk of the ongoing case or of Bill Green, who had recovered enough from his injuries to be awaiting his fate in a jail cell. Gary occupied similar quarters. The hunt was still on for Claude whom Bill accused of Gil's murder.

"You're thinking about it again." Spike had felt her concentration shift. "Nothing to worry about there anymore. I'd like to think Bonine wouldn't rear his head again after the graft charges, but he'll show up somewhere. Over the years he must have been on the take from every perp for miles around."

"Including the Martin boys and Gary," Vivian said quietly.

The ruckle was back between her eyebrows and he didn't like it one bit.

She looked toward Serenity House. "They're going to carry on with that place," she said. "Can you believe it? I thought they'd want to get away after Olympia was murdered. I thought they'd get a divorce."

He already knew what Morgan and Susan planned, just about everyone did, but he wasn't surprised by Vivian's thinking aloud about it. "Maybe that's why they're stayin'. If it hadn't been for that place and all the sneakin' around and lyin' she'd probably still be alive. Maybe they think they shouldn't leave now. But it's not our problem."

Wazoo came from the house carrying a

full bottle of champagne. She refilled their glasses and handed them over. "You two gotta grease the pump," she said.

"Sure that shouldn't be *prime?*" Spike asked her.

Her grin showed just how beautiful her teeth were — and she was pretty lovely herself, even if the red ribbon in her hair was her one concession to being at a wedding party. "I'd say it don't matter a whole lot what you do. Grease it, or prime it. Should do the trick."

Spike got a kick out of watching Vivian turn pink.

"I been meanin' to tell you how I've gone over every inch of this house," Wazoo said. "If there's one o' them foreign eggs here, I jest don't know where." If she thought about how she'd made off with Vivian's book, she never mentioned it and neither did Vivian.

"Forget the egg," Vivian said. "We have."

Spike didn't think that was entirely true but he was glad to hear it anyway. They figured that Guy Patin had hidden his precious egg as his own insurance against bad times. His riddle, dreamed up when he discovered he would soon die, hadn't been just a riddle, but a way to make the egg safe from a casual searcher who didn't have Guy's clues to follow.

The instant Wazoo was out of earshot he put an arm around Vivian and said in her ear, "Confession time. For a number of hours now, I've been seeing things."

Vivian looked at him sharply.

He nodded gravely. "Scenes. You're in all of them. Me, too. And I've been feelin' a certain way. And I've gotta tell you, *cher*, I think things are as greased and primed as they need to be."

She turned in his arm, rested her hands on his neck and kissed him until he moaned. "Time to go?" she whispered.

"Reckon so."

The guitarist had taken a break but from the open room behind them came the sound of the old piano. They peered around to see Cyrus, still wearing his collar but without his jacket, sitting there, bent over the keys. Madge perched on the end of his bench to watch.

Cyrus began to play, and to sing. Vivian hadn't known he sang. His voice was a warm tenor with a heart-squeezing break.

"Listen to him," she told Spike. "Is there anything he can't do?"

He glanced at her but didn't comment.

The piano needed tuning. Several notes didn't work at all but Cyrus kept right on singing "Your Love Amazes Me," and conducting with his spare hand during missing notes.

When it was over, everyone applauded and called for more, but he became bashful and wouldn't be persuaded.

"Hey, Spike." Marc bent over him and said quietly, "Is there anything I need to explain to you? Just so you'll feel you can take your bride wherever it is you're going?"

Spike smiled and shook his head. In fact he and Vivian didn't know just where they were going but that's the way they wanted it.

Joe approached next. "Nothing to worry about," he said. "Just follow your instincts." And Spike suspected a plot that was giving some people a good laugh.

"Ready, *cher?*" he asked Vivian.

She jumped up and pulled him with her, to the delight of the group gathered around them.

Wendy stood front and center, and accepted kisses from both of them, and hugs. "I'm not gonna ask to come with you again," she said, wrinkling her nose. "I'm staying with Gramps and Charlotte and they say I wouldn't like where you're going."

That brought a chuckle.

Cyrus tapped Charlotte's shoulder and gave her an envelope. Crimped up along its length, it was made of pale purple tissuelike paper. "Just tuned the piano for you," he said. He shot a glance at Spike and Vivian and rolled his eyes, making them both chortle. "Someone slid that in the works."

"I know what it is, me. I know what it is." Wazoo went into one of her famous capers. "Why didn't we think of that? The message was torn, remember? But it say, '. . . all the right notes.' So God man play the right notes and he don't get a thing 'cept that letter. It gonna tell us where that damn egg is, see if it don't." She waggled her head. "Excuse the language."

Charlotte worked open the flap, but gave the envelope to Vivian.

One sheet of paper, folded in half, slid from inside and she read it. Then she frowned.

"What it say?" Wazoo demanded.

Vivian cleared her throat.

"Last coming
First going.
First coming
Last going.
Which way?"

She folded the paper again.

"That's *it?*" Charlotte said.

"Uh-huh," Vivian told her, and gave back

the envelope and paper. "Have fun. I think it's time Spike and I got going." She put a hand under his arm.

The bags were already in Spike's pickup — now minus the boiling and barbecue equipment. The two of them had opted not to change, mainly because Vivian was too fond of her wedding dress.

Shouts and cheers went up and a few of the hardier guests ran beside the truck on its way down the drive, but eventually they fell back. Spike and Vivian waved to them from the windows. They had been spared the shaving cream announcements on the vehicle, but cans clattered and clanged behind.

When they approached the gates, they looked at each other and Spike stopped the truck. He climbed out to cut the cans free and toss them inside the back.

He looked over his shoulder to make sure he wasn't being watched from the driveway and heard Vivian's door slam. "Which way?" she asked. "Which way are we going?"

Spike shaded his eyes to look at her. "You get to pick, sweetheart. I'll follow you anywhere."

She stood there, her feet planted apart in strappy white sandals with high heels.

"Which way?" she said again and backed toward the road.

For a moment he thought she intended to run and have him chase her. He was game, but feared she might break an ankle.

Vivian went only as far as the gates and he caught up with her there. She crossed one foot over the other, leaned on one post and pointed upward.

"Have you changed your mind about this?" he asked, before he glanced above her head, at the stone finial on top of the post, one of the two pineapple-shaped ones that flanked the entrance. "Wow. Could it be . . . Last coming, first going. Which way?"

"All depends, doesn't it," she said. "Think we're right? Could it be in one of these?"

"Could be."

She ran around him and hopped back inside the truck. From the window she said, "Do you care?"

"Can't say I do much." He got in beside her and took off the brake. "Do you?"

"Not right now. Maybe later."

FABERGÉ EGG SOLD AT AUCTION

Bearing the stamp of Michael Perchin, supervising Fabergé goldsmith prior to 1903, a formerly unknown Fabergé egg (discovered in Louisiana) has been sold at auction for an undisclosed sum.

Experts attest that although the small (4½" high) masterpiece does not appear to be one of the eight eggs known to be missing from the Russian Czarist collection, this is indeed a Fabergé. Part of the egg's value, the experts say, results from its mystery.

18K gold beneath a shell of the master's unique oyster enamel (changes color in different lights), the piece is trellised with gold. At each trellis intersection are flowers of pearls with sapphire centers. The egg rests on three sapphire-encrusted cabriolet legs with rose diamond feet. A large rose diamond crowns the egg.

As with all formerly known Fabergé eggs, this one contains a "surprise," in this case a two-inch jade bowl containing a perfect miniature pineapple cast in gold with jade leaves.

The employees of Thorndike Press hope you have enjoyed this Large Print book. All our Thorndike and Wheeler Large Print titles are designed for easy reading, and all our books are made to last. Other Thorndike Press Large Print books are available at your library, through selected bookstores, or directly from us.

For information about titles, please call:

(800) 223-1244

or visit our Web site at:

www.gale.com/thorndike
www.gale.com/wheeler

To share your comments, please write:

Publisher
Thorndike Press
295 Kennedy Memorial Drive
Waterville, ME 04901